WILD
FLOWER
GRAVES

RITA HERRON

WILD FLOWER GRAVES

Bookouture

Published by Bookouture in 2020

An imprint of Storyfire Ltd.
Carmelite House
50 Victoria Embankment
London EC4Y 0DZ

www.bookouture.com

ISBN: 978-1-83888-987-6
eBook ISBN: 978-1-83888-986-9

*To my mother, who raised me during hard times,
taught me about country living, family,
being tough and about what's important in life.*

PROLOGUE

The angel's voice echoed in the mountain wind as he knelt and traced a finger over her tombstone. But the devil's sinister laughter rose above it. The devil had won. He had snatched her life before she even had a chance to live it.

Images of the dead children that had been found along the Appalachian Trail three weeks ago flashed behind his eyes. Their killer was in prison. But where was the justice? It didn't bring the little girls back.

His heart aching, he dropped tiny wildflowers over the small mound. Although lilies marked the front entrance of the graveyard, purple was her favorite color. She liked purple popsicles and purple headbands and her purple comforter. He pictured her smiling at him as he read her bedtime stories, mimicking the animal noises in the tales. She would giggle as he tickled her belly.

He'd grown up seeing the worst in life. He'd been beaten, taught to make the weak ones suffer. To make the women obey. To punish them.

Then *she* had come along.

He'd never thought he had a soft bone in his evil body. That he could care about anyone as much as he cared about her. And he'd tried his damnedest to save her.

But he'd failed.

No one knew the truth about what had happened. And if he told them, they wouldn't believe him.

Anger made him cold inside, cold all over. She shouldn't be dead. But she was gone. And it was time to make someone pay for it.

CHAPTER 1

Friday

Crooked Creek, Georgia

"How does it feel to know your parents covered for a serial killer?"

Detective Ellie Reeves shifted restlessly in her seat. That was a loaded question and one she didn't know how to answer. Not to the local press or to this therapist.

Not even to herself.

Nervous energy made her tap her foot on the wood floor of the counselor's office. She'd resisted seeing a shrink since her life had fallen apart three weeks ago, just as she'd resisted a tell-all with the press. They were already having a field day torching her parents for what they'd done.

She couldn't blame them either.

The therapist, a slender woman with a chin-length brown bob named Kennedy Sledge, cleared her throat.

"Take your time and tell me what happened," she said softly.

Ellie stared at her fingernails where she'd chewed them down to the nubs.

"I know you saw the news. A little girl named Penny Matthews went missing a few weeks ago. While looking for her, I learned she was part of a serial killer's pattern that went back two decades. They called him the Ghost. He lured his victims, all young girls, with small wooden dolls he carved."

"Yes, I saw the news." The counselor nodded encouragement. "But you saved and rescued Penny and another child that was taken."

Ellie nodded, taking some comfort in the fact that the little girls were back with their families. She'd thought once that case was solved Crooked Creek would return to normal, hosting small-town festivals, porch sitting and potluck dinners.

"Ellie?" the therapist prompted when the silence stretched between them.

Ellie took a deep breath. "I discovered that the man who took them was my mother's illegitimate son, who she gave up for adoption ten years before I was born. Mom was only a teenager when she got pregnant. Her parents, especially her father, insisted the baby, Hiram, would be better off in a home with two parents." Now that she'd started talking, the words spewed from her. "Although Mom thought he was in a happy family, she felt guilty about giving him up. So she adopted me when I was three."

Kennedy drummed two fingers on her desk, and Ellie noticed a tiny scar on her wrist. "So you are not blood related to Hiram?"

Ellie shook her head. "No, but that hasn't been made public knowledge yet. When Hiram was fourteen, he found out about me. He hated my mother, Vera. But most of all he resented me for taking her away from him."

"But you didn't take her away from him, Ellie."

Perspiration beaded on Ellie's forehead and she wiped it away with a shaky hand. "No, but he believed I did. Anyway, to cut a long story short. When I was five, he lured me into the woods and left me trapped in a cave. When my father found me, and I told him the boy's name was Hiram, my parents moved us to Stony Gap and changed our names." Her stomach churned. "Then Hiram started taking other little girls. He killed them because he… wanted to kill me."

Suddenly feeling ill, she remembered the sight of the children's graves she'd found in the woods of the Appalachian Mountains. She stood. "This is a waste of time. Talking won't change anything."

"Processing your feelings can help you move on," the counselor said. "I know you're angry with your parents."

"They lied to me all my life," Ellie said, her voice cracking. "And they suspected Hiram but didn't come forward." She pressed a hand to her chest. "People in town think I knew. And that we covered for a killer. I'm a detective—how does that make me look?"

Either complicit or incompetent. Neither elicited trust from the citizens of Bluff County.

The therapist made a note on her notepad. "How are your parents handling the accusations?"

Ellie picked at her cuticles. "They've been charged with withholding evidence and accessory to murder, but they've attained a big-shot attorney who promised he'd get the charges dropped, starting an uproar in town." Heat climbed her neck. "Everywhere I go, I hear the whispers and see the stares."

Through the window the sun was shining like a beacon, nearly blinding her just as her parents lies had.

Kennedy leaned forward, arms on the desk. "There's an online group you should join. Women talking to each other, sharing, offering support. It's secure, anonymous, so you don't have to divulge your real identity if you don't want to." The counselor pushed a business card toward her, and Ellie reluctantly slipped it into her pocket.

Unsettled at the idea of pouring out her heart to strangers, Ellie paced across the room, noting the woman's credentials on the wall and books that filled the bookshelf. They covered a range of psychological subjects—eating disorders, depression and anxiety, behavioral disorders.

She'd never been one to surround herself with female friends. Truth be known, Officer Shondra Eastwood, her colleague, was her *only* female friend. They'd bonded because of their mutual dislike for Bryce Waters, Bluff County's sheriff.

"I'll think about it. Right now, I just need to get back to work," Ellie finally answered.

Work was her salvation, even though her reputation with Crooked Creek's police department was shaky to say the least. Her own parents had fooled her. How could she trust her judgment now?

"So you're back at work already?" Kennedy asked.

Ellie bit down on her lower lip. "Actually, my boss, Captain Hale, ordered me to take time off to heal and let the dust settle." Or maybe he was questioning her abilities, too.

"How do you feel about being adopted?" the counselor pressed.

Ellie frowned. Rejected. "Like the woman who gave birth to me didn't want me."

But she'd said enough for the day. Emotions were battling their way to the surface, emotions she couldn't afford to confront.

"I need to go," she said. Not bothering to wait for a response, she stormed out the door.

CHAPTER 2

Saturday

Stony Gap, Georgia

The next morning, Ellie's stomach churned as she sped toward the sheriff's office. She should have laid off the vodka last night. Should have just left town.

But a glutton for punishment, here she was on her way to watch Bryce Waters be sworn in as the new sheriff of Bluff County, the job Ellie had wanted all her life.

Her phone buzzed as she turned onto Main Street. Looking down, she saw it was Angelica Gomez, from WRIX Channel 5 News. Dammit, the reporter wouldn't give up.

Shaking her head in irritation, she let it roll to voicemail. Remembering that Angelica was lining up an interview with Hiram, Ellie listened to the message. She wanted to know if he had divulged any more secrets, most specifically if he'd had an accomplice.

"*Detective, I'm meeting with Hiram,*" the reporter said in her message. "*But everyone wants to hear your side of the story. Call me.*"

Ellie muttered a curse. Angelica wanted answers. The town wanted answers. Ellie herself wanted answers. Who didn't?

Angelica's voice echoed in her ears. *Don't you want to set the record straight? Help people understand? Quiet the gossip?*

Gossip fueled by Meddlin' Maude and the busybodies in town who had nothing better to do than keep the rumor mill turning at the Beauty Barn while Carol Sue covered their gray with foils and teased the hell out of lifeless hair made worse by dye and lacquered spray.

Her mother's so-called friends, including Edwina the mayor's wife and the ladies at the Garden Club, had abandoned her the moment the news had broken. They no longer cared if Vera could win prizes with her violets. She had been ostracized like a wilted flower from the garden extravaganza they sponsored every year.

Ellie almost felt sorry for her.

But Vera's words reverberated in Ellie's mind like a bad horror movie. *I had to protect you because you were my daughter. I had to protect Hiram because he was my blood.*

Then the whispers in the town: *How could Ellie not know her brother was killing all those girls?*

Do you think she let her parents get away with covering for that monster?

It's her fault those little girls died.

Is she stupid? Or evil like Hiram?

A shudder coursed through Ellie.

You can't avoid the media forever, Angelica had said.

So far, she had. The pain cut too damn deep.

Hell yes, she wanted to quiet the talk in town. But opening up would only stoke the flames of suspicion.

Spring rain slashed the windshield, promising that the dead brown leaves scattering the ground would make way for green, but Ellie felt dead inside herself.

The sound of other cars around her and the presence of the news van made her stomach twist into a knot as she pulled into a parking spot in front of Town Hall.

Magically, as if Bryce had ordered the downpour to stop for his inauguration, the rain ceased. A commotion on the lawn jerked her back to the matter at hand, and she watched as locals flooded the square where Angelica and her cameraman had set up. Climbing from her Jeep, she inhaled the scent of rain and grass, which still remained brittle in the wake of the blizzard that had just raged along the east coast. The ground was slushy, the wind rolling off the mountain, a biting cold that had lingered as if the shadow of death hovered close by.

Pulling her ski hat over her ears, Ellie burrowed in her jacket and stood on the periphery of the crowd, hoping to go unnoticed. Voices and excited whispers floated in the wind as Bryce exited the building onto the steps of city hall.

Swallowing her bitterness over the fact that her father chose to endorse Bryce as his replacement instead of her, she quietly blended in with the spectators. Of course, Randall Reeves' support could have backfired after the truth about Hiram was exposed, but Bryce managed, as always, to put a positive spin on the situation. As the new sheriff, he intended to clean up the town. Get justice. Protect the towns along the trail.

He was the hero.

Maybe her father had been right. If the sheriff's job was about politics and publicity, Bryce had been the better choice. She wanted to concentrate on justice and the law.

Ever the charmer, Bryce saluted the people who'd gathered to watch him be sworn into office, sending cheers and applause across the lawn.

Ellie forced herself to breathe. As Bryce was now sheriff over the entire county which encompassed Crooked Creek's police department as well as Stony Gap's, technically she worked for him.

Shondra slipped up beside her, her scowl as disgusted as Ellie's. "He's always been a dick, but now he'll lord that power over all of us."

It didn't take a therapist to diagnose Bryce. "Narcissist chauvinist," Ellie muttered.

"You know during the investigation into the Ghost case, he had me working small details at the festival in town. Since then it's gotten worse. Last week, he assigned me to cover the garden show.

Apparently, Lily was afraid someone would steal the prize roses."
Shondra rolled her eyes. "Then I was assigned to the local nursing
home, where one of the patients was stealing the other patients'
afternoon ice-cream treats and cookies. All the while Bryce is
sending the other deputies out on domestic calls and to investigate
a drug ring he thinks has cropped up on the outskirts of town."

"That's not fair," Ellie said.

"Tell me about it," Shondra replied with a sigh. "I threatened
to file a complaint against him for gender bias if he didn't start
letting me work real cases."

A smile tugged at Ellie's mouth. "How did that go over?"

Shondra chuckled. "About like you'd expect. But hey, he finally
sent me on a couple of domestic calls."

Ellie admired Shondra. The woman had grown up in an abusive
home, and she was passionate about cracking down on domestic
violence.

Shondra nudged her arm, her smile fading. "How are you
doing?"

Ellie dug her hands into her pockets and shrugged. "Think I'm
going to hike the trail for a few days."

Just then, Bryce's gaze traveled across the crowd, settling on
Ellie. Some emotion she couldn't quite compute flickered across
his face, replaced with a wicked smile before he stepped behind
the microphone beside his father, Mayor Waters.

Anxiety pinched at Ellie's gut. Bryce had something up his
sleeve. That look… she knew it. He was going to make her life a
living hell now he was in charge, and there wasn't a damn thing
she could do about it—except quit and move away. Somewhere
no one knew her. Somewhere she could escape.

She'd been considering it for days now. She'd even pulled up a
map, trying to pick a location.

But with national news airing the story of the murdered little
girls, there was nowhere to hide.

CHAPTER 3

Marvin's Mobile Home Park, Crooked Creek

The dark, evil thoughts came out of nowhere. But they always lived in his head, whispering their insults, shouting that he was worthless, reminding him that he had no one. Voices that told him what to do, how to inflict pain.

Who to take.

They all had to suffer.

Glancing at the photographs on the seat beside him, the childhood rhyme about Monday's child taunted him.

"Monday's child is fair of face, Tuesday's child is full of grace, Wednesday's child is full of woe, Thursday's child has far to go, Friday's child is loving and giving, Saturday's child works hard for a living, And the child that is born on the Sabbath day, is bonny and blithe, and good and gay."

But the girls were none of those things, and never would be.

Night shadows hugged the exterior of the woman's trailer as he waited for her to come home. Overgrown weeds and patches of poison ivy choked the property, the mobile homes separated by broken-down cars, old tires, children's toys and junk.

With the streetlight burned out, he could easily hide in the dark corners of the yard. Aside from shouting two doors down and at least three or four dogs barking into the night, the area was quiet. No animals that he could see. Still, he knew how to handle dogs.

Slipping from his vehicle, armed with the chloroform rag, he crept into the shadows of the metal carport. Hunched behind a garbage can, he waited, anticipation building inside him and making his blood hot. His body hardened as he imagined pushing her to her knees and forcing her to beg for her life.

Wind rustled the trees, tossing a Bud Lite can from a neighbor's property across the graveled parking lot. An old man staggered from his trailer, stumbled, then grabbed the rail and wove to his pick-up truck.

The fool shouldn't be driving.

But he was not the problem tonight. Tonight was about taking Monday's child.

Tension coiled inside him as the minutes ticked by, and the rhyme played over and over in his head like a broken record, just like the country CDs she had played. Songs about drinking whiskey and cheating wives.

A half hour passed before the sound of an engine broke the silence. A black pick-up pulled into the carport.

His pulse jumped as she opened her car door and slid her legs over the side of the seat to the ground. A coal-black braid hung down her back, the car's interior light shimmering across ebony skin. Her full lips puckered into a frown as she slammed the door shut and stood, fiddling with her phone.

Anxious to take her and get the hell out of here before her neighbors got home, he lunged toward her, grabbing her around the neck in a chokehold. Quickly he pressed the rag over her face. She kicked, trying to elbow him, struggling to jerk his hands away, but he was stronger. He tightened his hold, cutting off her air until her body went limp, and her head lolled back.

Smiling to himself, he dragged her into the bushes. Then he scooped her into his arms and carried her to his car.

Opening the trunk, he shoved her inside, slamming the trunk shut.

Excitement made his cock throb as he drove away.

CHAPTER 4

Sunday

Springer Mountain, Georgia

Dawn cracked the sky, a sliver of sunlight seeping through the gray clouds as Ellie grabbed her backpack from the trunk of her Jeep. Wind shook the trees and rustled the bushes, the scent of rain filling the air.

Her gaze fell to the bundle of mail on her back seat. More hate mail.

Several letters had arrived yesterday, the ugly words taunting her and keeping her awake long into the night. Some sounded threatening, yet she'd hoped that folks were simply blowing off steam. She'd been too ashamed to show them to her boss or anyone else.

But as she was a cop, she'd kept every single one of them, and she'd also told the therapist about them just in case one of the threats became a reality.

What was she doing pouring out her heart to a shrink anyway? After Hiram trapped her in that cave, she'd been traumatized, repressing memories of what had happened. A few weeks later, her parents moved and changed her name from Mae to Ellie, so Hiram couldn't find her again. When she'd talked about Mae, they led her to believe that Mae was her imaginary friend.

Her childhood therapist had perpetuated her parents' lies under the guise of protecting her.

When, all those years later, the truth came out and Ellie realized the therapist helped her parents, she decided to report her to the board for unethical conduct. But she was too late. The counselor had left the job one day and virtually disappeared.

Ellie forced herself to return to the present. Knowing that cell service was spotty and deciding she needed a break from the countless calls from Angelica and disgruntled Bluff County residents, Ellie locked her phone in the glove compartment.

A few days off the grid, escaping into the mountains, would hopefully clear her head.

Still, dangers existed on the trail at every turn. There were steep ridges and drop-offs, wild animals, and drifters who sheltered in the mountains. Knowing some were mentally ill, and others were criminals hiding out, Ellie carried her weapon and extra ammo, as well as a flare gun, a Taser, and pepper spray.

A girl alone couldn't be too careful.

No fool herself, for emergency's sake, she snagged the handheld radio she used to communicate with the National Park Service. Early this morning, she'd texted Ranger Cord McClain with Search and Rescue to tell him where she was going, a deal they'd made long ago whenever she went hiking alone. The fact that he hadn't responded told her he was still angry with her. Maybe while she was out here, she'd figure out a way to mend their friendship.

Leaving her Jeep, she inhaled the crisp mountain air, bringing with it the scent of honeysuckle and ivy, and began her hike.

The steep inclines and twisting paths of the AT—the Appalachian Trail—led deep into the forest. Tall pines, hemlocks, oaks and cypresses filled her sightline and blocked out the sunlight, creating countless places to hide.

She'd never understood how a person could get so fed up with life they'd venture onto the trail and decide to stay.

But she got it now. She just wanted to be left alone. To get lost in the endless miles of woods and wilderness. To breathe in the scents of nature, watch the dandelions pop up, and forget that evil had torn her family apart.

Then maybe she could figure out what to do with her life, whether she wanted to search for her birth parents.

Because something told her it wasn't a good idea. If they hadn't wanted her as a baby, why the hell would they be interested in getting to know her now?

CHAPTER 5

Somewhere on the AT

The darkness closed around her. A cloying smell. Something wet. Dank. Rotten. She blinked to clear her vision, but there was no light. No sound.

Nothing.

Only the cold emptiness and hollow feeling of being alone.

Fear pulsed through her. The man had come out of nowhere. No… He'd been hiding at her place, waiting to ambush her.

A dizzy spell overcame her as she tried to sit up and determine her location. A metal chain clinked against the floor. A heavy weight circled her neck so tightly she could barely breathe. Blinking away tears of frustration, in the pitch black she felt the floor and walls surrounding her.

Cold. Steel. Bars.

Oh, God, she was in a cage.

Panic choking her, she forced herself to inhale deep breaths.

Heart racing, she lifted her hand to her neck, nausea rising to her throat. She knew what she was going to find.

A dog collar. Heavy metal linked to a chain.

What kind of sick pervert had put her in here?

Footsteps sounded above her, indicating she might be in a basement. Nearby the sound of water dripping echoed. A dog barked. And… did she hear another woman crying? Or… clawing at another cage?

The steps grew louder. The sound of a door creaking rent the air, floorboards groaning as he came down.

She glanced up, squinting to see his face. But it was too dark, and he closed the door, blocking out any light that might slip through the crack. A low whistle echoed as he walked down the stair, a happy whistle, as if he was excited.

Blinking, she forced herself to be still and choked back a cry. *Don't show fear.*

"Ahh, good, you're awake."

The sight of the knife in his hand made her snap. The cage rattled as he inserted a key into the lock. The scent of sweat and stale beer hit her.

"Why are you doing this?" she cried.

"Because Monday's child is fair of face," he murmured as he knelt in front of her and set a duffel bag on the floor. "And you're not."

With a sinister smile, he yanked her by the hair and pulled her from the cage, tearing a scream from her.

She couldn't see what was inside the bag, but her imagination went down a dark, terrifying path. Tears blurred her eyes, and she began to shake.

He snatched a whip from his belt and slapped it across her back. "You want to live, then beg."

The sharp sting of the whip sliced her back through her clothes, and she blinked back tears. But she refused to beg.

He brought the whip down again and again, slashing at her back. "I said beg!"

A sob escaped her, and she tasted blood, but she shook her head. Another crack of the whip, and he kicked her in the stomach. When she still refused to beg, he turned into a madman, shouting and pacing and slapping the wall with the whip.

Finally, he returned to stand over her, his breath panting out. With a yank of her head, he forced her to look at him. "All right, we'll play it your way. You won't beg for your life, then I'll keep you for a while. And we'll have fun." His menacing laugh pierced the air. "Oh, yes, we'll have so much fun, Cathy."

A shudder coursed through her. Her name was not Cathy. But she was too weak to say anything and he was lost in his madness. What did it matter anyway? She was chained in here like a dog.

"Now I'll have to find another," he sang as he dragged her back inside the cage. "Monday's child is waiting." The metal door clanged shut, then he stomped away, cracking the whip against the concrete wall as he climbed the steps and left her in darkness.

CHAPTER 6

Monday

The Reflection Pond

Last night he'd been forced to take another. But hell, this one was a better fit for Monday's child. Much better. She'd begged from the moment he'd taken her until he'd watched her draw her last breath.

He moved swiftly, juggling the dead woman in his arms as he climbed the hill, grateful for night and the canopy of trees hiding him from sight. Mosquitoes buzzed around his face, and a water moccasin snake glided across the crystal-clear water of the pond. Lily pads floated on the surface and wild mountain laurel sprang up around the bank.

The first woman he'd taken still lay waiting in the cage, suffering. But he would wear her down eventually.

The nursery rhyme flowed from his mouth in a singsong rhythm, and he eased the woman onto the ground, propping her against the thick trunk of an oak facing the water. *Women are special*, the voice inside his head said. *Monday's child is fair of face.*

He traced his thumb over her heart-shaped face. She truly looked angelic, her teeth as white as pearls, her skin ivory and as soft as satin, her hair as blonde as corn silk. But her eyes, the windows to the soul, looked blank and empty.

Smiling to himself, he carefully clipped her fingernails then stowed the clippings in a bag. No doubt she'd prefer a bright nail polish, but she would go to her grave with short, unvarnished nails void of color.

Prying her mouth open, he placed the folded scrap of paper with his message inside. He threaded the needle, stabbed it in the woman's lower lip, and pushed it upward into her top lip. Over and over he continued until her lips were completely sewn together. No more gossiping, talking back, or lying.

When he was finished, he stood back and admired his handiwork. His stitches were even, neat, seamless. Pulling the tube of lipstick from his duffel bag, he slowly painted her mouth ruby red until it looked as if she was bleeding.

The plain white panties and bra were something she'd never choose, but he slipped the underwear over her naked body, gently tracing his finger over her pale, cold stomach.

The olive-green dress came next. It looked sickly against her skin, which had already started turning blue. He smoothed the sheath down over her lifeless form, then slid simple black heels onto her delicate feet.

This dress would have been perfect for a funeral, if she was going to have one.

He unwound some bramble, wrapping it around her throat as a sign to the ones who found her. Let them figure out the meaning.

His pulse quickened as he remembered her scream of terror just before he'd slashed her throat. He dotted blusher along the cut on her cheek he'd made with the broken edge of a mirror, rouge the bright red of poppies. Then he folded her hands across her stomach in prayer form.

If she could see herself, she would not be happy with the way he'd fixed her.

A light rain began to fall, droplets clinging to her long blonde eyelashes. Any surface beauty she possessed would disintegrate quickly, turning her into dust and bone. The ugliness beneath would be revealed and everyone would know that Monday's child, who was supposed to be fair of face, was nothing but a disguise.

Pulling daffodils from his bag, he ripped off the petals and scattered them on the ground, spreading her on top of them and covering her with more of the bright yellow petals. The olive-green satin dress looked sickly beneath the soft wildflowers.

As stark and ugly as the woman wearing it.

CHAPTER 7

After hours of a punishing ten-mile hike in the drizzling rain, Ellie was bone tired. In spite of her experience on the trail, her muscles and feet ached, the blisters she'd acquired on her feet were raw, and a permanent chill had invaded her body.

Today the numbness had set in. Finally. She welcomed it, drowning out the pain of the past month.

Slogging through the mud and prickly brush, she used her flashlight to illuminate her path. All day she'd noted signs of spring in the budding trees and scent of damp grass as she strove to make it to the shelter ahead. Raindrops glistened on the leaves like tiny diamonds, and wild mushrooms pushed through the soil in various colors.

With the start of the season, eager adventure-seekers had begun their journey on the 2200-mile-long trail. Statistics showed that most would never make it the entire way. The challenging physical conditions made many give up. Worse, the isolation could turn a person's mind inside out. Getting lost in the endless stretches of untamed vegetation and smothering forests came with the territory. So did the craving for hot meals and warm beds.

At the moment, Ellie relished the solitude, although being alone with her thoughts could be a scary place.

Her mind kept turning to her birth parents. If she decided to search for them, who knew what she might find? Randall and Vera had seemed to love her, yet they'd kept secrets from her that had destroyed so many innocent lives.

How would total strangers feel?

Shivering as raindrops pinged off her waterproof jacket, she darted around a bend, using her knife to cut through the tangled vines that clawed at her feet like sharp tentacles. Stumbling over a rotting tree root, she pitched forward, getting caught in a mass of brambles. Thorns stabbed her palms, puncturing her skin and drawing blood as she righted herself and crossed over a fallen pine.

Dragging a handkerchief from her pocket, she dabbed at the beads of blood and plucked several thorns from her aching palms. Thunder boomed and lightning zigzagged across the perpetually gray sky, a deluge of more rain descending. Ignoring her throbbing calf muscles, she ran up the hill. A coyote howled in the distance. The fading sun and trees closing around her resurrected her fear of the dark, a fear that had begun when Hiram imprisoned her in the cave when she was small.

Pushing away the encroaching fear, she hiked on, searching for peace and answers that might not ever come.

Shadows flitted through the forest like black fireflies. She found one shelter, but it was infested with mice and nearby a group of hillbillies were drunk on moonshine, so she trudged on. Locals whispered of plants that strangled folks as they wove through the thick bush and untraveled terrain. Other foliage grew so dense it camouflaged the deep ravines and drop-offs, creating traps to ensnare a body in the dangerous hollows below, where they might disappear forever, never to be found.

Ellie climbed higher and higher, over the hill, and followed the narrow path toward the clearing where the pond lay. There she could pitch a tent for the night.

Suddenly a gust of wind stirred the leaves and brought raindrops from the treetops, something yellow fluttering to the ground at her feet as she made it over the hillcrest. Ellie paused, stooping to see what it was.

A daffodil.

The small yellow flower petal was damp and wilted. Another fluttered to her feet, followed by another. The soft swishing of the creek against the rocks echoed in the silence, and she peered through the fog towards the water. On the bank beneath a live oak, she thought she saw something… or someone.

Curious, she pulled her flashlight and shined it across the foliage and ground as she maneuvered her way toward the sea of yellow ahead.

As she neared, she had the uncanny sense that she wasn't alone. Pivoting, she scanned the woods. The sound of insects, frogs croaking, and the falling rain filled the muggy air.

Then she realized she was right—she wasn't alone.

CHAPTER 8

For a moment, Ellie simply stood, staring at the sight with a sickening, hollow feeling in her gut. She'd set out on the trail for peace, to decide what to do with her life, and to forget the grisly memory of the children's graves imprinted in her mind.

And now a young woman had been left here. It was no accident either. Judging from the deep slash on her throat, she'd been murdered. Even more disturbing was the way she was posed, laid out on the bed of flowers with a vine full of thorns wrapped around her neck, her hands in prayer.

Rocking back on her heels, Ellie's instincts kicked in, and she pulled her weapon from her pack and turned in a wide arc, searching the area. Leaves rustled, and tree limbs dipped and swayed from the force of the wind. Creek water gurgled over the rocks, spilling onto the bank, flooding caused by the recent snowstorm.

Slowly inching closer to the scene, she kept her gun at the ready, pivoting and scanning her surroundings and the woods beyond. Even with the sound of a coyote howling and rain drizzling, an eerie quiet enveloped the area, and the wind brought the pungent blend of wildflowers and brutal death.

She had to call this in. Get the Medical Examiner and an Evidence Response Team out here ASAP.

She had to get back to work, even if she wasn't ready.

Heart hammering, she radioed Cord. As a ranger with Search and Rescue, he worked odd hours and might not be on duty now. Hell, he might not even answer. During the last case, Derrick—FBI Special Agent Fox—had practically accused Cord of being involved in the Ghost's murders. When Ellie had asked Cord about it, he'd shut down, hurt that she hadn't trusted him.

But he was damn good at his job, and even if he was pissed at her, if someone needed help, he'd come.

Static crackled and popped, the wind rattling the airwaves. Finally, his voice echoed back.

"Ranger McClain, SAR."

"Cord, it's Ellie—"

"I'm working," he said in a clipped tone.

"Good. I need you to come to the Reflection Pond."

After an awkward pause, he heaved a breath. "What's wrong?"

Her chest clenched at the sight of the jagged red slash across the woman's neck. "I… found a body."

A hushed silence fell between them, the coyote's howl growing more eerie in the quiet.

"Did you hear me?" Ellie asked.

"Yeah," he muttered. "A hiker? Accident?"

"No accident," Ellie said. "It's a woman, Cord. She's been murdered." Her detective's brain finally overrode her emotions. "Request an ERT, the ME and a recovery team. We need to process her body and look for evidence before the rain kicks in again."

"Copy that," Cord said in a husky voice. "Did you see the killer?"

The concern in his voice gave her hope that he didn't totally hate her. "I don't see anyone," she replied. "Judging from the scene, she's probably been here a while."

Already petals had come loose and were floating in the pond, wilted and turning brown.

The radio crackled. "I'll call it in and be there ASAP."

Plunged into silence, Ellie pulled her camera from her pack, snapping pictures of the ground near the mound of flowers, the brush, and the trees that stood with their branches pointing toward the heavens, like natural grave markers.

Treading carefully, she aimed her flashlight at the ground in search of footprints or other forensics, but if the killer had left prints, the rain had already washed them away.

With so many hikers en route now, it would be hard to identify a specific print. Still, if forensics found one near the body, they'd certainly try.

Careful not to contaminate the scene, she inched closer to the body. The woman looked to be in her mid-twenties. She had silky blonde hair, and her skin had a faint blue tint although it appeared whoever had killed her had applied makeup: bright-blue eye shadow and reddish-orange blusher.

Then there was the lipstick. Bright red, the color of blood.

Even with the thorny bramble wrapped around her neck, Ellie could see a jagged knife wound had ripped her from ear to ear. She had to have bled a lot, but the killer had clearly cleaned it up, covering the slash mark with the vines.

She was striking, beautiful actually. But the olive dress, her plain clipped nails and simple black shoes made her look drab. It was as if she was dressed for church, yet she had been left exposed in the wilderness where she could be ravaged by animals, her body decomposing with the elements.

The murder scene appeared to be ritualistic. Although violent, it was not a crime of passion. There was only the one knife mark. If it had been personal, there most likely would have been multiple stab wounds. Whoever had murdered her was methodical, had meticulously planned out the kill. The back of Ellie's neck prickled as she snapped another photograph. The ritualistic nature suggested that he might have killed before.

And that he would certainly kill again.

CHAPTER 9

Ellie was relieved when she finally heard footsteps and voices echoing through the dense mass of red oaks and ash trees, flashlights flickering through the dark.

Cord led the team, his smoky eyes dark with wariness as he broke through the clearing. He was the best tracker in these parts, saving countless lives over the years.

His gaze locked with hers as he took in the scene. The ERT investigators paused, assessing silently, and Dr. Laney Whitefeather, the Medical Examiner, pressed a fist against her mouth as if to stifle a gasp. "Jesus, poor baby."

The male investigator began roping off the area with crime scene tape while the female, Sydney, pulled a camera from her pack. "I'll start photographing while you do your thing, Dr. Whitefeather," she said.

"I didn't see any ID on her, but like I said, I haven't touched her," Ellie said. "Keep an eye out in case the killer dumped her purse or ID here somewhere."

Sydney surveyed the area. "Do you think she was killed here?"

Ellie pursed her lips in thought, then shined the flashlight across the rocks and weeds. "No. With her throat slashed, there would have been blood spatter. She was killed somewhere else, then the bastard cleaned her up, dressed her, and brought her out here."

Laney's face was ashen. "How did you find her?"

"I've been hiking since yesterday, planned to pitch a tent by the pond tonight, then noticed the flowers in the wind. When I crossed the creek, there she was." She gestured toward the ground. "So far, there are no definitive footprints, although the rain could have washed them away."

Laney donned gloves and boot covers, then picked her way across the damp grass.

"How long do you think she's been here?" Cord asked.

"Hard to say with the cooler temperatures last night and this morning."

Laney used a flashlight to examine the woman's neck. "Initially, it appears she died of exsanguination; blood loss caused from having her throat slit. Although that's not official. We'll have to wait until I do the autopsy to determine exact cause of death, time of death, and whether or not she was drugged or sustained other injuries before she died." She gestured toward the clothing and makeup. "What do you make of this?"

Ellie shrugged. "The garish makeup has to mean something. Maybe he wanted to downplay her beauty because she'd wronged him somehow."

Laney shivered.

As disturbing as it was to dig into the mind of a killer, knowing what made him tick was essential to uncovering his identity and motive, to predict his next step. "His MO reads like a repeat killer."

Laney examined the woman's hands and wrists, and then her eyes, which were still open. "No petechial hemorrhaging." With gloved fingers she inched the woman's face left and right, noting slight bruising on her jaws. "Maybe we'll get lucky and pull a partial print or some DNA on her throat or clothing." She lifted one pale hand to examine it. "It looks like he cut her fingernails. Probably to eliminate evidence. But I'll try."

The sound of the workers combing the area echoed around them while Laney continued her initial exam, careful not to smear the blood-red lipstick as she used her fingers to open the woman's mouth. A gasp escaped her before she looked up at Ellie.

"What is it?" Ellie asked.

An odd look crossed Laney's face. "The bastard sewed her lips shut."

CHAPTER 10

"He sewed her lips closed?" Ellie asked, swallowing hard. "Like a mortician would?"

"Exactly," Laney said, nodding.

Ellie glanced at Cord, noticed an odd look on his face. But his radio crackled, and he walked over to a boulder several feet away to answer the call.

"That gives the MO a new meaning." Ellie's mind raced. Instead of dressing the women for an outing or church, the killer dressed and posed his victim for burial.

The realization made her skin crawl.

"Then we might be dealing with someone experienced in preparing dead bodies for burial or cremation." Ellie thought out loud.

"That's possible." A frown marred Laney's face. "Only, he left her eyes untouched, whereas a mortician would have glued her eyelids closed as well." Laney stood, pushing her glasses up with the back of her hand. "Although with the internet, El, anyone who wanted to know about preparing a body could find that information."

"True. He could just be some psycho intrigued by the death process. Or necrophilia. Or hell, he might have sewn her mouth closed because he didn't want her to talk."

"I'll definitely look for signs of sexual abuse, both pre- and postmortem." Laney gestured at the woman's throat. "There's a small line of bruising that may indicate he strangled her. Although this doesn't look like rope burns. Maybe something else."

Ellie winced at the thick, deep bruising. "Get me her prints right away. I need to notify the family and question them."

Laney nodded.

"Meanwhile, I'll search for other crimes bearing a similar MO."

"You think he's done this before?" asked Laney.

Ellie shrugged. "I don't know, but this type of display took planning and a certain kind of pathology. It wasn't just a crime of opportunity."

Special Agent Derrick Fox would be the best source for information on other similar cases, she thought, as the breeze swirled dead leaves and daffodil petals around her muddy boots. But Derrick Fox was the last person on earth she wanted anything to do with.

The memory of the last time she'd seen him taunted her. She'd stood on the periphery of a graveyard as he and his mother said their final goodbyes to Derrick's little sister, Kim, the first girl Hiram had murdered.

Derrick had come to Crooked Creek with the theory of a serial killer, opening her eyes to the truth about her father. He blamed Randall for closing Kim's case too soon, then later for keeping suspicions about Hiram from the police. She and Derrick had spent a heated night together in the mountains during the investigation—and then he'd accused her of sleeping with him to distract him, so she could protect her dad.

He'd been right about everything except the latter. But it didn't matter now. He hated her and her family—and she could hardly blame him.

She'd do some research on her own, she told herself. Meanwhile, she watched as the crime team scoured the area and Laney finished her initial exam.

Cord returned, frowning. "I have to go. There's trouble over at Rattlesnake Ridge."

"What kind of trouble?" Ellie asked.

"Couple of hikers lost their footing and one broke his ankle." He took off on the path south, and Ellie followed Laney down the mountain, where Laney drove Ellie to her Jeep.

"I'll send those prints in ASAP," Laney said as Ellie got out.

Thanking her, Ellie climbed into her Jeep, and retrieved her phone from the glove compartment. She had to call her captain immediately. He'd ordered her to take some time off but she'd just stumbled on a gruesome murder and she couldn't ignore it. The poor woman needed justice.

CHAPTER 11

Pigeon Lake

Skinny Minnie Whiny Vinny. Skinny Minnie Whiny Vinny. You're so stupid, you don't know when to get out of the rain.

The voice chimed in Vinny Holcomb's ears as he rocked back and forth in the old dilapidated house. He hated the nickname. Hated the house.

The one that held the memories of all the bad things.

Blood dripped through his fingers and dotted his clothes, but he didn't care. She had deserved to die for what she'd done.

Her ugly laugh echoed in his ears, a sound that gnawed on his nerve endings like a falcon sinking its talons into its prey.

You're a loser, boy. You don't have any friends. You'll never have any.

But she was wrong. He'd made friends with Hiram. Hiram was like him. He'd suffered and been locked away by the woman who was supposed to love him.

He pulled the article about the Ghost from his wet pocket, unfolded it and smiled at the headline.

"I'll be your friend if you'll be mine," Hiram had said as they'd ditched their pills in the potted plants in the solarium.

Vinny promised he would. He'd do anything for Hiram. Anything.

CHAPTER 12

Between Springer Mountain and Crooked Creek

Dammit. Her phone was dead.

Ellie snagged her charger and plugged it in, starting the Jeep and flooring the engine. Nerves on edge, she sped around the twisting mountain road back toward Crooked Creek as night hugged the forest. Wind whipped through the towering trees and howled off the steep mountain ridges, tree limbs rocking back and forth.

Self-doubt warred with Ellie's stubbornness. She should call Bryce. She would have no choice but to deal with him on the case.

But not tonight.

Tonight she'd call the captain and let him deal with the new sheriff. Deputy Heath Landrum who'd joined Crooked Creek's police department a few months ago, was young and green, but he was working out as a decent cop. Still, his expertise was in technology, and he hadn't worked the field on a big case. Not to mention the fact that her gut was telling her this one would be big.

Her tires screeched as she swerved up the drive to her bungalow. Her body ached from hiking, and a hot shower and a strong vodka beckoned.

Grabbing her phone and her backpack from the trunk, she dragged herself up the porch steps and let herself inside.

The sound of the furnace's rumble was comforting as she entered, and she carried her bag to the laundry room, dumping it there. She'd unpack tomorrow.

With her phone battery still low, the hot shower came first. Stripping her soggy clothing, she stepped beneath the warm spray of water and scrubbed her skin raw, desperate to cleanse the sweat and dirt from her pores.

And the horrific images of that dead woman from her mind.

After soaping her hair, she rinsed it, then conditioned the hell out of it, before rinsing again. Stepping out of the shower, she pulled on a pair of sweats and after a quick towel dry of her hair, she walked to the kitchen, grabbed a frozen pizza from the freezer and stuck it in the oven.

While the pizza cooked, Ellie poured herself a chilled vodka, carrying it to her den, where she flipped on the gas logs. Already the dark shadows of death were stampeding around her, reminding her of the screams of dead children that she couldn't shake from her head.

Now the screams of the murdered woman on the bed of daffodils were added to the haunting collection.

Fortifying herself with the drink, she grabbed her phone and called her boss. He sounded a little groggy when he answered. "I'm sorry if I woke you, Captain. But it's important."

"I thought you were on vacation," he growled.

Ellie rolled her eyes. It was hardly a vacation. "It got cut short when I found a woman murdered today."

"What?" He spewed a string of expletives. "How? Where?"

She explained about the dead woman and the MO. "It looks ritualistic, Captain. Like he might have done this before."

"Aww, geesh. The dust hasn't settled from the Ghost case yet."

"Tell me about it," Ellie said sardonically.

"Are you ready to take this on, or do you want me to hand it over to the sheriff?"

Hell, no she didn't. "I can handle it." Besides, something about the woman had spoken to her. Those terrified eyes, as if she hadn't known such horror existed. "I'm going to run a search for cases with similar MOs," she carried on. "Hopefully, Dr. Whitefeather will have her autopsy complete tomorrow and we can get an ID. Then I can notify and question the family."

"I'll call Bryce and inform him," Captain Hale said. "Meanwhile, get some rest and let me know what else you need."

Ellie thanked him, then hung up and checked her voicemail. There were two more messages from Angelica Gomez. Both the same, wanting to tell Ellie's story.

But Ellie didn't have the energy to deal with the journalist now. She'd been crucified enough already.

The next message was from her father: "*Hey, honey. I know you're still upset, but your mom is so torn up, and that reporter is hounding her. Please don't tell the press about the adoption yet. I don't think your mother is ready for all that to come out.*"

Ellie deleted the message. Of course Vera wasn't ready. Her fall from society had hit her hard.

There were two more voicemails from her counselor asking if she wanted to reschedule along with a reminder about the group therapy session.

She deleted them, then discovered a text from an unsaved number. The hate mail she'd received about the Ghost case sprung to mind, messages that left her sleepless, searching her house every time she entered and leaving the lights on all night long.

Taking a deep breath, she opened the message, expecting more hate. But it was even more chilling.

Monday's child is fair of face. Did you find her, Detective Reeves?

CHAPTER 13

Somewhere on the AT

The screams of the other woman reverberated over and over in her head as he tied her arms and legs spread-eagle inside the cage.

The beating last night had been bad. But whatever he had in store for her now was going to be worse.

"It's your fault she had to die, Cathy," he spat. "Your fault I have to do this."

Terror washed over her as he tied the restraints tighter. The screech of the door swinging back and forth at the top of the stairs bounced off the cold dank walls, the crack of the whip against the floor echoing around the basement.

Tears pooled in her eyes as she braced herself for the sharp sting of leather cutting into bare skin, but instead he knelt beside her. All she could see were dark eyes boring through the holes of his mask, but his voice sounded familiar, and he smelled of wood, sweat and dirt, as if he'd been outdoors.

Grunting, he bent beside her, and she saw something rubbery between his teeth. Some kind of tubing… a tourniquet.

He peeled it from his mouth and with gloved hands wrapped the tube around her upper arm, tying it so tightly that she sucked in a sharp breath. A second later, silver glinted in the dark and she saw the needle.

Terrified of what he was going to inject her with, she gritted her teeth as he jabbed the needle into her arm. But instead of the slow burn of drugs seeping into her, she realized he was drawing blood.

Helpless to do anything but lie at his mercy, she searched her memory for where she'd heard his voice before.

But as he drew vial after vial of blood, she grew weaker and weaker...

CHAPTER 14

Tuesday

Crooked Creek

Ellie rubbed her bleary eyes. She'd spent half the night searching every database she had access to for crimes even remotely similar to the MO of the murdered woman she'd found at Reflection Pond.

Although there were a few scattered cases in other states involving necrophilia, nothing fit with the way the killer had posed his victim.

She was aching from exhaustion, yet wired from wondering why the killer had contacted her personally, as she met Heath and her captain at the station first thing.

The sheriff stormed in within minutes of her arrival. "Detective Reeves," Bryce said, his voice loud, irritated, "why didn't you call me yesterday about that body?"

Ellie tensed and poured herself a cup of coffee, determined to stay calm. Bryce liked goading her and she refused to rise to it. "Because I could handle it alone. I figured you were busy anyway." Probably busy drinking on the job. "Besides, I knew the captain would get in touch with you."

Bryce glared at her, then followed her into her office, where Captain Hale and Deputy Landrum were waiting. She explained about the message from the killer. "We'll try to trace the call," Ellie said. "But this guy is smart. Most likely he used a burner phone." She paused. "I need to meet Dr. Whitefeather soon."

Deputy Landrum looked up from his laptop. "I think I have an ID on the victim. I ran her face through facial recognition software and got a hit."

That was fast. She'd thought they'd have to wait on DNA or prints. "Who is she?"

Heath angled his laptop for her to see. "Her name is Courtney Wooten. She's twenty-nine, developed her own makeup line and is trending on YouTube and Twitter. She's also apparently working on a line of party dresses."

No wonder her face had popped up so quickly.

"Is she local?"

"Home address is Atlanta, but she has one sister, Renee, who lives a few miles outside Crooked Creek. Parents were killed in a car crash when she was ten, so she and her sister went to live with the grandmother. Grandma died last year."

"We need to talk to Renee."

"I'll send you her contact information," Heath said. "I'm studying the vic's social media for love interests, but so far, she's all over the map in her dating."

Bryce looked down at the photos of Courtney and whistled. "A pretty girl, talented. I guess she has lots of interest."

Heath nodded, a frown creasing his eyes. "I've just started digging into her personal life and business. There could be something there."

Maybe it was something to do with the makeup line, Ellie thought. All beauty and fashion, yet look at how the killer had posed her.

A noise in the bullpen made them all look up, and Angelica Gomez appeared, her cameraman in tow. Ellie clenched her hands by her sides. She had been running from the press for weeks now. She'd gone as far as hiding in the woods to escape it all. But there was no escape. And she refused to tuck her tail and run now when Courtney Wooten needed her. The reporter was tenacious but she had been helpful in the last case—Ellie just had to manage her.

"I'd talk to her, but since you obviously left me out of the loop yesterday, I guess you'll have to," Bryce said to Ellie.

"No problem. I've got it." The whir of phones and computers buzzed in the room as Ellie crossed to the reporter. Two new deputies had been brought in and were in training to assist on routine calls.

"Detective Reeves," Angelica said. "Do you have a minute?"

"If this is personal, then no," Ellie replied, arching a brow.

Angelica's dark eyes narrowed. "It's about the body you found yesterday."

She was about to ask how Angelica knew, but the reporter could have spoken to the sheriff. Many journalists had police scanners and picked up information that way. Besides, it didn't really matter. The public would find out. It was best to get ahead of it.

Angelica pushed her microphone towards Ellie. "This is Angelica Gomez, WRIX Channel Five news coming to you live with Detective Ellie Reeves." Angelica smiled for the camera. "Many of you remember her as the detective who broke the Ghost case a few weeks ago. But just yesterday, in Bluff County, another murder has occurred. This time the body of a young female." She gestured to Ellie. "Detective?"

Ellie hated the limelight, but she forced herself to concentrate on the job. "Yes, I'm sorry to say that a woman's body was found on the Appalachian Trail late yesterday. I cannot divulge details of the case until family has been notified, but if you have any information regarding a crime committed in the area, please call the local police department."

Her phone buzzed on her hip. "I will make a statement once we learn more," she said, pushing the mic aside and checking the message.

Laney was almost finished with the autopsy. She had to go.

CHAPTER 15

Bluff County Medical Examiner's Office

Ellie would never get used to the morgue. Formaldehyde blended with cleaning chemicals, made more potent by the scent of decomp clogging the air in the sterile room.

Laney's office, the autopsy room and refrigerators were housed on the same floor.

The walls had been freshly painted, and the stainless-steel table and its instruments shone beneath the bright light.

Lifting her face shield as Ellie approached, Laney wore a scowl.

"I have a likely ID on her," Ellie said as she moved up beside the woman's body. Her blue skin accentuated bruises on her torso that Ellie hadn't seen when the woman was clothed. Now she lay draped in a sheet, the Y incision Laney had made snaking down her chest.

"Is she from the area?" Laney asked.

"Atlanta," Ellie said. "Heath is digging into her. But her sister lives not too far from town."

Laney gently brushed her hand over the woman's pale blonde hair. "She was pretty," she said, a sad note to her voice. "And so young."

"Twenty-nine," Ellie replied, explaining about the YouTube makeup videos. "Now, what can you tell me?"

Laney sighed. "Just as I initially thought, she died of exsanguination due to her throat being slashed." She pointed to the laceration on the woman's throat. "He went deep, but it appears to be one clean cut, not multiple stab wounds. Looks like a hunting knife of some kind."

"Fast and efficient, and hunting knives are a dime a dozen in these parts," Ellie murmured. She even had one. "And the bramble around her neck. That has to mean something."

"That was postmortem, so he didn't strangle her with it." Laney angled the woman's head to the side. "There's also a deeper line of bruising around her throat, as if he put something around her neck."

Ellie leaned closer to examine it. "It's wide, almost like a band."

"Possible asphyxiation sex gone bad," Laney suggested. "Although there were no signs of sexual activity or abuse. But he did beat her." As Laney lowered the sheet, Ellie saw black and purple bruises on the victim's arms and legs. Then she tilted her sideways to reveal deep slash marks.

A sick feeling washed over Ellie. "He whipped her."

Her thoughts took a twisted turn as she struggled to understand the evidence. "That bruising… It could have been a choker of some kind. Like one used in S and M, or a dog collar."

Laney pressed the back of her hand over her forehead and exhaled. "You'd think we'd become immune to this stuff," she said. "But the depravity still gets to me."

Ellie simply nodded agreement. When the cruelty of what one human could inflict on another stopped bothering them, it would be time to quit. "Time of death?"

"Monday, sometime between four p.m. and six p.m." Laney lifted a small scrap of paper. "This was in her mouth."

Ellie clenched her teeth and read the message which appeared to have been written on an old typewriter. *Monday's child is fair of face.*

"She hadn't been dead long when I found her."

Yet she'd missed him, and the killer could have been close by, hiding in the woods, watching…

CHAPTER 16

Rocky Forge, Georgia

Mid-morning sunshine slanted golden rays across the mountains as Ellie parked at Renee Wooten's clapboard house. Courtney's sister lived in a small, older neighborhood called Rocky Forge where the houses had been built in the fifties and looked as if they were stacked on the rising hills like stair steps.

According to Heath's last text, Renee cleaned rooms at a local motel, but today was her day off. The photograph he sent made it hard to believe Courtney and Renee were sisters. Where Courtney was five-ten, thin, blonde and model-pretty, Renee was barely five feet, slightly chubby, and had muddy brown hair.

A green Chevy sat in the drive, and the front door was open as if to let fresh air into the house. A tabby cat lay curled on a tattered straight chair by the door.

Ellie's stomach knotted as she got out of the vehicle. Notifying family of a loved one's death was never easy or pleasant, but it had to be done.

Gravel crunched beneath her feet as she walked to the stoop and climbed the two steps, knocking on the screen door, and tapping her foot as she waited. After a few minutes, she knocked again and called out Renee's name. But there was nothing. Maybe she wasn't home after all.

A noise from the rear caught her attention, and Ellie went down the steps, walking around the side of the house. A clothesline was strung between two trees, and she spotted a young brunette hanging sheets on the line, her ponytail swinging as she worked.

A stiff breeze caught the material and sent it flapping, the woman struggling to untangle it.

Ellie called her name and Renee turned with a surprised look. "Yes. Who are you?"

"Detective Ellie Reeves," Ellie said, gesturing to the shield attached to her belt. "Crooked Creek Police Department."

The woman's face suddenly paled. "Oh, my word. You're that detective who solved the Ghost case?"

Ellie nodded. "Yes, I am. But I'm not here about that." She hesitated, waiting to see if Renee made the connection from the morning news. A second later, the woman swayed slightly, indicating she had.

"I'm sorry to have to tell you this, Renee. But yesterday we found a body we believe to be your sister in the woods not far from here." Ellie showed Renee a picture of the woman's face. "This is your sister Courtney, correct?"

"Yes." Dropping the fitted sheet she'd been hanging, Renee staggered over to a metal chair beside a fire pit made from an old metal tire rim.

Ellie hurried to her, bending down beside her. "I'm so sorry for your loss, Renee."

Tears pooled in the woman's brown eyes, her hand trembling as she wiped at them. "Wh-what happened?" she asked in a whisper.

Ellie didn't intend to share the details. "I'm afraid she was murdered. At the moment, her body is at the morgue, but I can let you know when she's ready to be released so you can make arrangements."

Renee nodded, her lip quivering.

"Is there anyone I can call for you?" Ellie asked.

The woman gave her a blank look, denial and shock glazing her eyes. "You said she was found near here, not in Atlanta."

Ellie nodded. "Was she coming to see you?"

Surprise flashed in Renee's eyes. "If she was, I didn't know anything about it."

"I understand you need time," Ellie said softly. "But I have to ask you some questions…"

Nodding again, Renee blinked as if to clear her mind. "What can I do?"

"Tell me about Courtney," Ellie said. "Were you two close?"

Renee shrugged. "Not really. Courtney was gorgeous and cared more about her looks and her business than her own family."

Ellie's heart clenched. "I'm sure she cared about you," she said.

Renee lifted her head, and Ellie noticed the woman's skin was pockmarked, as if she'd suffered badly with acne. "She was embarrassed by me."

"That must have hurt." Ellie knew all about family dysfunction. After wanting a sibling all her life, she finally had one. One who'd wanted her dead.

"I accepted how she was a long time ago," Renee said with a shrug.

Ellie hesitated at the resignation in the woman's voice. An image of the way Courtney had been dressed—in a plain dress and shoes, even plain underwear—taunted Ellie. The killer had chosen those garments for a reason.

"Did Courtney have a boyfriend or girlfriend? Anyone special in her life?" Ellie asked.

"Not that I know of." Renee shrugged again. "She changed guys like she changed her shoes, always looking for a new style or prettier one."

"How about enemies? Maybe a jilted lover?"

"Like I said, I don't know about her personal life. We haven't talked in months." Renee stood, wiping her hands down her sides. "Although she did make a few enemies with her business."

Ellie raised a brow, her interest piqued. "Tell me about that."

With a sigh, Renee walked back to the laundry basket, picked up the fitted sheet and stretched it out to hang on the line. "Courtney's makeup line made her wealthy," she said, her tone tinged with disapproval. "Some people loved her products, but at least a couple of women had adverse reactions to some chemical in the foundation."

Heading over, Ellie snagged the opposite end of the sheet and helped Renee even it out so she could hang it on the line. "What happened?"

Renee's gaze met hers. "The women's faces were scarred. A couple had plastic surgery to repair the damage. They sued Courtney, but she paid them off and made them sign NDAs saying they'd keep quiet." Renee released a sigh. "But Courtney just kept on making the product without changing anything."

"If you two didn't talk, how do you know about this?" Ellie asked.

Renee lifted her hand to her cheek. "Because I was one of them."

CHAPTER 17

The Men's Den, Bluff County

The darkness called him again. He'd fought it for years, but those little girls' graves had stirred up all the pain and anguish he'd suffered. Suffering he'd hidden for so long that he'd become adept at wearing a disguise.

Even the ones closest to him had no idea the evil thoughts that consumed him.

"Tuesday's child is full of grace," he silently chanted as he swirled the amber whiskey in his glass. Country music boomed through the speakers of the titty bar that was situated off the highway drawing locals and truckers. Women twirled and gyrated, showing off oil-slick bodies that tempted the audience to reach for their wallets and throw cash on the wooden floor of the stage or stuff it in their G-strings. The dim lights meant to enhance the atmosphere and provide cover for the patrons who wanted to remain anonymous made him relax, even as stage lights painted the dancers' bodies in a rainbow of colors.

The one he'd come to see finally took center stage. Her lithe form was silhouetted by the haze of light, the sheer beauty of her striking him as she glided like a cat from the shadows.

He sat up straighter. He was not here for pleasure, but to watch for the perfect moment to strike.

But hell, who said a man couldn't enjoy his work?

Adorned in a skimpy black negligee with red sparkly heels and silver glitter shimmering off her inch-long eyelashes, her gaze spanned the room. It was as if she was a bloodthirsty vampire sniffing out the tastiest piece of meat in the house.

The music piped up, and she spun around, dropped to the floor and crawled across the stage, her head lifted, tongue flitting in and out like a serpent's. When she reached the edge of the stage, she stood, twisted around, then dropped her head forward. Her long dark hair grazed the floor as she shook her ass in his face.

Shouts and jeers erupted from the men in the room, and an old fat guy at the table in the corner rubbed his cock.

The woman was definitely comfortable with her body.

Anticipation heated his blood, but not for sex. To have her chained, at his command.

Would she fight or succumb?

Checking his watch, he tossed back his drink, then waved his hand to order another. She had another number after the next performer. But when she finished the show, she would be his.

CHAPTER 18

Decatur, Georgia

Special Agent Derrick Fox slid onto the barstool at Manuel's Tavern, palmed a handful of nuts from the bowl on the bar, tossed a few in his mouth, then waved at his partner as he loped in. Special Agent Bennett Sanders joined him, ordering a scotch. It was a little early for Derrick to drink, so he asked for a club soda with a twist of lime.

A news report flashed on the TV screen hanging over the bar, and he went still as Detective Ellie Reeves appeared. Angelica Gomez, the same reporter who'd covered the serial case involving his sister Kim and was covering the court case against Ellie's father, thrust her mic at Ellie.

He braced himself for a story about the dismissal of the charges against Randall Reeves, or one focusing on the victims' families, who'd screamed incompetence at law enforcement in the Ghost case. Not that he could blame them.

His own family had suffered at their hands for years. His sister was Hiram's first victim twenty-five years ago, prompting his father to kill himself out of guilt because he'd been the primary suspect at the time.

"Isn't that the detective you worked with?" Bennett asked.

"Yes." Derrick grimaced. He hadn't spoken to her since he'd left Crooked Creek.

He'd suspected Reeves had covered for Hiram and he'd torn her family apart in the investigation. Still, he'd do it again if he had to. He'd gotten justice for Kim and nearly a dozen other little girls.

He and Bennett both quieted as Ellie responded to the reporter.

"Well, that was brief," Bennett muttered, as Ellie pushed the mic away.

The ice in his glass clinked as Derrick swirled it around. His curiosity was definitely piqued. The investigation had obviously just begun, but Ellie already looked worn down.

"Why don't you call the detective and ask for the details?" Bennett asked.

Derrick shook his head, tension forming a knot in his belly at the thought of talking to Ellie again. Too much had happened between them when he was in Crooked Creek. They had nothing to talk about now.

He was a by-the-book agent, and her parents had crossed the line.

Then again, he'd crossed it himself by sleeping with her. It wouldn't happen again.

CHAPTER 19

Crooked Creek

Stopping for a late lunch at the Corner Café on the way back to Crooked Creek, Ellie's phone buzzed as she climbed from her Jeep.

It was Kennedy Sledge. She let it go to voicemail, then listened to the message before she entered the café.

"Ellie, this is Kennedy Sledge. I thought you were taking some time off work, but I saw your interview this morning. If you want to talk about what happened, please feel free to call me anytime day or night."

Putting her phone away, Ellie briefly considered a chat, but had no time now. Whispers and stares met her as she entered the café, Meddlin' Maude and her brood growing hushed as Ellie seated herself at the counter. The nosy busybodies had nothing better to do, she guessed.

"I can't believe she's still working for the police department after what her daddy did," Maude groused.

"How can we trust her?" one of Maude's hens murmured.

"You saw her on the news. She wouldn't tell anyone what's going on," Fanny Mae, one half of the Stichin' Sisters who owned the quilt shop in town, muttered. "For all we know, all our daughters and granddaughters are in danger now."

Ellie curled her fingers into fists. She wanted to tell the gossipmongers to back off, but losing her temper would only feed the rumor mill. Someone had already gotten hold of the fact that she'd seen a child therapist and it had snowballed. It was a game of Chinese whispers, the story growing more dramatic each time it was shared. The latest was that Ellie had had a nervous breakdown and was going to be institutionalized. That was another reason she'd kept her sessions with Kennedy Sledge to herself.

"What'll you have, hon?" Lola, the owner asked with a sympathetic smile.

"A chicken salad sandwich to go." There was no way would she eat in here with those ladies. It was a wonder she didn't totally combust as their fiery stares pierced her back.

Lola returned a moment later with a bag and a Diet Soda. "I threw in a slice of peach pie for you, Ellie. You look like you need it."

Ellie bit back a laugh. Southern folks thought food fixed everything. Casseroles and pies and sweet tea were staples delivered to your door whenever someone died. Widowed men were buried beneath them before their wives' bodies even got cold.

Tossing some cash, including a generous tip, onto the counter, Ellie snatched her food and hurried back outside. Ten minutes later, she wolfed down the sandwich and pie in her office, then filled Heath and her captain in on what she'd learned from Renee Wooten.

"I've already checked Renee's alibi, and it's rock solid, but the other women who filed lawsuits against Courtney have motive," Ellie said. "We need to find out who they are."

"That'll be hard if what you said is true about the non-disclosure agreement," replied Captain Hale, "although under the circumstances, we can probably convince a judge to issue warrants and force the lawyer who drew up the papers to talk."

"You'd think he'd want to know who killed Courtney," Ellie said. "But if he's invested in the company, he may not want the truth to come out. The company might have to be shut down and that could mean big money."

Captain Hale popped a mint into his mouth, his replacement for his life-long smoking habit. "I'll handle that," he said, pulling his phone from his pocket and leaving.

"I'm still looking at her social media for clues," Heath said. "But so far, nothing from a man who might have been a stalker." He hesitated. "You mentioned bruising that looked like a collar… I'll see what I can find on sex clubs in the area. There's an adult toyshop called The Love Shack on the highway near a strip club. Maybe our perpetrator bought something from there."

"According to Laney, there wasn't evidence of recent sexual activity or abuse," Ellie said. "Although the collar could be about domination and not sex. Go check out that place and see what the owner has to say. Maybe he's got a customer who's into Dominatrix or S and M."

Heath agreed, then left, and Ellie turned to her computer. The killer's signature was important. He'd clearly chosen the plain, drab clothing because it was the opposite of Courtney. But what did the bed of daffodils mean?

Determined to understand what made this monster tick, she ran a search for the symbolism of the wildflowers.

Her eyes widened as she began to read.

Daffodils are known as a schizophrenic flower which symbolize resurrection and rebirth, or self-love and vanity. They are also the flower of the underworld.

Ellie threaded her fingers through her hair. This killer was definitely trying to tell them something about his view of the victim. Was he a religious man?

Her curiosity raised, she googled the meaning of thorny bramble. A quick search yielded results.

Thorns symbolize grief, difficulties and sin. The thorns represent minor sins. Bramble represents major sins.

Ellie sat back with a weary sigh. Did the killer see himself as some kind of saint who'd been chosen to dole out punishment to sinners?

CHAPTER 20

Red River, Georgia

The ice-cold water lapped back and forth against the riverbank—a peaceful, reverent sound against the call of the wild inside him.

He carefully laid the woman onto the moss-covered ground, his teeth clenched as he dressed her in the plain cotton panties. Before he fitted her with the bra, he made x's with his knife on her breasts, x's to expose the implants she'd gotten to enhance her chest. Another fake, just like Cathy. He punctured them with his knife, smiling as the saline began to leak down her tattered skin.

Then came the simple white bra. For her, he'd chosen a deep crimson dress which seemed fitting for her occupation, but he buttoned the dress up to her neck. The red color blended with the jagged bloody cut on her neck, and he carefully wound the bramble around her throat, then placed a red poppy in her hair. But instead of the silver sparkly heels she would have chosen, he completed the outfit with simple black flats. She had to be humbled somehow.

While she lay silently, eyes staring at the roving clouds above as if she could see the heavens but she knew she'd never make it there, he scattered the daffodils across the ground by the river's edge. A beautiful blanket of yellow dotted the green, then he lifted the woman and placed her on the bed. Spreading more daffodils across her lifeless body, he buried her in the yellow petals until only slivers of red peeked through the wildflowers.

Folding her hands in prayer fashion, he tucked a Bible page between her fingers, then removed his needle and suture thread and sewed her lips together.

Smiling at his handiwork, he stood, then decided to send Detective Reeves a text.

Laughing as he hit send, he grabbed his duffel bag and headed back onto the trail with a hitch in his step. One still waited in the cage for him. She still hadn't broken, and that meant more fun and games tonight.

Then tomorrow another woman would have to die.

CHAPTER 21

Crooked Creek

Night was falling, and Ellie was still at the office. Frustrated, she still had no real lead in the Courtney Wooten murder. Her phone beeped with a text. Hoping for good news from Heath, she quickly checked the message.

But her heart stuttered when she saw the wording.

Tuesday's child is full of grace. Can you find her, Detective Reeves?

Her hand trembled, and her stomach pitched to her throat. It was *him*. He'd already killed again.

And now he was taunting her.

She tried messaging back, but it was undeliverable, and just as before, when she called the number, it was unavailable. It was most likely another burner phone.

Her body tight with tension, she stood and hurried to inform her boss. "Captain Hale, look at this. He's killed again."

He ran a hand over his balding head as he glanced at the message. "By God, I was afraid of that."

She had been, too.

"I'm still working on the warrants to find out who all filed lawsuits against Ms. Wooten," the captain said. "Maybe the killer took another victim to throw us off?"

"Maybe," Ellie conceded, although she sensed there was more to it. "But that would be risky. This man is methodical, a planner, detail oriented. It's like he's playing a game."

Captain Hale sucked air through his teeth. "What is he trying to tell us with that rhyme?"

Ellie shook her head. "I don't know for sure. But he left victim number one, a beauty expert, at the Reflection Pond, as if to imply she needed to look within herself." She scratched her hair, mind racing. "Tuesday's child is full of grace—does he mean she's full of grace or lacking it?"

She paced across his office, struggling to understand the killer's message.

"Falling from grace means losing God's favor," Captain Hale said.

Ellie snapped her fingers. "Right. Then perhaps he's leaving her at a church or some place of religious significance."

"I'll call Sheriff Waters and let him know what's going on. We need deputies out searching."

"Ask him to put Shondra on it," Ellie said. "And I'll research local churches." While he called Bryce, she returned to her office. Victim one had been found on the AT, and her gut told her to look there now.

She studied the map on her wall, using pushpins to mark the potential spots she recalled, but she couldn't remember them all. On her laptop, she googled churches within a twenty-mile radius and came up with ten.

Her phone jangled. It was the sheriff.

"Ellie, what the hell!" Bryce yelled the moment she answered. "Captain Hale just called and said another woman has been murdered."

"I think so," Ellie said, relaying the message she'd received. "So far, we haven't found her body, but we need to begin looking. We might catch him in the act. I'm sending you a list of churches to forward to your deputies. We need all hands on deck, Bryce. Including Shondra."

"You don't have to tell me how to run the investigation," Bryce replied. "And FYI, Shondra didn't show up to work the last two days and didn't bother to call either. If you talk to her, tell her she's on thin ice."

Ellie frowned. Shondra must be really pissed at Bryce not to even call. Worry flitted through her, and she tried Shondra's number. She got her voicemail and left a message.

Hanging up, her gaze scanned the names of the churches again, and her pulse clamored as one name jumped out. *Tuesday's child is full of grace.* There was a church called Church of Grace at the edge of the Blue Ridge mountains, about fifteen miles north of Crooked Creek.

She phoned Cord, but he didn't answer, so she left a message for him to spread the word to the park service to be on the lookout for a second body. She snatched her keys and jacket and went to tell the captain where she was going.

Twenty minutes later, the image of Courtney Wooten lying on the grave of wildflowers taunted Ellie as she maneuvered the drive to the Baptist church. Night had set in, stars glittering above the lawn, which was dotted with white tents.

The parking lot was packed with cars, and a sign welcomed people of all walks to the Tent Revival. Two tables selling homemade baked goods for the youth group sat in front, manned by teenagers passing out fliers about an upcoming mission trip to Honduras.

As she climbed from her Jeep, old-time gospel singing echoed from the large tent, drowning out sounds of the cicadas and crickets. Growing up, she'd attended revivals with her parents and always felt uncomfortable, as if the preacher's sermon and Bible thumping were directed at her. The born-again preachers used to rove the aisles, preaching hellfire and damnation, eyes boring into her as if to call her a sinner and suggest she should throw herself on the altar for mercy. Even from the parking lot, she spotted parishioners waving hands in the air and shouting their "Amens" as the reverend began to suck wind.

According to the sign, the revival had started an hour ago, and judging from the enthusiasm, emotions were building. The killer would not have come near this place, not with this many people around.

Still, she decided to look around the property. A graveyard bathed in darkness occupied one side of the property, artificial flowers waving back and forth in the wind. She headed in that direction, veering away from the revival and the holy rollers who'd begun crying and speaking in tongues.

Just as she reached the gate to the cemetery, her phone buzzed. Dread tightened her stomach as she answered. "Cord?"

"I got your message about another victim."

"I'm at the Church of Grace now," Ellie said.

"She's not there," Cord said.

Ellie stilled, her gaze skipping over names carved on tombstones with dates going back to the early 1900s. "How do you know?"

"Because I found her."

CHAPTER 22

Ole Glory Church

Perspiration beaded on Ellie's skin as she pulled down the graveled road to the old-as-dirt chapel at the edge of Red River, named so because at dusk the water shimmered with red streaks. Some attributed the color to the Georgia red clay soil although others professed it was blood shed by Jesus. The ways of the church dated back centuries, with rumors that snake handling and exorcisms abounded in the parish. The men were heads of the households and in total control, while the women were not allowed to wear pants or makeup, subservient to their husbands.

The small white wooden building was nestled in the woods and known for its traditional baptisms. At the water's edge, people gathered to sing hymns while the Southern Baptist preacher dunked lost souls beneath the icy water to cleanse their sins.

Cord's truck was parked beneath a live oak. She'd called the captain on her way, and he was sending out Laney and the Evidence Response Team. Getting out with her flashlight, Ellie walked down the hill to meet him. For a moment, she was struck by the odd way he was stooped beside the body, staring at the woman.

Cord knew better than to disturb a crime scene, but there was something strange about the intense look on his face and his breathing, which sounded erratic.

The whoosh of the water rushing over the jagged river rocks blended with the whistle of the wind. Slowly, she approached, her boots skidding on the damp ground as she went down the hill.

Algae and stonewort crept along the riverbank and she knew from fishing with her father that trout, bass and carp swam below the surface. At the thought of her father, her stomach churned.

Moonlight glowed through the tree branches, shimmering along the water and illuminating the wildflowers covering the ground.

"Cord?"

As if he'd been lost somewhere in his mind, he startled and turned his head towards her.

A haunted look darkened his eyes, and he stood, jamming his hands inside his jeans pockets, and slowly backed away from the body.

The image of the crime scene soaked into Ellie's subconscious. "Are you okay?"

Cord glanced back down at the woman, his jaw clenched, then gave a little nod. "When you called and talked about churches, I… thought about this place."

"Have you been here before?" Ellie asked.

His shoulders lifted in a shrug. "A couple of times."

She didn't see Cord as a church-going kind of guy. But then again, he never talked about his past. She knew he'd been in foster care. Maybe one of those families brought him here.

"I didn't touch her," Cord said, as if he suddenly realized he'd been close to the body when Ellie arrived.

"Good. We'll need your boot prints though, to eliminate you in case we find others."

He nodded, and slowly she walked nearer, careful to look for prints on the wet moss and noting disturbed patches of weeds. Emotions warred with her professionalism as she paused to study the body.

This woman had dark brown hair, long legs, and deep brown eyes that looked tormented in death. This time, the killer had dressed her in a crimson dress with tiny white pearl buttons that fastened up to her neck, and simple black flats. Her nails were clipped short again, and her hands were folded in prayer. A page from the Bible was tucked between her fingers. Leaning forward, she realized it was from Genesis, where Eve took a bite of the forbidden fruit.

Red lipstick and rouge completed her makeup, which was smeared, resembling blood.

The location of her body beside the Red River, where baptisms took place, fit with Tuesday's child, and the MO was similar enough to tell her they were dealing with one killer.

The rhyme taunted her again. *Monday's child is fair of face, Tuesday's child is full of grace, Wednesday's child is full of woe, Thursday's child has far to go, Friday's child is loving and giving, Saturday's child works hard for a living, And the child that is born on the Sabbath day, is bonny and blithe, and good and gay.*

Ellie shivered as the implication set in. If the killer stayed true to the nursery rhyme, five more women would die unless she stopped him.

CHAPTER 23

Twenty minutes later, Ellie guided Laney and the Evidence Response Team to the body, while Cord stood staring out into the woods, the same brooding, intense expression on his face. Something was clearly bothering him.

Hell, the grisly sight of the dead woman buried beneath the wildflowers *was* disturbing.

"We're dealing with the same offender, aren't we?" Laney asked as she knelt beside the victim.

Ellie nodded, explaining about the text.

Worry lines creased Laney's forehead. "It's interesting that he's chosen to contact you personally."

Ellie pursed her lips. Why her? Why not Bryce, the new sheriff? He'd been all over the media.

"COD looks the same, exsanguination from blood loss," said Laney, examining the victim. "Although he didn't clean her injuries. Blood is smeared down her neck into that red dress." She unfastened the pearl buttons and eased the fabric away. "Similar plain white bra, although…" She adjusted her glasses and peered closer.

Ellie leaned over for a closer look. "Although what?"

"Look at this." Laney pointed out x's that had been carved into the woman's breasts. "She had implants."

"Good Lord, he punctured them," Ellie muttered.

"He sure did." Laney sighed. "But the implants will help us identify her more quickly."

"Was that done before he killed her?"

"No, there would be more blood loss if that was the case."

More questions pummeled Ellie as Laney finished and the crime techs began to gather the flower petals to bag for analysis. Courtney's past had revealed the lawsuits, which meant she had enemies.

What about this victim?

At first glance, their hair color and body types were different.

So what was it about these two women that made the killer choose them?

CHAPTER 24

Haints Bar

The first one he'd taken was a tough one. She hadn't broken yet. Hadn't begged or pleaded or prayed.

But she would. They all did at some point. It was just a matter of time.

His hand palmed his phone where the message to Detective Reeves waited. He'd send it later. For now, he reveled in the fact that Reeves might be looking at Tuesday's victim.

Now he had a short window of time to take Wednesday's child. He had to stay on schedule.

Eagerly he slipped inside Haints, a local bar and the best place for hardworking men to gather and shoot the shit. The place where booze made loose tongues wag.

Places had great meaning, just as the places he chose to dispose of his victims.

A few females dared to grace the establishment, but most learned their place real quick and decided to take their business to the local wine bar or Bulls, the honkytonk down the street. Women from all over Bluff County met there to vent, male bash and flirt with the rowdy cowboys. Testosterone and estrogen flowed as freely as the liquor and spirits, egged on by the soft croon of male country stars who sang of beer, whiskey, trucks, dogs, love and, of course, cheating women.

Voices dragged him back to the moment, and he turned to scan the crowd. There were a few women here.

Tonight, one of them would be leaving with him.

All he had to do was paste on a smile, buy her a drink, and use his smoky-eyed look to draw her under his spell.

He already knew her name. Knew her weaknesses.

Parking himself on a bar stool, he nudged his Stetson hat lower to shade his face, then scanned the gyrating bodies and the bar for the woman he'd come to find.

He was a patient man. He'd wait until the time was right. Then he'd take her home and she would be his for the night—and forevermore.

CHAPTER 25

Crooked Creek

Her body throbbing with fatigue and debating her plan of action, Ellie let herself inside her bungalow.

There was no doubt in her mind she was dealing with a serial killer. Although Heath was still looking into the first victim's enemies, she thought they could safely put that theory on the back burner. If killing Courtney had been personal, there was no reason to kill another woman.

Yet self-doubt nagged at her. Was she equipped to handle another big case?

Pouring herself a vodka, she carried it to her back deck and curled onto the glider. Tonight the sharp mountains towered toward the dark sky, tall and ominous.

Knowing the images of the wildflower graves would haunt her sleep, she grabbed her phone and debated calling her therapist. She'd said to call anytime, day or night.

But first she needed to process the crime scenes herself.

Inhaling the crisp citrusy scent of her favorite Ketel One, Ellie took a long slow sip before booting up her laptop and making notes about the latest crime scene for the file she'd created for the Wooten murder. She listed each detail of the woman's appearance, outfit, injuries and the location where the body had been left.

Laney's earlier comment echoed in her head. Why had the killer sent her the message instead of the sheriff? She had been thrust into the limelight, but so had Bryce.

With the bodies being left on the AT, she had to consider the fact that the perp might live in Bluff County. Or perhaps he'd seen the story about the Ghost case and was drawn to the area because of it, researching locations of significance that fit his pathology.

And why the nursery rhyme? It had to mean something. In itself, it wasn't creepy. But the sinister aspect came from the fact that the rhyme didn't fit the victim, that it seemed to contrast. So what had this woman done to fall from grace?

Leaning back, Ellie rubbed her temples. The one thing she knew for certain was that he was going to kill again. And if he stuck with his pattern, another woman would die tomorrow. At that thought, Derrick Fox's face floated through her mind. He was more experienced with serial predators and profiling. But did she want to invite him back into her life, even just for work?

Her phone buzzed, dragging her away from thoughts of Derrick. She checked the number calling. It was unknown.

Her stomach tightened. Was it the killer?

She clenched her drink in one hand, then pressed accept, her pulse hammering.

"Ellie… help me."

The glass slipped through Ellie's fingers and crashed to the floor, spilling vodka across the wood. The citrus odor flooded her senses, growing stronger as it splashed on her legs.

"Shondra?"

"Help," her friend cried.

A second later, there was another voice, an altered one.

"Wednesday's child is full of woe," the voice said. "Will you find her in time, Detective?"

CHAPTER 26

Nerves clawed at Ellie as she phoned back. If the killer was taunting her, maybe he'd want to talk. But yet again the call didn't go through.

Shaking all over, she stabbed the sheriff's number, pacing in front of the doors leading to her back deck. A plane buzzed above, disappearing into the clouds that crept across the sky, obliterating the stars and the moonlight, casting the mountains in gray.

"Dammit, Bryce, where are you?"

The call rolled to voicemail, and she hung up and rung again. Finally, he answered.

"Sheriff Waters."

Her stomach curled at his voice, but she steeled herself. Shondra needed her to be strong. "It's Ellie."

"Are you finally calling to tell me you found another body?"

"I just got home," she said, irritated at his tone. "The victim is on her way to the morgue. But that's not the reason I'm calling." Panic made it hard to breathe. "It's Shondra."

"Shondra?" He made a disgruntled noise. "So you talked to her and what? Does she want me to beg her to work for me? Because I'm about to fire her ass."

"Listen to me, Bryce. *He* has her."

The sheriff cleared his throat. "What the hell are you talking about?"

"I just got a call. It was her... crying for help."

A tense heartbeat of silence passed. "Are you sure? Shondra was pissed at me and probably just went off to pout."

She inwardly cursed. Why did she think Bryce would actually care?

"I know it was her. I'm going to her place to look around."

"I'm tied up right now or I'd meet you there," Bryce said. "But keep me posted."

"You could put her on the missing persons list and spread the word."

"Don't tell me how to do my job. Find some proof that she's actually missing and I will."

Technically he was right. But that call… it had been real. If the killer had abducted Shondra and they waited too long, she might already be dead.

CHAPTER 27

Marvin's Mobile Home Park

Her anxiety rocket-high, Ellie raced to Shondra's trailer. The mobile home park had seen better days. The owner, Marvin, charged too much for rent, and last year, Ellie had busted him for using two trailers in the rear as brothels. But Shondra was not one to complain or to care about material things—and she felt like her presence might keep the other single women living there safe from the pimps that came around at all hours of the night to collect their cut and beat up on the girls.

Shondra had grown up with no one to look out for her, so she'd learned to do that herself. She was as independent as they came.

But lately, she'd hinted about a girlfriend.

What was her name?

Self-recriminations screamed in Ellie's head. She'd been so caught up in her own problems, she hadn't been a good friend. She'd only half listened when Shondra mentioned her new love interest.

If Shondra was dead, she'd never forgive herself.

As Ellie climbed from her jeep, three black crows gathered on the power line, giving her an eerie feeling. According to a high school teacher, crows were symbols of danger and death, said to be God's messengers to the mortal world.

Ellie had never been superstitious, but she couldn't shake the sensation that they were here for a reason.

Shondra's black pick-up truck was parked beneath the carport, and the sound of dogs barking filled the air, the wind slapping a loose awning against the metal structure.

Unease crawled up her spine as she gauged the property. The grass needed cutting, the side of the trailer was splattered with mud from the recent thunderstorms. An animal had foraged through the trash, strewing plastic bottles, fast food wrappers, and beer cans everywhere.

Walking up to the carport, Ellie used her flashlight to peer inside Shondra's truck from the passenger side.

Candy wrappers were discarded on the passenger seat, a reusable water bottle was in the console, with a Warriors hat from the girls' soccer team she helped coach beside it. As far as Ellie could see, there was nothing amiss.

As she headed to the driver's side, Ellie's foot hit something and sent the object skidding. Looking down, she spotted Shondra's cell phone in its silver sparkly case. Scuff marks darkened the area by the driver's door and the keys to the truck glinted from the weeds.

Her breathing growing labored, she pulled latex gloves from her pocket and retrieved the phone and keys. A quick check revealed the cell battery was dead.

Ellie moved toward the front door of the trailer, glancing through the window. There was no movement inside. Raising her hand, she knocked, then tapped her foot while she waited. Seconds passed. No one answered.

She pounded the door again with her fist. "Shondra, if you're in there, open up. It's El."

But the knot in her chest told her no one was inside. Her friend would never just disappear, never give Bryce the satisfaction of allowing him to think he'd run her off.

And that had been Shondra's voice. There was no doubt in her mind.

Wind whistled in the silence, and a stray cat meowed from somewhere nearby. Worry knotting her muscles, Ellie walked to the opposite window, which offered a view of the living area. Remembering that her friend left a key beneath the bird feeder in the side yard, Ellie hurried to retrieve it. Seconds later, she snagged the key and let herself inside, checking the living room and kitchen, both of which were empty.

Turning into the hallway, she held her breath as she spotted a trail of daffodil petals—leading all the way to Shondra's bedroom.

She followed the trail, her pulse clamoring. Stopping in the doorway, she saw that her friend's bed and the entire floor were covered in petals.

CHAPTER 28

Somewhere on the AT

Shondra lay curled on the floor in the metal cage, shivering from the cold and pain. Her shoulder was twisted and aching, her ribs bruised, maybe even broken, and her fingers bloody from trying to claw open the metal cage.

Her arm throbbed and she felt weak from losing so much blood. Blood he'd taken from her in vials. He'd been collecting it ever since he locked her down here, though she had no idea what he was going to do with it. Maybe he was just going to drain her blood until she had none left, leaving her to slowly die.

Ellie had probably gotten the message by now. She'd come looking for her, and the thought comforted Shondra.

Memories of lying in the dark as a child, listening to the sound of her father beating up her mother, taunted her. His drunken rages, breaking dishes, punching walls. Why did some men use their fists to make a point?

Hysterical laughter bubbled in her throat as she recalled the rage flaring in her abductor's soulless eyes when he realized she wasn't going to obey or beg or kiss his ass.

Closing her eyes, she forced her breathing to steady. He'd gone out again. He would be drinking. Would come home with another woman tonight. One a day for seven days, he'd told her.

Which day would she die?

The sound of an old furnace rumbling—or was it thunder?—resounded through the damp basement. There were more rooms down here, other cages.

She'd heard the other women he'd brought here, crying and screaming, begging for their lives. He'd killed them anyway. There was no doubt about that.

She had been here the longest, she thought, although she couldn't be sure. What was he waiting for?

Closing her eyes in case she needed energy later to fight him—and you can bet she would fight if she got the chance—her father's sneering voice echoed in her head.

"You're trash, girl. You ain't going nowhere."

Anger strengthened her resolve. She'd proved him wrong. She had made it as a cop. She had arrested countless cowards like him.

And she'd found love. It was a surprise, even to herself, but a few months ago, she'd met Melissa. Melissa with soft hair the color of raw honey. Melissa with sky-blue eyes and the voice of an angel.

Melissa, who she'd told all her secrets to.

Shondra had expected her to run as far away as she could, or to look at her with disgust or pity.

Instead she had pulled Shondra into her arms, declaring her love. That was only two months ago, but now they were planning to move in together. They'd even talked about a wedding.

Fear pressed against her chest. She was so close to having the family she'd always wanted, she couldn't die now.

The last night she'd seen Melissa haunted her, regret consuming her. Melissa had been hesitant to tell her family about the two of them. "They just won't understand," she had said through tears. "They're old fashioned and my dad is set in his ways. They'll probably disown me."

"If they do, then you've got me," Shondra argued. "We'll make our own family."

At that, Melissa had burst into tears and run from the room. The next morning when Shondra got up, she was gone.

Shondra squeezed her eyes shut, wishing she could take back the things she'd said. She hoped that Melissa could forgive her—that she'd get to see her again. That she'd live long enough.

Just then the screech of the door made her tense, pulling her back to her dark surroundings. *He has returned.*

Footsteps. Shuffling. Another woman's scream piercing the air.

"Let me go. Why are you doing this?" The woman's cries tore through the silence. "Please don't hurt me…"

Tears blurred Shondra's eyes as she heard the grating sound of another metal cage being slammed shut in the dark.

CHAPTER 29

Marvin's Mobile Home Park

Ellie grabbed the wall to steady herself.

Find me proof, Bryce had said.

This was proof. The fucking phone call was proof. The bastard had been inside Shondra's house—the daffodils were his calling card.

Fingers shaking, she snatched her phone. She should call the sheriff, but he'd already told her he was tied-up. Probably tying one on, was more like it.

So she called her boss. Shondra needed her to do her job, not fall apart.

Captain Hale sounded winded when he answered. "Ellie?"

"The killer has Deputy Eastwood, Captain."

"What?"

Ellie heard the sound of Captain Hale cracking his knuckles. Struggling to steady her breathing, she explained about the phone call and what she'd found at Shondra's.

"Did you call Sheriff Waters?" Hale asked.

"Yes, I told him about the message, but he blew me off. Said to bring him evidence." She kicked at the floor with her boot. "So I came to Shondra's and found it."

"I'll let him know, then send a team to process Shondra's trailer right away." He hesitated. "And Ellie, for God's sake, be careful. If this killer sent you those messages, he may be watching you."

A shiver rippled through her. He was right. The killer wanted her involved in this case.

That was his first mistake.

Later, while the crime team—fresh from the body at Ole Glory—processed the place, Ellie pulled herself together enough to canvass the neighbors. That turned out to be a bust.

The lady two trailers down had coke-bottle glasses and a hearing aid. The man on the other side of Shondra was three sheets to the wind. The two millennials next door claimed they'd been at a keg party the night Shondra disappeared, and the middle-aged couple with the two Labradors across the street had been at the ER because the man had a gallstone attack.

Exhausted and with her head crowded with images of what might be happening to her friend, Ellie returned to the trailer and found one of the crime techs deep in Shondra's closet.

"Does Shondra have any kin or family to call?" he asked.

"No," Ellie said. "She lives alone."

"Are you sure? There are clothes in a size two and others in size twelve."

Ellie checked the tags. He was right. The smaller sized clothes were also a more feminine style than the staple jeans and shirts Shondra wore.

Ellie scratched her head, trying to remember what Shondra had said about meeting someone. But then Penny Matthews had gone missing, and after that, she'd forgotten to ask her friend about it.

"She may have a girlfriend," she murmured. "Check her phone when you get it charged and let me know what you find."

He nodded, and Ellie went to the kitchen, finding the calendar Shondra kept on her desk. Quickly thumbing through it, she saw several notations about meeting a woman named Melissa White. A phone number had been scribbled below one of the dates.

Lifting her phone from her pocket, she stepped onto the front stoop. It was 11 p.m., and Melissa might be in bed. But she couldn't put off the call. If Shondra had met her abductor before she'd been taken, Melissa might have helpful information.

Dialing the number, Ellie saw that the crows were still perched on the power line, their eyes darting towards her as if they were trying to tell her something.

Something she didn't want to know.

Shivering, she yanked her gaze back to the driveway, tensing as a woman answered in a clipped tone.

"Hello?"

"Is this Melissa?"

"Yes."

"Detective Ellie Reeves. I'm at Shondra Eastwood's home, and I found your number."

A shaky breath rattled over the line. "You're that cop friend of Shondra's, aren't you?"

"Yes, and—"

"What is this about? Is Shondra okay?" Melissa cut her off, her voice rising with panic.

"I don't know. When did you last see her?"

"A little over a week ago," Melissa replied. "But I've been calling and calling and she hasn't answered." A cry escaped her. "I thought she was just mad and not picking up because we had an argument."

"What did you argue about?"

"It was stupid," Melissa said, tears lacing her voice. "We were talking about moving in together, and she wanted me to tell my parents, but I knew they wouldn't approve." So they were together, and Ellie had been barely paying attention. Guilt crushed her. "What happened to her?"

Ellie inhaled sharply and glanced at the crows, unable to shake off the antsy feeling. "Did Shondra mention anything strange happening to her lately? Did she say anything about someone stalking her or bothering her?"

"No… I mean she was upset with her boss, but that was nothing new. Now tell me what's going on."

"I don't want to panic you, but I think she's been taken." Typically, she would hold back information, treat Melissa like a suspect. But this was no ordinary case or an instance of love gone awry—she'd received a message from the killer himself.

And he had her friend.

CHAPTER 30

Crooked Creek

Two hours later, Ellie sank onto her couch, still reeling from shock. Her hands were shaking as she dialed her therapist's emergency number. Kennedy had given it to her the first time they'd met and promised they could do an online health video-call session anytime she needed.

Ellie had balked, thinking she'd never resort to calling it.

But with her best friend's life in the hands of a serial killer, she had nowhere to turn.

With a pang, she remembered the first time she'd met Shondra. Ellie had tracked a meth dealer to a house in the hills and Shondra had shown up at the scene because of a domestic call at the same address. The meth dealer's brother was in the main house beating up on his girlfriend, and Shondra had charged in, tough as nails, trussed him up like a pig and dragged the creep out by his hair.

They'd bonded on the spot.

A message told her the therapist was ready, so she phoned the number and seconds later, Kennedy Sledge's face appeared. "Hello, Ellie. What's going on?"

Tears flooded Ellie as she pictured the murder scenes with the grave of wildflowers, and she explained about Shondra's abduction.

"You and Deputy Eastwood are friends?"

Ellie nodded and took a sip of the vodka she had poured for herself, the ice clinking. "Yeah. I guess I don't make friends easily. Seems like I piss everyone off."

"What makes you say that?"

"Butting heads with Sheriff Waters just like I did some of the trainees at the police academy. Shondra and the sheriff go at it, too. He thinks he's superior because he's a man."

"But you stand up to him?"

"Hell, yeah," Ellie muttered. "I'm just as good a cop as him, or better. Except…"

"Except what, Ellie?"

"Except that I was so blind to my father's secrets that two little girls nearly died before I figured out the truth." Emotions choked her. "And now what if I'm too late for Shondra?"

CHAPTER 31

An hour of sleep, at a push. That's all Ellie had gotten.

She'd rest later. After all, what was loss of sleep when god knows what Shondra might be suffering?

Ironically, bright sunshine shimmered across the concrete parking lot of the morgue, and sunflowers poked through the planters flanking the grassy area where benches offered seating and a reprieve for workers to escape the gruesome happenings inside.

Still, even the sun couldn't alter her mood this morning. Anxiety coiled inside her as she entered the morgue, followed by shock when she found Special Agent Derrick Fox waiting outside Laney's office.

Seeing him in person again resurrected memories of their one night together, wreaking havoc on her already frayed nerves. His dark hair was combed back from his forehead, his charcoal shirt accentuating his deep brown eyes. He stood ramrod straight, his jaw clenched as if he didn't want to be here.

Remember, he hates you. And he destroyed your family.

Although really, had he? Her family had done that themselves with their decades-long deceit.

Ellie folded her arms. "What are you doing here?"

A small sardonic smile tilted the corners of his mouth. "Your boss called me," he said in a gruff voice.

Damn, she hadn't seen that coming. "You could have sent another agent."

His brow rose, some emotion she didn't recognize flickering in his eyes before his professional mask slid back into place. "You didn't know he asked for me?"

She shook her head. "I've been busy."

He cleared his throat. "He called me early this morning, said he thinks you have another serial killer in Bluff County."

Ellie gave a clipped nod. Although technically it took three kills to constitute a serial killer, these crimes had the markings of one—and they had to act fast. "It looks that way. He also abducted one of our deputies, Shondra Eastwood."

"You know that for sure?" Derrick asked.

"I got a phone call from her, asking for help. Then I searched her place and found signs of foul play." She hesitated as the images of the daffodils floated through her mind. "Signs matching his signature."

"Which is?"

"I'll explain all of it later," Ellie said. "I need to brief the sheriff and Deputy Landrum once we leave here." She might as well do it all at once.

The door opened, and Laney appeared, a frown crinkling her forehead. She looked exhausted and Ellie realized she must have worked through the night. "I'm ready, Ellie." A hint of recognition shone in her eyes as she glanced at Derrick. "Agent Fox, I wasn't expecting you."

"Captain Hale called him." Ellie gestured toward the office. "Do you have autopsy results? An ID?"

Laney nodded, her deep chocolate eyes troubled. Ellie and Derrick followed the medical examiner inside the autopsy room. The acrid odor of body waste, decay, blood and formaldehyde assaulted Ellie as they approached the lifeless woman lying on the metal slab. A sheet covered her lower extremities, and Laney had carefully executed the Y incision. Pans holding the woman's organs sat to the side, and her breasts were exposed, where Laney had removed the remains of the implants. Her skin was blue and marred with black and purple bruising, both on her neck and torso. The young woman couldn't be more than thirty years old and had her entire life ahead of her.

Just like Shondra did.

Derrick remained rigid, his expression giving nothing away, while Ellie used a handkerchief to cover her mouth and nose. She didn't know if she'd ever get used to the heinous smells in the morgue, or the sight of a human body dissected.

"What can you tell me from the body?" Ellie asked, gesturing toward the corpse.

"I sent her bloodwork, prints and DNA to the lab." With gloved hands, Laney lifted one of the implants. "These helped identify her. Her name is Carrie Winters."

Adjusting her glasses, Laney carefully opened the woman's mouth with gloved hands. Using a pair of tweezers, she removed a small folded piece of paper, then dropped it into a metal bin.

Derrick made a low sound in his throat as Laney used the tweezers to unfold it.

Tuesday's child is full of grace.

"You know the nursery rhyme?" Ellie asked Derrick.

Arms crossed in front of him, he nodded. "It goes through all seven days of the week."

"Exactly," Ellie said. "It appears our killer is using the nursery rhyme as a blueprint for murder."

CHAPTER 32

Sunlight glimmered off the asphalt as Ellie drove toward Crooked Creek Police Station. Derrick was on her tail, and she'd stalled answering his questions until the briefing. There was no need to repeat herself a dozen times, and it wasn't like she'd invited him.

No, her captain had done that.

He told you to take some time off.

Didn't he think she could handle the investigation?

Forced to drive past the sheriff's office in Stony Gap on the way, Ellie noticed the street in front of the courthouse had been blocked off. Protestors had gathered, waving signs and shouting as they marched back and forth. Her stomach lurched at the sight of the signs urging the prosecutor to come down hard on her father.

Randall Reeves is a child killer!
Reeves deserves to rot in jail.
Give him the death penalty.

She spotted her father exiting the courthouse with his attorney, and recognized parents of some of the Ghost's victims. She saw Darnell Purcell, the brother of little Millie Purcell. The man looked stoop-shouldered and frail now, his wiry brown hair standing out in tufts. She'd heard he'd had drug issues after his sister disappeared but was supposedly in rehab now. Philip Paulson, Ansley Paulson's father, looked angry as he stomped back and forth. Ginger Williams' mother, Lynn, held a poster with her daughter's face on it, a reminder of her devastating loss.

In spite of the shouts against him, her father held his head high. But he looked tired, worn down, and… guilt stricken.

Sympathy tugged at Ellie. Despite everything, occasionally sweet memories of her childhood broke through her anger. The day she'd learned to ride her bike, she'd been terrified of going downhill. But he'd run along beside her and steadied her, holding onto the seat until she was finally ready for him to let go. In middle school, she'd been dared to jump from a rocky ledge into the swimming hole where all the kids gathered, and she'd broken her foot. He'd held her hand in the hospital while they'd rushed her into surgery to set it. In high school, when her independent streak had surfaced and she'd rebelled against Vera's smothering, he'd been her rock.

Pulling her gaze from him, Ellie drove on and turned down a side street before she was seen by the mob then sped onto the winding road between the two small towns.

Once upon a time, everyone in Bluff County loved and respected her father. He'd been a town hero. He'd taught Ellie how to shoot a gun and how to read maps when they ventured onto the trail and its treacherous terrain. She'd wanted to be just like him when she grew up.

But now… she could barely even look at him.

Ellie told herself to focus. *You have to find Shondra and stop the madman who took her from killing again.*

Or worse… From killing her friend.

Turning into the parking lot for the Crooked Police Station, she took a steadying breath before climbing out the Jeep. Chin in the air, she avoided looking at Derrick as he parked and followed her into the station. He must have seen the protestors—and he'd definitely agree that Randall should serve time. But thankfully he said nothing.

Captain Hale greeted her as they entered the conference room, and Heath glanced up from his computer and two other officers joined them. Derrick made himself at home by taking a section of the conference table, setting up his laptop.

Just as she started to attach photos of the first two victims to the whiteboard, footsteps pounded in the hall. A second later, the sheriff's voice boomed as he stormed into the room. He stopped in his tracks when he spotted Derrick.

"What the fuck is going on, Detective Reeves?" Bryce shouted. "You called in the feds without asking me?"

Ellie stiffened, but Captain Hale stood. "I called him in, Sheriff. And I'll thank you not to talk to my detectives like that."

Bryce glanced at Ellie, his feathers ruffled, and she couldn't resist. "We've got a serial killer here, and he took one of our own, your very own deputy," Ellie said. "We're going to be spread thin, as I know you'll make finding Shondra a priority."

The darkening of Bryce's eyes indicated she'd touched a nerve, and a warning flickered in his eyes as well.

Derrick cleared his throat. "I am here to assist, Sheriff," he said calmly. "Any way I can."

Ellie bit back a smile. How could the sheriff argue with that?

Hell, she wanted to point out his incompetence, how he'd blown her off the night before when she'd first called him about Shondra. How she knew Shondra had threatened to file a complaint against him for gender bias. That she knew he was just looking for a reason to get rid of her.

But she kept her mouth shut. She'd dealt with her share of bullies at the police academy. Men who thought they were stronger and smarter and more resilient than her. She'd had to work harder, think fast on her feet, and develop a thick skin. A few had even exerted their power and physical strength to intimidate her. Sexual harassment had even been part of their tactical game. They'd cornered her in the locker room once and pushed her around, had teamed up to cut her off when they'd gone on runs, had even tried to grab a feel when they'd practiced defense moves.

But she hadn't allowed them to make her quit, and she sure as heck wouldn't let Bryce Waters intimidate her either.

The killer had challenged her. And Ellie Reeves did not back down from a challenge.

CHAPTER 33

Ellie opened her mouth to speak, but Bryce cut her off. "As a matter of fact, I've got men searching for Deputy Eastwood now. We're looking at abandoned properties and rentals in case this maniac is hiding out in the county somewhere."

Chair legs scraped the floor as Bryce seated himself at the head of the table, marking his territory as the leader. His arrogance knew no boundaries.

While everyone else claimed seats, she handed Heath a sticky note with the name Carrie Winters on it.

"Dr. Whitefeather identified our second vic. See what you can find on her."

The deputy nodded and instantly went to work on his computer.

"All right, then," Ellie said as she stepped to the front of the conference room. "It appears that we have a serial killer targeting young women in the county. If he holds true to his pattern, we may be looking for another body today." She paused for effect. "So let's see if we can find him first."

She wrote the nursery rhyme on the whiteboard, reciting it as she did.

"Monday—Monday's child is fair of face.

Tuesday—Tuesday's child is full of grace.

Wednesday—Wednesday's child is full of woe.

Thursday—Thursday's child has far to go.

Friday—Friday's child is loving and giving.

Saturday—Saturday's child works hard for a living.

Sunday—And the child that is born on the Sabbath day, is bonny and blithe, good and gay."

Next, Ellie attached a photograph of Courtney Wooten to the board underneath the heading "VICTIM 1". The stark sight of the dead woman with the bramble wrapped around her neck, smothered in unsightly makeup and her hands in prayer, silenced the room.

"Monday, we found our first victim, twenty-nine-year-old Courtney Wooten, at a place on the AT called the Reflection Pond. Inside her mouth, he left a piece of paper with the 'Monday's child' part of the rhyme typed on it." She explained what they'd learned about Courtney from Heath's research and her conversation with Courtney's sister.

"We are looking into the lawsuit angle," Captain Hale interjected. "So far no one is talking. The lawyer insists that Courtney settled because the complaints were bogus, and that the women who sued were money-hungry."

Anger twinged inside Ellie. Courtney's sister told a different story.

"We'll keep pursuing it," Hale added, "but given how things are developing, it feels less likely than it did on Monday that it'll lead to our killer."

Moving on, Ellie said, "Dr. Whitefeather also found a thick band of bruising around the victim's neck, which could be consistent with a dog collar or a choker that might be used in sexual play." Ellie gestured to Heath. "Did you find anything on that?"

"Nothing definitive," the deputy said. "The adult shop on the interstate sells several versions that might fit the crime, although most of his customers pay in cash, as they don't want to give their names."

"Or their wives to see the shop on the credit card bill," Bryce muttered.

"And he said a lot of the trade is online anyway these days," Heath continued, ignoring him. "A collar or choker could have been ordered from countless online stores."

"The killer texted me personally," Ellie went on, also ignoring the sheriff. "The number was from a burner phone, which as you all know is difficult if not impossible to trace to the owner." Ellie released a breath. "The message on the paper found in the victim's mouth appears to have been written on a typewriter. The lab is analyzing it now, along with the wounds on the woman's throat, to pinpoint what kind of knife he used. Although the striations look like a regular hunting knife."

"Send everything to my people," Derrick said. "Maybe they can trace the type of typewriter and who bought it."

Ellie motioned for Heath to handle it.

"What's this place called the Reflection Pond?" Derrick asked.

Ellie explained about the folklore associated with the area. "Locals claim that if you look at your reflection in the water there you see a mirror of your inner soul. I think our killer knew about the flaws with Courtney's makeup line, and that she was lying to her customer base to sell her product."

Ellie pinned up a photograph of victim number two. "This is Tuesday's victim. Her name is Carrie Winters." She glanced at Heath.

Heath looked up from his laptop. "She's a stripper," Heath said. "Works as a dancer at a place called the Men's Den."

"They do more than dance there," Bryce muttered with a chuckle.

Ellie barely resisted an eye roll. Of course he would know that. "That could mean something to our killer. I believe the way he poses the victim, the wording of each day's rhyme, and the locations where he chooses to leave the body are significant."

Out of the corner of her eyes, she saw Derrick making a note. "Where did he leave victim number two?" he asked.

"At a primitive Baptist church called Ole Glory, by Red River." She filled him in on the folklore about the color of the water and the baptisms held there. "Tuesday's child is full of grace," she said as she gestured to the whiteboard. "My working theory is that our killer must have thought Carrie had fallen from grace, so he left her at a church which has old-school, traditional values and would be a place to repent." She tapped the photograph of Carrie. "He also left a Bible page from Genesis in her hands. The very page where Eve took a bite of the forbidden fruit."

A heavy silence settled over the room as everyone absorbed the information. Derrick was making copious notes and Heath was tapping away. Over his shoulder, she saw him studying Carrie's social media.

"Did you find Ms. Winters' next of kin?" she asked.

Heath shook his head. "According to records, her parents are dead, and she has no siblings."

"I'll talk to her coworkers," the sheriff offered. "Maybe one of her customers is this perv."

Of course he'd volunteer to go to the strip club.

But they had to divide up manpower, so she said nothing.

"Why wrap thorns around their necks when he'd already slashed their throats?" Captain Hale asked.

Deputy Landrum cleared his throat and spoke before Ellie could. "According to Biblical symbolism, thorns represent sin."

"Which means our killer could be religious, or he's studied its symbolism," added Ellie.

Derrick drummed his fingers on the table. "Your theory sounds right, Detective Reeves. The posing and places are definitely significant. He may have some kind of God complex where he believes he's punishing these women for perceived sins."

Ellie relaxed slightly. She was accustomed to being underestimated by her peers, and it was refreshing for someone to respect her opinion.

"What is the importance of the wildflowers?" Captain Hale asked.

Ellie raised a finger. "Daffodils are what's called a schizophrenic flower, which can either have the attributes of rebirth and resurrection or the negative connotations of vanity. It's also considered the flower of the underworld."

"So we're dealing with a religious freak who's into nature?" Bryce muttered.

Ellie shrugged. "Or one who has knowledge of nature's symbolism and mythology. Its symbolism comes from the Greek legend of the youth Narcissus, who was admiring his own image in a pool of water and drowned. At the spot where he fell in, a flower emerged, giving it the attributes of love and sacrifice over vanity."

"You seem to know a lot about this," the sheriff said.

"Research," Ellie said. "When the killer contacts you personally, you can't waste time." Her father had also taught her some about plants, flowers and trees in the forest, and she pushed away the pain that surfaced at the thought of him.

Another tense silence fell for a second.

"What about the dress color?" Heath asked. "It seems to vary. Monday is dressed in olive green, Tuesday in red."

"That I don't know," Ellie admitted.

"I'll have my people look into it," Derrick offered. "If the clothing doesn't belong to the victims, maybe we can pinpoint where he's purchasing the dresses."

Ellie's mind turned to Shondra and she attached her photograph to the board. "At this point, we have reason to believe that he abducted Deputy Shondra Eastwood." She filled them in on her phone call. "It's Wednesday already, so he's going to kill again."

"A victim a day for a week," Bryce said. "The Weekday Killer."

Ellie hated to glorify this sicko with a name, but the press would name him if they didn't. And that name reminded her of the urgency of the investigation.

She tilted her head toward Derrick. "Perhaps you can work on a profile of the perpetrator while Deputy Landrum looks for connections between the victims."

Derrick tapped his notepad with his pen. "Already working on it."

Bryce's cell phone buzzed on his hip, and he glanced at it. "Hold on, I've got to take this."

"Let's take five," Derrick said.

The captain excused himself for a minute, and Deputy Landrum turned back to his computer.

As Derrick made a phone call, Ellie remained silent, watching Bryce.

Just like him to storm in, assert himself, then expect everyone to wait on him. He stepped to the doorway and spoke in a hushed tone, his body tensing. When he glanced up at Ellie, his eyes flickered with wariness.

Ellie's pulse jumped. Something was wrong.

A second later, Bryce hung up and stepped back into the room. "The protest at the courtroom turned violent. I have to go."

Remembering the scene she'd witnessed on her way to the station, Ellie stood quickly. "Is my father all right?"

Bryce shrugged. "I don't know yet. But I'll keep you posted."

"Maybe I should go," Ellie murmured.

He shook his head. "No, stay away. You'll only make things worse."

CHAPTER 34

Derrick struggled to control his temper at Bryce's callous remark. He'd seen those damn protestors and understood their anger. God knows he detested Randall Reeves himself.

But group mentality could be dangerous—it was best that Ellie stayed away.

Captain Hale loped back in, and as everyone convened again, Ellie gestured to the whiteboard, indicating where the victims' remains were found.

"Special Agent Fox, what can you tell us about the killer from the information we have so far?"

Admiration for Ellie's ability to focus on the case stirred inside him, and he forced himself into analytical mode. Derrick eyed the details on the whiteboard and the photos of the crime scene, disturbed by the images. He was tempted to say the bastard was FIH—fucked in the head. But that much was obvious.

"I would say that our unsub is a male—he appears to have a hatred for women, given the manner he is posing them and almost punishing them for what he perceives as their sins. I would guess he's probably early to mid-thirties. There's a level of sophistication about the crime scenes that suggests this man has been around the block. He's highly organized, intelligent, and methodical, which could be reflected in his job. He carefully chooses the locations where he disposes of the bodies and is meticulous in the details of how he poses them. He could be choosing the victims randomly, spontaneously, although the rhyme and the potential meaning of the victims you've noted indicates he's researched them. It's possible he meets them in person or online somehow." He exhaled. "We'll be able to tell more once we dig deeper into the victims. Did Courtney have a business partner?"

Ellie glanced at the captain.

"Yes, but the partner is a she. So is her accountant."

So that almost certainly ruled them out.

"We need the vics' computers and cell phones," Derrick said.

"I'll call the Atlanta PD to go to Ms. Wooten's residence and obtain them, then have them sent to the Bureau," replied Captain Hale.

"I'll check out Ms. Winter's residence and canvass her neighbors," said Ellie, before addressing Heath. "Pull together a list of all the members of the Ole Glory Church. Ask them to go back twenty-five years. Our killer could attend there now, or it's possible that he attended as a child."

Deputy Landrum nodded.

Captain Hale gestured to the clock. "I guess we should start considering places where he might leave Wednesday's victim."

Ellie paled, and Derrick knew what she was thinking. They wanted to find Deputy Eastwood alive, not to be looking for her body.

"*Wednesday's child is full of woe*," she said, thinking out loud.

Derrick squared his shoulders. "Perhaps the unsub plans to leave her at a place of mourning."

"Possibly a cemetery," Captain Hale suggested. "I'll send my new deputies to stake out graveyards and churches with cemeteries."

"I'll call Ranger McClain and see if he has any ideas," said Ellie.

Derrick stiffened at the mention of the ranger. He hadn't liked McClain when he'd met him on the last case, certain he was hiding something.

The ranger clearly had a thing for Ellie, too. A tiny seed of some feeling he didn't want to analyze gnawed at him, but he quickly dismissed it. It didn't matter if they were involved.

All that mattered was stopping the Weekday Killer and finding the missing deputy.

CHAPTER 35

Stony Gap

Snap, snap, snap. Vinny clicked his fingers. *Snap, snap, snap.* Over and over and over.

He always snapped them three times in a row when he was nervous or excited. Couldn't help himself. *Snap, snap, snap. Snap, snap, snap.*

As the crowd outside the courthouse chanted and waved their homemade protest signs, Vinny moved into the shadows. He had the kind of face that went unnoticed. It used to bother him that he was bland and boring. That was when he took those damn stupid pills though. Not anymore.

When he flushed them down the toilet, he became another man. Full of life and energy and action. Nothing—and nobody—got in his way.

No more Skinny Minnie Whiny Vinny.

Snap, snap, snap.

Wheezing out a breath, he lifted his phone and took a picture of Vera and Randall Reeves as they slipped into their Lincoln town car. They couldn't hide from what they'd done. The cameras were watching. Following. The crowds were chasing. The demons would get them one day.

Just like the old hag. She'd gotten what was coming. Now she was rotting, her bones turning to dust.

Her words chimed in his ears. *No friends. No friends. No friends.*

But she was wrong. He had a friend. The best kind. They would do anything for one another. Anything.

They would kill for each other.

CHAPTER 36

Crooked Creek

Before Ellie could make the call to Cord, her phone buzzed. Hoping for a lead, she connected.

"Detective Reeves speaking."

"It's Melissa White," the young woman cried. "Have you found Shondra?"

"Not yet, but we're looking for her," Ellie said in a calming tone. "Trust me. Shondra and I are friends. I want to find her as much as you do."

"If you're such good friends, why haven't we met before?" Melissa asked, her voice accusatory.

Her jab struck home. "I don't know," Ellie said. "Shondra mentioned she had a girlfriend, but the last few weeks we were busy investigating the Ghost case."

"That's right," she said in a shaky voice. "I'm s-sorry. I'm a mess. I… just can't believe she's missing."

"Why don't you come into the station and talk to my deputy? Maybe you'll recall something you haven't thought of before."

"I can't," Melissa cried. "My mom isn't doing well right now. I can't leave her."

"I'm sorry to hear that. Maybe you can talk to him on the phone instead? We'd like to show you some photos of the victims, see if that sparks anything," Ellie said. "I know that's tough, but it might help us. Would you be okay with that?"

Melissa's breathing rattled out. "All right, but I don't really think I can help."

"Sometimes we know things we don't even realize," Ellie said. "I'm going to get him now and have him call you back."

Hanging up, Ellie hurried over to Heath. "Heath, send Melissa pics of the victims and see if she recognizes either of them. We have to find out if there's a link between the women."

Giving a nod of understanding, Heath returned to his desk with Melissa's number. Grateful he was detail-oriented, Ellie headed back to her office to call Cord.

The day was getting away from her. Just like the killer.

CHAPTER 37

"I need your help, Cord."

His heavy breathing echoed back, and she pictured him chopping wood for his stove. It was a less unsettling image than the taxidermy wildcats he kept in his dark house. Lately, she'd had nightmares where she woke up and the feral animals were watching her, teeth bared, ready to tear her apart.

"What is it?" Cord asked.

Fear made her voice crack. "The man who killed those two women—he took Shondra."

"What?"

Ellie closed her eyes. She suddenly felt as if she was suffocating. When she'd rescued Penny Matthews and the other little girl after Hiram took them, Hiram had buried her alive. Cord had literally dug her from the ground and saved her. He also admired her father, who'd been a mentor to him over the years. But she'd been so wrapped up in her own shock and pain she hadn't considered how the fallout had affected him.

Forcing aside the thoughts, Ellie exhaled. "Special Agent Fox, the captain and Deputy Landrum just met for a briefing. We know where he left the first two victims. If he's true to pattern, the nursery rhyme 'Monday's child' is a clue. And he's going to kill a woman for each day of the week. The sheriff has already named him the Weekday Killer."

Emotions threatened to overcome her. "Shondra may be next, Cord." Her voice cracked. "Bryce has deputies searching abandoned buildings and properties. But the rhyme may be a clue."

"What can I do?" Cord asked gruffly.

"Help me think. According to the rhyme, Wednesday's child is full of woe. The captain is dispatching deputies to cover local cemeteries and church graveyards. Woe means sadness, so look at the map and see if any place strikes you as significant."

"I'll get right on it," Cord agreed.

"Good. Agent Fox and I are going to search the second victim's house and look for her computer and phone. Call me if you come up with anything."

"Sure." His voice rasped out as if he was hurrying somewhere. "And Ellie, this man is dangerous. If he contacted you, he may be trying to lure you into a trap."

"I survived my own brother's attempt to kill me," Ellie said. "This son of a bitch is not about to make me back down."

CHAPTER 38

Somewhere on the AT

Shondra jerked at the chain around her neck, desperate to escape. All night long she'd listened to the other woman crying, weeping as the hours crept by.

Her heart ached. She'd tried to call out to her, to let her know that she wasn't alone.

But her voice had made the woman only sob harder.

Shondra knew that her days were numbered. But for some reason, the monster was holding her, making her suffer first. Not like the others, who he kept a day or two before killing them. Why didn't he just kill her, too?

Damn him to hell and back. He'd shown her the pictures of the women after he'd cut their throats. The sick way he'd posed them on beds of daffodils. The bramble around their necks.

He was sadistic. He killed for the thrill. Enjoyed watching a woman beg to live as she drew her last breath.

A noise sounded above, jerking Shondra from her thoughts. He was back. Storming through the house. Shouting and stomping and throwing something.

Frantic to free herself, she fumbled yet again in the dark for a way to release the chain, but there was no way to loosen it. Her fingers were bloody and raw from prying endlessly at the cage door. Summoning her strength, she struggled to loosen one of the screws holding the cage door shut, but it wouldn't budge.

The sharp metal stabbed the tip of her finger and blood trickled down her hand.

Exhausted and sore, she clenched her teeth and sagged against the floor of the cage, tears of anger filling her eyes.

You're trash, her daddy used to say. *Good for nothing trash.*

When she was little, she'd believed it. She'd worn thrift-store clothes and used an outdoor toilet. She had free lunches at school, and the other kids made fun of her.

One day she'd had enough of being pushed around and she'd fought back. Sure, she'd gotten suspended for three days, but it was worth it. The bullies left her alone after that.

A crash sounded above, then the door creaked open. A sliver of light wormed its way through the opening, then his heavy breathing punctuated the silence. She thought she heard a dog barking again. But it sounded far away, outside somewhere.

She craned her neck to see her abductor's face, but then the door slammed shut and blackness engulfed him.

His sinister chanting filled the shadows, the wood steps squeaking as he descended.

In spite of her training, fear seized her.

You're a survivor, she told herself. *Look for your opening and attack.*

Sucking in a breath, she steeled herself to take whatever he dished out. She'd grown up tough. She'd play along with him if necessary, get him to talk, get inside his head.

And when she got her chance, she'd claw his damn eyes out.

But instead of coming to her, footsteps echoed in the opposite direction. He kept more cages in there. More screaming women—his next victims.

"Wednesday's child is full of woe…" he chanted.

A shrill shriek made chills rip through Shondra, as the woman cried and pleaded, "Please don't do this, please let me go."

A sob welled in Shondra's throat.

The chain around her neck rattled as she yanked at the metal bars of the cage. As a police officer, she'd vowed to protect others.

But helpless frustration seized her. She couldn't save this woman now. She couldn't even save herself.

CHAPTER 39

Crooked Creek

Ellie retrieved Carrie Winters' address from the file before striding back to the conference room. She tensed at the sight of the TV airing a late breaking news story. Derrick and her captain were watching it with solemn faces, and her stomach pitched as she realized it was the reason the sheriff had left so abruptly.

"*This is Angelica Gomez coming to you live outside the Bluff County courthouse, where this morning former Sheriff Randall Reeves and his wife met with the DA in hopes of settling the court case that has rocked the good citizens of Bluff County.*"

In horror, Ellie watched as the protestors chanted and waved signs condemning her father. The mayor, Bryce's father, who'd been friends with her own dad for years, stood to the side at a distance. Several women from the Garden Club, who'd hosted charity events with her mother for a decade, held signs slandering her family.

"*As you can see, the county is vocal over their desire to see that Sheriff Reeves is punished for allegedly withholding information regarding the search for the serial killer who killed a dozen small children over the span of twenty-five years.*"

In the footage the doors to the courthouse suddenly opened, Ellie's father and mother emerging, both looking haggard, flanked by two deputies. Angelica and her cameraman hurried toward them, more shouts and ugly comments erupting from the crowd.

"*Sheriff Reeves, Mrs. Reeves,*" Angelica said. "*Would you like to make a statement to the public?*"

Vera clung to Ellie's father, and he tenderly patted her hand, then stared into the camera. Ellie had never seen him look so tormented. And her mother… She looked weak-eyed, disoriented.

Randall cleared his throat. "*I want everyone in the county to know that I deeply regret the fact that so many children's lives were lost. My wife and I would do anything to bring back those little girls. While we did not know the whereabouts of Hiram, the man who took those innocent children, as sheriff I was working behind the scenes to investigate each murder.*" He paused, his voice hoarse. "*I'm truly sorry for the families who suffered.*"

More noises and angry comments filled the air, and Angelica pushed the microphone closer to Ellie's father. "*Sheriff Reeves, we understand a deal is in the works regarding the charges you face. Can you elaborate on that?*"

Her father's lawyer laid a hand on his arm, before he addressed the reporter. "*We are working swiftly and with respect toward all parties to see that justice is served. Please bear in mind that our country is founded on the principle of innocent until proven guilty.*"

A litany of shouts filled the air and the crowd's attitude morphed into mob-like rage as two men pushed through the crowd and came at Randall.

"*Killer!*"

"*You murdered our little girls!*"

"*Your daughter is no better!*"

One man lunged toward her father, while the other attacked her mother. Vera screamed and her father threw his arm in front of her to protect her, as deputies rushed to contain the crowd and usher her parents into their vehicle.

As three men stormed her parents' car, rocking it back and forth in an attempt to block them from leaving, Ellie realized she was shaking. Bryce and his men took charge, with the sheriff personally guarding the driver's side as her father started the engine and slowly pulled away.

"Jesus, Ellie, things are getting out of hand," Captain Hale muttered.

Suddenly Ellie was finding it difficult to breathe. She walked into the hallway, Hale following. She pinched the bridge of her nose to stem her panic.

Bryce was taking care of her parents, she told herself. For now, she had to focus on finding Shondra and the killer.

"I have to get back to work, Captain," she finally said.

"Are you sure you're up to it?"

"Is that the reason you called Fox? You don't think I can handle this case?"

He ran a hand over his balding head. "You've been through a lot lately, Detective. I thought you and Agent Fox made a good team."

"He hates my family, or have you forgotten that?"

"I'm not saying there isn't tension, but you both handled it and got the job done." He reached into his pocket for a mint. "Now is not the time to let personal feelings interfere."

Pulling herself together, Ellie walked back into the conference room to Derrick, and cleared her throat. "I talked to Cord. He's looking for places that might fit our rhyme. Meanwhile, I'm going to Carrie Winters' place."

"Let's go."

Laney's comment about the killer contacting her personally played through her head. Did he have some personal vendetta against her? At that thought, the hate mail she'd received taunted her.

"Let me get something I need you to look at while I drive."

A puzzled expression flashed on Derrick's face but he simply followed her to her office.

Opening a drawer, Ellie took out a folder. "I've been thinking about the killer, why he'd contact me. It could have something to do with the hate mail I received."

Derrick went stone still, eyes narrowing. "What hate mail?"

She hadn't wanted to share this with him—with anyone. It was humiliating. But if it helped find the Weekday Killer, she had to suck up her pride. "The last couple of weeks, I've received several letters blaming me for those little girls' deaths. Some accuse me of knowing and covering up." Just like Derrick had at one point.

A muscle twitched in his jaw, as if he remembered his accusations. Maybe he still believed them.

"What if one of the people who wrote to me is killing these women to punish me? Or to make me look incompetent?"

A tense heartbeat passed between them. "That seems extreme."

"Maybe. But you saw how the people in the county are reacting to my family."

He exhaled. "Let me take a look at the letters."

Heat climbed Ellie's neck as she handed over the folder. He gripped it and followed her back through the bullpen and outside to her car.

Derrick slid into the passenger side, and she got in, started the engine and headed toward Carrie Winters' address. Pulling on latex gloves, he shook out the individual envelopes, his jaw stiff as he saw the pile. "Did you send these to the lab to be analyzed?"

Ellie bit her lip. "No."

His gaze jerked to hers. "Why the hell not?"

"I figured people were just blowing off steam." Besides, maybe she deserved their wrath.

Derrick's eyes darkened as he studied her for a moment. Then he released a breath and returned to the mail. The letters held no return addresses and, barring a couple of people, no one had signed their names.

There was no way to trace the sender just as there was no way to trace the burner phone the Weekday Killer used to taunt her.

One by one, he unfolded the letters, his expression growing more intense as he skimmed the contents. She didn't have to read them twice. The hate-filled words were seared into her brain.

Your family killed those girls. Go to hell.
You should have died instead of my daughter.
I hope your family rots in prison for what they did.
Evil runs in your blood.
Leave town and never come back.
Tell the truth for once and beg God for forgiveness.
You'll be sorry.
You have to pay.
A good cop would have stopped the Ghost long ago.
How could you cover for a killer?
You should be buried on the trail like the children.

Sometimes even Ellie had trouble not believing that last one.

CHAPTER 40

Clifton Heights

"That mail is going to the lab," Derrick said.

"It could be unrelated, but at this point, I guess we have to examine every angle," Ellie agreed.

"What do you know about Ms. Winters?" Derrick asked as he checked the front door and found it locked.

"She owns her own house," Ellie said. Clifton Heights, which was situated on a cliff with a seventy-five-feet overhang, consisted of small rustic townhomes and cluster homes with manicured lawns and flower beds filled with purple, red and yellow petunias and red-tipped azaleas that provided privacy for the individual homes. Nestled close to the parkway, they were close to the highway for easy access to both the mountains and the small-town tourist attractions along the highway running from Atlanta to North Georgia.

Considering how well-to-do the area was, it struck Ellie as odd Carrie Winters, with her career as an exotic dancer, would have lived in the neighborhood.

As they walked around the side of the property, Ellie noted that the closest unit to Carrie's was empty while the one on the right had lights on. Stopping at each window to search for clues indicating the killer had abducted Carrie from her home, Ellie didn't see a broken window or signs of forced entry. Needing a look inside, she jimmied the door open, wincing when it screeched and a gray cat meowed, rubbing up against her leg.

"Hey, kitty," she said as she petted the shorthaired animal.

An array of scents hit her—some kind of potpourri and burned coffee and the litter box, which needed to be cleaned.

Ellie scanned the kitchen but nothing seemed amiss. They moved onto the living area, where there was a plush black leather sofa, a white leather club chair, and a cowskin rug. Carrie clearly had expensive taste and the décor of the place was very contemporary, at odds with its rustic exterior.

Derrick gestured toward the hallway and Ellie inched to the right, with Derrick following. The first room was a guest room, with a white desk and daybed. Everything neat and orderly.

In the master suite, the king-sized iron bed was draped in a bright red comforter with an accent wall of black. Again, sleek and modern.

Everything was perfectly in place, as if Carrie hadn't been here for some time. Or perhaps she was OCD or had a housekeeper.

The bathroom held an array of cosmetics, perfume, and lipsticks in a dozen different colors, all expensive brands. Derrick ducked into the closet while Ellie checked the dresser. Sexy, lacy lingerie was folded neatly in the drawers—the opposite of the plain white cotton panties and bra she'd been dressed in by the killer.

"Did you find anything?" Ellie asked Derrick as she looked over his shoulder into the closet.

He stepped aside with an eyebrow raise and indicated the wall of wigs and dance costumes, complete with feathered boas, sequin bras, and tiaras.

"Well," she said wryly. "She obviously dressed the part."

Just as she was feeling uncomfortable, looking at lingerie with a man she had slept with, Ellie's phone vibrated. Glad to escape the closet, she stepped back into the bedroom to answer the call. It was the sheriff.

"Hey," she muttered as she imagined him at the strip club where Carrie worked. Loud music boomed in the background, blending with male jeers. Bryce was probably front and center tossing dollar bills at the young women who gyrated and shook their tasseled tits.

Shoving the images aside, she said, "We're at Ms. Winters' house. I don't think she was taken from here."

"Me neither," Bryce said. "Her car is still at the club. Manager said sometimes she leaves it here after work for *extracurricular activities*, then comes back for the car in the night. I took a look at it and found her purse and phone in the alley. Doesn't look like she made it to her car at all."

Ellie sucked in her frustration. "Did the manager or any of the employees see her leave with anyone?"

"No, but they're all protective of the clientele."

"Cameras?"

"Not working," Bryce said. "They're there to deter crime, but again, he doesn't want customers shying away because they're on film."

"He's more worried about protecting the men who frequent the bar than his employees," Ellie said in disgust.

"It's adult entertainment, Ellie," Bryce said sardonically. "The men have a right to go to a bar without worrying about being blackmailed by someone who might extort them."

Ellie rolled her eyes. "Talk to the waitresses and bartenders and other dancers. Dust her dressing room and look for DNA left by one of her clients." She shook her head at the fact that she was going to suggest this but did it anyway. "Do whatever you have to, Bryce, but find out if one of the customers is the man you dubbed the Weekday Killer. For all we know, she could have been blackmailing him and he decided to kill her. The other murders could be a ruse to cover up his real target."

Although that sounded far-fetched, she was trying to be open-minded and not miss anything.

"You don't tell me what to do," Bryce snapped. "Remember, I'm the sheriff."

How could she forget?

A text dinged from Cord, and she muttered that she had to go.

CHAPTER 41

Somewhere on the AT

His latest victim twisted at the bindings around her wrists and feet as she struggled to open her eyes. Darkness swallowed her, the sickening scent of his sweat and a musk-like odor filling her nostrils.

Slowly the truth registered. She was moving. Locked in the trunk of a car, the tires were grinding over ruts in the road, swerving and spinning in a dizzying winding pattern that indicated she was somewhere in the mountains.

Somewhere far away from home.

How long had she been unconscious?

Her brain felt foggy, her eyes swollen from crying, her voice hoarse from screaming at the man to release her before she'd eventually passed out. He'd laughed in her face. Chanted some rhyme to her that she'd heard when she was a little girl. He'd yanked her hair, jammed a knife at her throat, stuffed a rag into her mouth. The world swirled, stars exploded behind her eyes, and she hadn't been able to breathe. Then everything faded to nothing.

She blinked again, struggling to recall the details of the night before.

But everything was a fog.

Tears trickled from her eyes, trailing down her cheeks.

Suddenly the car screeched to a stop, slamming her sideways. Pain ricocheted through her. Choking back a cry, she twisted and tugged at the ropes.

But there was no time. The trunk opened and a hulking gray shadow loomed over her. Tall trees shrouded what little sunlight seeped through the treetops. He wore a dark ski mask so she couldn't see his face, even though she had seen it last night.

The realization hit her. That meant he didn't intend to let her live.

Summoning her courage, she raised her legs and kicked at him as she reached for her. He grunted, stepping to the side to dodge the blow, then pulled her to a sitting position. She pushed at him with her bound hands, but he was strong and snatched her hair.

The knife blade glinted against the darkness. "Wednesday's child is full of woe," he murmured. "But you aren't, are you?"

With a sinister laugh, he dragged her from the car. Her scream was drowned out by the sound of a waterfall nearby, and she inhaled the sickening sweet scent of wildflowers.

CHAPTER 42

Teardrop Falls

A man of few words, Cord's text to Ellie was short and to the point:

Teardrop Falls. Locals who've lost loved ones go there to pray and mourn their loss. Meet at Springer Mountain and I'll guide you there.

Ellie's lungs squeezed for air as she parked at the base of the mountain a short while later. The falls were roughly five miles north of Springer Mountain. After leaving Carrie Winters' house, she and Derrick had dropped her hate mail at the station to be forwarded to the lab at the Bureau and he'd sent Bryce a message to have any mail her father had received sent there as well.

Derrick had found Carrie's laptop in her bedroom. It was password protected, so he'd also sent it to the lab.

"If Bryce comes up empty at the Men's Den, maybe we'll find a calendar of Carrie's clients," Derrick said.

Ellie nodded. "If one of them wanted more than Carrie offered, or stalked her and she rejected him, it could have triggered his rage. Although if that's the case, why didn't he start with Carrie?"

"It's true that a killer's first victim is often more personal," Derrick said. "But not always the case. Sometimes the other victims are a replacement for the one he really wants to kill."

Ellie inhaled a painful breath, an awkward silence falling between them. Hiram had killed all those little girls, including Derrick's sister, as a replacement for her. She didn't need a reminder. She'd never forget it.

The sound of Cord's truck pulling up beside them saved her from the memory.

As she climbed from the vehicle, the giant rocky ridges of the mountains climbed toward the sky. Wildflowers dotted the expanse of green, poking up through the grass and weeds, adding shades of purple, yellow, white and red as vibrant as the sunrise.

Although majestic in beauty, the shadowed, isolated areas in the dense thickets provided countless places to hide. There were drop-offs and ledges so narrow that crossing them meant plastering your body against the wall of stone and sliding one foot at a time. Even seasoned hikers like Ellie held their breath as they negotiated them. Praying folks swore that they got one step closer to Jesus as they crossed to the other side.

As she took in the view, she tried not to imagine what Shondra might be going through, but no matter how hard she tried, she couldn't shake the fear from her mind. She'd seen those whip marks on Courtney.

"He didn't keep the other women long before he killed them," she commented as they set off on the trail. "Yet Shondra has already been gone three days."

Derrick adjusted his pack. "I know. It's doesn't fit his MO, does it? But we're doing everything we can, Ellie."

They lapsed into silence again as Cord got out. Dressed for the hike in insulated pants, a navy flannel shirt and North Face jacket, he grabbed his backpack from his trunk. Mud already caked his boots and dirt streaked his jacket as if he'd taken an early morning hike before meeting them. He threw the bag over his shoulder, and she thought she saw blood beneath his fingernails. Though with Derrick present, she decided not to probe. She'd learned that the hard way last time.

His deep scowl indicated he was about as happy to see Derrick with her as she was to be with both men. But this was about the job, so she asked Cord to lead the way. Derrick took the rear, staying close behind her and keeping up as they wove through the narrow paths carved between the giant oaks, pine trees and cypresses.

Although it was April now, the crisp mountain air was cool, especially under the shade of the canopy of trees, sending a shiver through Ellie.

Three miles in, Cord paused to take a sip of water, his throat muscles working as he swallowed. Derrick constantly scanned the woods, and Ellie did the same. If the perpetrator had already murdered another victim, he could be out here somewhere, looking for the perfect spot to dump the body.

The Weekday Killer's message taunted her. *Will you find her in time, Detective?*

CHAPTER 43

Preacher's Circle

Eula Ann Frampton sat in a rocking chair beside Preacher Ray, her gnarled hands clasped. The voices of the dead whispered in the old lady's mind as the sun slipped behind a cloud.

Most folks around Bluff County thought she was crazy as a loon, and some were downright scared of her, even dragging their children to the other side of the street when they saw her coming, as if she was the bad witch in Hansel and Gretel.

Silly fools.

It all started with the rumor Meddlin' Maude had started years ago. The gossipmongers jumped on Maude's words, and the legend blew up from there, spreading through the town like wildfire.

Apparently, Eula killed her old man and buried him in their rose garden.

The Porch Sitters, what the prayer chain called themselves, gathered for weeks on different porches to pray for her lost soul.

While she did grow the prettiest blood-red roses in these parts, only she and Ernie knew what had happened. Dust to dust though. And a dead body did make for decent fertilizer.

Laughter bubbled in her throat as Preacher Ray handed her a cup of herbal tea, that he swore helped heal the soul. Although preachers weren't supposed to swear, he'd had his own share of the rough life, and he made his own set of rules while living on the trail.

"Ms. Eula, you said you been hearing the spirits again?"

Eula tucked a strand of her wiry gray hair back into her bun, then sipped her tea. "Afraid so. You know I don't ask for this," she said. "They just come to me in the crevices of my mind. Unsettled and searching for some kind of peace or guidance." Not that she could help. She had no control over heaven and earth or sin and sinner.

Not when she was one herself.

Preacher Ray patted her shoulder. "Only God can give them that," he murmured. "Do you want to talk about it?"

Eula forced down the tea, wishing Ray had some honey or sugar. He swore it wasn't bitter to him, just to those who needed cleansing.

Like everyone else, he wanted to know the truth about Ernie.

But even in death, he would never pry that from her cold, dead lips.

"I did. Happened just a little bit ago," Eula said, the sound of the woman's scream reverberating in her head. "She's some place close by."

A noise rustled outside, and Preacher Ray stood inside the shelter he'd built from the pines and hobbled toward the doorway. After a quick peek outside, he angled his head toward her. "A bunch of the Shadow People have come for my sermon."

It was time for Eula to go. Even Preacher Ray's sermons couldn't save her. But maybe he'd pray for the young women this latest monster was after—even if it would soon be too late.

CHAPTER 44

Teardrop Falls

Derrick kept a close eye on Ranger McClain as they wove through the knee-high weeds. Perspiration trickled down the side of his face, and he waved mosquitoes and no-see 'ems away. He'd made an enemy of the ranger on the last case when he'd questioned him about his past, and the fact that he'd worked multiple Search and Rescue missions involving the missing children. McClain was intense, a loner, and had grown up in foster care. He also had a history in juvie and one of his foster fathers owned a mortuary.

The fact that the Weekday Killer sewed the victims' mouths shut as a mortician would do wasn't lost on Derrick. There was no telling what atrocities McClain had seen—or done—growing up living above a funeral home.

He'd also led Ellie to the second victim. "McClain, what made you think of this place?" Derrick asked.

The ranger cut his brooding eyes toward Derrick. "Ellie told me about the rhyme, so I looked at the map. This place is known around these parts for mourners who want to grieve the loss of their loved one."

"Isn't there some legend about the tears forming the falls?" Ellie asked.

Cord gave a small shrug, then hacked at the overgrown path to clear their way up the hill. "Some say that the overhang from the falls used to be dry until three teenagers years ago formed a suicide pact and jumped to their deaths." His voice turned gruff. "Supposedly the families and the girls' classmates joined here for a prayer vigil, and there were so many tears shed that it looked like a waterfall. Ever since then the waterfalls run and pool in the gorge below."

They stepped over a rocky creek bed, where the water was so clear you could see minnows swimming below, and a nest of turtles on the muddy bank. As they climbed the next hill, black-eyed Susans sprang up along the path, and a sudden breeze stirred the scent of honeysuckle and something murky, like a dead animal.

Ellie's breath punctuated the air as they climbed the last incline and she came to an abrupt halt. She stopped so suddenly Derrick almost ran into her.

"This is it," Ellie said in a strained voice.

Derrick glanced over her shoulder and saw the base of the falls, water dripping over the ridge below and splashing into the pool beneath. A sea of yellow covered the ground, and beside the pool of water lay another woman on a bed of daffodils.

CHAPTER 45

"It's not Shondra," Ellie said breathlessly.

No, this woman was a redhead. Medium build, with freckled ivory skin that looked ghostly against the stark blackness of her dress.

Guilt at her relief that the woman wasn't Shondra seized Ellie, and immediately she took in the details of the scene. Just as before, daffodil petals dotted the body and the woman's hands were folded in prayer fashion, yet this time the slash on her throat was more jagged. The makeup had escalated too—the killer had painted red streaks down her cheeks, as if she was crying blood.

He'd also left her dress open at the top, revealing a dark purple bruise. Leaning closer to examine it, she realized he'd carved the shape of a heart into her chest.

"Look at that, Derrick."

His brows rose. "Maybe a tattoo, and he removed it."

"Maybe." Or maybe he was escalating to torture. Ellie laid two fingers against the woman's skin and went still. "Her body is cool, but not completely cold." Pulling her weapon, Ellie pivoted to scan the surrounding area. "She hasn't been dead long. He might still be somewhere in the woods."

Derrick grabbed his gun from his holster, surveying the area. There was a noise from somewhere, leaves rustling, twigs snapping.

Ellie gestured to Cord. "Stay here and call it in." She motioned to both men that she was going to search the area, then craned her neck as she inched further up the hill. The ash trees and red oaks shrouded the sunlight, making it hard to see, but the movement of foliage broke the silence.

Charging forward, she tripped over a tree stump, but grabbed a vine to keep from tumbling down the ravine. Derrick was close behind her, his movements as stealthy as a cat's.

Ellie reached a section where the creek was overflowing again. There was no time to take the long way around, so she trudged through the ankle-deep frigid water, shivering as a bone-deep cold seeped through her.

Peering ahead, she spotted movement. It was a tall figure, with broad shoulders. A man wearing a black ski cap. But he was so fast she couldn't distinguish any details.

Snatching a tree limb, she hoisted herself up a steep incline, hoping for a better vantage point. A few more feet, and she'd reach the crest of the hill, where she'd hopefully be able to catch a glimpse of his face.

But just as she latched onto a vine to swing herself across the ravine, which fell a good seventy-five feet below, a shot rang out. The bullet pinged by Ellie's head, then another one zinged, snapping past her. Derrick cursed as he ducked. Using her feet, she swung her body in an attempt to propel herself to the other side. Another bullet skimmed her hand, the sound vibrating in her ears, and the vine slipped between her fingers.

Flailing to hang on, her body swung back and forth, and she attempted to jump back onto the ground beside Derrick. He lurched to his knees, firing at the shooter, who'd run up the hill.

Her feet finally connected with vines and weeds, and she released the vine in her hand, but she missed the edge and hit the side. Frantically trying to slow her descent, she tucked her body and curled on her side, rolling down the hill.

As she descended, her vision blurred and she crashed headfirst into a jagged rock.

CHAPTER 46

"Ellie!" Derrick's heart raced as she slammed against the boulder. For a second, she lay so still, he thought she'd passed out. His foot skidded on the ledge, sending rocks crumbling down, and he barely stopped himself from toppling down the hill himself.

Ellie lifted her head slightly, yelling for him to go after the man. He sprinted up the next hill, pushing through weeds and brush, shoving tree branches aside as he scanned the woods for the shooter. A shift of the bushes to the right caught his eye, and he veered around a cluster of rocks. Behind him, the sound of vultures hissing and grunting filled the silence.

Sweat trickled down his neck as he ran, his gun at the ready as he examined the landscape. His boots pounded the foliage, snapping twigs and sticks, the soggy ground near the creek sucking at his feet like quicksand.

Before he could land a clean shot, another bullet pinged toward him. He ducked behind a pine, swung his gun up and fired at the shooter. Chasing the shadowy figure, he maneuvered from one tree to the next until he reached the crest. A trail led to the left.

Suddenly the sound of a motor firing up rent the air, and he rushed toward the source.

It was an ATV. *Dammit.* Although the NPS protected the wilderness and vehicles were illegal on the trail, some sections were so deserted that people used them anyway.

Darting ahead, he aimed his gun, but another bullet narrowly missed his cheek, thudding into a tree trunk next to him and sending wood splinters into his face. He kept moving.

Just as he reached the clearing, the ATV sped into the dense woods ahead. He fired another round at the shooter, but he was too far away.

A second later, he disappeared in a cloud of dust.

CHAPTER 47

Battling a wave of dizziness, Ellie pushed herself to a sitting position. She swiped at the blood trickling down her forehead, then wiped the residue on her pants.

Blinking to clear her vision, she inhaled several deep breaths, struggling to stand. The ground swayed, the world foggy, so she grabbed a tree limb to steady herself, then judged the distance up the hill. A steep incline, but she thought she could make it.

Pulling her gloves from her bag, she tugged them on. The first step made her ankle throb, and she realized she might have a slight sprain. Ignoring the pain, she put more weight on her left foot, snagged a hefty tree branch and used it to propel herself upwards.

One foot at a time, one more… another… perspiration beaded on her skin and she heaved a breath. Her muscles protested the steep climb, but the image of the dead women played through her head, driving her forward.

By the time she reached the edge of the ridge, her hands were aching, her head was pounding, and her gloves were ripped from clawing at the rough bark and bramble. Reaching for leverage to pull her the rest of the way, she held onto a thick tree root and dragged her body over the side. Swinging her leg up, she managed to crawl over the edge and then collapsed, her breath panting out.

Bushes rustled ahead, and she spotted Derrick running toward her.

Shoving her tangled hair from her face where it had come loose from her ponytail, she tried to stand. The world swayed again, and she cursed, then blinked, determined to stay strong as he approached.

But the fact that he was alone made her stomach clench. "What happened?" she wheezed out.

Derrick's dark eyes skated over her. "He got away. Had an ATV parked off the way."

"He hasn't used a gun with his victims." Ellie gestured towards the falls. "But the close proximity to the woman's body suggests he could be the killer."

"If he wanted us to find her, why shoot at us?" Derrick questioned.

Ellie shook her head. "It's a game to him, and he isn't finished. He wants to play out the days of the week."

"You're probably right." Derrick walked toward her, halting a foot away, his frown deepening. "You're bleeding."

"I'm fine," Ellie said, shrugging him off. She zeroed in on his cheek. "You're hit?"

"Just a shrapnel graze," he muttered, his voice edged with frustration. He pulled a handkerchief from his pocket and offered it to her. "Let me take a look."

"I'm fine," she repeated through gritted teeth. The sound of the vultures swooping, their wings flapping in the silence, made her turn. "Let's get back to the body."

Derrick nodded, then lifted his hand. "I collected a couple of bullet casings. Looks like he was using a .45 caliber pistol."

"So, he has a gun, but he doesn't use it to kill the women," Ellie said, frowning. "He slashes their throats instead."

"Maybe he uses the gun to force them into going with him," Derrick suggested.

"I guess he could be hiding out and stalking them before he ambushes them."

"This guy is a sociopath," Derrick pointed out. "They can be charming, handsome, look perfectly normal."

"That's the reason he can stalk them without anyone noticing," Ellie said. "Because he doesn't look threatening."

"The worst kind," Derrick replied. "He could be sitting right next to you and you'd never suspect him."

CHAPTER 48

By the time Ellie and Derrick made it back to Teardrop Falls, the Evidence Response Team had arrived, along with Laney.

Cord met them, his phone in hand. "I have to go, Ellie. A hiker fell off the ledge at Rattlesnake Ridge."

"Then go, and Cord," Ellie said, "thanks for your help here."

Darkness tinged his eyes and he turned away quickly, leaving her to wonder again if he was still angry with her. But she didn't have time to analyze it now. They both had their secrets.

The investigators were combing the area for evidence, and Ellie had the instinctive urge to wrap a blanket around the poor woman's body, even though she knew better than anyone not to compromise the scene.

The ME looked up from where she was examining the victim, her eyes widening slightly, and Ellie realized she must look a mess. Hazard of the job.

"Are you all right?" Laney asked.

Ellie shrugged, although her head was thumping like someone had hit her with a hammer. "Took a roll down a hill, but I'm fine, unlike our poor lady here. Are her lips sewn shut like the others?"

Laney nodded confirmation. "But this scene feels even more brutal than the last one," she said, pointing toward the blood that had dried on the woman's neck and torso. "What do you think this means?" Laney asked.

Ellie cleared her throat. "He carved a heart on her chest because he thinks she doesn't have one."

CHAPTER 49

Skinny Minnie Whiny Vinny. Skinny Minnie Whiny Vinny.

No, no, no, no! He was not Skinny Minnie Whiny Vinny. Not anymore. The doctor at that nuthouse said he was like two different people, and he was the other one now.

The strong, smart one. The one who'd make all the women who'd wronged him pay.

He had friends now, too. Maybe *two* friends. Yes, yes, yes, the man who'd come to see him at the sanitarium was his friend, too. He never could have gotten out without him. And now here he was, doing favors for him and Hiram. That's what friends were for.

Gripping the jar of blood in his hands, he crept through the bushes in front of Ellie Reeves' house. A car sounded down the road, and he hunkered down and stayed hidden as it passed. A lizard slithered across his foot, and he caught it by its tail and flung it into the yard.

Dark shadows clung to the front porch as he crept up the steps. The damn front light had been on, but he'd taken care of that with a rock. Inside, a light burned from the kitchen but he could see there was no one inside, just like Ellie's Jeep was missing.

Clutching the blood in one hand, he hovered in the shadow, then opened the mason jar. The coppery smell suffused his senses, and he breathed it in, remembering how the woman he'd punished had bled all over him. He'd tasted it when it spurted from her body and spattered his face, a sweet taste he would savor because it meant she was dead.

Dipping his finger into the jar of blood, he lifted it and began to smear it across her door. He wished he could be a fly on the wall, to see Ellie's reaction when she got the present he'd left for her.

CHAPTER 50

Stony Gap

Three hours later, after the crime scene team finished, Ellie and Derrick parked at Haints. Bryce wanted an update on the case and said to meet him at the bar. Hopefully he had something to share from his interviews with the other dancers and bartender at the Men's Den.

"I can't believe he's here drinking on the job while we're hunting a serial killer," said Ellie.

Derrick didn't like Waters, but he was too busy studying the cemetery across from the bar to comment. A wrought-iron gate surrounded the hilly plot of land which was well manicured, with statues of angels and Jesus and holy crosses decorating the various sections. A fog had rolled in, casting the grounds in a dull gray, and wind battered the flowers in the vases at the heads of the graves. "It seems odd to build a bar across from a graveyard," he said.

Ellie shrugged. "It's called White Lilies Cemetery and has a special section for children, called 'Loving Arms'. Apparently, the bar owner built it so he could watch over his daughter, who's buried there."

Derrick tightened his hands into fists as an image of his little sister flitted through his mind.

"Some say at night you can see the little angels running through the white lilies," Ellie said with a thoughtful look. "Others say the bar is haunted."

Derrick wanted to believe that Kim was somewhere magical surrounded by other children, running and playing together. But he'd seen enough of the hell and the evil on earth that his faith was shaken.

"Might as well get this over with," Ellie said.

Derrick followed her into the bar. He'd disliked Waters even more than Cord McClain, but for different reasons. He couldn't quite put his finger on it, but he sensed the new sheriff had some kind of vendetta against Ellie.

Even though he and Ellie had their differences, he knew she'd been clueless about her parents' actions and admired her grit.

Bryce Waters, son of the mayor, struck him as an entitled, spoiled kid who always got his way, no matter what he had to do in order to get it.

He noticed Ellie turning her attention to her phone as they walked to the bar and, a second later, wide eyed, she turned it to show him, the color draining from her face. His heart dipped as he read the message on the screen.

Shondra says hello. You were too late again. Just like you'll be tomorrow.

CHAPTER 51

Haints Bar

He'd barely escaped tonight. Detective Reeves was fast. But he was faster. Faster and smarter.

And he would win this game.

He swirled the drink around in his glass, grateful for the cover of the crowded bar as he spotted the detective and that agent walk in. Their gaze scanned the room, the detective's eyes scrutinizing every man inside as if she found them lacking.

Averting his gaze, he tossed back the drink, pretending she didn't exist. He'd have to deal with her.

But not quite yet.

From his vantage point, he looked through the open-air side of the bar and saw the twinkling lights glittering above the graveyard, sparkling as night fell and the ghostly shadows of the dead rose from the dirt. The statuesque angel stood watch over the little ones buried there.

He knew just the right woman to take as Thursday's child. It was time to get back to work.

CHAPTER 52

"He's toying with me," Ellie said in a low voice. "Torturing me by making me wonder when he's going to kill Shondra."

"Bastard. We're going to find him, Ellie."

Ellie wanted to believe Derrick, but they needed something concrete. So far, they were running around chasing their tails, looking for bodies, and had no real suspect.

Pausing to scan the crowded bar for Bryce, hushed whispers floated around her, and a couple of deputies she recognized gave her skeptical looks as she crossed the room.

As a teenager, boys had steered clear of her because her father was sheriff. At the academy, she'd had to fight harder, be tougher, and prove she could hold her own with her fellow officers as well as the criminals. When she returned from the academy, they assumed she'd survived because of who her daddy was. When she'd made detective, the scrutiny had gotten even worse.

Working for Crooked Creek's police department instead of the sheriff's office in Stony Gap had given her a reprieve. Until the Ghost case.

Now stares and suspicious looks dogged her everywhere. Bryce looked up with an eyebrow raise, then a frown at the sight of Derrick. All these damn testosterone-laden men were too territorial.

The guy beside Bryce moved over to flirt with a thirty-something female, and Ellie slid onto the seat.

"You wanted an update. Here we are." She didn't bother to hide her disdain that he was here drinking on the job.

"You found another victim," Bryce said.

She nodded and showed him the text. "It wasn't Shondra though. She's still out there."

Bryce plucked a French fry from his plate and wolfed it down. "You're sure it's the same killer?"

"Same signature, with the lips sewn shut. Although this time he carved a heart on her chest."

Bryce's eyes darkened, then he tossed back a shot of whiskey. "Any clue who she is?"

"Not yet," Ellie said. "Dr. Whitefeather will let us know lab results after the autopsy." She gritted her teeth as he ordered another drink.

"I thought you were working, too," Ellie said, indicating the shot. "He's going to kill again. And if Shondra is still alive, the next victim could be her."

"For your information, my people are still searching for Shondra and locations where this killer might be hiding out." He arched a brow. "But a man has to eat." He shot her a sarcastic look. "Or don't you have to, Ellie?"

He made her blood boil. "Food is one thing. Whiskey is another."

"You're walking the line here, Detective," said Bryce, gripping her wrist. "Being insubordinate could be dangerous."

"Is that a threat?" Ellie asked, lifting her chin in challenge.

Bryce's eyes narrowed. "A warning."

Derrick's expression was lethal as he noticed the sheriff's hand clenching Ellie's wrist. He started to speak, but Ellie held up a warning hand and shook her arm away.

She didn't want—or need—a man fighting her battles.

"Did you learn anything from talking to Carrie's coworkers or the staff at the club where she worked?" Derrick asked, clearing his throat.

A vein throbbed in Bryce's neck as he tilted his head toward Derrick. "Bartender said she was a good dancer, liked entertaining the men. Took some lap dances and did some after-hours work but was always discreet."

"He give up the names of any of her special clients?" Ellie asked.

Bryce accepted the second shot and swirled it around in the glass. "No, said she handled her own business and respected her clients' privacy. I searched her dressing room and car but didn't find a client list anywhere." He downed the whiskey. "Although one of the other girls said she was saving up enough money to get out of the business. She planned to go to college and study finance."

Ellie rubbed her throbbing head. So Bryce had actually done some background work. That was something, at least.

"A special guy in her life who inspired this decision?" Derrick asked.

Bryce shook his head. "Not that she knew of. Said Carrie's friend Samantha might know, but I've called her and she didn't answer. When she phones back, I'll go by her place and find out what she knows."

"Be sure to ask her if one of her clients is into domination or S & M," Ellie said.

"Don't worry," Bryce said with a sly smile. "I've got it covered."

She just bet he did.

Frustration knotted her shoulders as she turned and left. Three women were already dead, their lives on her head. There had to be some clues in the Weekday Killer's MO or the victims themselves. What in the hell were they missing?

CHAPTER 53

River's Edge

Cord let himself inside his cabin, the scent of dirt and blood clinging to his skin just as the images of the dead women lingered in his mind and their screams had reverberated through the pines and hemlocks.

The evil voices from his past had spoken to him all day and night. Evil voices that ordered him to do things he knew were not right. Evil things he'd been taught to do as a child.

He'd lied to Ellie again. There hadn't been a call for a hiker in trouble.

But the sight of the woman's shocked eyes and painted lips had forced him to leave before Ellie saw who he really was.

She would figure it out one day. She was smart.

But he wasn't ready to share that side of himself with her yet.

Ripping off his gloves and bloody clothes, he threw them in the wash, added detergent and turned it on. For a second, he stood and watched the machine fill with water, the soapy bubbles building as the crimson stain bled from his clothes, turning the water bright red.

Another woman would die tomorrow. Somewhere on the trail. The place he now called home.

With blood and dirt still stained on his body, Cord stepped into the shower and ran the water as hot as he could. The sharp bite of heat blasted him, stinging the scratches on his hands and arms, and he scrubbed his skin until it was raw. Blood and grime swirled around the tile floor, disappearing down the drain, but he couldn't erase the memory of what he'd done from his brain.

Or maybe it was the pull of evil inside him that kept it running through his mind.

CHAPTER 54

Crooked Creek

Night brought the cloying darkness that cloaked the mountains and felt suffocating to Ellie as she pulled into her drive. On the way home, she'd heard Angelica Gomez's latest report from the sheriff.

For a moment the world spun, threatening to paralyze her. Déjà vu struck her and sent her spiraling back to the Ghost case.

Closing her eyes, she forced deep breaths in to stem the panic, just as Kennedy Sledge had suggested the first time they'd met. She wanted to teach Ellie the power of mind over body, and that she could fight her own weaknesses if she focused.

Her nails dug into her palms as she practiced counting with each breath, then exhaling slowly, giving her brain time to adapt. But as her breathing steadied, the images of the dead women slipped through the calm. The gaudy makeup, the daffodil petals, and the thorny bramble formed a gruesome picture in her mind that she couldn't erase.

Shondra was out there somewhere with the killer. Would she live through the night? Or was she already dead? Ellie's head swirled with it all.

Rain drizzled down steadily, the gray clouds robbing the sky of moonlight. A frown pulled at her mouth as she cut the engine and realized her porch light was off. So was the light inside her kitchen. Not wanting to come home to a dark house, she always left the outside light on and one burning in her kitchen.

The hairs on the back of her neck prickled as she scanned her property for signs someone had been there. There were no vehicles or tire marks in sight.

Pulling her gun at the ready, she tugged her jacket on, then slowly maneuvered down the path to her porch. The steps were slick with rain, and she paused to listen at the top for sounds someone was inside.

Fear pounded at her as she touched the doorknob, and her hand came away sticky. Jerking her fingers back, she pulled her flashlight and shined it on the door. The coppery scent of blood inundated her as she saw what was there.

Dear God. Someone had written the words "It's Your Fault" in blood on her door.

For a second, she was too stunned to do anything but stare. Her own voice of guilt whispered through her mind followed by the sound of the protestors in town and the hate mail she'd received.

Fury that this bastard was toying with her triggered her into detective mode.

She wiped her hand on her pants, then yanked on latex gloves. Careful not to touch the blood, she jiggled the doorknob, and the door swung open. *Dammit.* Her alarm was off.

A slight musky odor wafted through the house, an earthy scent of wood, sweat and oil. And she was sure she could also detect the faint odor of the ointment her mother had slathered on her when she'd been stung by a bee and broke out in hives.

Someone had been inside.

Gripping her gun at the ready, she eased inside her hall. The pungent scent assaulted her again, and she shivered as the pitch black swallowed her. For a moment, she forgot to breathe.

Memories of Hiram trapping her in the dark tunnel, and the faces of the terrified little girls he'd kidnapped flooded her. Then the image. She could hear Hiram's shrill voice, the sound of his knife shaving away wood as he carved the little dolls he'd used to lure her and his other victims to follow him into the forest. He'd promised a pretty pink dollhouse with furniture and doll clothes, but that had all been a lie.

Her body trembled. Nausea climbed her throat.

A noise from the back of the house jarred her from her fear-induced stupor, and she shined her flashlight around the space, scanning the living area and kitchen. After a quick sweep of the hall, she crept to the bedrooms.

The wood floor creaked as she crossed her room, searching her closet and the master bath.

The rooms were empty. Nothing seemed out of place.

Releasing a breath, she relaxed slightly, then made her way back to the living room. In the kitchen, a damp breeze blew through a window which stood wide-open, cold night air filling the room and giving her a chill.

She'd left the window locked, she was sure of that.

Flipping on the light, she gasped. A small wooden doll lay on the kitchen table. It was on top of a bed of daffodils with a river rock tombstone marker at the head of the grave.

On the stone her name was drawn in blood.

CHAPTER 55

Thursday

Crooked Creek

The next morning, worry for Shondra dominated Ellie as she and Derrick stopped at the Corner Café for breakfast. She'd barely slept for the nightmares. It had literally taken half the night for the crime team to process her house, and the doll and blood had been sent to the lab.

She and Derrick had theorized while the crime team worked. Could Hiram possibly be behind all this? He'd gotten away with a dozen murders over a twenty-five year span. And if the killer was taunting her because of his hatred of her, it was part of his pathology. The only person Ellie could think of who hated her enough was Hiram.

But how could he orchestrate multiple murders from prison?

Then she'd seen the news, where Bryce had addressed the press. He'd informed them that now they had three victims, but at least he'd kept his mouth shut regarding MO, details they intentionally decided to keep from the media and public in case some lunatic attention-seeker decided to take credit as the Weekday Killer.

She rubbed her aching head, hoping the painkillers would kick in soon. Last night in her dream, the mountain trail was a dumping ground for bodies. Dead women were everywhere. Laid along the paths, deep in the woods, hanging from trees, floating in the river. Bugs and insects feasting on the remains. Just as she left one, she turned and saw another. Sightless eyes stared up at her begging for help, mouths stood wide open in silent screams.

Terrorized cries echoed through the long dark night as she stumbled to escape them.

"You okay?" Derrick asked as they entered the café.

She nodded, although they both knew she was lying. Inside, she spotted Angelica at a table where she was deep in conversation with someone. Always working her story. The strong scent of sausage gravy and homemade biscuits made her mouth water. Lola waved from the counter, and she and Derrick headed to a booth in the back. All eyes and heads turned their way, wary looks passing among the patrons.

Willie Grace, Fanny Mae's twin and the other half of the Stitchin' Sisters, pointed a crooked finger at Ellie. "What's she doing here?"

"She ought to be looking for that killer."

"Just as sorry as her daddy."

Ellie gritted her teeth, telling herself to ignore them. But Meddlin' Maude had the nerve to stand up and block her way. The woman's hot-pink warm-up suit made her look like a raspberry Popsicle, but there was no sweetness in Maude's cutting tone. "I hope you do a better job finding this maniac hurting our young women than you did saving all those poor children."

Edwina Waters, Bryce's mother, tugged at Maude's arm. "Come on, Maude. Bryce will find this killer, then our kids and families will be safe again." She threw a nasty look over her shoulder and Ellie, stomach in knots, for the first time spotted her parents huddled together in the back corner of the room.

Maude lifted a haughty head and strutted past Ellie, with Carol Sue, Lily and other gossipmongers trailing after her like a brood of hens.

Derrick took Ellie's arm, guiding her to their booth.

From the back of the café where her parents sat, she heard crying, before her mother jumped up from the table and ran out the back door.

Pulse racing, Ellie's gaze met her father's worried one, then he chased after her. At the back door, she heard raised voices and saw Philip Paulson, the father of one of the Ghost's victims, and another man she didn't recognize accost her dad.

So much pain caused by Hiram, she thought with a heavy heart. She wanted to talk to him today. Make him look her in the eye and see if he was behind these latest murders. If he had an accomplice or had garnered an apprentice.

"I heard you're making a deal," Paulson shouted. "How can they let you off for letting our little girls die?"

"Let's get food to go," Ellie muttered as she saw Angelica Gomez rush from her table to cover the debacle. "I want to question Hiram and see if he has something to do with this."

He could not fight the demons inside him any longer. They ate at him like live beasts, tormenting him with the need to get justice for the one he hadn't been able to save.

Gripping the woman's face so tightly he thought her jawbone might crack, he stooped down to look at her. She disgusted him. They all did. "Do you know why I chose you, Cathy?"

Her hazel eyes were glazed with shock and defiance. "My name is not Cathy," she snarled. "Now, let me go."

"The only place you're going to is hell." His laughter boomed off the concrete walls, and he fastened the metal collar around her neck, making sure the chain was securely attached. She dug her fingernails into his gloved hands and spat at him.

"You bitch," he said, giving her a hard slap across the face. "You're a fighter, aren't you?"

"Is that how you get off?" she asked as she turned a hate-filled look toward him. "Beating up on women?"

He dragged her toward the cage. "You talk like you're some fucking saint." He raised the whip and slapped it across her back. "Thursday's child has far to go. But you're going to hell, Cathy."

He shoved her in the cage, then locked it. "You know what the Ten Commandments are, don't you?" His laugh boomed from him. "You must not, because you didn't obey them."

CHAPTER 57

Bluff County Prison

An hour later, after Ellie and Derrick downed their dinner, they arrived at the county prison where Hiram was being held until he could be transferred to a federal facility. "Let's get this over with," Derrick said as he climbed from the car.

"You don't have to go in there and face him after everything he did to you. I can handle it," Ellie said, reaching out and touching his arm.

Derrick's gaze locked with hers. "I was going to tell you the same thing, Ellie. After all, he tried to kill you."

Ellie licked her suddenly dry lips. He didn't have to remind her what Hiram had done. All the sweet children's lives lost because of her. "All the more reason to confront him. I want to show him I'm not afraid of him anymore. And if he's somehow pulling strings from in here to help this killer, or if they were working together, then I want to know."

When they reached the front steps of the prison, Angelica Gomez was exiting the building. Damn, the reporter seemed to be everywhere they were.

Ellie's first instinct was to run, but the reporter might have persuaded Hiram to talk about an accomplice in the Ghost murders, so she forged ahead.

"Detective Reeves, Special Agent Fox, nice to see you," Angelica said.

Ellie couldn't say the same. "You just interviewed Hiram?"

Angelica nodded, tucking a strand of her long ebony hair behind one ear. Her coal black pantsuit and heels looked expensive and sophisticated, out of place against the aging stone prison walls behind her.

"He's interesting," Angelica said. "He wants me to tell his side of the story."

Ellie stiffened. "Interesting? That's a strange choice of word for a serial killer. Did he give you any information about a possible accomplice?"

Angelica shook her head. "He mostly wanted to talk about his childhood. I think it's going to take several visits before he gets past that and we can discuss the details of the crimes. He likes the attention, so we can use that to our advantage."

Ellie raised a brow at Angelica using the word *we*, as if they were partners.

"He did hint that he had a fan, although he refused to divulge his name," the reporter said, twisting the strap of her handbag.

Surprise fluttered through Ellie. "This fan could be the Weekday Killer."

Angelica nodded. "I thought of that, and I'll keep pushing. Do you have any updates?"

"You talked to the sheriff, you heard what he had to say," Ellie pointed out.

"I was hoping you had more," Angelica said with an eyebrow lift.

Derrick squared his shoulders. "We're exploring possibilities."

Angelica glanced back at Ellie. "He also talked about your family. He said they had more secrets."

Ellie grinded her teeth. "You know you can't go public with any of this right now. If you do, you could jeopardize the case against my parents."

"I'm surprised you want to protect them," Angelica said. "Considering."

Ellie shot her a warning look, daring her to say more.

The journalist remained cool, but she'd made her point. "I hope you find Deputy Eastwood."

"We will," Ellie said. She just prayed they found her alive.

As Angelica headed off, Ellie motioned at Derrick to head inside. Maybe talking to the reporter had warmed Hiram up enough to spill his guts to her.

Remaining silent as they entered the prison and went through security, Derrick's face was a mask of control. While his mind must be occupied with thoughts of his sister and the fact that he was about to confront the man who'd killed her, he never once showed it.

The warden steepled his hands on his desk as they were shown into his office. The man was big and brawny, a former cop with mammoth-sized hands and arms, and eyes the color of cold steel.

"We think Hiram has a follower," Derrick said. "Do you know anything about that?"

"Captain Hale asked me to check Hiram's correspondence. He's received hate mail for the crimes he committed. And also some fan mail. Disgusting." He gestured toward a folder on the desk. "And last week, a man tried to visit him. Gave the name Vinny Harper, although he didn't have proper ID or clearance, so we turned him away."

"Can you have your people pull security footage from when he tried to enter?" Derrick asked.

"Certainly." The warden buzzed security, asking them to locate the recording.

"Has he had any other visitors?" Ellie asked.

"Your mother came once," the warden said. "But Hiram refused to see her."

Ellie squeezed her fingers around the chair edge, stifling her reaction.

"What about his cellmate?" Derrick asked. "Or friends? Has Hiram made any since he's been locked up?"

The warden shook his head. "Child molesters and killers are considered the lowest of the low, even to other felon offenders. His first cellmate tried to shank him, so we had to move him to a cell by himself instead of being in the general population."

The warden buzzed for a security guard, who escorted them through the dingy halls to the main security office where dozens of cameras displayed various areas of the prison, including individual cells, the common areas, the yard and mess hall. He pulled up the footage of the main entrance and security station, zeroing in on the man who'd called himself Vinny.

The man, dressed in dark clothes, looked wiry and jumpy. He had a pointed chin, shifting eyes set a little too far apart and a ruddy complexion.

Derrick had the guard send the footage to the Bureau so they could run it through facial recognition software, while Ellie texted Heath and asked him to find out what he could on the man.

A coldness swept over Ellie as they were escorted through another dank cement hallway that smelled of sweat, urine and feces.

She and Derrick seated themselves at a metal table attached to the floor, and a guard brought Hiram in. Nerves pinched at Ellie, the memory of Hiram throwing her body into that hole and burying her alive returning to make her sweat.

Handcuffs and shackles clinked and clanged as he shuffled toward the chair. His limp seemed more pronounced today and a fresh scar marked his cheek, as if he'd been cut by a razor.

His crazed eyes skated over Ellie with a mixture of disdain and victory. "Hello, sis," he said with a smile as he slid onto the chair across from her. "I've been expecting you."

CHAPTER 58

Derrick barely controlled his rage as he stared at the sick son of a bitch who'd murdered his little sister. His mother had talked to him about letting go of his hatred, but Hiram's lack of remorse for the girls he'd killed made that impossible.

Still, he had another case to solve, so he pasted on his game face, shoving aside his fury.

Hiram spread his scarred hands on the table, the nervous twitch to his eye adding to his sinister look. The orange jumpsuit made his skin look even more sallow.

"How's Mommy dearest?" Hiram asked Ellie with a toothy grin.

"I'm not here to discuss the family," she said sharply. "I'm here for information."

Hiram's bushy brow rose. "Information about what? About where you came from?"

As anger flashed across Ellie's face, Derrick realized the man was playing games. What did Hiram mean?

"About the Weekday Killer," Ellie replied, leaning forward.

Hiram stretched his hands out to touch her. The minute he did, Ellie leaned back, just out of reach. "Do you know who he is?" she asked.

Hiram smiled. "Don't know what you're talking about."

Derrick removed photographs of the victims from his briefcase and spread them on the table. The pictures were black and whites of the women's faces, their bodies covered in a sheet on the autopsy table. "Each of these women was brutally murdered a day apart," Derrick said.

Excitement lit Hiram's eyes at the sight of the women's corpses, and Derrick barely restrained himself from jerking him across the table and pounding his face.

Sometimes at night, he fantasized about killing Hiram. He'd almost done so when he'd caught him but, in the end, he'd managed to stop himself, for his mother's sake. She'd grieved so much over her daughter and her husband, he hadn't wanted her to lose her son too. He'd never forgive himself for that.

But now the urge hit him full force again, tightening his lungs.

"Pretty ladies," Hiram sneered. "Just like you, Ellie."

"They look nothing like me," Ellie said. "But they are dead because some madman slashed their throats. That madman also texted me to tell me about them. The only person I can think of that would want to torment me is you."

Hiram threw up his hands, the handcuffs clanging. "Wish I could take the credit, but I've been right here." He glanced at the pictures with a sick smile. "Besides, I like them younger."

Derrick stood, leaning over and grabbing Hiram by the neck of his jumpsuit. "So it's your partner who likes them older?"

The prison guard took half a step forward, and Derrick released Hiram and sat back down before giving the guard an apologetic nod.

"Who said I had a partner?" Hiram asked with another smirk.

Ellie slapped the table with her palm. "Stop playing games, Hiram. Someone buried those children we found, and I think you know who it was." It was how they'd found the little girls, their bones buried recently on the Appalachian Trail, as if someone wanted them to be found. "If someone helped you, speak up. The media will make you even more famous for cooperating."

Hiram's eyes turned menacing as he glared at Ellie. "Whoever dug those graves did it on their own. But this Weekday Killer—I want to meet him when you find him."

"Not going to happen," Ellie said.

Hiram chuckled. "Now, Ellie, why don't you ask me what you really want to know?"

"This is a waste of time. Let's go, Agent Fox." Ellie stood, turning away from Hiram.

"You wanna know who you are, don't you? You and Mommy dearest not so chummy anymore?" Hiram called from his seat as Ellie walked toward the door.

Shooting him a warning look, Ellie hit the buzzer to be let out. Derrick picked up the photographs, stuffing them back in his briefcase and followed Ellie outside while another guard entered to help escort Hiram back to his cell.

When Derrick stepped into the hallway, Ellie was leaning against the wall with her eyes closed, her breathing erratic.

"What was that about?" he asked.

A second later, Ellie opened her eyes, pain lingering in the blue irises. "Nothing." Spinning around with a sigh, she headed down the hall, leaving him with more questions than answers.

CHAPTER 59

Ellie was shaking as she stormed down the prison hallway. Damn Hiram for bringing up her family in front of Derrick.

Her secrets should be her own to keep. She'd reveal them when she was good and ready.

Retrieving her weapon at the security checkpoint, an instinct to run pulled at her. But running anywhere near a prison with armed guards was a good way to get herself shot.

Walking at a brisk pace, she ignored the way Derrick was watching her as they exited the building and crossed the parking lot.

When she climbed into the car, she sat gripping her phone, wishing like hell that she'd driven and she could punch the gas and speed along the highway to vent her stress.

Derrick started the engine, and passed through the security gate, heading back toward town. A tense silence stretched between them, the air vibrating with the unsaid and her labored breathing.

Drumming his fingers on the steering wheel as he drove, Derrick's expression was angry, although she had no clue as to why.

Maybe he'd wanted to stay and push Hiram harder. But she'd sensed Hiram didn't plan to add any helpful information to the case. He was having too much fun tormenting her.

At odds with her dismal mood, sunlight flickered off the asphalt, creating rainbow-like patterns. Spring flowers that should have been blooming were late due to the freak March snowstorm, yet the dogwoods blossomed and tiny purple buds were beginning to open up on the pear trees that dotted the side of the mountain.

Derrick swung into the parking lot of a convenience store, then turned to face her. "What aren't you telling me, Ellie?"

She turned to him in shock. "I don't know what you're talking about."

"Now you're flat out lying," he said, his voice hard. "Angelica knows it, too. That's why you cut her off. You're keeping something from me. Either about the Ghost case, or your family, or this case, and I want to know what it is. Don't let another woman die because you kept secrets like your father did."

His words stabbed at her heart. "I've told you everything I know about the case. I realize seeing Hiram wasn't easy for you, and it sure as hell wasn't easy for me, but I did it to find answers." She crossed her arms. "I'm sorry he refused to cooperate."

Derrick's gaze locked with hers for a long moment. "What did he mean—that you want to know who you are? And what did Angelica mean, that you have other secrets?"

Emotions flooded Ellie. The shock of her parents' deceit still stung so strongly that she blinked back tears. She reached for the door handle, but Derrick gripped her arm. "Did you find evidence against your father that you're holding back?"

Perspiration trickled down the back of Ellie's neck. "No…"

"Don't lie to me, Ellie," Derrick said. "I deserve to know the truth."

He didn't have to remind her how much he'd suffered. That it was her fault his sister was dead.

"I didn't find evidence, but if I did, I'd turn it over," she said. "Besides, I haven't talked to my parents since the arrest."

"Then what is it? If it's something that might help with this case, you have to share it. We can't let this maniac get away."

"It's not about the case," Ellie said finally. "It's about me."

"What about you?"

Ellie's stomach churned. He wasn't going to give it up. "Vera and Randall are not my birth parents," she said in a whisper. "They adopted me. That's the reason he hates me so much." Her voice cracked. "And the reason he killed Kim."

CHAPTER 60

"The reason he killed Kim?" Derrick asked, running his fingers through his hair.

She nodded, misery on her face. "Vera gave Hiram up for adoption when he was a baby because she was a teenager. Later, she felt guilty and decided to look for him, but she'd signed all rights away and thought he was in a good home. So I was matched with her."

The remorse in her broken tone made his chest clench. Though he had absolutely zero compassion for Hiram, he understood more now why he'd come after Ellie.

"Does anyone else know?" he asked.

Ellie shook her head. "Angelica wants a tell-all, but I haven't agreed. And my parents have asked me to keep it between us."

"So you're protecting them?" He couldn't keep the anger from his tone.

"No, it's just there's already enough gossip about my family running wild in this town. I needed time to process the truth myself."

"Secrets have a way of coming out, Ellie. The best thing to do is get out in front of them."

"Maybe, when this is all over," she replied, biting down on her bottom lip.

"Have you asked Vera or Randall about your birth parents?"

"They claim they don't know," Ellie said. "But how can I believe anything they said after all their lies?"

In spite of the fact that he'd vowed not to touch her again, the pain on her face and the anguish in her voice made him want to reach out to her. For a brief second, he pulled her up against him.

"I'm sorry, Ellie. It's… not your fault. What he did."

"It is, though. If Vera hadn't adopted me, he wouldn't have killed Kim or any of those other children. They were a substitute for me."

"You were a child. You were helpless. That's not your fault."

He knew what it was like to suffer from guilt.

A person could suffocate beneath the weight.

Her body trembled against him, then she pulled away and released a sigh. "I can't talk about this right now, especially with you. Let's just focus on the case. Time may be running out for Shondra."

Especially you. Her words were like a slap to his face.

Before he could respond, her phone buzzed, and she snatched it. "Yes, Heath, what do you have?"

Ellie's face paled. When she looked up, fear darkened her eyes.

"There's a fire at my parents' house. I need to go there now."

CHAPTER 61

Stony Gap

Thirty minutes later, as they sped up the drive, Ellie clenched the seat edge in a white-knuckled grip. Perched on a hill with the towering mountains behind it, her childhood home had always looked as welcoming as a Norman Rockwell painting.

But now thick plumes of smoke curled into the gray late-morning skies, and orange, red and yellow flames shot upward, raging above the rooftop and trees as the wind fed the blaze.

A Bluff County fire engine screeched ahead of her, brakes squealing as it slammed to a stop near the burning house. Frantically scanning the property for her parents, Ellie didn't see them anywhere on the lawn.

Derrick barreled to a stop a few feet away from the fire engine, and the sheriff's car zoomed up the drive. After swerving to park, Bryce threw his car door open just as she slammed her own shut and ran toward the house.

The wind swirled the fire higher into the sky, wood crackling and popping as the ferocious flames ate at the wood frame. The firemen jumped from the truck engine, the captain barking orders as workers rolled out hoses to try to douse the carnage.

Heat seared Ellie's skin as she approached the house, and the windows exploded, shattering glass everywhere. "Mom? Dad?" Ellie shouted.

"Stay here, miss," one of the firefighters yelled as she stepped forward. But if her parents were in there, she had to save them.

Ignoring the warning, she ran towards the back of the house to see if the fire had spread there, but Derrick dragged her away as the roof collapsed in a mind-numbing roar.

Shock robbed her breath, and she gasped, coughing as smoke filled her lungs. Derrick hauled her toward a live oak to the side of the house while two of the firemen rushed up the porch steps, using axes to hack away the door and spraying water as they entered. Bryce stood by the fire truck, swiping a hand across his face as he watched the chaos.

Fear clogged Ellie's throat, paralyzing her. She'd been so angry at her parents the last few weeks she hadn't spoken to them.

But she didn't want them to die.

"I'm going to talk to Waters," Derrick said. "Stay here, Ellie. Let the firemen do their jobs."

Dizzy with emotions and from the smoke, she didn't argue. Her eyes were glued to the door to see if her parents made it outside. Unbidden, images of her past flickered in her head.

Running through the front yard chasing fireflies and collecting them in mason jars. Her father tossing the softball in the yard with her. Digging for worms behind the house to fish in the pond.

Her mother decorating the lawn with silly Christmas blowups in spite of the fact that the other ladies at the garden club had disapproved. Every Easter when she'd begged Ellie to wear a frilly dress…

The memory tickled her conscience with sudden affection for her mother. Vera had actually caved one time, telling her interfering friends that little girls didn't always have to wear dresses. It had been out of character, but that gesture had given Ellie hope that they wouldn't always be at odds. A hope that soon fizzled.

Wood splintered and the flames popped, shattering Ellie's memories. The right side of the house collapsed, her childhood bedroom engulfed in the blaze. Flames licked at the windows and the fire hissed into the night as if it was a live, breathing monster.

Despite being entranced by the horror unfolding, a movement to the right suddenly caught Ellie's eye.

She quickly turned, spotting someone running away. They were heading toward the woods behind the house.

Ellie sprinted after them, dodging falling debris and embers as the walls collapsed, destroying all her memories. Scanning the property, she saw the man again. But she couldn't tell who it was.

He was wearing a dark hoody, ski mask and black sweats, his face in the shadows as he glanced back at the burning house, then at her. His body went rigid, then he darted through a thicket of pines.

Ellie dashed toward him through the smoke-filled air, her feet flying as she wove between the trees and bushes. He veered to the right, and she snaked her way through the woods, keeping her eyes trained on him and closing the distance. Nearing him, panting with the exertion, she managed to catch him just as he began to climb a hill.

Snagging his jacket and yanking at him, he tumbled backward with a grunt, then spun around and came at her with his fists. Ellie threw her arm up to deflect the blow and managed to knee him in the groin.

His bellow of rage rent the air, his fury seemed to be fueled, and he dove at her headfirst, knocking the air from her lungs. Before she could reach her gun, he threw her to the ground and closed his hands around her neck. His fingers dug into her windpipe, cutting off her air.

CHAPTER 62

"Do you know what happened here?" Derrick asked Bryce, studying the smoky scene before him. "Was it started by one of the protestors in town?"

Bryce rubbed a hand over his clean-shaven jaw. "I don't know, but I intend to find out. The protests against Randall have gotten out of hand. I've broken up two now that have almost turned violent."

"I requested copies of the hate mail he received," Derrick said.

"Why do you want them? So you can gloat?"

The sheriff definitely had a chip on his shoulder. "Because it could be possible that one of them is the Weekday Killer. And he's targeting Ellie to get back at Randall."

Bryce's eyes narrowed. "I asked Randall about the mail, but he hasn't sent it to me."

Two of the firefighters emerged from the front of the house, one carrying Vera, who appeared to be unconscious. The other was helping Randall through the clouds of smoke to the safety of the lawn.

Glancing back at Ellie, Derrick realized she was gone.

"Where's Ellie?"

Bryce snapped to attention. "Did Detective Reeves go inside?" he shouted to the firefighters, who shook their heads.

Hearing a strangled sound, Derrick turned, spotting Ellie coming round the side of the house through the smoke. She looked like a ghost rising from the ashes. But she staggered slightly. Something was wrong.

An ambulance careened up the driveway, siren wailing, lights twirling, as he sprinted towards Ellie.

When he reached her, he noticed a dark bruise forming on her cheek. Her breathing was unsteady. "What the hell happened?"

She pushed her hair from her face. "A man, saw him running out back," Ellie said breathlessly, her troubled gaze meeting his. "I tackled him but he got away."

"Did you recognize him?"

"No, his face was covered." She wiped at the blood on her lip. "But he set that fire and tried to kill my parents."

CHAPTER 63

Ellie watched with a sickening feeling as her family home crumbled to the ground. All the memories, the holidays, her whole childhood was wrapped up in those rooms. It would soon be nothing but dust.

But she didn't have time to dwell on it. Her parents' lives were at stake.

Hurriedly, she crossed the lawn to check on them, relieved that they were out of the burning building, her heart thudding as the medics placed an oxygen mask on her mother's face. Derrick followed her, watching stoically as she approached her parents.

"Good lord, Ellie, what happened?" her father asked, looking up at her.

"I chased a man leaving the scene. I think he set the fire."

"Are you all right?"

"Yes." Ellie's heart shattered as she glanced at her mother. "Are you okay? How's Mom?'

"I'm… I'm fine. But your mom, I don't know." Her father's voice cracked. "I found her passed out in the dining room and they barely got her out."

Vera lay limp, eyes closed, her skin a ghostly white. Ash stained her cheeks and her mint-green warm-up suit was covered in black dust.

Ellie's gaze met her father's terrified one. Bruises darkened his face, soot covered his skin and clothing, and blood seeped from a gash on his forehead.

"Vera, honey, wake up," Randall whispered to his wife.

"Sir, we need to get her to a hospital," one of the medics said. "Her blood pressure is dangerously low."

Randall nodded. "I'm going with you."

"You need to be examined yourself," the medic replied.

"At the hospital," Randall insisted. "First, take care of my wife."

Ellie momentarily froze, memories flashing in her mind. Family Christmases, with twinkling icicle lights on the house, Santa on the roof, carolers in the yard.

Other special times together. Her mother making hot chocolate and bringing it to her in bed when she had a cold. Crafting a superhero costume at the last minute when Ellie refused to wear the princess dress Vera had chosen.

When had she forgotten there were tender moments among the battles with her mother? Moments where Vera almost put aside her desire to impress the ladies in her social world and simply let Ellie be a child. Moments before teenage angst and rebellion had set in. She hadn't been the easiest of kids.

There were times she'd waded in the creek and caught frogs and come home all muddy and excited, her hair full of pine straw, and Vera had ushered her into the bath without worrying about her polished floors and gleaming crystal.

Gathering her composure, Ellie finally found her voice. "What happened?"

Her father's hand shook as he threaded it through his hair. "Someone threw a pipe bomb into the living room and through the bedroom window. It exploded and the place went up quickly."

"Did you see who it was?"

"No." Frustration hardened his voice. "Probably one of those protestors. They've been pretty riled up."

She couldn't argue with that. She'd seen their anger firsthand. Right now, though, she needed to remember whatever details she could. "I saw a man running into the woods behind the house. I gave chase and caught up with him, but he got away."

Bryce had been talking to one of the firefighters but joined them in time to overhear the conversation. "Did you recognize him?"

Ellie shook her head. "He was wearing a hoody and ski mask, but I think I scratched his chin." She spread her hands in front of her, palms up. "Hopefully I got his DNA."

Bryce's jaw clenched. "I'll get my kit to take samples to send to the lab."

"You know it could be Paulson," she continued. "I saw him at the café earlier. He seemed furious over the possibility of the charges against Dad being dropped."

Her father's breathing was erratic, his eyes growing glassy. Just a few short weeks ago, he'd been shot by Hiram and nearly died. Now he was facing this.

"You should go to the hospital and be examined," Ellie said. "I'll make sure the ERT and arson investigator are thorough."

"Ellie," said Bryce gently. "Go to the hospital with your folks, and get yourself examined, too. I can handle it here."

Ellie swallowed against the emotions crowding in on her. Bryce almost sounded as if he cared. "There are women's lives at stake," she said. "I need to work. For all we know, the Weekday Killer may be the same man who set this fire. And he may already be holding his next victim somewhere."

"Why do you think it's the same person?"

"Because of those personal messages. Maybe it's his way of punishing me for the deaths of those little girls. He hates my parents and me."

For a brief moment, Bryce's gaze locked with hers and she thought she saw concern. "You should have told me."

She shrugged. Confiding in the sheriff was the last thing she'd do.

When she didn't respond, his look hardened. "I'll get my kit." Bryce squared his shoulders and walked back to his squad car.

"The Weekday Killer contacted you personally?" Ellie's father asked, his brows furrowing.

"Yes," Ellie said, and that was just the tip of the iceberg.

"Jesus, Ellie," her father said. "You almost died on that last case. Are you trying to get yourself killed now?"

The sound of an engine rumbling up the drive made Ellie turn toward the approaching vehicle. WRIX Channel 5 news. As the van stopped, the cameraman and Angelica hopped out, making a beeline for Ellie.

She couldn't deal with the press at the moment, so turned, following her father toward the ambulance, determined to escape. Bryce was in his element. He could handle Angelica.

She had police work to do. And angry as she was with her parents, she had to make sure they were all right.

The roof and walls of their home had collapsed and the furniture inside was turning to rubble and black ash. Heat still poured from the blaze, the air was hot and sticky.

Her father turned to her from the ambulance doors, his face as ashen as the charred remains of the belongings in their house. "Ellie, your mom just had a heart attack."

Ellie's pulse clamored, and she was unable to speak as her father jumped into the back of the ambulance. She stood staring as it sped off, its siren roaring.

CHAPTER 64

Ellie had been so angry with her mother the last few weeks. Could not talk to her or even look at her. It had hurt to even think about Vera.

But despite everything, she didn't want her to die. Of course she didn't.

Memories swamped her again. She saw herself as a little girl, five years old, standing on the back porch looking out at the woods, too terrified to venture into them. As much as she was scared, she was intrigued by the twisting paths and gigantic trees that offered adventures.

But that day her mother encouraged her not to be afraid of anything.

Then everything changed the day Hiram lured her away.

"You okay?" Derrick asked.

She wasn't. But she couldn't cry on his shoulder, so she gave a quick nod, biting back the pain. He pushed his keys into her hand. "Go. We have the whole county working on the case. I'll follow up here."

The need to be alone suddenly seized her. She couldn't break down, especially not in front of him.

His fingers brushed hers as he handed her the keys, and her hand shook as she gripped them, hurrying to his car.

Climbing in, she sent a text to her captain filling him in on her parents' condition.

Stomach knotted, she started the engine then pulled down the drive. Smoke billowed in the sky behind her, obscuring the view of the mountains beyond, while her parents' home continued to burn, the embers glowing orange and red across the lawn. Would the firefighters be able to save the commendations her father had received? And the hand-carved chess set her grandfather had made? What about her photos from the police academy?

It didn't matter, she told herself. They were only things. Her mother's life was at stake.

Ten minutes later, she forced deep breaths as she parked at the hospital and rushed inside. Her legs felt wooden, a numbness washing over her, dread curling in her belly.

She flashed her badge at the nurses' station and was quickly sent back to an ER exam room. For a moment, she stood outside the door watching as her father hovered by her mother's bed. He looked ragged, his clothes torn and dirty, his face thin and drawn. He must have lost at least fifteen pounds in the last few weeks, the stress and his surgery having taken its toll.

Machines beeped and whirred, providing her mother with oxygen and monitoring her vitals. The scent of disinfectant and sickness permeated the air. Muffled voices and the sound of a rolling cart rattled in the hallway. A woman's heart-wrenching crying seeped into the milieu.

Ellie's breathing grew erratic as she watched her father squeeze her mother's hand. As if he sensed her presence, Randall turned to look at her. The fear in his eyes was so stark that her knees nearly buckled.

Blinking away tears, Ellie willed her feet to move. For her to dig deep and find some semblance of forgiveness for her mother. But she remained immobile, stuck in the doorway. The betrayal and lies that had destroyed her world, ripped apart her family—and cost so many innocent lives—were still so raw, paralyzing her.

CHAPTER 65

Somewhere on the AT

Please don't do this, she silently begged. *I don't want to die.*

His next victim tried to struggle against the ropes tied around her wrists, but she was powerless—he had drugged her. Her arms and legs were dead weights and she couldn't move her fingers. Her vocal cords seemed to be frozen so she couldn't scream even though every nerve in her body desperately wanted to.

"Thursday's child has far to go, and that's you. So far to go to get to heaven that you'll never get there." He slapped her face so hard her ears rang and stars danced in her eyes. Then he stuffed her in the trunk and slammed it shut. Silent tears trickled down her face.

A horrifying realization dawned. He was that maniac she'd heard about on the news—the Weekday Killer. She'd heard he did awful things to his victims, slashing their throats and leaving them out in the woods. All the women at the Beauty Barn were talking about him—they were buying mace now and one girl had even bought a gun.

Now she wished she'd listened to them.

She tried to move her limbs again, but to no avail, sending a cold terror through her.

The burlap sack he'd stuffed her in before he'd carried her to the car was suffocating. Through the tiny holes in the fabric, she had seen a hint of the sun as he'd hauled her to his car. Ever since he'd taken her, she'd been in and out of consciousness, stirring when a camera flashed. The twisted creep was taking photographs of her.

His words echoed in her head. *It was your fault, Cathy. I have to teach you a lesson.*

Who was Cathy? He was deranged.

Then he'd forced her on all fours with that dog collar and chain, dragging her until she begged for him to stop.

God help her. She had too much living to do to die.

The engine burst to life, tires grinding, and the vehicle bumped along a graveled road, then began winding back and forth. With each turn, her body bounced against the interior of the trunk, her stomach recoiling from the movement. The sounds of traffic whizzed past her and, along with the wind, she inhaled the scent of gasoline.

The car suddenly screeched to a stop, and fear choked her as he yanked opened the trunk of the car. He lifted her and threw her over his shoulder as if she weighed nothing, then began walking. She struggled to regain movement, frantic to fight back, but her hands and legs were useless.

The scent of his sweat and some kind of strong aftershave nauseated her. He grunted as he climbed a hill, occasionally halting as if to draw a breath. Twice, she'd heard him muttering like a mad man about someone, about why she'd done this to him.

Summoning every ounce of courage she possessed, she opened her mouth to scream, but her voice emerged as nothing more than a whisper. He threw her on the ground, dragging her across it. Her body bumped along, hitting rocks and tree stumps and tree limbs, slogging through damp ground and mud. Pain ricocheted through her.

The drug must finally be wearing off, as she felt sharp needles stabbing at her skin through the burlap. The mistakes she'd made returned to taunt her. But even with those, she didn't deserve to die alone in the woods at the hands of a monster.

Suddenly, he stopped.

His loud breathing rattled in the air, mingling with the fluttery sound of the breeze and tree branches creaking somewhere in the forest. She felt him kneeling beside her, untying the sack and sliding it down over her body.

Determination and panic drove her, and she finally moved a finger. Just one. Then another.

Tears blurred her vision as she struggled against the numbing drug to make her hands work so she could fight him. "Please," she managed to whisper. "Let me… g-go."

His sinister laugh bounced through the pine trees, his evil black eyes boring holes into her.

Dragging her over to a cluster of weeping willow trees, he propped her against a trunk. Her fingers and toes were starting to tingle as the feeling returned, but they were still bound. Cold air brushed her face. Something was crawling on her, too.

Fear seized her as he stripped her clothes, then took a gray dress from his duffel bag and pulled it over her head. His fingers felt ice cold as he buttoned the buttons and tugged the skirt down over her bare legs.

Next, he pulled out a lipstick, rolled it from the tube and smiled as he held it up to the light. "Red lipstick—the color of blood," he muttered.

He gripped her face tightly, and pain shot all the way from her jaw to her ear as he slowly began to trace her lips with the lipstick. He filled them in, running the makeup above her lips and below them, smearing it with his fingers.

Tears blurred her eyes and trickled down her cheeks, and he wiped them away with a white handkerchief.

"No, no, you mustn't cry. I'm going to make you pretty, you'll mess up your face." A dark chuckle rumbled from him as he used a makeup brush and smudged red rouge all over her cheeks.

A cry lodged in her throat as he strewed daffodils on the ground beside her. Darting her eyes around the area, she prayed for a hiker to come by and find her, to save her. But except for the rustle of leaves and the sound of animals scurrying for food, the forest was eerily quiet.

His dark hair gleamed in the sliver of sunlight fighting through the clouds and the spindly willow branches, his chiseled jaw clenched in concentration as if his mind had taken him to a dark world far away.

Terror stole through her as he picked her up and settled her on the ground on top of the petals. Smiling, he spread more of the dying flowers across her body.

He pulled a bramble vine from another bag and laid it on the ground. The sharp blade of a knife glinted.

Then there was a bright light. The flash of a camera. He walked around her, taking photos of her posed on the bed of daffodils.

"Scream for the video, Cathy," he murmured as he drew closer.

Opening her mouth to scream, the sound died in her throat as he raised the knife and held it above her head.

She managed a tiny shake of her head and a guttural sound of protest, but he showed no mercy, only judgment in his menacing eyes as the blade plunged into her.

CHAPTER 66

Marvin's Mobile Home Park

Derrick studied a text from his partner as Bryce pulled into the mobile home park where Philip Paulson lived. Shondra had been abducted from this very place.

According to Bennett, a print he'd found at the fire belonged to Paulson, whose six-year-old daughter had been one of Hiram's victims.

"Do you know this man?" Derrick asked Bryce, showing the sheriff footage of the protests where Paulson had been present.

Bryce pinned him with an angry look. "I know *of* Paulson, but if you're asking if I saw this coming, I didn't."

"According to the man's neighbors," Derrick said, reading the message, "when they were questioned during the Ghost case, he and his wife divorced two years after their daughter disappeared." He skimmed further. "The wife filed for divorce, claiming her husband was an alcoholic. According to Paulson's boss at the time, he went off the deep end and he had to fire him last year. The wife moved away with their son and refused to let him see the boy."

"So his life spiraled because his daughter went missing," Bryce said. "When her body was found, it triggered his rage toward Randall."

"He needed someone to blame." Derrick gave a brief nod.

"I know you think we're small-town here, Agent Fox, but this is my county and I run it," said the sheriff, his eyes hardening. "You can't just come in and take over."

Derrick's anger spiked. "The feds are brought in to assist with cases that are wide-scoped and when police departments need help. It seems to me like you need all the manpower you can get to find this serial killer."

"We'd find him without you."

"Maybe so. But how many more women would die first?"

"Fuck you," Bryce said, getting out and slamming the door.

The feeling was mutual. "Let's just work the case," Derrick replied, climbing from the vehicle. "If he's not connected to the Weekday Killer, I need to get back to it and to Ellie."

The sheriff's look was scathing. "You should leave Ellie alone."

"What's it to you? At least I respect her work ethic."

"What goes on between me and Ellie is none of your goddamn business," Waters muttered.

Derrick ended the discussion by moving towards their target. While the sheriff went to the front door, Derrick moved to the right side of the trailer.

After knocking, Bryce signaled that he heard something, and Derrick hurried around back. Movement through the side window caught his eye, and he saw Paulson throwing clothes into a duffel bag as fast as he could. Another knock from the sheriff made Paulson jerk his head up, eyes wide and wild-looking, and he snatched the bag and darted into the hallway.

Hiding beside the rail to the back stoop, Derrick pressed his back against the wall, waiting. There was a crashing sound as Bryce kicked in the front door. His shout echoed from indoors, and he heard running, before the back door burst open, and Paulson staggered outside.

Derrick stepped from the shadows, aiming his weapon. "FBI, we need to talk, Paulson."

The man froze for a brief second, confusion on his soot-streaked face.

Sensing he was on the verge of running, Derrick called out, "Don't do it."

Panicking, Paulson gripped the rail and stumbled down the steps. Derrick snatched him with one hand and threw him up against the wall. "You're not going anywhere."

Paulson shoved at him like an animal, but Derrick slammed his fist into his gut, making him double over with a groan. Jogging down the steps toward them, Bryce snagged his handcuffs from his belt and tossed them to Derrick.

Catching them, Derrick turned Paulson around and slapped the cuffs on him. He had no doubt this man set the fire at the Reeves' house. He reeked of smoke and sweat, his clothes and skin stained with soot.

Bryce gave the man a venomous look then read him his Miranda rights as he hauled him toward the squad car.

"I hope that bastard died today!" Paulson shouted as Bryce shoved him in the back seat and slammed the door shut.

Derrick understood his hatred. Hell, he detested the fact that Randall was still walking around while his sister and nearly a dozen other little girls were dead at the hands of a monster.

But he'd joined law enforcement because he believed in it. If people took it into their own hands, there would be no safe place for anyone to go.

CHAPTER 67

Marvin's Mobile Home Park

Derrick wanted to shake some sense into Paulson, to get some answers. But the look that Bryce gave him warned him not to.

He'd give him five minutes, then he'd take over. He'd already watched Randall, one small-town sheriff, screw up a case and let a killer roam free for decades—tearing his family apart in the process. This one was too important to mess around.

"Okay, Paulson, we know this," Bryce said.

The man didn't look so intimidating now he was cuffed. He was older than both Waters and Fox, and skinnier. He reeked of smoke and sweat, and his eyes looked glassy, as if he was too wasted to realize just how much trouble he was in.

"I lost my daughter because of that man." Paulson's voice shook with rage. "He was supposed to protect little girls like Ansley, but he let that psycho get away."

Derrick understood his fury. He felt it too—it had haunted him for decades. Sometimes at night he woke in a cold sweat, wishing he could kill Hiram and Randall, wishing he could make them pay for his sister's fate.

"I know you're angry," the sheriff said. "But the law says a man is innocent until proven guilty. And I've known Randall Reeves a long time. He didn't turn a blind eye to justice. He was searching for your daughter's killer all those years."

"That's bullshit," Paulson spat. "They covered it all up, then protected their own daughter at the expense of everyone else's. And now they're going to get off scot free."

"The law will decide what is true," Sheriff Waters said bluntly. "You can't go around threatening people and burning down their houses. For God's sake, Randall and his wife might have died." Bryce leaned closer. "Vera Randall almost did die. She's in the hospital now fighting for her life."

Paulson's handcuffs clanged as he shook his fists. "Do you think I give a shit about that bitch? She gave birth to an evil monster. That means the devil is in her blood." He grunted in disgust. "That means Ellie Reeves is evil, too."

Derrick dragged him to his feet, his patience worn thin. "You hate Randall and Vera, I get it," Derrick growled. "But their daughter had no idea what was going on. She risked her life to save those children."

The sheriff cleared his throat. "He's right." Bryce moved up beside him. "And if you decided to kill these other women to get back at her, you're going to prison for the rest of your life."

Paulson's eyes widened, snot dripping from his nose. "What the hell are you talking about?"

"Did you send Randall and Ellie Reeves threats?" Bryce asked.

Paulson's yellowed teeth clamped together, a vein throbbing in his neck.

"I take that as a yes," Bryce said. "Then when you thought he might get the charges dropped you killed those women to get revenge against the Reeveses?"

Paulson began to shake his head. "No, goddammit, I… set that fire, but that was all I did."

CHAPTER 68

Rose Hill

Eula Ann stood in the midst of the rose garden, her body jolting as fear swept over her.

As she closed her eyes, she swore she heard the shrill scream of a woman as she drew her last breath. There was so much evil out there in the forest.

There was goodness, too, like that Ellie Reeves girl. And the others who were hunting this latest killer.

Kneeling, she plucked a red rose from the bush, then plucked the petals one by one. Holding them in her palm, she raised her fingers and let the wind pick them up and carry them into the forest.

Folks thought she was touched in the head. But she found solace in knowing the spirits turned to her when they were lost between the darkness and the light.

Tree branches cracked and snapped in the wind, footsteps crunching dried leaves somewhere nearby. She pivoted. Someone was there. Someone watching her.

She'd sensed his presence many times. Heard some of the Shadow People called him the Watcher. Although she hadn't seen him in some time now.

No one knew if he was good or evil. But he roamed among them all the same. Lurking and watching. Hiding from something.

She didn't think he was this latest killer. A sorrowful aura radiated from him as if pain and life had been too hard on him, and he was lost.

Softly, as the rose petals fluttered around her, she began to hum her favorite gospel hymn, willing Ellie Reeves to find answers fast before another woman was taken, another innocent life over too soon. Before the evil created a permanent stain on the trail.

CHAPTER 69

North Georgia State Hospital

Ellie looked up at the forbidding mental institution.

While pacing the waiting room at the hospital, anticipating news about her mother, she'd received word from Derrick that he had an ID on the man who'd visited Hiram in prison. As Bryce booked Paulson for arson, she swung by and picked up Derrick.

"The man's name is Vinny Holcomb," Derrick said as they parked. "He has a record for assault against women, and he attacked his own mother, who called the police. He's institutionalized in the same mental facility where Hiram had first been sent for evaluation." He hesitated. "He escaped last week, Ellie."

Derrick had already checked to make sure a bulletin had been issued for the escaped mental patient and all authorities at the airports, ports, and borders were notified. It was still active, but with everything else going on it wasn't something Ellie had been made aware of. Although if Holcomb was the Weekday Killer, he must be hiding out somewhere in the mountains.

The gray stone hospital, located in a neighboring county about twenty minutes away, resembled a haunted castle, with turrets and a spiked roof. An electric fence surrounded the property, which backed up to the river and the sprawling forest behind it. A few who'd managed to get past the guards and the electric fence had plunged to their death in the raging river as they tried to escape.

"I've heard about this place," Derrick said as he parked.

"I'm not surprised," Ellie said. "It definitely has a reputation. There are rumors that in the fifties and sixties they used to try out experimental procedures on prisoners being treated here."

Ellie shivered as they entered, the giant stone walls closing in on her. She could practically hear the screams of patients who'd suffered in this place, ones who might have been locked away for life.

The director of the hospital, a tall, thick-chested man with a gray beard and bulbous nose, met them at the front door, introducing himself as Carlton Hudson.

"We're here about your patient who escaped," Ellie said.

"Yes, I figured you'd show up sooner or later," Mr. Hudson replied.

"How did he get away?" Derrick asked.

The director made a low sound in his throat. "The details are sketchy. Happened at night after the patients were on lockdown in their rooms. We think he somehow overcame a guard, stole his gun and then his uniform. Drove out of here in the man's car."

"You alerted the police?" Ellie asked.

"Of course. The sheriff over in Ellijay."

How hadn't they heard about this?

"What about the Marshal Service?"

He shook his head. "Vinny wasn't a prisoner, Detective Reeves. It's true that we temporarily assess and treat convicts here—hence the security measures—but we specialize in long-term, secure treatment of the mentally ill."

They followed the director through a security area and down a long dark hallway. Voices, medicine carts and a loud banging sound from inside one of the rooms echoed around them. The scent of dust and medicines and something rancid that Ellie couldn't define permeated the air.

They passed a solarium with potted plants, tables where patients gathered for card and board games, and an area for arts and crafts, complete with easels for painting. Floor-to-ceiling windows allowed sunlight to flood the room, which made Ellie breathe a little easier.

Staff members supervised the small groups and a guard stood by the door, his eyes on the room.

Unease grew inside Ellie as they veered down another hallway, then stopped at another security station.

"Behind these doors, we keep the most dangerous of our patients," Mr. Hudson said. "Ones who have a history of violence against others. It's also where convicts who we are assessing or treating are held. Suicidal patients are housed in another section for twenty-four-hour monitoring."

The second they crossed through the double doors, the atmosphere changed. The space felt cold, isolated, closed off from the world. Ellie had the fleeting thought that this was the stuff horror movies were made of, creepy dungeons where one could easily make an unwanted family member disappear.

An armed guard greeted them, and the rooms had metal doors that were locked, offering no light from the hallway.

Ellie wouldn't survive being shut in like that.

The sound of someone screaming and another person banging on a closed door made her stomach twist into knots.

The director used his key card to unlock the door, gesturing that they could go in. Inside, the walls were bare, concrete and painted a faded pea-green. The floors were a cold, rough cement and there wasn't a single window. Other than the cot with a sheet and thin blanket on it, the room was bare. Scratches made by human fingernails marred the walls, and dark copper stains streaked the area near the door, as if Vinny had tried to claw his way out.

"Our people searched the room for some sign as to where Vinny might go, but found nothing," the director said.

Ellie pulled on gloves, then crossed the space, checking below the bed and under the mattress while Derrick searched the closet.

Three pairs of sweatpants, the strings removed, and t-shirts that had seen better days hung in the closet.

Turning in a wide arc, Ellie glanced up at the ceiling. A vent was directly above the bed. Climbing on top of it, she tried to reach it, but she was too short.

"Let me." Derrick stepped onto the bed, stood on tiptoe, then pulled out a pocketknife. Flipping it open, he used the tip of one of the tools to loosen the screws.

Dust floated down from the ceiling as he removed the vent, then he raked his hand on the inside. Seconds later, he removed a folder and handed it to Ellie.

Her breath caught as she opened it. There were dozens of articles about her and the Ghost case. Her parents and their arrest. Hiram in shackles and chains as he'd been escorted into the courthouse to be arraigned. And pictures of the small graves where the girls had been found.

Below them, she discovered a series of crude sketches of women who'd been tied down and gagged, lying in the brush and wilderness. Women who looked as if they'd been beaten to death.

Another one was a close up of Ellie at Hiram's arraignment. An X had been drawn across her face in blood-red lipstick.

CHAPTER 70

"He's coming for me," Ellie said, her voice riddled with contempt.

"That's not going to happen," Derrick assured her, his hands knotting into fists.

Ellie lifted a skeptical brow, and he grimaced, pushing a business card toward the director of the hospital. "Send Holcomb's medical files to me."

"We can't do that without a warrant," Hudson said.

"You'll have one by the time you pull them together. What else you can tell me about Mr. Holcomb? Did he have visitors? Family?"

"His mother washed her hands of him when he was committed. Apparently, she'd been through years of trying to help him, but he'd go on and off his meds. When he's off them, he's psychotic and violent. His physical attack against her led him here."

"Did he have contact with anyone outside the hospital, or perhaps a staff member who might have helped him escape?"

"My staff have been questioned and cleared. As far as mail and outside correspondence, Vinny didn't receive any."

"I assume you have surveillance cameras. Have you looked at those to determine if anyone approached him or came in and out of his room, someone suspicious?"

"One of our guards looked at them after he escaped," the director said. "But he said he didn't see anything."

"Yet somehow Holcomb got hold of those newspaper articles," Derrick pointed out. "And the ease with which we found them doesn't say much for the thoroughness of your staff."

An ashen look settled across the man's face. "True."

"I want to take a look."

Ellie's phone buzzed, and she glanced down at it. "The reporter," she muttered, letting it go to voicemail. "While Special Agent Fox reviews the tapes, I'd like to speak to Holcomb's therapist."

"All right. But without a warrant, she can't tell you much."

"I still need to speak to her," Ellie said firmly.

Derrick sent a quick text to his partner asking him to work on the warrants. "That warrant is coming forthwith," he said. "Now show me the security tapes."

The director led them down the hall, through the double doors and security checkpoints, to a cleaner section of the building which held offices and two large rooms that he explained were used for group therapy sessions.

He knocked on a door with a brass nameplate indicating it belonged to Grace Wiggins, Mental Health Counselor. A minute later, she invited them to come in.

While Ellie slipped inside to interview the therapist, the director escorted Derrick to the security office and introduced him to the chief of security, a frail-looking man named Roger who looked about ninety. The security system was old and outdated, the camera footage grainy and choppy.

Derrick spent the next half hour reviewing CCTV, focusing on Holcomb's every movement. Although Roger looked feeble, he did know the names of all the employees and vouched for them.

As the footage from the night Holcomb escaped appeared, the old man adjusted his bifocals, then pulled at his chin. The camera revealed a man dressed in scrubs entering Holcomb's room, but his boots didn't match the clothing.

"Who is that?" Derrick asked.

Roger made a clicking sound with his teeth. "I don't know. Can't see his face."

"That's because he'd intentionally avoided the camera. I want to send this film to my people," Derrick said. "Maybe they can do something to identify the man. He may have helped Holcomb escape."

CHAPTER 71

Ellie scrutinized Grace Wiggins, the mental health counselor, as she seated herself in the office.

The middle-aged woman had choppy graying hair, tortoiseshell glasses and her stiff posture radiated a tough exterior that she no doubt had to possess to do her job. Yet when she spoke, her voice was as soft as butter.

"You're here about Vinny Holcomb?"

"Yes, he's a person of interest in a homicide investigation." Ellie gave her a moment to absorb that information. "I need to know everything you can tell me about him."

The woman's fingers worried the pen she gripped in one hand. "I'm afraid HIPAA prohibits me from divulging a patient's personal medical information."

"Yes, I'm aware." Ellie lifted her chin, determined to extract some information from her. "I'm not asking for his diagnosis or details of his treatment." They would look at that when Derrick got the warrant for the man's medical records. "But if you feel he's a threat to himself or others, you have to talk to us. And we believe he may be the perpetrator we're hunting in the Weekday Killer murders."

Dr. Wiggins blinked as if to control her reaction and failed, nerves flashing in her eyes.

"The killer has texted me personally, taunting me about the murders," Ellie continued. "The fact that we found articles about the Ghost in Vinny's room raises suspicions. The director said Vinny was obsessed with that case. And the warden at the prison where Hiram is currently being held informed us that he tried to visit Hiram there."

"Oh, my goodness." Wiggins fidgeted with the pen again. "I didn't assess Hiram, but he would have been allowed access to the solarium, under observation. He could have met Vinny there, or in the secure wing."

"Hiram murdered those girls as a replacement for me, because I'm the one he wanted. Now I'm receiving texts from the Weekday Killer, and a mental patient who was obsessed with that case is on the loose." She tilted her head, gauging the woman's reaction. "You see where I'm going with this?"

The therapist sighed wearily. "Yes, I understand how you might make a connection."

Laying her phone on the desk in front of the woman, Ellie scrolled through the photos of the victims. "Here are the faces of the women the Weekday Killer murdered. What I need to know is if you think Vinny Holcomb is capable of sadistically slashing these women's throats and posing them in ritualistic fashion."

Dr. Wiggins' face whitened. Finally, she set the pen down and folded her hands on the desk. "We are speaking hypothetically, of course."

"Of course," Ellie replied, raising a brow.

Wiggins' sigh hinted she wanted to say more than she could. As a patient in therapy, Ellie understood and appreciated patient–doctor privilege. But there were gray areas where a counsellor had to report a patient if they presented a danger to themselves or someone else.

"Hypothetically, a patient with a history of OCD and schizophrenia, off his medication, might become violent."

Ellie nodded. "This is in strict confidence, and off the record," she told the woman. "The killer exhibits ritualistic behavior. He dresses his victims in Sunday clothes as if preparing them for a viewing, poses their hands in prayer, and lies them on a bed of wildflowers."

Despite her calm demeanor, a shocked sound escaped the therapist.

"He also smears lipstick and rouge on them. Would those actions fit with Mr. Holcomb's behavior?"

"Again, I can only speak in hypotheticals, but it's possible."

"Is there anything you could tell me about these rituals? What they might mean?"

Wiggins tapped her fingers on her temple. "It's possible the women represent someone else in the killer's life who wronged him or hurt him. He's obviously obsessed with death. Have you considered the fact that he might work in the medical field, maybe as an ME? Or that his job has something to do with preparing bodies for burial, like a mortician? He could even be a body mover."

Cord McClain immediately came to mind. But she trusted him. Didn't she?

"You should also talk to the police officer who handled his arrest," Dr. Wiggins added.

Ellie nodded, frustrated that the therapist had danced around her questions, but respecting her reasons for doing so. "Do you keep recordings of your sessions with the patients?"

Wiggins twisted her hands together. "I do."

"Could I listen to them?"

"You know I can't release them without a warrant."

Leaning across the desk, Ellie gave her an imploring look. "Listen to me—this man has murdered three women so far and we're expecting to find another victim today. Every minute you drag your feet could cost that woman her life."

Suddenly, the therapist turned to her keyboard.

"I keep digital and physical copies of the recordings. I'll ensure a physical copy is included with the files you've requested. But some sessions are likely to be of more interest than others."

Ellie thought the therapist was going to dismiss her, but instead Wiggins asked for her email address. A moment later, Ellie's phone vibrated. An email with an audio file attached.

She looked back up at the doctor. Their gazes locked, then Ellie hurried from the office, anxious to hear what was on the tape.

CHAPTER 72

Ellie and Derrick convened in the car outside the hospital, and Ellie started the recording of one of Vinny Holcomb's therapy session. The therapist started with an introduction.

"Vinny, would you like to talk about the reason you're here today?"

"Talk? I only talk to my friend. I have a friend now, Hiram. You know Hiram. He's brave and smart and so am I now." The man's voice sounded almost childish, obsessive. *"They used to call me Skinny Minnie Whiny Vinny. But I'm not skinny or minnie or whiny."* A clicking sound echoed, and Ellie realized he was snapping his fingers. *"See, I've got muscles now. And friends. Hiram likes me and so does my other friend."*

"What friend are you referring to?" Dr. Wiggins asked.

"My other friend, you know, he says Mama shouldn't have thrown me away in here. Mamas are supposed to be loving and kind, but she was bad, real bad, and she has to be punished."

"Your mother put you here because you attacked her," Wiggins pointed out.

"She was bad, just like the other ones. Like Hiram's mama and sister. Look what they did to him!" His voice rose with rage. *"They can't get away with what they did to us. They have to pay."*

"Vinny," Wiggins said in a calm but authoritative voice. *"Please sit down. I need you to stay calm so we can talk."*

"You sound like my mama!" Vinny bellowed, then she heard Wiggins shout for him to stop, and suddenly footsteps as someone rushed in.

"We've got him!" a man shouted.

"*Sedating him now,*" the other one said.

Vinny screeched like an animal, the sound of struggling ensued, followed by more noise as he was clearly dragged from the room.

"*They have to pay!*" Vinny yelled. "*All of them have to pay!*"

As the door closed and the recording ended, Ellie released a breath she didn't even realize she'd been holding. "He's definitely violent and hates women."

Derrick looked worried. "He fits the profile."

And he had drawn an X on her in red, the same red the victims' lips were painted. Which meant he was targeting Ellie.

"He mentioned another friend," Derrick said. "When I looked at those security tapes, there was a man who came into his room the night he escaped. He stayed in the shadows, as if he knew where the cameras were and was avoiding him. The head of security couldn't be sure who he was."

"You think this man helped him escape?" Ellie asked.

Derrick nodded. "Which means we could be looking for a team who planned these murders together."

CHAPTER 73

Ellijay, Georgia

The police station in Ellijay was only fifteen minutes away.

A deputy showed them to Sheriff Miller's desk, and Ellie introduced herself and Derrick, explaining they'd just come from the secure hospital.

The man was middle-aged, tall and bald, and judging from the tattoo on his forearm, ex-military. His gold wedding band looked too small, digging into his fleshy fingers, and a picture of a woman with brown curly hair sat on his desk along with a photo of a French bulldog.

Derrick had phoned ahead, and the man had agreed to pull Holcomb's file so they could discuss it. Derrick had also called Vinny's mother, but she hadn't answered so he'd left a message asking her to contact them.

Opening the file, Miller clicked his teeth. "That was some crazy dude," he said. "When I showed up at his mother's house, he had her cornered with a butcher knife to her throat."

"Go on," Ellie said.

"Twice before we'd been called out there. Once when he'd beaten the hell out of a girlfriend. Put her in the hospital with a broken arm and broken nose. She also needed dozens of stitches on her arms where he'd cut her."

She and Derrick watched as he laid the photos of the girlfriend on the table. The woman appeared to be undernourished and her hair looked like straw, as if Vinny had kept her locked up and hadn't fed her.

"Next time, it was his mama, but she decided not to press charges. Said he was sick and off his meds, and she was going to try to get him into treatment."

"So he has a pattern of violence," Derrick said.

Miller nodded. "We looked back and found two other domestic calls, but the police backed off because the women chose not to follow through. Abusers seem to have some kind of hold on women. Or maybe the women think they can save them."

That never worked out, Ellie thought.

"What happened the last time?" Derrick asked.

"He went too far with his mother," the officer said. "Beat her to a bloody pulp. She managed to get to the phone and called 911. Upon arrival, from the yard we heard him ranting about how she was white trash and he knew she'd cheated on his daddy, how God wanted women to obey their husbands and sons. He'd locked her in so we had to break down the door. He had her by the hair with that butcher knife to her throat. Had already nicked her twice and was screaming that he was going to kill her."

The officer displayed another set of photos, this one of an older woman, her hair matted with blood, her face and body bruised, a red line rimming her throat where he'd cut her. "It was a wonder she survived."

"Any idea what set him off?" Derrick asked.

Miller shook his head. "Said he was at her house trying to get his ex's address, but she refused to give it to him. Said she knew he'd kill her if she did."

"Do you know where this woman is now?" Ellie asked.

"Afraid not. The mother said she went to a women's shelter and begged us to leave her be."

"Have you sent anyone to check on the mother since Vinny escaped?" Ellie asked, folding her arms across her chest.

"I called her and left a message warning her, but she didn't answer."

"And you didn't think to go out and check on her?" Ellie asked in disbelief.

He looked contrite for a moment, then shuffled some papers and shook his head.

Sorry son of a bitch. No wonder some people criticized small-town law enforcement.

CHAPTER 74

Pigeon Lake

Ellie swung the Jeep down the graveled drive of the clapboard house belonging to Vinny Holcomb's mother and came to a stop. Pigeon Lake, a small lake only a short drive from Stony Gap, was named for the pigeons that gathered in flocks, circling the muddy water.

A dark green sedan streaked with filth was parked beneath a carport.

"Mother's name is Martha. She worked at a dry cleaners a few miles away," Derrick said, skimming the information Sheriff Miller had given them.

"Poor woman," Ellie muttered. "Couldn't be easy being attacked and nearly killed by your own son." She had to live with the fact that her son was a murderer, just like Ellie needed to live with her own parents' betrayal—and her own mother was paying for that right now, fighting for her life.

"His rage against women fits the profile," Derrick agreed. "But he strikes me as too impulsive, not a planner."

Ellie opened the car door and climbed out, the afternoon breeze swirling leaves around her feet and bringing the scent of rotting garbage. A spider web clung to the awning over the front door and the windows looked foggy. Pigeons had nested on the windowsills.

Derrick scanned the yard and property while she knocked. Once, twice, three times, but no one answered.

"Ms. Holcomb, it's the police. We need to talk," Ellie said.

Another knock, then she leaned against the door and listened. Nothing but the sound of water dripping from inside.

Twisting the knob, Ellie pushed the door and it creaked open. She covered her nose and mouth at the terrible stench that assaulted her. She and Derrick held their weapons at the ready as they crept inside.

"Police. Is anyone home?"

Ellie's shout was met with silence, the sound of dripping water echoing from down the hall. Derrick motioned that he'd check the kitchen and she inched towards where she assumed the bedrooms were. The first one held assorted junk, magazines and a twin-sized bed. It looked as if it hadn't been dusted in months, a thick layer of grime covering every surface.

Creeping slowly, Ellie pivoted and paused at the second bedroom. The ancient bed was made, the corners of a faded floral bedspread neatly tucked in. There was no one in the room.

But the stench grew stronger. A buzzing sound mingled with the dripping water.

Bile rose to her throat as she paused in the bathroom doorway. The scent of death and body waste permeated the air.

Flies buzzed around the woman's body, which was sprawled on the bathroom floor in a pool of dark blood.

CHAPTER 75

Ellie's shout sent Derrick racing down the hallway.

The buzz of insects resounded from the back room and the stench of death hit him as he rushed to the bathroom. Already the body was decomposing, maggots crawling in the woman's hair and clothing. Dried blood spread over the floor, cabinet and the side of the tub where it looked as if she'd tried to pull herself up to stand, before collapsing back down.

"Fuck, this is messy. He must have killed her right after he escaped."

"My guess, too." Ellie nodded toward the dozens of stab wounds in the woman's chest and stomach. "This is definitely personal, a crime of passion. You can see the rage in the number of times he stabbed her and the viciousness of the attack."

"Assuming Vinny did this, it's not the MO of the Weekday Killer," Derrick agreed. "No posing. No daffodils. Nothing staged or symbolic in this chaos." Which meant the unsub was still out there. "His mother sent him away, so he had motive to want her dead."

"Could it be possible that he purged his rage on his mother, then planned the others?"

"Possible, but not likely," Derrick said. "A perp doesn't go from this type of spontaneous violence to methodical planning. Just look at the way he left her, lying in her own blood and waste. The other victims were left on petals, dressed for their funerals, adorned with makeup. And he took the time to sew their lips shut, leaving the rhyme in their mouths."

"You're right. He'd also need time to get the makeup, research the trail, buy or gather the dresses."

"But if he was working with someone else, the other man could be the planner."

As Ellie stepped into the hallway, Derrick began capturing the crime scene on his phone. The room was a mess. Toiletries strewn across the counter, a can of hair spray on the floor, manicure scissors in the sink, as if, in desperation, she'd tried to find something to defend herself with. The towel bar had been ripped from the wall, with a bloody towel on the floor, the sink dripping and slowly leaking.

He stepped closer, peering inside the sink and noting blood droplets in the basin.

The killer had tried to wash the blood from his hands. Another glance at the hardware and he noted a bloody print on the faucet.

If Vinny's DNA was here, they'd soon confirm that he'd killed his mother.

And if he was working with a partner, the man who'd helped him escape, it couldn't be Hiram, since he was locked away. So who the hell was it?

CHAPTER 76

Crooked Creek

While crime investigators processed Martha Holcomb's house, Ellie and Derrick stopped to grab sandwiches at the Corner Café.

Lola greeted Ellie with a worried look. "Hey, Ellie, any word on Shondra?"

Ellie's heart stuttered. Every second that passed lessened their chances of finding her alive. "Not yet, but we're still looking."

Hushed whispers rippled through the room, and Ellie felt all eyes on them. She caught a glimpse of the mayor's wife, the local librarian Gertrude Cunningham and Lily Hanover, the president of the garden club, seated in a booth. Meddlin' Maude fluttered in and joined them, her mouth wagging as she glanced at Ellie.

Irritated, Ellie stared at them, but the women quickly looked away, disapproval radiating in the vicious stares they threw in her direction.

Ellie rubbed a finger over her shield. Dammit, she didn't care what those old biddies said. Except her mother had once thought they were her friends and they'd completely turned on her.

Just like you did, a guilty voice in her chided. And now, who knew if her mother would survive, she thought, pain-stricken.

"Let's get the food to go," Ellie said. She'd probably never be able to eat inside a restaurant in town again.

Derrick agreed and they quickly ordered, Lola shoving a disposable cup of coffee toward Ellie. "Here, you look like you could use this. I'll throw in some pastries, too."

Thanking her, Ellie grabbed their food and started toward the door, when Emily Nettles, the wife of the youth minister in town, stopped them. "Ellie, I want you to know the Porch Sitters have started a prayer chain for Shondra and for your mama." She squeezed Ellie's arm. "We're also praying for you and Agent Fox."

Emotion welled in Ellie, and she murmured thanks. Maybe soon enough she'd turn into a praying girl herself.

Hell, she closed her eyes for a brief second and decided to try it now. A quick prayer for her mother chimed in her head, and she glanced at the heavens, wondering if anyone up there was listening.

CHAPTER 77

Somewhere on the AT

Every cell in Shondra's body hurt. Her skin was raw where he'd whipped her, the sting constant from the relentless beatings. Her eye was swollen shut, and she could barely move her jaw.

He'd taken her clothes now, leaving her lying on the floor of the cold metal cage, naked and alone for hours with nothing to do but dread his next visit.

He'd sworn he would break her.

She'd vowed he wouldn't.

But she was growing weaker and weaker. She understood now. Once she begged, he would finally kill her.

Then the pain would end.

And so would her chance for a future. She had to escape, stop him from claiming any more lives.

Tears choked her. But how? He never let her off the chain and he had a camera watching her now. She imagined him sitting upstairs drinking whiskey with a smirk, watching as she lay curled on the floor in her own blood.

Her mouth was so dry it felt like cotton balls inside, and her throat hurt from holding back a scream. The water bowl he'd left for her sat in the corner.

A dog's water bowl.

Humiliation climbed her neck as she dragged herself over to it. Metal clanged against metal, the thick band around her neck cutting into her already raw skin. She loathed the sheer idea of drinking from the dog bowl, but she had no choice—she had to survive.

She raised her head and stared into the camera, knowing he was watching, getting off on her pain. It was a twisted game to him. Her hatred for him made her stronger, and she gave him a determined half smile.

She wasn't ready to give up yet.

CHAPTER 78

Crooked Creek

Anxious to escape prying eyes, Ellie and Derrick sat in the car and ate their sandwiches in silence. Ten minutes later, they met Angelica Gomez at the Crooked Creek Police Department to make a statement to the public about Holcomb.

Evening shadows clung to the building in the fading sun, and a slight breeze rocked a traffic light back and forth as leaves swirled across the park.

Angelica and her cameraman looked hungry for news. They rushed towards Ellie, the reporter's face etched with determination and the realization that she was onto another big story.

Ellie motioned for her to step aside for a moment away from the camera. "You were right," she told the reporter. "Hiram had a follower. That's the reason we're here."

Interest sparked in Angelica's eyes. "Are you ready to report on it?"

She had to. The people in Bluff County needed to be warned. "Yes, I'll give a statement." Angelica signaled to the cameraman to start filming. "This is Angelica Gomez coming to you live for WRIX Channel 5 news with FBI Special Agent Derrick Fox and Detective Ellie Reeves, who are investigating the case of the Weekday Killer. Already this man has murdered three women and is still at large." She pushed the mic toward Ellie. "Can you give us an update?"

"The FBI, along with local Bluff County law enforcement, are doing everything possible to find this killer and make it safe for women in the county again. Currently we are exploring several leads and persons of interest, one of which includes escaped psychiatric patient Vinny Holcomb," Ellie paused.

"Mr. Holcomb has a history of violence against women and is extremely dangerous. If you have any knowledge of him or his whereabouts, please contact the police." She glanced at the clock in the middle of the square—every single second counted in a case like this. "Once again, he is considered extremely dangerous. Do not attempt to apprehend him yourself. Alert authorities immediately."

Ellie's mind turned to the photo of her, branded with a X. He might be coming after her right now.

"One last thing, Mr. Holcomb, if you see this, please contact us. No one else has to be hurt. If you want me, then call me and we'll talk."

As she wrapped up, Ellie noticed a muscle ticking in Derrick's jaw. She didn't give a damn if the killer came after her if she could save Shondra's life.

Leaving Derrick to finish dealing with Angelica, Ellie ducked into the station.

Deputy Landrum looked up from his desk. "Are you sure you should be here instead of the hospital?"

Ellie battled guilt. "Right now, Shondra needs me more. I can do something for her—but I can't help my mother right now." She licked her dry lips. "There's something I want you to do."

He murmured agreement. "What is it?"

"Both Dr. Whitefeather and the therapist at the mental hospital suggested the killer might have worked in the medical field or a funeral home. I want you to look into those, any that are close by, and any medical personnel or funeral directors who've had complaints filed against them. Also compare those names to anyone connected to the Ole Glory Church. Even one of the body movers who transports bodies to the funeral home." She rubbed her forehead.

"Still working on getting a complete list of the parishioners and staff of Ole Glory," he replied. "Apparently, someone recently broke into their office and stole files, but the historian of the church is trying to compile a list from memory."

That could take time. Time they didn't have.

A text dinged on Ellie's phone, and she opened it, her heart pummeling her chest when she saw what it was.

Dear God. It was a video of a young dark-haired woman somewhere in the woods, tied up in the midst of a cluster of weeping willow trees. Spidery moss hung to the ground, the willows' limbs bowed with the weight. Terror filled the woman's eyes and her cheeks were stained with tears.

"Please don't kill me," the woman cried, her voice jagged with desperation. "Please, I don't want to die."

Ellie gasped as the camera showed a man's hand gripping a knife, glinting. "Thursday's child has far to go," the masked man sang creepily. "Too far to go for redemption."

"Someone help me!" the woman screamed.

He swung the knife down in one quick motion, slashing the woman's throat.

Blood spattered across the ground and dripped down her neck, staining the grave of wildflowers.

CHAPTER 79

Weeping Willow Holler

Ellie replayed the woman's death in her mind as Cord led her toward Weeping Willow Holler. She'd recognized the place the moment she'd seen the video and had called Cord immediately.

Before she left, tips from the public had started coming in about Vinny, and Derrick had gotten word that a man fitting his description had been spotted at a property near a small country store. He had gone to check it out.

Meanwhile, Paulson had been ruled out as the Weekday Killer. Evidence proved he'd set the fire at her parents' house, but he had alibis for the other murders.

Although Ellie was relieved Shondra hadn't been in the video, watching another young woman die at the hands of this monster had torn her up inside. How many other innocent victims would die under her watch?

Derrick's team was analyzing the video to see if it was real time, and nausea rolled through Ellie at the thought.

Dusk had set in, casting the forest in gloom as the moss from the weeping willows draped the ground and formed a circle near the creek bed. They passed a group of hikers setting up camp, and Ellie paused to ask them if they'd seen anyone suspicious, but no one had.

Ellie, the ERT, ME and recovery team followed Cord as he led them deeper into the woods. Other than the frogs croaking and crickets chirping, it was so quiet Ellie could hear her own breath puffing out and Cord's soft footfalls in front of her.

"Do you recognize the woman in the video?" Cord asked as he maneuvered across a rocky section of the creek.

"No," Ellie said, uncomfortable discussing the details of the case with Cord. Once she'd trusted him completely and as a teenager had a crush on the enigmatic man. Later, they'd slept together, but when she'd tried to get him to open up about his past, everything came to an abrupt halt.

The mental health counselor's comment about the killer's professional affiliation with a mortician nagged at her. She considered asking Cord about his foster father now, but their friendship was tenuous enough already.

"Why is he contacting you?" Cord asked.

"In case you haven't noticed, my parents and I have been in the spotlight lately. It's possible he's doing this to hurt me or show my incompetence because he believes I failed to protect those children. That he's a family member, father or brother maybe, of the Ghost victims."

"What about the man who set your parents' place on fire?"

"He's doesn't fit the profile and has alibis," Ellie said, knowing they had to move on. Then she explained about Vinny Holcomb.

Cord paused and looked down at her, his smoky eyes intense. "You think he's coming for you, Ellie?"

"I don't know," she said. "If he does, maybe I can put an end to this nightmare."

At his penetrating stare, Ellie felt guilty for questioning his past. But she pushed it aside and forged on. She had to explore every single lead, and she had to focus.

Except the image of her mother dying in the hospital bed kept playing through Ellie's mind as she crossed the rugged terrain, slashing at brush and bramble. The thorny bushes reminded her of the vines wrapped around the women's throats and the sins they represented.

Mentally she reviewed the case. Victim one, fair of face, found at the Reflection Pond, was vain and made her money off hocking shoddy beauty products. She'd deceived her clients, caused them physical and emotional suffering and then paid them off, leaving her own family member in pain. Victim two, full of grace, found at Ole Glory, had fallen from grace by selling her body for money. Victim three, Wednesday's child, full of woe, was found at Teardrop Falls and they were still waiting on information about her. But according to his pattern, she must have lacked sorrow.

With night falling, the dark shadows of the forest felt eerie now, making her skin prickle with unease.

The tops of the trees grazed each other as they rose toward the sky above, casting the mountain in an ominous gloom, the sky growing even more gray as they descended into Weeping Willow Holler.

The lush, overgrown greenery of the holler surrounded by the dripping weeping willows was an area of natural beauty. According to locals, people traveled here to mourn lost ones. Legend claimed their tears dampened the earth and made the weeping willows grow. Tonight Ellie swore she heard a mournful wail of sorrow permeating the air. The team with her remained silent, as if in reverence to the dead woman they were searching for.

"Thursday's child has far to go," Ellie said, thinking out loud. "So why leave her body here?"

Cord wiped perspiration from his forehead, and she noticed scars on his thumbs and a long scratch on his forearm. "Symbolically, the brown of the tree trunk stands for strength, and green leaves symbolize life. The weeping willow is the only tree that can bend like this without snapping," he continued in a low monotone. "It's supposed to signify being adaptive, as one survives challenges."

"We need to learn more about this woman to see how the rhyme fits her," Ellie said with a sigh.

The call of a bird of prey in the night sky added to the dread in Ellie's stomach as they broke into the clearing and she spotted the woman's body.

Grief for the woman struck her. A simple gold bracelet circled her wrists, shoes a plain black. Again, she was dressed in funeral attire, this time wearing a brown dress. But unique to this victim, he'd placed a copy of the Ten Commandments between her hands.

Which commandment had she broken?

Wildflowers covered the ground below her and a single daffodil had been placed in her light brown hair. Blood dried on her throat, and the bramble he'd wrapped around her neck was tied in a knot. Her eyes were so wide open that it looked as if she was silently begging for help.

"She didn't deserve this," Laney said quietly.

Ellie studied the victim for a moment. She was slender, her face oval-shaped, eyes a dark brown, darker than her hair.

As Laney began her initial assessment, Ellie leaned closer to photograph the bruises on the woman's arms. A darker, deeper one circled her neck. The impression was so grisly that once again she was struck by the fact that the killer might have been into S and M… or… what if the collar was actually a dog collar? What if the killer raised and trained—or abused—animals?

Laney pointed to the woman's fingernails, which were painted a shocking pink but were jagged on the ends. "Acrylic nails. Looks like he ripped some of them off. Her fingers are dark with blood."

"He's escalating. Growing more cruel. Time of death?"

"She's not in full rigor yet," Laney said. "So I'd say two to four hours at the most."

Dammit. They were close again.

As she looked around the scene, wondering how recently he had been here, something caught her eye in a patch of weeds nearby. Walking over to look at it, with gloved hands and a pair of tweezers, she plucked it from the grass. It was a small piece of a fingernail, painted hot pink. Either it had broken off in the struggle or the unsub had dropped it after he'd clipped the woman's nails.

Hope flared in her. If she'd scratched him, maybe they could get DNA.

CHAPTER 80

North Georgia

"This is Cara Soronto, your local meteorologist with an update of the storm system traveling through the southeast. Tornados have been spotted in Alabama and Tennessee with wind gusts of up to a hundred fifteen miles per hour. Thunderstorms are rolling through North Georgia and conditions in the next two days could be ripe for tornadoes in the mountain region. Stay tuned to your local news and weather station for updates."

Ignoring the wicked-looking clouds gathering above, Derrick flipped off the radio, pulling his gun as he scanned the property north of Crooked Creek where Vinny had apparently been spotted. The clerk of the nearby country store had said the building he'd seen the man near contained abandoned chicken houses. The area was isolated, with tumbledown houses set miles apart, and many appeared to be abandoned.

Meanwhile, Sheriff Waters was going through the list of family members who'd lost children in the Ghost case, checking their whereabouts and alibis.

Looking around, Derrick didn't spot any cars but saw an ATV parked to one side of the outbuilding. He remembered then that Hiram had used a similar vehicle to escape through the woods. Could it have been the same vehicle that had sped away the other day?

Slowly, Derrick crept through the property, shining his flashlight across the wild bushes and weeds choking the nearby farmhouse.

Peeling paint and loose shutters gave it a run-down appearance and the sound of dogs barking echoed from a nearby barn. The outbuilding might be derelict, but the property wasn't totally abandoned.

He inched up to the house and climbed the side steps to the porch, staying alert. The place sounded quiet, lights off, and looked deserted, but he eased to the door and carefully twisted the knob. A quick turn and the door opened with a groan. Derrick slipped inside, moving as quietly as possible, listening for sounds of Holcomb or a hostage in the place.

There was an old mattress where it appeared someone had been recently sleeping, and discarded food containers littered the room.

With the house empty, he headed back outside. Holding his gun at the ready, he crossed the yard to the barn. A rattling sound shattered the silence, followed by barking, and the noise grew louder as he approached. Pausing to peer through the cracks, he spotted several cages holding pitbulls. The animals were barking, howling and banging at the cages to get out.

Stepping inside, his senses were alert for Vinny, but the animals were the only creatures to be seen. A deep rage set in as he shined his light on the cages and realized that the animals had clearly been abused. Whips hung on a ladder propped against the wall, and the animals cowered as he approached. Their coats were missing patches of hair, burn marks and bruises marring their skin.

Someone was training them to be fighting dogs. It was a common problem in rural areas, where illegal dog fighting was on the rise.

"Don't worry, guys, I'll be back for you," he said quietly to the barking and growling dogs, who were clearly terrified.

Next, he moved to the chicken house, looking through one of the low windows with his light. At first glance the interior appeared empty, the light illuminating the metal coops.

A sick feeling knotted his stomach as he entered the space. He expected more dogs, but there was another, larger cage in the corner.

Although it was empty, he spotted blood on the door and crouching, he examined it. At first glance, he assumed it was animal blood, and a dog collar and chain lay inside the cage.

But his pulse jumped. Strands of long, wavy, blonde hair were caught in the metal. Human hair.

CHAPTER 81

Bluff County Hospital

The sight of another dead woman on the trail and seeing Vinny's mother brutally murdered was too much to handle in one day. With no word from her father, after Ellie had returned wearily from the trail and phoned her captain to update him, she stopped by the hospital and went straight to the Cardiac Critical Care unit.

Nurses' voices, rolling medicine carts and endless machines beeping added to Ellie's frayed nerves. When the ICU nurse buzzed her in, she found her father slumped in the chair by her mother's side, his head lolled back, mouth slack with sleep.

Tiptoeing over to her mother's bed, Ellie stared at the heart monitor and oxygen tubes, feeling helpless. When she was four, she had chicken pox, and she remembered Vera rubbing lotion on her arms and legs to keep her from scratching, then sitting and reading stories to her for hours to distract her. At eight, she'd had a bike wreck and had busted her knee. Her father carried her around when it hurt too badly to walk and had tacked a map on the wall so they could plan their next trip when she got better. But here she was, powerless to do anything to help.

A tear escaped her eye and she brushed it away, lifting her mother's hand in her own. Vera's fingers felt unnaturally cold, her complexion milky white, her normally coiffured hair mussed messily on the pillow. A strand of gray peeked through the brown, a sign the always-pristine Vera had missed her standing hair appointment at the Beauty Barn.

The image of Ellie's childhood home being swept away in a blaze, flames engulfing so many memories, taunted her. She didn't know if her parents could salvage anything from that fire.

Or if they could salvage their family if Vera survived.

CHAPTER 82

Somewhere on the AT

She didn't want to do it anymore. Could not live with the guilt. She'd traded her own soul to the devil, and watched the other women die.

He'd said to beg. And she had. Oh, how she'd begged. She'd begged for her life, begged to be spared, begged to survive.

She had to save herself. No one was coming for her. No one cared. They probably didn't even know she was missing.

What was her life worth now? If she ever escaped, she'd carry the spine-chilling screams of the other women with her. She'd see their faces, hear their pleas to live, bear the smell of their blood. She would never sleep again.

Closing her eyes, she vowed to fight back this time.

Footsteps pounded above. She was in the locked room, the one that no one knew about.

The one that had, when she made her grave mistake, intrigued her.

Until she'd seen what was inside.

When she'd tried to run, he'd dragged her to the chicken house, where she'd lived alone in the cage and he'd beaten her down. Then he'd brought her here.

He didn't let the others out until it was time for their death. Until he was ready to execute them.

But she had other uses.

The door screeched open, a splinter of light worming its way down the steps. In the other room, she heard Shondra banging against the cage. *Oh, god, what he'd done to her…*

And the other woman… what was her name?

She didn't know. He called her Cathy. He called them all Cathy.

She had no idea who Cathy was, what Cathy had done to him, or why he hated her so much. But the name Cathy tore through the air every day, labeling the women with their fates.

Bracing herself to fight him this time, she straightened inside her cage and balled her hands into fists. His feet shuffled across the floor, then he shined a light into her eyes, blinding her.

"Come on, Cathy. I need you."

She bit her tongue so hard she tasted blood as he yanked her from the cage, dragging her up the steps. The house was so dark she couldn't see a thing, then he pulled on the choker around her neck. Pain shot through her as he hauled her into another dark room.

Summoning every last vestige of strength she possessed, she lashed out and pushed at him. His hands quickly circled her throat and he wrenched her head back.

"You don't want to fight me, Cathy," he hissed.

"You're a monster," she cried as she lifted a knee and jabbed him in the groin. He bellowed, releasing her slightly as he reeled with pain, then she grabbed the heavy chain and swung it up, hoping to connect with his face.

It hit him in the chest, and she tried with all her might to crawl away. But he lunged on top of her and pinned her down, his hands tightening around her throat again.

"You'll pay for that."

A sob tore from her as he yanked a needle from his pocket and jabbed it in her neck. Seconds later, the scream in her throat died as her body went numb.

CHAPTER 83

Crooked Creek

It was the middle of the night by the time Ellie made it home.

Rain had set in, forcing her to crawl around the mountain roads. She'd had to maneuver around a vehicle that had stalled in the road.

Derrick had left a message that he'd uncovered evidence that might pertain to the case. Already they'd found a woman's hair and blood that appeared to be human. Hopefully they'd find some forensics to lead to the killer and pinpoint if it was Vinny. A local rescue shelter had also picked up the abused animals.

Exhausted, she tugged her jacket over her head to ward off the rain and hurried up to the porch. Her skin crawled as she noticed the lights were off again.

Had the storm knocked out the power or had someone been in her house?

Pulse pounding, she drew her flashlight, gripped her weapon in one hand and checked the door. No blood this time, but the bushes by the house rustled. She pivoted to check it out, but a loud roar came from the boxwoods, a shadowy figure lunging toward her. Big. Brawny. Wet dark hair clung to his bearded face. His crazed eyes looked as if he was high. Swinging her arm up in defense, she raised her gun with the other, but he knocked it from her hand.

The gun fired into the air with a deafening shot then hit the ground with a clatter as he grabbed her around the neck in a chokehold. She clawed at his hands to free herself, but he tightened his grip, shutting off her windpipe. Gasping and struggling against him, she saw stars.

She couldn't let him win. Self-preservation instincts fueled her, and she rammed her elbow backward into his belly, lifted one foot and kicked at his knee. The blows made him loosen his hold, and she grabbed his arm, flipping him to the ground.

He quickly recovered and kicked her in the stomach, sending her flying backward as she wheezed, winded. Digging frantically at the wet ground, she scrambled for her gun, which had fallen into the bushes.

With an animal-like howl, he pushed up and jumped her again, slamming his boot into her back. Pain shot through her kidneys, blinding her. Sucking in an uncomfortable breath, she rolled onto her back, then used her feet to shove him away. He stumbled sideways, but righted himself quickly, then grabbed her hair and snatched it so hard, her skull felt as if it might split in two.

Still, she pushed past the panic, managing to punch him in the face. Blood spurted from his nose and dripped down his chin, merging with the rain. It was coming down so hard now that she could barely see. Mud and water soaked through her clothing as she threw him off her and ran for her gun. He yelled again and chased her, closing in. Her foot slipped in the mud, and she went down just as she reached the bushes.

He was fast, grabbing her leg and dragging her toward him.

Desperate, she kicked him in the face with her free foot, then groped around and snagged her weapon. A second later, she angled her body and released a round. A shocked grunt ripped from him as his body collapsed to the ground, splattering mud everywhere, blood gushing from his chest.

Adrenaline surged through Ellie, and she pushed to her feet, wincing, then aimed the gun at him again as she staggered toward him.

A streak of lightning zigzagged across the sky, lighting his face. It was Vinny Holcomb.

"Where's Shondra?" she yelled, filled with a fury that set her alight.

His cold expression sent fear trickling down her spine. "Hiram says hi," he said with a sick smile.

Fuck him. Fuck Hiram. She knelt, rain battering her, and shoved the gun to his temple. "Where is Shondra?" she screamed.

A sinister laugh emerged from him, blood gurgling from his mouth and nose. Ellie shook him. "Where is she?"

But his breath rattled out, and his eyes went still as death claimed him.

CHAPTER 84

Crooked Creek

After an exhaustive search at the barn and chicken house, Derrick had just reached Crooked Creek when the call came from Ellie. Vinny Holcomb had attacked her at her house and she'd shot him to death.

When he pulled into her drive and hurried to her, she looked as numb as she'd sounded on the phone. She was sitting on the ground beside Holcomb as if she couldn't drag herself away from his dead body.

He steeled himself as he approached, furious at the sight of her battered face and shocked stupor. Ellie was a fighter, but right now she looked defeated.

He approached quietly, noting the details of the scene. Holcomb lay soaked in blood on the ground near her porch. Ellie's gun was still clenched in her hand, her knuckles white from gripping it so hard.

"An ambulance is on its way," he said, hoping she heard him through the shock.

She didn't respond, so he stooped down and gently eased the weapon from her hand. "The crime team and ambulance will be here soon." Fearing she needed medical attention, he gently pushed her hair from her face where strands escaped her ponytail. A bruise was blossoming on her jaw, and blood stained her forehead and cheek.

Gently, he took her hands in his to warm them. "Ellie," he said softly.

For a brief second, she simply stared at him as if she didn't hear him, but he continued to rub her hands between his and finally she shook herself from the fog.

"Are you okay?" he asked, his gaze skimming her for any further injuries.

She nodded, although the quiver of her lip told him more.

"Did you get hit?" he asked.

"No," she said in a whisper. "I'm okay."

He cupped her face in his hands, aching to comfort her, but knowing she was off limits. The case was all that mattered. Anything else was a mistake—he'd learned that the hard way.

Even so, he removed his jacket, settled it around her shoulders and tugged up the hood to shield her from the worst of the rain. "Listen to me, you had no choice. He attacked you."

"He was out of control," she murmured. "Crazed."

"He must have been off his meds like the director at the hospital said."

Her chin trembled. "But now he's dead, what if Shondra is still alive and we don't find her in time?"

The sound of a siren wailing burst between bouts of thunder, the rain still pouring down.

"We will find her," Derrick said. Although in all honesty, he had no idea how. At the moment, they'd exhausted one lead after another—and he didn't know which way to turn.

CHAPTER 85

Friday

Crooked Creek

Ellie had stared at the ceiling for hours when she'd finally crawled into bed, every muscle in her body aching. Derrick had insisted on sleeping on her couch, and she was so shaken she couldn't even bring herself to argue.

She tossed and turned all night, questions railing through her head. *Hiram says hi.*

Something didn't feel right. The way the bodies were posed, the elaborate details of the graves, the painstaking way he dressed them in Sunday dresses—it read nothing like the violent, erratic crime scene they'd witnessed at Mrs. Holcomb's house.

Or the animal-like way Vinny had attacked her.

Around 4 a.m. she finally collapsed into a deep sleep, but by seven she lurched awake to the sound of footsteps in her den. For a brief moment, she thought there was an intruder, until she remembered Derrick had stayed over.

The scent of coffee drifted to her. Craving the rich pecan taste and desperate for a jolt of caffeine, she rose in her pjs and went to the kitchen. Rubbing the sleep from her eyes, she poured a cup into her favorite mug, savoring a long slow sip.

Derrick stood on her back deck, a mug in hand, staring into the expanse of woods behind her house. Morning sunlight struggled to peek through gray, unforgiving storm clouds overhead.

"Tornadoes are traveling across the southeast," he murmured. "They might be headed this way."

The past two weeks of sunny spring days had faded. She'd seen bad twisters in her day, entire neighborhoods flattened and wiped out. The mobile homes where Shondra lived didn't stand a chance.

But a storm was the last of her worries at the moment.

Ellie rubbed her forehead, where a headache pulsed. Her cheek was throbbing.

The press hadn't released the news that Holcomb was dead yet, that Ellie might have killed their last chance of finding Shondra. Guilt surfaced once more, that she had yet again failed her friend.

Derrick arched a brow. "Did you get any sleep?"

She shrugged. "A couple of hours. You?"

"The same."

"I've been thinking," Ellie said. "The crazed psychotic man I shot last night just doesn't fit the profile of the killer. Like we said yesterday, if Vinny was part of this, he's working with someone who is a planner, detail-oriented. Considering what you found last night at those chicken houses, we should search for priors involving men arrested for animal cruelty and dog fighting. This man may have transferred his behavior toward women."

"My partner is already on it."

Ellie nodded. Her boss had been right. As far as work went, she and Fox made decent partners.

"We should probably prepare for another press conference with Angelica," Ellie said, dreading the onslaught she would get from the media. "I'll grab a shower."

Back inside, Ellie read a text Heath had just sent.

Have been digging into the mortuary angle. Did you know Ranger McClain grew up in the system? His foster father, Felix Finton, owned Finton's Final Resting Home. His son Roy now runs the business. Two complaints filed against the father for desecrating female bodies but no convictions.

A chill splintered any semblance of calm Ellie felt. She knew more than anyone how much betrayal stung, and she didn't want to hurt Cord any more than she already had. But she owed it to all the murdered women claimed by the Weekday Killer to chase it up—she had to.

And if nothing came of it, Cord wouldn't have to know.

Her phone beeped with another text from Heath. The message took her breath away.

DNA results for the blood on the door at your house. Belonged to Deputy Eastwood.

CHAPTER 86

Every time he thought he'd seen the worst of mankind, another sinister villain surfaced to show him an even sicker side. And this one had them chasing their tails.

Derrick couldn't erase the images of those dogs from his mind. They had been brutally abused, but a call to the vet assured him that physically, at least, the dogs would survive.

A quick call to Dr. Whitefeather confirmed scarring on the victims' necks was consistent with a dog collar used in training dogs to fight.

Ellie returned from the bedroom, freshly showered with her hair still damp. Compared to the stench of what he'd seen last night at that old farm, she smelled like sunshine and rosewater. The bruise on her face was stark, though, and the purple smudges beneath her eyes confirmed she had barely slept the last few days.

Neither one of them would until Shondra was found and the killer stopped.

"Heath texted with the DNA results from the blood on my door," she said in a raw whisper. "It was Shondra's."

Derrick's fingers tightened around his coffee cup. "I'm sorry, Ellie. But that doesn't confirm that she's dead."

Her defeated, blank stare betrayed her disbelief.

A text from Bennett came through, and he skimmed it. "I just got the name of a possible person of interest—Karl Little, the brother of another Ghost victim. He was arrested for animal cruelty and dog fighting a couple of times but keeps cropping up in different locations and starting all over again."

"Interesting," Ellie said. "I'm going to call the hospital and check on my mother. Then I'll talk to Cord about ideas where this maniac might leave Friday's child."

He nodded, although he didn't like it. His jaw was tense. "Are you sure you should be talking to him?"

"He knows more about the places along the trail than anyone I know." Ellie's brows pinched together. "We have to use all our resources."

She was right. Time was running out, and they had to divide up tasks. If Shondra was still alive, one thing was certain: she didn't have long left.

Four women had died already. He wanted to find the killer today, not another helpless victim. But his gut was churning with the fear that they were already too late.

CHAPTER 87

River's Edge

"Go ahead, touch her body. Feel how cold her skin is."

Cord stared at the dead girl, his stomach knotted. She was pretty—or at least she had been before death claimed her. Long glossy black hair hung over her shoulders. She was tiny, with big dark eyes and a heart-shaped face. She must have been beautiful when she smiled.

Just a teenager, like him.

But her face had been cut badly when she'd been thrown through the windshield of her boyfriend's car, her body crunched between it and the tree where the crash happened. The boyfriend had been drinking. She hadn't worn a seat belt. Now the boy sat in a jail cell for manslaughter while she lay in the prep room, waiting to be dressed for her burial.

Worse, the old man had sat with the mother and held her while she cried. Assured her he'd take care of her daughter.

"She was so young and sweet," the mother had cried. "Why did God have to take her now?"

"It's so hard when we lose a loved one," the old man had said. "But we must have faith."

She'd nodded and cried some more and he'd patted her hand and brought her coffee and then promised he would treat the daughter with special care.

But as soon as he made it to the basement, his kindness and promises faded. Special care *meant something different—something awful.*

The old man grabbed Cord's hand and pushed it toward the steel table where she lay. He'd already forced Cord to watch as he drained her blood and pumped her full of embalming fluid.

"Go ahead, touch her," the old man said. "She doesn't know what's happening now and can't fight you."

The hair on the nape of Cord's neck prickled as his fingers brushed the girl's cheek.

The old man set out his tools and supplies. First the pancake makeup he would use to cover the scarring on her face. Then a bright red lipstick to match the color of nail polish he'd chosen. The blusher to bring some life to her cheeks. Then she'd be dressed—her mother had sent a soft red dress for her to wear and little black sandals.

"The mother wants an open casket," he told Cord. "When we're finished playing with her, we'll make her pretty for her mama."

CHAPTER 88

Before heading to Cord's, Ellie called about her mother, hearing that her condition was the same.

Next, she phoned the captain and filled him in on everything that had happened. According to him, Angelica had already phoned wanting a statement, and he agreed to update Bryce and let him handle her.

Kennedy Sledge had also left another message, asking if she wanted to talk. But her emotions were too raw at the moment. She felt like she was unraveling, like the yarn in one of her old sweaters.

Pounding on the door to Cord's house, Ellie noted it was dark inside. But it was always dark at his place. She had no idea why he refused to turn lights on, but the one time she'd spent the night with him, when she'd flipped them on, he had immediately turned them off. Only when she explained her phobia of the dark, and where it stemmed from, did he finally relent.

For a moment, she considered that he might not be home, but his truck was in the driveway. If he'd had a late call that kept him up all night, he could still be asleep.

She'd just turned to go when he opened the door, his shaggy mahogany hair and stubble adding a hint of danger to his rugged appearance. He was the most alpha male she'd ever met. Muscles strained the confines of his black t-shirt and the sweatpants that hung low on his lean hips.

He scrubbed a hand over his face, and she realized she'd woken him. "Ellie, what are you doing here?"

"Can we talk?"

His dark eyes contracted, then he stepped sideways for her to come in. "Holy crap, have you seen your face?"

Ellie traced a finger over the knot on her head. "Seen it and felt it."

"What the hell happened?" He crossed to the kitchen, then started a pot of coffee brewing while Ellie quickly explained about Vinny Holcomb's attack and Shondra's blood being left on her door.

Cord's fingers clenched the counter for a moment in a white-knuckled grip, drawing her attention to the scrapes and scratches on his hands, and his thumbs, which always seemed to be bruised. "Do you think he's the Weekday Killer?" he finally asked.

"He's violent and was mentally ill, but if he's part of this, he didn't do it alone. His violence was erratic. Our killer is a planner."

His look hardened. "Let me wash my face. I'll be right back."

As he left the room, Ellie's phone pinged. It was Heath again.

Just heard from the lab. Prints on Deputy Eastwood's truck belong to Ranger McClain.

The words sucked the air from Ellie's lungs. *What?* Why would Cord's prints be on Shondra's truck? There had to be an explanation.

By the time Cord returned, the coffee was ready, the air filled with the aromatic, nutty scent. He poured himself a cup and offered her one. Shaken from the text, she gladly took it and cradled the warm mug between her hands.

A quick glance around his family room, and she noted the taxidermy animals were missing. The bookshelf housing all its usual titles on nature, graveyard symbols and burial rituals was a mess, with books on their sides and askew. Her gaze was drawn to a closed door leading off the living space. She knew it didn't lead to the bathroom or the bedroom, and Cord had never told her what was on the other side. She couldn't remember ever having seen the door open.

For the second time, she wondered what was inside, what he didn't want her to see.

Cord leaned his back against the kitchen counter and simply waited, with a guarded look.

"Why did you really come, Ellie?"

His words sounded like an accusation, a reminder that he was still on edge from the last case, when Derrick had questioned him. He wasn't going to like her doing the same now, she knew that.

But it had to be done.

She relayed her conversation with the psychiatrist. "That leads me to dig deeper into the profile and look at his MO."

"You're talking about the wildflowers and the way he dresses them, as if he's preparing their bodies for a funeral?" Cord asked through clenched teeth.

"It's possible that he learned all of that online, but we have to consider the fact that he could have worked in the field, perhaps as a medical examiner, a mortician or funeral home director. Or he… grew up around that kind of work."

Angry heat flared in Cord's eyes. "That's the reason you're here? You think I had something to do with those women's deaths?"

Ellie grimaced at the vehemence in his tone. "That's not what I said." She hesitated, knowing she was stepping into unwanted territory. "I know one of your foster fathers was Felix Finton and that he owned Finton's Final Resting Home when you lived with him. What can you tell me about him?"

"You've been researching my background?"

Ellie released a slow breath. "It came up when the deputy was looking into the funeral home angle." A tense heartbeat passed. "I'm sorry, but I have to ask."

Cord's throat muscles worked as he swallowed, then he spun away from her and dumped his coffee in the sink. "What can I tell you?" he said in a low but lethal tone. "I can tell you that you should stay away from him."

"Why, Cord?" Ellie pressed. "Is he dangerous? Do you think he's killing these women?"

"Not him," he ground out. "He would be in his sixties by now." Slowly he turned back toward her, his calm mask tacked in place, although the rigid set of his body suggested he was holding back.

"How about his son? He runs the funeral home now." She couldn't back down now. She had to push for the truth. "Did you know him, Cord?"

Cord's grim look told her everything. "Yeah, he's just as mean as his old man."

CHAPTER 89

Dahlonega, Georgia

Derrick found Karl Little's house on the outskirts of Dahlonega, where his family had lived all their lives.

Although Derrick's mother had mourned her little girl for two decades, she felt some semblance of peace in the closure that they'd finally found, after so many years. She'd been able to bring her daughter home and give her a proper burial.

Apparently, Mrs. Little had the opposite reaction. The week after Hiram was arrested, Karl's mother had taken her own life.

The property was overgrown with weeds, and the cornfields that had once probably supplied the family's income had long since died. To the right of the house sat a silo, and an old barn that tilted to one side as if the ground was going to swallow it.

A mangy dog loped up to Derrick when he got out, and he leaned down to examine it. It was dirty, its skin patchy and dry, but there were no cigarette burns or scars indicating the dog had been abused.

The strong scent of moonshine filled the air as Derrick walked toward the barn, and a quick glimpse inside confirmed there was a still. Judging from the odor, Karl Little was brewing apple pie, a favorite in the mountainous, rural parts.

Before he reached the porch, the front screen door screeched open and the barrel of a shotgun poked through the opening. "Stop right there!" a gray-haired man called.

Derrick halted, raising his hand. "Don't shoot," he called out. "I just want to talk."

"We got nothing to say to you. This is my land and if I want to run a still, I aim to."

"I don't care about the still," Derrick shouted. "I need to talk to Karl. Is he around?"

"Sure as hell is. Passed out in the barn. Told that boy to sell the liquor, not to drink it, but he's been on a binge ever since our daughter's killer was found. Hasn't left the farm."

"I'd like to talk to him anyway." Derrick knew better than to take the man's word for it. Parents covered for their kids all the time.

"Sure. Knock yourself out," the old man said, gesturing toward the dilapidated outbuilding.

Derrick turned and picked his way across the patchy grass, stepping over litter and dog crap. The stench of corn liquor brewing clogged his nostrils, and he breathed out the fumes.

As he neared the building, he kept one hand on his weapon, just in case. Easing open the barn door, he shined his flashlight inside and scanned the interior. No dog cages.

The ground was littered in hay, farm equipment, the man's still and moonshine-lined shelves in one corner.

"Karl?" he called. "I'm Special Agent Fox, I need to talk to you."

He inched inside, then heard a noise coming from one corner. A rumbling sound. Walking closer, he spotted a heavyset man in overalls passed out on a ratty blanket, snoring. The pungent odor of apple pie, cigarette smoke and sweat wafted toward him, and one look told him the man's clothes hadn't been changed in days.

Losing his mother could well have been a trigger for him to murder. But if he'd been drunk and passed out here for days on end, he wasn't the killer they were looking for.

Which meant he'd just wasted time chasing another dead end.

CHAPTER 90

Thirty miles north of Crooked Creek – Elm Grove

Ellie felt the tension between Cord and her intensify as they parked at Finton's Final Resting Home, which was in a small community called Elm Grove. She shuddered at the sight of the morbid exterior where Cord had once lived.

She'd seen enough death the last few weeks to last a lifetime. What exactly had he seen growing up? She'd asked him to explain on the drive and he'd completely clammed-up, becoming even more sullen.

The parking lot was empty, and on the front door of the red-brick building was a sign that read "CLOSED FOR RENOVATIONS". A blue tarp covered the roof, and building supplies were dotted around. An empty mortuary would be the perfect place to hide hostages or a body until the perp was ready to dump it.

"Tell me the layout of the building," Ellie said as she surveyed the property.

"The top floor was living quarters for Finton and his wife and however many kids he took in," Cord said. "The ground floor houses the funeral parlor, with visitation rooms, Finton's office and a kitchen. The cold room where bodies are stored until he can process them for burial and the prep room are downstairs, in the basement."

Ellie cringed at the thought of what actually took place between those walls. "I take it the basement is insulated for odor and sound proofing?"

Cord nodded. "You could scream your lungs off down there and no one upstairs would come."

She sensed he was speaking from experience and her gaze swung to his, goose bumps skating up her arms.

But he stood ramrod straight, his expression grim, a million miles away.

"Let's search the downstairs first," Ellie said. "If he's holding someone here, that's where he'd keep the bodies."

Thinking about the Weekday Killer's victims, she asked, "Did he ever defile the bodies he had in his care?"

Cord made a low sound in his throat. "I can't talk about what he did, Ellie. Let's just go."

"No." She reached for the doorknob, but it was locked. "If Finton is sadistic, and his son is like him, he could have escalated from prepping dead bodies to murder." With a sigh, she went to find another way into the building. Technically she needed a search warrant, but these were exigent circumstances. "And if he is our killer, Shondra could be somewhere inside."

CHAPTER 91

Ellie checked the back door of the main building, but as expected, it was locked. A quick trip to all the side doors yielded the same results. Deciding the best method of entry without drawing suspicions from any passersby would be the basement, she asked Cord to show her the way.

The exterior door was locked, and the windows were set three feet apart on either side of the door. Ellie pulled a tool from her pocket, and jimmied it between the ledge and sill, prying it until the lock snapped. Thankfully the building was old, the lock half broken and easy to trigger open. Slowly she pushed up the window while Cord kept guard. She hoisted herself inside, then dropped to the cement floor.

Darkness coated the interior, and she froze, the space closing around her with its acrid odors and memories of death clinging to the walls. Ellie swayed, haunted by an image of the countless people who'd been laid out here, their final hours before interment spent naked and cold and left in the hands of the mortician as they were prepared to be laid to rest. Suddenly she felt trapped, suffocating, locked in the dark with no way out.

"Ellie?"

The sound of Cord's breathing echoed around her, a comfort as the cloying tentacles of fear wound around her throat.

Dragging herself from the waves of fear swirling around her, she listened for signs that someone was inside. A dripping sound echoed in the silence. Holding her breath, she inched down the hall, using her flashlight to lead her and listening closely for any sounds of a woman crying or calling out for help.

Cord pointed toward the prep rooms and the strong scent of formaldehyde and body decay permeated the air, making Ellie's stomach twist. Tiptoeing inside, she glanced at the metal tables, but to her relief there were no bodies laid out.

"The cold room," she whispered as she crept toward the refrigerated area where bodies were stored until they were released for viewings or burial.

Cord led the way, his jaw set in stone as he pushed open the door. Holding her breath, Ellie prayed that she didn't see Shondra inside but braced herself for the worst.

The room was ice cold, the frosty air slamming into Ellie, and it was lined with metal tables ready for multiple bodies to be stored. But it was empty. Ellie breathed a sigh of relief.

Ducking back into the hallway, she scanned the sign at the end of the hall. It was the room which stored the coffins for families to choose from. Tension knotted her shoulders as she pushed open the door.

Her flashlight darted across the eerie scene of a row of coffins. Pewter, silver, bronzed, some of the lids open, some of them shut.

Shondra's face taunted her and she stepped forward to search the caskets. She imagined opening a coffin and seeing her friend, pale and lifeless, lying there.

But just as she shoved aside the image, Cord grunted. Suddenly something hard slammed against the back of her head and she let out a yelp of pain. Her flashlight fell to the floor, immediately going out and enveloping them in darkness. Ellie tried to reach out for Cord, to call for help.

But her hand connected with empty air and spots danced behind her eyes as she collapsed on the floor with a thud.

CHAPTER 92

Entering Crooked Creek's police station, Derrick hoped to meet up with Ellie. He'd phoned her on the way back to town but gotten her voicemail. A quick check with the hospital, and he learned she wasn't there. She'd mentioned talking to McClain about a place to look for Friday's victim. Was she out looking now?

Captain Hale was in a meeting with the mayor and the sheriff when he arrived, heated voices coming from his office, and Deputy Landrum was hunched over his computer, his face pinched with worry.

"Have you heard from Detective Reeves?" Derrick asked.

The deputy gave him a quick glance, then his eye twitched as he looked away, as if he didn't know how to answer.

"Where is she?" Derrick asked again.

"I don't exactly know."

Derrick threw an accusing stare. The sheriff, the mayor and Ellie's captain stepped from the office and went still, listening. "Listen to me, Deputy. Someone tried to kill her last night, and we think he may have a partner. If you know something, tell me. She could be in trouble."

The deputy rocked back in his chair, his expression worried. "She asked me to look into funeral homes and morticians in the area. I dug around and learned Ranger McClain grew up above a funeral home. A place called Finton's Final Resting Home. It's run now by the old man's son, Roy. He's had complaints filed against him for desecration of female corpses. I think she was going to question him about it."

Holy shit. "You let her go alone?"

"She didn't ask me to go with her."

Of course she wouldn't. She was independent and stubborn and would never ask for help.

"She should have called me," the sheriff said.

"You need to get your people under control," the mayor told the captain.

Captain Hale cut him a sharp look. "What else did you learn about the Fintons?" he asked Deputy Landrum.

The deputy ran his fingers through his hair. "Felix Finton was one of Ranger McClain's foster fathers, but Cord was sent to juvie at age fourteen for assault. Finton told the social worker that Cord had a sick obsession with the bodies he brought in for preparation. That he found him running his fingers over the corpses of the females. And that twice he caught him dressing the bodies in pretty clothes and making up their faces."

"Did Ellie know all this?"

The deputy shook his head. "Some of it. I tried to call and tell her the rest, but she didn't answer."

"What happened after McClain got out of juvie?" Derrick asked. "Any arrests?"

"Not that I found." The deputy exhaled. "Although I can't seem to find anything on him until he started working for FEMA."

"What about Finton?"

"Can't find a current address on the father. But the funeral home is not far from Crooked Creek, and the son, Roy, still runs it. And there's something else."

Derrick traded looks with the captain and the sheriff. "What?"

"The lab called earlier about prints found on Deputy Eastwood's truck. They belonged to Ranger McClain."

The sheriff muttered an obscenity while Captain Hale shook his head in denial and the mayor wiped a hand down his chin. He was starting to sweat profusely.

Derrick mentally reviewed what he'd just learned, fitting pieces together. McClain knew all about Ellie's family issues, about Hiram and the dolls, about the locations on the trail. He was a loner who disappeared into the woods for god knows how long and would know the perfect places in the wilderness to hide a hostage or plant bodies. And no one knew where he had been or what he'd done for years.

Ellie had defended him on the Ghost case. But lightning doesn't strike twice.

CHAPTER 93

Finton's Final Resting Home

Ellie slowly roused back to consciousness, confused and disoriented. Her head throbbed, and it was so dark she blinked to bring the world back into focus. But her head and memory were fuzzy.

Closing her eyes, she struggled to remember the last few minutes before she'd passed out. Slowly they came back to her, the scenes reeling through her head. She and Cord had come to Finton's funeral home to search for Shondra. They'd searched the prep room and cold room, finding them empty. Then they'd entered the room housing the caskets. And everything went black.

Panicking suddenly, she attempted to sit up but realized there was no room, her head banging on something hard. Heart racing, she reached out to either side and felt the slick coldness of satin. Choking on a sob, she lifted her hands above her but could only reach a few inches. More satin.

God help her… she was in one of the coffins.

The cave where she'd been trapped as a child had been tight, but she couldn't even sit up or turn over in here. It was so black, she found herself paralyzed with fear.

Tense seconds passed as she lay frozen in horror. Her chest constricted as she worked to catch her breath. The top of the casket seemed to slowly drop closer to her face. The sides closed in, and her lungs strained for air.

Where was Cord? Had he been assaulted, too? Had Finton been here and caught them looking for Shondra?

Fighting hysteria, she finally forced herself to move, lifting her hand and feeling along inside the coffin for a release button. Surely there had to be one. Her fingers brushed over the satin lining below her and on the side panels, then she ran her fingers frantically along the top.

The small space shifted around her again, robbing her of breath, and she gasped.

Think, Ellie, think. Breathe through the panic.

Slowly her breathing steadied, and she remembered a class discussion at the academy. Someone had asked the instructor how long a person could survive if they were buried alive. The time frame varied depending on a person's body size, and rate of oxygen consumption per minute. She couldn't remember the exact formula, but she thought a person could survive about five hours on average.

A shudder coursed through her. She couldn't stay in here for five hours, couldn't just lie here and slowly suffocate in the dark. Perspiration beaded on her forehead, sweat trickling down her back.

Frantically she ran her fingers along the interior, this time focusing on the edge of the coffin lid.

Forcing slow, even breaths in to calm herself and preserve air, she fumbled across the lining. Finally, she felt a tiny metal clasp. She almost cried with relief, feeling the cool steel in her hand.

Running her fingers around it, she pushed the edge and shoved the top of the casket at the same time. But the clasp broke, snapping in her fingers, and the lid refused to budge.

Her breath quickened, and silent tears ran down her face.

She was trapped.

CHAPTER 94

Finton's Final Resting Home

Derrick glared at Sheriff Waters, who'd insisted on driving and checking out the funeral home with him.

"Did you know about this?" he asked him.

"Detective Reeves doesn't share well," Waters said in an irritated voice. "And I was checking out a couple of Carrie Winters' clients."

"Any leads?" Derrick could barely concentrate for the worry eating at him.

The sheriff shook his head. "For a hooker, she seemed to have morals. No extortion or threats to expose her clients. And I ran backgrounds on the few names but no one with a history of violence against women."

That they knew of. After all, men with money could pay to have their illicit activities covered up.

The sheriff's siren wailed as they careened into the parking lot for the funeral home.

"Ellie's Jeep," Derrick said, pointing to her parked vehicle.

"I'll look around out here if you want to check inside." Bryce pulled his weapon and scoped out the property. Woods backed up to the brick structure, heavy gray clouds overhead threatening a downpour and casting the exterior in deep pockets of gray.

Senses honed, Derrick held his gun at the ready while Bryce headed toward the woods. First, he climbed the steps to the outside entrance of the apartment but found it was locked and boarded up. A quick look through the window revealed it was empty, so he went back down the steps. If Finton had someone here, he'd probably put them in the basement. Ellie might be there now in trouble.

Walking around the outside of the building, he checked doors and windows for a point of entry. He finally found a lock broken, the window half open and dusted with footprints. Two sets. A woman's boots and a larger set that had to belong to a man.

Crawling inside, he shined his flashlight around the dank interior, the acrid odors of body waste and chemicals permeating the concrete walls so strongly that he briefly gagged.

Moving slowly, he listened for any indication that Ellie was inside, or that another woman might be here needing help. The furnace clanged, and somewhere he heard a mouse skittering along the floor. He followed the hall to the prep room and looked inside, but it appeared to be empty. Still, he ducked inside and checked the storage room, careful not to touch any of the instruments or supplies.

Forcing himself not to think about the fact that this place had seen countless dead bodies, he continued on to the refrigerated room.

Dread made his stomach cramp, but he opened the heavy door and looked inside. A blast of frigid air assaulted him, but the steel shelves and tables were bare.

A noise from down the hall made him step back outside, closing the door then creeping past an office. Eyes peeled for an ambush, he eased open the door and shined the light inside. Dingy yellowed walls, a cold tile floor, and a room full of caskets.

There was the noise again, and he spotted McClain dragging himself up from behind one of the coffins and staggering toward the door.

"McClain?" Derrick went still. "Where the hell is Ellie?"

The ranger rubbed the back of his head with his hand. Looking confused and dazed, he slumped against a gray coffin, leaning over as if struggling to focus.

Just as Derrick moved toward him, he thought he heard a sound again. A squeaking sound. Or was it scratching?

"Ellie?" he shouted. "Are you in here?"

Quickly glancing around, he realized there was no one else in view. If someone was in the room, they had to be in in one of the caskets. Stowing his gun, he hurried toward a bronzed coffin against the wall. He quickly lifted the lid. Cream-colored lining, gold around the edges. But it was empty. Fear pulsed through him as he raced to the next casket, a dark charcoal one with a silver bracket closing it. Heart hammering, he raised the lid and found ivory satin pillow and lining. No one was inside.

"Ellie!" he yelled as he moved onto another. He jerked it open, expecting to find Ellie. Or… Shondra.

But there was no one.

Rapidly exhaling a breath, he ran to the last one in the corner. Polished nickel.

The shrill sound echoed again and his hand shook as he jerked the lid up.

Ellie lay inside, gasping for a breath, her eyes wide in terror, hands clawing to get out.

CHAPTER 95

Ellie screamed and grasped at Derrick to help her out. With the latch broken and the lower half of the casket closed, her legs were trapped. He gently helped her, lifting her free.

Tears trailing down her face, she gulped for air, the claustrophobic darkness finally giving way to light.

"I've got you," Derrick said as he hauled her limp body toward the door and held her. "You're okay, Ellie. You're safe now."

Unable to help herself, she sobbed against him, tremors running through her at the terror of being locked inside.

Derrick carried her into the hall. She blinked back tears, unable to stop trembling.

Her fingers ached where she'd tried to claw her way out, and her nails had broken off, her fingers bleeding from scratching at the interior.

Footsteps echoed behind them, and Cord shuffled into the hall, rubbing the back of his head. "Ellie?" he said in a thick voice. "El?"

"She's right here," Derrick replied, his tone harsh. "What happened, Ellie? Did McClain lock you in there?"

Ellie's head swirled with confusion. One minute she and Cord had been searching the space, then the next, someone had jumped her from behind.

"Ellie?" Derrick asked. "Talk to me. Tell me what happened."

"I don't know," she whispered. Cord wouldn't have hurt her. Would he?

Footsteps pounded, then another male voice sounded from nearby. "Agent Fox? Ellie?" A second later, Bryce ran into the hall, his gun drawn.

"I found her," Derrick shouted. "She was assaulted and locked in one of the damn caskets."

Hurrying toward them, the sheriff's jaw was set tight as he took in the scene.

"Arrest him," Derrick ordered, staring at McClain. "I think he attacked Ellie because she got too close to the truth."

"What?" McClain said, his voice slurred. "No. That's not true."

Ellie opened her mouth to argue but she was still struggling to breathe as Bryce handcuffed Cord and hauled him down the hall.

CHAPTER 96

Stony Gap

An hour later, after Ellie had been examined by the medics, she and Derrick made it back to the sheriff's office. Derrick was unable to erase the image of finding Ellie trapped in the casket, panicked, gasping for air.

"I'm telling you, you should be looking for Finton," Ellie said. "Cord wouldn't hurt me."

"We're issuing an all-points bulletin for him and his son Roy," the sheriff replied, clearly annoyed at her defense of McClain.

"Let me talk to Cord," Ellie said.

"He's in an interrogation room. Stay here, Ellie." Sheriff Waters disappeared through the double doors that led to the interrogation rooms and holding cells.

After hesitating for a second, clearly recovering from her ordeal, Ellie took off after the sheriff. "I want to watch the interview."

Dammit to hell, she is stubborn, Derrick thought as he followed her. The first interrogation room was open, so they went to the second and Ellie knocked.

The sheriff opened the door. Cord was already handcuffed and seated at a table, his expression sullen.

"I want to be in there," Ellie said, trying to push past the sheriff.

"No way," Bryce said, blocking her entrance. "I know you two are friends. I'll handle this."

Cord didn't even look up.

"I'm going to sit in," Derrick said, clearing his throat. "I have information that might be helpful."

Ellie's face paled as she looked at him, but he couldn't apologize for doing his job. He was just following the evidence. If McClain had anything to do with the Weekday Killer murders, he had to be stopped.

"Turn on the camera so I can observe in the other room," Ellie said through clenched teeth.

Bryce tensed, but nodded in concession.

"Cord is not the Weekday Killer," she said with as much conviction as she could muster.

"This is why women shouldn't be cops. You let your emotions get in the way," the sheriff said sharply.

"It's not emotion. It's instinct," Ellie said with a glare.

Her comeback made Bryce's eyes flare with anger. Saying nothing, Derrick followed the sheriff into the room while Ellie spun around and headed to take her place and watch.

Waters claimed the chair opposite McClain, but Derrick remained standing.

"All right, Cord," the sheriff began. "What the hell happened today?"

"Ellie wanted to go to Finton's funeral home," Cord's expression was as flat as his voice. "I went with her. We got jumped from behind." He rubbed his head. "When I came to, Agent Fox was there shouting Ellie's name, and I finally roused."

Walking over to Cord, Derrick stared down at him.

"We know about your foster family, the Fintons. Felix Finton told your caseworker about how you enjoyed dressing the female bodies."

Silence engulfed the room, tension building.

"Did you take your habit of playing with dead bodies to the next level and start murdering women?"

McClain hissed between his teeth but said nothing. He just folded and unfolded his hands, staring into his lap.

"We checked. Finton's has been closed for renovations for the past two weeks, like the sign said." Derrick slapped his palms on the table. McClain didn't flinch. "Have you been hiding the bodies at the funeral home after you murder the women, then returning to move them when you're ready for them to be found? Is that why you have blood under your fingernails?"

Curling his fingers into fists, Cord remained silent.

"Come on, McClain, talk to us," the sheriff said. "You were caught red-handed in that home. Now we know you're a pervert."

Rage burned in Cord's eyes. Derrick thought he was going to jump up and grab Bryce, but he wheezed out a breath instead.

"Your print was found on Shondra's vehicle," Derrick said. "Tell us where Shondra is and if she's still alive, and we might help you out."

Cord's brows furrowed and he went very still. Either he was surprised that the print was his or surprised that he'd been caught, Derrick reasoned.

"Why would I take Shondra?" he finally said.

"You tell us," Derrick said. "And while you're at it, tell us where you were on the nights of these killings." He laid a photograph of each victim on the table.

Staring at the pictures, Cord's expression was a mask of barely controlled emotion. But he didn't respond, remaining tight-lipped.

The sheriff stood abruptly, pushed away from the table, circled around and wrenched Cord from the chair. "You don't want to talk, fine. Maybe a night in a cell will change your mind," he said, dragging him from the room.

Derrick followed them into the hallway, where Ellie rushed toward them, a mixture of disbelief and panic on her face.

"Bryce, let me talk to him," she said.

The sheriff shook his head. "No way. Go home, Ellie. I've got this," he said, shoving McClain through another set of doors to the cells in back.

As Ellie clenched her hands by her side, Derrick saw the blood on her fingers and his stomach twisted. If McClain had done that to Ellie, he felt like killing the man.

"Cord might talk to me if Bryce would just let him," Ellie said, her tone full of angst.

"If he is innocent, why isn't he defending himself?" Derrick asked. "Why not answer my questions?"

Ellie pressed her lips into a thin line.

"I'll drive you home, Ellie. You need rest," Derrick said. "Then I'm going to get a search warrant and search McClain's house tonight. If you're right, there may be something there that can exclude him, or, if my gut is right, there could be something to tell us where Shondra is."

"I'll go with you," she replied. "If something's there, I need to see it for myself."

CHAPTER 97

River's Edge

Denial stabbed at Ellie as she drove to Cord's. Gray skies promised a deluge at any minute, painting the woods in an oppressive gray. Though she wanted to take her own car, Derrick insisted on driving in case she was concussed.

Being locked in that coffin reminded her of just how much she didn't want to have to bury her mother. She made a quick call to her father on the way. "Hey, Dad."

"It's good to hear your voice," her father said. "I miss you, El."

Emotions overwhelmed her, but she swallowed them back. "I don't have much time. We're working the case, but I wanted to check on Mom."

"Her vitals aren't good, honey. They're doing all kinds of tests. She might need open heart surgery."

That was a scary thought. "When will you know?"

"Hopefully in the next few hours. I'll call when I hear." He hesitated. "And thanks for calling. I'll tell your mother. It might cheer her up."

Ellie hung up, her heart in her throat. Damn her parents for lying to her. Damn Paulson for setting fire to their house.

Damn Bryce for not allowing her to speak to Cord. He'd worked with the ranger on rescue missions and had to know in his gut that Cord wouldn't kill anyone, much less commit multiple murders—or hurt her.

Something was going on here, something that wasn't right. It was almost like the killer was lobbing grenades at her with clues pointing to different suspects. Was that part of his game?

They parked at Cord's cabin and got out. Ellie shivered as she hurried up to the front porch.

As usual, darkness bathed Cord's rustic log cabin, which was nestled between the oaks and pines as if it had been carved from the forest.

"I got the warrants," Derrick said as he removed a lock-picking tool and jimmied the front door open.

Ellie scanned the front porch, then the surrounding area. The grass had been mown recently, bushes trimmed, and firewood that Cord cut himself for his stove was stacked by the house.

Derrick pushed the door open, and she flipped on the light in the entry. The sense that she was violating Cord overcame her, reminding her she'd felt the same way when she'd combed her parents' home—now up in smoke—for evidence of Hiram.

That search hadn't ended well. She hoped today yielded better results.

They both pulled on gloves, and stepped into the house. The minimalistic décor screamed that Cord was a loner. There were no personal photographs of family, friends or trips.

Derrick gestured to a book on plant and flower symbolism, then he flipped it open and found a page about daffodils.

His gaze met hers. "Right in line with the MO."

"Okay, we know his background," Ellie conceded, unable to keep the anger from her voice. "That doesn't mean he killed those women or took Shondra. The AT has been his home—of course he's bound to be interested in this kind of stuff."

"Heath did some digging. He can't find anything on McClain after he left juvie. There are years missing in his life, Ellie. Years before he met your father and started working for FEMA." He paused. "Has he ever talked to you about that time?"

Ellie's heart gave a pang, but she shook her head. He'd never talked about Finton either.

With a grunt, Derrick headed back to the bedroom. Ellie had been inside there once, right before she left for the police academy. The only night they'd spent together.

She tapped into her memory bank for any red flags, any warning signs. Cord had been gruff and adamant about leaving the lights off.

But that didn't make him a killer.

While Derrick searched the bedroom, Ellie checked the kitchen. A few groceries, beer cans and whiskey, steaks. Nothing odd. Rooting through the drawers, she spotted a small wooden box in one of them. She opened it and found a key, and instinctively knew what room it opened. She strode across to the door she'd never seen open and turned the key in the lock. The door opened creakily, and she was pitched into darkness. For a moment, the world spun, like she was trapped in the coffin all over again.

Gripping the door frame to steady herself, she inhaled deep breaths to calm the suffocating sensation. Seconds passed. The blood roared in her ears. Fingers of fear crawled along her spine.

"Ellie?"

Derrick's brusque voice cut through the fog and she swallowed hard, biting back her terror.

"What's in there?"

"I don't know," she said. Suddenly she wasn't sure she wanted to know.

Running his hand along the wall, Derrick flipped on a light. Ellie blinked as the warm light filled the room. One wall held an assortment of knives—jackknives, hunting knives, a Buck 110 folding knife with a wood grain handle and brass bolsters, and an assortment of carving knives, tools and pocketknives. She knew that Cord usually carried the Buck 110 on his hikes.

Derrick gestured toward the collection. "Laney said the lacerations on the victims probably came from a hunting knife."

Inhaling, Ellie continued studying the room, desperately searching for some clue to help Cord prove his innocence.

One corner held wood shavings, another section a table where he must do his taxidermy. Two wild cats sat there now, tools lined up neatly next to them, along with a jar of glass eyes.

Derrick marched across the room, lifted another jar that sat on the shelves by the table and held it up to examine it.

"Blood." His gaze swung to her. "Could be the blood he used to write on your door." Derrick looked grim. "Shondra's."

Nausea climbed Ellie's throat while Derrick opened the doors to a metal cabinet.

Inside, fixed to a cork board, were photographs of all the Weekday Killer's victims posed on the daffodils. Four dead women so far, four gruesome images.

And there were two more pictures—of Shondra and Ellie.

CHAPTER 98

Derrick stared at the photos. Finding them here made McClain look as guilty as sin, and he was shocked to read denial on Ellie's stunned face.

"These pictures are his souvenirs," he said.

"I can't believe Cord would do this," Ellie replied, a tremble in her voice.

"He fits the profile of the killer," Derrick added. "He lives out here alone, knows the AT, led us to bodies, has knowledge and books on the symbolism used in the unsub's MO, and allegedly liked to dress up corpses. Evidence doesn't lie, Ellie." He pointed toward the shelf of taxidermy tools. The jar of eyes was downright disturbing. "Just look at his hobby. Taxidermy." How on earth did she need convincing?

Walking over, Ellie studied the tools. "I've known him since I was a teenager, and he's never seemed violent. He's risked his life on rescue missions, carried lost hikers and children for miles to get them medical attention." She shook her head. "It just doesn't fit with the man I know."

"Sometimes we're too close to people to see who they really are. We just see what we want to see in them."

She flinched. His comment had clearly struck a nerve about her parents.

"I know it looks bad," she said in a low voice. "But this is all circumstantial."

"His past suggests he's troubled. Maybe those crimes with the girls triggered something in him—you know about the cycle of the abuse. And these photographs are of the crime scenes. He had to be present to have taken them."

"Where's his camera, then?" Ellie said. "And the dresses? If he prepares ahead, why aren't those things here?"

Derrick chewed the inside of his cheek. "Maybe he keeps them somewhere else. He could have a secret place on the AT that we don't know about."

"The perp could have planted these pictures to frame Cord," Ellie said.

She had her head in the sand. "Did he plant those books on symbolism, too? And what about how he grew up? And the fact that he won't talk now?"

Ellie cut him a venomous look. "I'm calling a team to process the house."

"I was just going to do the same thing." She could argue Cord's innocence all day long.

But he went by the book. Evidence told the story. And right now, it was stacked against Cord McClain.

CHAPTER 99

Crooked Creek

He'd heard those old biddies gossiping in town. One of them, that crazy-mean old Maude Hazelnut who liked to dish about everyone in town, pointing fingers here and there and airing everyone's dirty laundry when she was nothing but a fraud herself, had gotten under his skin.

Her granddaughter was just like her.

Except she was as pretty as a peach. She knew it, too. Used her good looks to lure men into sleeping with her until she got knocked up. Then she robbed them blind.

It was time she got a lesson of her own.

He jimmied the lock on the door to her plush bedroom. He knew it was plush because he'd been here before. He knew all about the women he took. His feet sank into three-inch deep white carpet and the smell of some expensive perfume nearly knocked him over as he tiptoed to her underwear drawer to rifle through it. He was sure it was full of sheer lace and satin.

But she wouldn't be wearing any of that when he was finished with her.

And Meddlin' Maude would be screaming at the heavens, wondering why God had forsaken her and brought evil into her family's life.

Truth was, Maude was evil herself. And one day everyone would know it.

Exposing her was just icing on the cake.

CHAPTER 100

Stony Gap

Ellie was not only confused as hell but pissed too as she and Derrick entered the sheriff's office. Her parents' betrayal had nearly destroyed her. Cord couldn't have committed these heinous crimes, he just couldn't have. This devastating blow would be one too many.

"You have something I can use?" asked Bryce.

Derrick filled Bryce in on what they'd discovered at Cord's. "I'm going to lay our cards on the table and show him the evidence we have against him."

"You can go in with me. But not Ellie," Bryce said, tugging at the waistband of his pants.

Outrage seethed through Ellie. "That's not right, Sheriff. Cord might talk to me."

"You're not objective," Bryce replied.

Ellie opened her mouth to protest, but Derrick touched her arm. "Watch the interrogation and let us know if you pick up on anything."

So, he thought she shouldn't be in there either. "Just be fair," she said. "We want the truth, not to railroad an innocent man into jail for a crime he didn't commit. Shondra's life depends on it."

Bryce's look said he didn't appreciate her comment, but she didn't give a damn. Cord was not a killer. He couldn't be.

Yet you believed in your father, and he betrayed you.

She shook her head. No, it couldn't happen again.

As Derrick followed Bryce through the double doors, Ellie slipped into the observation room. Five minutes later, Bryce escorted a handcuffed Cord in and Ellie wanted to scream at Bryce to remove them.

But, despite her faith, questions nagged at her. Like where had Cord been all those years between juvie and meeting her father? Had he suffered a trauma that had turned him into a monster? Had he been able to hide the truth from her? Had she, yet again, been blind?

The questions piled up in her head. What motive would he have to take Shondra and the others? Why had he refused to answer Derrick's questions? And who would know enough about Cord to frame him?

The ranger dropped into the chair with a sullen expression, anger radiating from him in waves. He spotted the small camera in the corner and turned his brooding eyes toward her.

Derrick claimed the chair across from him while the sheriff stood, as if to intimidate Cord by towering over him. But Cord simply stared at his battered hands, which he flexed on the wooden table. The scratches there looked fresh. She remembered seeing blood on his hands before when they met on the trail. He'd been running, panting, sweating.

"Why don't you start by telling us the truth?" Bryce began.

"The truth is that you're wasting your time. You have the wrong guy."

"Really?" the sheriff asked in a sardonic tone. "Because all the evidence we found points to you."

A twitch of Cord's mouth was his only reaction.

Derrick laid the pictures of the victims on the table, naming them as he did. "These are the four women the Weekday Killer has killed so far."

Cord stared at them, saying nothing.

"Ellie received texts about the murders," Derrick paused, then added photos they'd found at Cord's. "Look at these," Derrick said. "We found these at your house."

"That's impossible," Cord said. "I've never seen them before."

"They were in your workroom, McClain, along with all those knives you collect."

Sweat beaded on Cord's upper lip, and he rubbed his hand over it, distressed.

"We believe the killer took Shondra to get Ellie's attention."

Cord lifted his head and stared directly at Derrick. "Why would I do anything to torment Ellie?"

"Because you want in her pants but she turned you down," the sheriff snapped.

Ellie gritted her teeth at Bryce's crude remark, while Cord gave the sheriff the coldest look Ellie had ever seen. "That's your problem, Waters, not mine."

Bryce pounded the table with his fist. "You'd better watch it, McClain. We have enough evidence to put you away for life."

As Derrick held up a warning hand to silence Bryce, he laid the photos of the jar of blood and the fingerprint evidence on the table. "When we searched your house, we found your collection of books, which matches the MO. And when we test this blood, I have a feeling it's going to match the blood left on Ellie's door. Blood that was Shondra Eastwood's."

"I don't know what you're talking about," Cord said, shaking his head in denial.

"We also have your print on Shondra's truck," Bryce said with a smug look.

Cord blinked, his expression earnest. "I didn't kill those women, and I sure as hell wouldn't hurt Ellie."

"Come on, these photographs are proof, what we call souvenirs," Derrick said tersely. "We know about your foster father. That he told the social worker you liked to play with the dead bodies. You dressed them up and put makeup on them and—"

"No," Cord said through clenched teeth. "That wasn't me."

"You're accusing the social worker of lying?" Derrick asked.

The handcuffs clinked as Cord flexed and unflexed his hands. "No, my foster father did. He was a sick son of a bitch who liked to touch the dead women. He dressed them up in lingerie and laid beside them and did… other things."

A tense silence descended.

"Let's say, for a minute, that's true," the sheriff interjected. "It still doesn't explain the evidence we found at your house. For all we know, you joined in with him and had a party."

Cord blinked, heaving a labored breath. Slowly he angled his head and looked at the camera, as if he knew he was cornered, a deer in the woods. "I'll talk. But only to Ellie."

CHAPTER 101

Ellie met Bryce and Derrick in the hallway. Both men looked grim-faced and disapproving, but resigned that if they wanted information from Cord, they had to use her.

"I'm surprised he didn't lawyer up," the sheriff said.

"Be careful, Ellie," Derrick said, nodding in agreement. "He might be asking for you because he thinks he can manipulate you."

Ellie crossed her arms, immediately defensive. Although she guessed she couldn't blame them, after she'd failed to see her parents' lies. Just like at the academy, she had to work harder to overcome their scrutiny. "Believe me, I want the truth as much as you do."

"We'll be watching," Bryce replied.

"Don't you trust me?" Ellie asked, raising a brow.

"About as much as you trust me."

Well, there you have it. They were in a standoff.

Derrick glanced between them. "Just get him to talk, Detective."

Shooting Derrick a look of contempt, Ellie squared her shoulders and walked to the interrogation room. Before entering, she braced herself for whatever Cord had to say. She could handle the truth, she told herself.

At least she hoped she could. If it turned out he was a murderer...

Pushing her doubts aside, she entered the room. Cord drew in a breath, his gaze so intense it sent a chill up her spine.

Her heart pounded as she slipped into the chair across from him.

"They're watching, listening, aren't they?" he asked in a gruff tone.

Ellie nodded. "I'm sorry."

Cord's eyes flickered with regret. "You have nothing to be sorry about. I should have told you earlier."

"Told me what?" she asked, gently laying her hand on his. He tensed, but instead of pulling away, he leaned closer and lowered his voice.

"About my past," he said in a strained voice. "But you have to believe me. I didn't kill those women, Ellie. I swear I didn't."

Relief flitted through Ellie—she believed him—but she steeled herself again. Something was still very wrong here, her instincts were alight. "Then how did those pictures and that blood get in your locked workroom?"

"I don't know."

"Come on, Cord, you asked to talk to me," she said quietly. "So talk."

"Someone's framing me."

"I had the same thought initially. But who would go to all those lengths to set you up? And how would that person know about your past, how you grew up?"

"I can't be sure. But I have an idea."

"Go on."

His breathing became unsteady, as if he was lost in the throes of a dark memory. "Felix Finton was a sadistic monster. He did all kinds of sick things to the bodies before preparing them for visitation. He liked to play with the corpses, especially the women. One night I caught him violating a young girl and he wanted me to join in the fun. When I refused and threatened to tell, he was furious, and then he told the social worker I did it."

The grisly images played through Ellie's mind like a horror show.

"Do you think he's capable of committing these crimes?"

Cord gave a slight shake of his head. "Mentally, yes. But he was in poor health back then so I doubt he could pull it off now. But his son Roy hated me. And he took after the old man."

"Why did he hate you?"

"Finton took in a little girl, eight years old. I caught Roy pulling her into the prep room. He wanted to show her what he liked to do with the bodies. Sick fuck. But I intervened."

"You protected her?"

He turned his hands over, staring at the nicks on his fingers. She'd asked him once how he got them, and he said he cut himself when he was whittling.

"She was so little and scared, I had to. Roy liked to dress the bodies with his father. He'd spend hours combing their hair and painting their lips."

He stuttered, as if the memory pained him, then continued. "He was a year older than me and a mean bully. We fought a lot, especially that night." His voice sounded tormented. "That's another reason his father told the social worker I was the one who played with the bodies. He wanted to protect himself and his son."

The tension in Ellie's chest eased slightly. She believed him. And if he was right, Roy Finton might be the unsub. "Where's Roy now?"

"He used to live in the apartment above the funeral home, but I have no idea where he is now." Cord's shoulders slumped. "When I saw the way the bodies were left, the ghoulish makeup and the flowers, I thought about Roy, though. Sometimes he stole flowers from the arrangements people sent into the funeral home and spread them on the bodies."

Ellie felt nauseated. She remembered the odd way Cord had been looking at the victims they'd found—suddenly it made sense.

"Why didn't you tell me then?" Ellie asked.

Cord averted his eyes. "Growing up, seeing that, it's not exactly the happy childhood you want to share." His throat muscles worked as he swallowed, his voice like gravel. "Besides, I was afraid if you knew, you'd think I was like them."

CHAPTER 102

Somewhere on the AT

"It's time to go, Cathy."

Cold fear swept through her. He called them all Cathy. And if she tried to tell him her real name, tried to convince him to see her as the person she really was, it only made him angrier. It only made him beat her harder.

But she had to fight. Knowing every second counted, she struggled against the masked man as he hauled her into the woods.

Guilt over not being able to help the others weighed on her, but survival instincts kicked in.

He was almost done with the game, he'd told her. Now it was her time to die.

She kicked and fought and screamed, but he simply laughed, dragging her through the forest. That damn rhyme was on repeat in her head. She'd asked him about it, but the only talking he did was with his fists.

Her body ached and she was sure her ribs were cracked. But physical pain was nothing compared to what she'd witnessed.

She could still see the blood draining from Shondra. Hear the steady drip of it and see the blood spattered on the wall from where he'd beaten the others.

Ignoring her agony, he hacked away weeds and hauled her over a tree stump. Rough stones stabbed at her and a tree limb smacked her in the face. Insects buzzed around her face, worsened by the wet ground and mud.

She tried to resist him, but he carried her like a sack of flour over his shoulder. Ahead she heard the rush of water over rocks.

"Help!" she screamed. "Somebody help me!"

The wind whistled, and the other women's shrill screams echoed in her ears, just as her own boomeranged off the sharp mountain ridges and faded into nothing. No one else was out here. No one would hear her.

She was going to die, just like the others.

He'd only kept her as leverage if he needed it. Now he didn't need her anymore she would simply become another part of his ritual. Another one bites the dust.

He reached a clearing near a waterfall, stopped beside a large boulder and propped her against it.

Slowly he began to pull the bag of wildflowers from his duffel bag, then a red dress and the makeup. He'd shown her the photos of his handiwork.

It was the only time she'd seen him smile. Even through the eyeholes of his facemask, a perverse exhilaration lit his eyes. She could sense his pulse quickening, his body radiating heat and excitement. The sharp knife blade glinted in the shadows as he laid it on the rock.

Panicked and knowing she only had minutes, maybe seconds to live, she wrestled with the ropes behind her back. She rubbed her hands against the sharp edge of the rock, sawing back and forth. The stone cut into her wrists and hands, blood trickling down her fingers. But she moved her hands up and down, sawing away at the ropes, biting at her lip to mask the pain.

He lifted the knife up to examine it, then removed a tool and began to sharpen the edge. The sound of metal against metal echoed in the quiet but helped to disguise her uneven breathing as she worked to loosen the ropes. Finally, she felt the rope fray, and she gently jerked her hands free, beginning to steadily unravel the knots at her feet.

"Monday's child is fair of face. Tuesday's child is full of grace. Wednesday's child is full of woe. Thursday's child has far to go. Friday's child is loving and giving…"

She knew she was going to be Friday's child.

Slowly, she loosened the ropes from her feet. He was looking at the flowers now, lost in total madness, in the fervor of what was about to unfold.

Spurred on by fear, she stood, her head rushing with the movement, then turned and fled into the forest, as fast as her feet would carry her. Maybe she'd find help. A hiker. A ranger. A path back to the road. Anything.

Footsteps echoed behind her. His howl. Bushes being slashed with his knife as he chased her.

The need to survive overcame her, and she picked up her pace, slogging through the slushy ground and knee-high weeds. Wet moss made her trek slippery, and mosquitos swarmed her face, but she let the sound of the river nearby guide her. Patches of briars and poison ivy clawed at her bare legs, sharp stones jutting between the damp grass.

Her limbs felt heavy, her body weak from lack of food and water, the earth shifting sideways as a dizzy spell nearly overcame her.

Clawing at the trees to stay on her feet, she pushed on, weaving between the tall pines towering over her. The sharp brittle pinecones stabbed at her bare feet as she ran, the scent of rain and wet ground cloying.

"You can run, but you can't hide." The voice of the monster who'd taken her drifted through the trees. He was right behind her. Closing in.

Her feet sank into mud, and tree branches slapped her in the face, but she forged ahead and found a rough trail.

"You won't escape." His voice resounded through the woods again.

Bile clogged her throat as she followed the overgrown path, suddenly coming to a cliff. The sight of it robbed her breath. The ground dropped hundreds of feet into the icy river below. Jagged rocks and overflowing water awaited her, and the current was so strong she'd probably never survive.

She turned to run back the other way, but his silhouette appeared in the shadows a few feet away. The blade of his knife blade glimmered as he lunged toward her.

Glancing at the drop-off again, she gauged the distance, and her chances. Certain death if she jumped and hit the rocks. If that didn't kill her, the paralyzing temperature of the water would.

He caught her arm, but she swung her fist up and knocked him backward, turning and throwing herself over the edge. Her scream died in the wind as she plunged into the depths of the raging water below.

CHAPTER 103

He teetered on the edge of the cliff, enraged that she'd gotten away from him. "No, Cathy! No, no, no, no, no."

As her body disappeared below the surface of the raging water, he looked for her to surface. Balling his hands into fists, he banged them against his thighs then ran along the embankment in the direction the current would carry her.

Wind spun through the trees, shaking them and tossing twigs down into the river, but as far as he could see she didn't surface. Below there was nothing but murky water. With the steep drop off, she'd probably hit rocks when she landed. The sheer impact of the fall would have likely killed her.

Sweat soaked his shirt and hair as he continued to follow the current nonetheless. What if she wasn't dead? What if she survived and told everyone where he'd kept her? What if she could identify him?

"Cathy!" he bellowed. "You shouldn't have left me!"

Jumping over rocks and broken tree limbs, and pushing through the tall briars, he followed the river for miles, chasing the current and stopping every few feet to see if her head appeared or if she washed up.

But after four heart-pounding miles where he hadn't seen her surface, he knew she had to be dead. She'd been weak already—he'd made sure of that. There was no way she could have swum underwater that far without him seeing her come up for air. Even if she survived the fall, the raging current would have swept her under. And hypothermia would get her.

Shaking with rage, he ripped vines from the ground with his bare hands, throwing a clump of them over the edge of the cliff and watching them fall into the rocky water.

She had just messed up his plans. She thought she was smart, running like that. Thought she'd escaped him.

But he was smarter.

He'd covered his tracks. Hidden his face from her.

And he had another. One who was even more fitting to be Friday's child than she had been. She'd served her purpose.

It was time for her to meet her fate.

CHAPTER 104

Elm Grove

Finton no longer lived above the funeral home. He owned a house although the outside of it looked as bleak as the funeral home. Made of stacked stone in a dull gray, with overgrown weeds and backed by the woods, it seemed to disappear into the foliage. Kudzu had taken over, snaking up the sides, winding around the railings.

Derrick had called to request warrants for Finton's home and computer while Ellie drove, his address easy enough to find. He'd also downloaded a photograph from the funeral home's website. In the picture, Roy Finton was dressed in a gray pinstriped suit with his hair clipped short and a sympathetic smile on his face. On the surface he looked like a nice, empathetic undertaker—*With our loving hands, your loved ones will rest in peace.*

But if what Cord said was true, it was all a lie.

"I don't see any cars," Derrick said as she parked.

"No lights on inside either. If he's not at the funeral home or here, where is he?"

"Who knows? The man might have a life. A girlfriend."

"No one in their right mind would want to be with a creep like him," said Ellie, with a shudder.

"That's assuming McClain is telling the truth."

Ellie threw a glare at him, then opened her car door and climbed out. He followed, examining the property for any signs Finton was around. An outbuilding sat to the side of the house, but it was dark and windowless.

Braced for an attack, they drew their weapons and eased up the drive. A stray cat loped across the front yard, then darted into the woods, and wind tore through the ancient trees, slamming a shutter on the house back and forth.

Cobwebs clung to the window to the side of the porch and Ellie noted rotting window casings that looked termite-infested. She reached the door and knocked, while Derrick continued to scope out the property. Set apart from other houses by at least a couple of miles, it would be easy for Finton to hide here or hold a victim without anyone being aware. If she screamed, the sound would dissolve into the wind and trees.

Ellie knocked again. There was no answer, so she jiggled the door. Locked. Derrick used his lock-picking tool and opened the heavy wooden door. The interior was an inky black, an odd odor permeating the air.

Freezing for a second, the darkness closed around Ellie and choked the air from her lungs. Dammit, she was working hard to overcome her fear, but sometimes it snuck out and curled around her like a snake winding its way around her throat.

"Roy Finton, this is the FBI!" Derrick shouted as she entered the space.

The sound of a clock ticking somewhere echoed as the wind wailed, gaining in intensity.

No one appeared to be inside.

Using his flashlight to illuminate the interior, Derrick cast a beam across the cement floor. A shiver rippled through Ellie as cold air wafted around her. The mausoleum-like house was like a refrigerator, carrying the scent of death and a deep kind of evil she'd never felt before.

Satisfied no one was inside, Derrick flipped on a light in the hall as they crossed through the entryway to the living area. More cement floors, and a black leather chair and stone countertop sat in an empty, plain kitchen.

Ellie forced herself to go to the refrigerator, half expecting to find jars of blood inside, but it was almost bare. A few condiments, sandwich meat and a leftover slice of pizza.

The desk in the corner held stacks of papers and bills. No typewriter to make the notes. No daffodils anywhere.

They moved down the hall to a bedroom. A king-sized oak bed was draped in a black comforter and the closet revealed pairs of jeans and work shirts, boots covered in mud, and an army-green duffel bag.

Ellie tugged on gloves and inspected the inside of the bag. There was some dried blood inside, but no knives or evidence he'd used the bag to carry wildflowers or bramble. In the outside pocket she found a suture kit that he could have used to sew the victims' mouths shut.

Derrick snapped close-ups of the mud on the boots. "We'll send these to the lab and have them tested to see if the soil matches our crime scenes."

Ellie checked the dresser drawers for photographs of the victims but found none. But her stomach knotted as she discovered bags of women's underwear, all lacy and risqué, along with makeup and tubes of lipstick in varied shades, from hot pink to coral to red.

Derrick's brow climbed his forehead as he lifted a sheer black thong. "Doesn't match the underwear on the vics."

"I know, but he could dress them in this for play, then change when he disposed of the bodies."

Ellie gestured to the caddy of lipsticks.

"We need to compare the red lipstick here to the blood-red colour the killer uses." A shiver rippled through her as she spotted combs, brushes, and hair spray. "These brushes should have DNA." If the hair collected matched the victims, they'd have Finton.

Where the hell was the man? Was he out on the trail with his next victim, posing her body right now?

Derrick gestured toward a small bookshelf, making a low sound of disgust as he lifted one of the titles. A book on necrophilia. "There are others along similar lines: *Dressing the Dead, Hairstyles for the Viewing, Makeup to Make Her Pretty, Preserving the Dead*," Derrick muttered. "*Ancient Burial Rituals*."

Spotting a laptop, Ellie crossed to it, booted it up, and began to scroll through his browsing history. "Good god," she whispered as she found chat rooms where he'd communicated with others whose proclivities included necrophilia.

Cord was right.

"He's a sick perv," Ellie said, her skin crawling as she skimmed several posts. "Just the kind of man who'd leave women posed the way we found the Weekday victims."

"Let's search that shed outside," Derrick said.

Dread clawed at Ellie, but she led the way.

Outside, thunder rumbled, the wind bowing trees, leaves flying across the yard. Crossing to the shed, they found it chained with a padlock. Ellie retrieved an ax from the trunk of her Jeep, using it to hack the padlock open.

Shining her flashlight into the dark space, her stomach rose to her throat. A steel table sat in the middle of the wide-open room, a silver-gray coffin against the back wall.

On the opposite wall hung pictures of dead, naked women with Finton touching and kissing their pale, lifeless bodies.

Sickened, she had to look away for a second. But the coffin drew her. If Finton was the killer, then Shondra might be in there.

Shaking with the memory of being locked in the casket, she held her breath as she reached to open it.

CHAPTER 105

"Thank you, God." Ellie sagged as they saw that the casket was empty. Knowing she must be reliving the trauma of being locked inside one herself, Derrick caught her arm to steady her.

So McClain hadn't lied about Roy Finton being a sick son of a bitch.

Ellie mopped sweat from her forehead, her breathing erratic, and closed her eyes.

"Are you okay?" Derrick asked.

She shook her head, surprising him, then spoke in a brittle tone. "Even if Shondra is still alive and we find her, there's no telling what he did with her all this time."

"She's tough, Ellie, just like you are," Derrick murmured. "And you'll be there for her."

"Like I was when he took her?"

He squeezed her shoulder. "You had no idea he would target her."

"Like you had no idea a predator would take Kim," Ellie said softly.

Their gazes locked, bonded for a moment by their shared memories, their guilt.

"We have to find Finton." Pulling away from her, Derrick moved to the wall and studied the photographs. All women, twenties to thirties. Pretty, busty and blonde.

But none were of the Weekday Killer victims.

Finton seemed to have a type, unlike the killer. Then again, these could have been women he'd mistreated but hadn't murdered. Perhaps he even chose the opposite type, and that was part of his pathology—he killed women who didn't fit the image of the ones that aroused him.

Ellie released a long sigh. "I wonder if the families know what he's up to."

"Two complaints were filed, but somehow the charges were dropped," Derrick said. "But he's not getting off this time."

"Or going back to his business," Ellie said, her voice determined as she grabbed her phone.

She called a crime scene team, alerting Bryce and her captain that Finton still had to be found and brought in.

"Get his picture and issue an all-points bulletin on his car," she told the sheriff. "I'm sure Angelica Gomez will be glad to run with the story."

Derrick's mind raced with questions as she hung up.

"Finton fits the profile," Ellie said.

"Then why didn't he keep the pictures of the victims? And why contact you personally?" Derrick asked. Something still wasn't adding up.

"Because he hated Cord and wanted to frame him. Maybe he saw me in the news with Cord when we rescued Hiram's victims. At one point Angelica even called Cord a hero," Ellie said. "That could have triggered his rage."

Derrick conceded with a shrug, but he still wasn't convinced. "McClain directed us to Finton. Have you considered that he may be framing Finton to save his own ass?"

"No." Ellie's face blanched. "Cord may be troubled, but he's not a killer."

"Are you sure about that?"

She turned away, her mouth tightening into an angry scowl. "Like you said, let's just follow the evidence."

"What if the evidence proves it's McClain? Or what if he and Finton have stayed in touch and they're committing the crimes together? Each one could be pointing evidence at the other to confuse the police."

The sound of the forensics van rumbled outside, and he tore his eyes away from a stricken-looking Ellie to greet the team at the door. The shock on the techs' faces said they were just as disgusted by Finton's activities as he and Ellie were.

Suddenly Ellie looked down at her phone, pivoting towards him.

"We have to go. A Jane Doe was brought to Bluff County Hospital. Possible victim of the Weekday Killer."

CHAPTER 106

Bluff County Hospital

Dark clouds rolled across the sky, obliterating the stars, and the wind gusts ferociously picked up as Ellie parked at the Bluff County Hospital. A piece of trash tumbled across the parking lot, the wind slapping at the overhead power lines.

"Why do they think she might be one of our vics?" Derrick asked.

"They aren't sure." Ellie re-read the text. "But according to the doctor, she has bruises consistent with being restrained and held captive."

Pulling up her hood, she climbed from her vehicle, hoping the twisters that had been barreling through the south didn't decide to sweep through the mountains here. Some were so strong they took out entire neighborhoods and dropped trees like they were matchsticks.

They rushed to the nurses' station, and Derrick explained who they'd come to visit. Hurrying to the second floor where the woman had been admitted, they spoke with the attending doctor. "Do you have an ID yet?" Ellie asked.

"No, but we immediately contacted the authorities and they're circulating her picture to see if anyone comes forward to identify her. We've also collected blood samples and DNA."

"Thank you for being on top of the situation. What can you tell us about her condition?" Derrick asked.

The doctor frowned. "Judging from the bruising on her wrists and ankles and the whip marks on her back, she was physically restrained and abused. She was unconscious when she was brought in. Her nails were torn, and the scrapes on her body indicated she'd fought through the woods to escape. Bug bites, bruising and scratches are consistent with the fact that she was found by the river. She was soaking wet when she was found. With no ID and judging from her condition, I had to report her." The doctor fiddled with her stethoscope. "The deputy I spoke with thinks she might be one of the Weekday Killer's victims. Is that right?'

"That's what we're here to find out," Ellie said. "Can we see her now?"

The doctor nodded. "This way. But don't expect her to talk. She's been severely traumatized, is suffering from hypothermia and had water in her lungs."

Walking over to the bed, Ellie looked down at the pale brunette. Bruises marked her neck, hands and arms, and a thick purple mark roped around her neck, consistent with the other victims. An IV dripped fluids into her, and oxygen tubes fed air to her.

"How serious is her condition?" Ellie asked. The poor woman looked as if she'd been through hell.

"The hiker who found her said she'd either fallen or jumped over a hundred feet into the river. She hit rocks when she landed, sustained multiple injuries and a concussion. We're checking for other internal injuries. At this point, all we can do is run tests and wait."

CHAPTER 107

While Ellie waited for the young woman, praying for her to wake up, she made a trip to her mother's room—relieved that she could at least check in while she was here. She hesitated at the door, her gut churning as her mother struggled to breathe.

"She needs the surgery," her father said. "I'm waiting on her to wake up to tell her."

Ellie blinked away tears. "Let me know if she comes to. They brought in a woman who might be a victim of our killer. She's unconscious but hopefully can tell us something when she regains consciousness."

"Be careful, El," her father said.

"Don't worry about me. I can take care of myself," she replied, her voice thick with emotion as she tore herself away from the room.

Back in the victim's room, she got a text update from Captain Hale.

Have IDs on both Wednesday's child and Thursday's child. Victim three is Samantha Jennings. According to a neighbor, she cheated on her husband, triggering him to commit suicide, but instead of mourning him, she seemed relieved he was gone.

That explained the killer carving the heart into her chest—to indicate she didn't have one.

Victim four, Thursday's child, was thirty-two-year-old Valerie Patterson. She was accused of killing her father when she was twenty,

*but got probation on the grounds that he'd molested her as a child
and had then tried to molest her own daughter.*

Ellie hissed. That explained the Ten Commandments, although
the homicide sounded justified. The lowlife man should have been
castrated.

It also lent credence to their theory that this man had a God
complex and assigned himself as judge, jury and executioner. But
how did he have so much personal information about the victims
before he'd taken them?

Turning towards the latest victim, Ellie spoke softly. "I'm so
sorry for what happened to you. When you wake up and tell me
who hurt you, I'll make sure he pays."

As Shondra's face flashed in her mind, she had the sickest feeling
that time was running out for her friend, that she was missing
something. But what? Her head hurt with it all.

Derrick returned, pushing a cup of coffee into her hand. "They're
analyzing Finton's computer. Although it's odd that we found
nothing about the trail in his place—no maps, no notes about
locations and their meanings. That seems to be McClain's territory."

She bit down on her lower lip. Why would Cord kill those
women and taunt her with the crimes? Why would he take Shondra?
They'd always been friendly.

Which meant Shondra might have gone with him if he'd asked,
a little voice in her head whispered.

But no…

Derrick's phone beeped, and he checked an incoming text.
"Well, this is something. We have an ID for Jane Doe."

"Who is she?" Ellie asked, her pulse jumping.

"Her name is Kennedy Sledge."

CHAPTER 108

Ellie gasped. "This isn't Kennedy Sledge."

"What?" Derrick handed her his phone. "Yes, it is. There's a photo of her on LinkedIn with her business profile and her prints matched."

Stunned, Ellie's mind raced, and she quickly punched Heath's number. "Heath, check and see if any of the victims saw a therapist. Look for the name Kennedy Sledge."

"On it."

"And get me her home and business address."

"Will send ASAP."

"What's going on?" Derrick asked as she hung up.

"If this is Kennedy Sledge, then someone else is using her identity and credentials to see patients." Unsuspecting women like her, who unknowingly spilled their guts to a stranger.

"How do you know that?"

Ellie spun around, her mind racing. "After what happened with my family, Shondra encouraged me to talk to a counselor. She'd been seeing one because of her family's reaction to her sexuality." She exhaled. No wonder he'd taken Shondra. "Oh, my word," she muttered. "That's how he knew all about me. What makes me tick, what triggers me, about the dolls and Hiram and Cord and my friendship with Shondra." She'd unknowingly told the bastard everything.

She turned and looked at the unconscious woman in the bed. "He abducted the real Kennedy Sledge and used another woman to pretend to be her."

Derrick's eyes widened. "That means we're looking at a female accomplice."

CHAPTER 109

Thirty minutes later, as the police artist arrived, Ellie's disgust at the thought of a woman helping a monster to lure and kill others intensified.

Derrick had already asked his people to analyze her computer for links to the IP address of the PC the impersonator had used. He'd also alerted her captain to search the office where Ellie had first met the woman claiming to be Kennedy Sledge.

"Was their anything distinctive about the office?" Derrick asked.

"Not really. There were credentials on the wall, and books about therapy techniques, eating disorders, I think, and one about hypnotism."

"How about when you talked on the phone? Any sounds in the background? Traffic? A train?"

Ellie massaged her temple, where a headache was starting to fester. "Just a clock ticking." A reminder now that time was running out for Shondra—if it hadn't already.

The police artist, Sienna Redding, appeared at the doorway. She was a curvy woman with coppery hair and wore a dozen bracelets. She and Ellie had worked together before—Redding was talented. "Why don't we walk to the cafeteria and find a quiet spot to work?" she suggested.

Ellie glanced at the real Kennedy Sledge.

"I'll let you know if she comes to," Derrick said.

Nodding as she left the room, Ellie's stomach roiled at the thought she'd been tricked. Despite her better instincts, she'd halfway trusted the woman who'd pretended to be the therapist, when all along she'd been probing Ellie for information to use against her. How many more people would she be blind to? Could she trust herself anymore?

"Take your time," Sienna said in a quiet tone once they were seated in the cafeteria. "Just tell me what you remember and we'll work from that."

Closing her eyes, she pictured the woman's face.

"She was slender, had an oval-shaped face, a button-like nose, thin lips, hair cut in a dark brown bob. Although she could have been wearing a wig. Her complexion was slightly tanned. Dark brown eyes."

She glanced at the sketch the artist had been working on, studying it.

"She's tall," Ellie said. "And… her lips were a little thinner, eyes set slightly further apart."

By the time the artist was finished, Ellie was nodding her head. The sketch looked very much like the woman who'd claimed to be Kennedy Sledge.

She and Sienna returned to the hospital room, where the artist handed the drawing to Derrick. While he sent it to the Bureau, Ellie dialed the number she had for Kennedy Sledge, but it was dead.

Heart racing, she called Angelica.

"Hello, Detective. I was just about to call you. My boss wants me to run human-interest pieces on each of the victims and their families. We're putting it together now."

Ellie sighed. "I understand. If anyone remembers something useful, please keep me informed."

"Of course. You have information for me?" Angelica asked.

"I do." Ellie explained about Kennedy Sledge and the woman impersonating her.

"Oh, my goodness," Angelica said in a horrified voice.

"Don't reveal that to the public yet. Run the sketch I'm sending you on the news with the message that she is a person of interest in the Weekday Killer investigation."

"Got it. How do you think she's involved?" Angelica asked.

"This is just between you and me," Ellie said. "But she's either voluntarily working with the killer or he's forcing her to help."

CHAPTER 110

Somewhere on the AT

Shondra spit blood as her abductor swung his fist against her mouth. Her jaw cracked beneath the force, pain shooting through her cheek. He enjoyed making her suffer, his eyes alight with every blow.

Her body had to be black and blue. Every bone and muscle in her screamed with pain.

And she was still weak from when he'd drawn the blood. Tubes and tubes of it. What did he want it for?

"Coward," she snapped. "Take off that damn ski mask and show your face."

"I'll show you who's a coward," he growled as he yanked her by the hair and slammed her head against the wall. "I'm the strong one. You want to live, beg for your life."

Shondra forced herself not to cower from him. She refused to beg. That had only enraged her old man more.

"That was a mistake." He hauled her out of the cage and toward the steps.

"Men like you think they have to prove their power by using brute force," Shondra spat. "Real men don't need to do that."

"Real men have to teach their women how to behave," he said. "But you and Ellie never learned that lesson."

Oh, God, Ellie. She was Shondra's only chance at survival. She would search for her, Shondra knew it. She wouldn't give up either, just like she hadn't given up when those little girls went missing.

"Ellie is better than you," she said with a challenging lift of her chin.

"She will fucking learn she's not, just like you will." With an animal-like rage, he landed another blow to the side of her face. "Now get down on your knees and beg like a dog."

Shondra's head was spinning. Blood gushed from her nose and cheek, and she tasted it in her mouth. Her body was so sore she couldn't tell where one ache ended and the other one began.

Jerking her by the hair again, he tightened the dog collar around her neck, forcing her on all fours. "Beg."

Her tears were flowing freely now, and she coughed up blood as he shoved her face to the floor, setting his foot on the back of her neck. "Beg."

Closing her eyes, Shondra willed herself to be strong, but he'd already attached chains to her wrists, tightening them so she couldn't claw at him. A sob wrenched from her gut as he stomped on her neck and then she crumpled to the cold cement floor, curled into the pain.

"You will," he shouted. "You will beg. Or you will die today and, unlike the others, no one will ever find you."

CHAPTER 111

Saturday

Bluff County Hospital

The next morning Kennedy Sledge still showed no sign of coming to.

The doctor warned them that her physical injuries coupled with the trauma were severe, and they had to be patient. But it was damn hard to be patient when another woman's life—and countless others—depended on you.

"I talked to Captain Hale," Derrick said. "He said that office was empty, cleaned out as if no one had ever been there."

"It was all bogus," Ellie said bitterly.

Derrick nodded. "The crime scene team is going over it."

Heading to the cafeteria, Derrick brought them back sandwiches, and they ate and waited some more. Ellie didn't have an appetite but she knew she needed her strength, so she forced the food down, barely tasting the turkey sandwich. Flipping on the TV to see the news, they exchanged grim looks.

Angelica Gomez stood with the sheriff, giving her usual lead-in. "*Folks, four women have died at the hands of the Weekday Killer so far, and he's still out there hunting.*"

"She's stirring panic," Derrick said, his jaw clenched.

"She's just reporting the truth," Ellie replied. "Those people lost loved ones, young women with their lives ahead of them, all because of me. And I haven't done a damn thing to stop him."

"Those people lost their loved ones because a crazed psycho is murdering women, Ellie. The blame goes on him, not you."

Ellie shook her head. Logically that was true, but the killer targeted her with his messages for a reason. He took her friend for a reason too.

"*Sheriff Waters, do you have an update on the Weekday Killer investigation?*"

Ellie knotted her hands in her laps as Bryce addressed the mic. "*Yes, I do.*" One by one, he put a name to the women's faces as photographs appeared on the screen.

"*Do you have a suspect?*" Angelica asked.

"*At the moment, we are working several theories and have two persons of interest. But we can use your help out there, folks. This killer is leaving his victims on the Appalachian Trail in a ritualistic manner. If you have any idea who he is or see anyone suspicious in town or while hiking or camping, please call the sheriff's office immediately.*"

As Bryce started to walk away, Angelica stopped him. "*One more thing, Sheriff. I received a copy of this sketch with information that this woman is wanted for questioning in the murders. Can you tell us more about her?*"

A muscle in Bryce's cheek twitched, and Ellie realized he would have her head for not informing him first. "*I have no statement regarding her at this time.*"

Fury snapped in his eyes as he clicked his boots and turned and strode back into the sheriff's office.

"He's pissed," Derrick muttered.

Let him be.

Just then, Ellie's phone dinged and she stared at the screen in horror. It was a picture of Shondra, deathly pale, her ebony hair spread across her shoulders as she lay on a bed of daffodils in a grove of cypress trees, bramble wrapped around her throat.

CHAPTER 112

Derrick's gut clenched. "What's wrong?"

"I just got this." Ellie's hand trembled as she lifted her phone, but it slid from her hand and hit the floor.

He wanted to reach for her but grabbed the phone, looking at it first. With Vinny dead and ruled out as a suspect, Finton could be the killer.

His stomach plummeted when he saw the photo—they were too late for the deputy.

Pressing her fist to her mouth, Ellie stifled a sob. Unable to stop himself, Derrick wrapped his arms around her. She trembled, clutching his shirt and crying into his chest. They sat like that for several minutes, absorbing the news and settling into the shock.

Ellie didn't deserve to be tormented like this. She was estranged from her family and guilt-ridden over all the girls' deaths. Her family was torn apart and she might lose her mother. And now Shondra, her friend. Anger took root in his soul.

"Poor Shondra," Ellie murmured. "And Melissa. Oh, God, oh, God, oh, God. How am I going to tell her?"

"We aren't telling her anything yet." Derrick studied the picture while Ellie lifted her head and wiped at her eyes. "I know it's difficult to look at, but can you tell where this is?"

Her erratic breathing punctuated the air as she struggled to pull herself together. Finally, she gripped the phone with quivering fingers, narrowing her eyes as she analyzed the scene.

"Do you recognize any landmarks?" Derrick asked.

Wiping at her eyes, Ellie took a closer look. "Those cypress trees. They seem familiar."

"Keep thinking about it," he said. "My partner just texted that Finton's truck was spotted. I'm going to track him down."

Ellie eased away from him and stood, looking at Kennedy Sledge as if debating what to do.

Derrick shook his head. "Stay here with her. She might be the answer to all this, Ellie."

"I have an idea," Ellie replied. "Why don't we release information that we found a surviving victim?"

"Then he might come after her."

"Exactly," Ellie said. "I can take her place and wait and when he comes after her, grab him."

"No, Ellie, that's too dangerous," Derrick replied, his eyes darkening.

"But it might work," Ellie argued.

"I am not letting you use yourself as bait," he said. "Look what happened last time you pulled that stunt. You were almost buried alive. Stay here and don't do anything stupid, like going off on your own."

Ellie lifted a brow in challenge.

"I mean it, Ellie. I'll call a guard for Ms. Sledge's room. For both of you."

His gut was screaming at him—Ellie might be the killer's next target.

CHAPTER 113

Rose Hill

Eula Ann clamped her hands over her ears to drown out the sobs of the latest young women who'd died. Terrible, gut wrenching wails that cut through the air like knives cracking glass.

Just like the little girls, the victims of the Weekday Killer were finding their way among the dead. Trapped between two worlds where peace could not be found, they huddled together, writhing in pain and shock.

In her mind, she saw the blood trickling down pale, slender throats, mouths opened in screams of horror, eyes flashing with the lives they were meant to have, the lives that were stolen from them.

Yes, some were sinners. Yet weren't we all?

She knew all about sinning herself. About crossing the line and keeping secrets.

Out on the mountain, she saw the clouds darkening and rumbling across the skies. The creek was overflowing and the trail was due for more bad weather, tornadoes closing in.

Cold air and hot air melded together, blending with the anger of the Gods, funnel clouds forming. Gray skies and bare trees that should be blooming by now cast a gloom over the wilderness.

A killer roamed the mountains. Sometimes, in her mind, she heard his feet snapping tree limbs and twigs as he dragged a body through woods and ridges. One night she heard the slosh of creek water on the bank as he tromped through it.

She stared out into the forest, willing God to let her see his face. To hear his voice. To recognize the killer among them.

But she saw nothing. God's punishment to her for her sins.

So be it. She'd long accepted her fate.

Once again, Ellie Reeves was steeped in the investigation. Trouble and death seemed to follow that girl everywhere, and Eula felt a strong connection to her.

She knotted her gnarled fingers together as yellow daffodil petals floated in the air toward her like little drops of honey in the wind—except these petals symbolized nothing but death. A cluster landed on her rose bushes, the bright sunny yellow contrasting with the blood-red roses.

A sign of evil. An evil that she feared would get Ellie Reeves in the end.

CHAPTER 114

Cord twisted his hands together, silently cursing himself for ever befriending Ellie. He couldn't help but think about the call he'd gotten when he was at the Reflection Pond with Ellie and they'd found the first victim. The call from Roy.

"You're not a hero, McClain," his foster brother Roy had said. "Someday everyone will know it."

Cord ran his hand through his hair. If Roy Finton was killing women to get back at him, their deaths were on him.

Ellie was the only good thing that had ever been in his life. He'd never told her that, and he didn't intend to put that weight on her, but if something happened to her because of him or his past, he'd never forgive himself.

He sank onto the cell cot, knowing that Waters enjoyed seeing him locked away. Ellie seemed oblivious, but he suspected Bryce wanted her for himself. No matter he acted like a bastard. He was a control freak, a man who used his power over women. The fact that Ellie hadn't fallen at his feet with admiration rankled Bryce's pride.

Memories of Roy and his foster father's perversions slammed into him. Roy was a year older than him and already entrenched in his father's sick ways when Cord had come to live with them. Before then, Cord had been tossed from one place to another, dragging his hand-me-down clothes and too-small shoes in a trash bag just like the one his mother had abandoned him in when he was a baby. She'd thrown him out like garbage, starting a pattern that had lasted his whole life until he'd been released from juvie. He'd lived on his own ever since, chasing his own demons.

The first night he'd been at the Fintons he'd heard Roy and his father laughing as they defiled a young woman's body. He'd hidden in the corner behind a curtain and watched, biting his tongue until it bled, as Felix crawled on top of the woman and ran his tongue over her. His foster father had stripped his pants, grunting as he'd humped her. Then he'd invited Roy to join them. "Go ahead, son. Have fun. This one can't fight back."

Nausea rose in Cord's throat, and he choked back the need to vomit as the images played in his mind.

He'd tried to tell Roy's mother, but she was too deep in the bottle to know or care what was going on.

He'd run to the social worker to tell her the next day. But she'd told him to behave, that he was lucky the Fintons had taken him in, since no one else wanted him.

What the Fintons really wanted was free labor to help prepare the dead and keep their disgusting secrets. There was no love for Cord in that home—only trauma.

He studied the scars on his hands. He'd let the rage and beatings get to him. Done unforgiveable things.

Maybe he deserved to rot in here after all.

CHAPTER 115

Crooked Creek

Ellie waited until the guard arrived to watch Kennedy Sledge, then drove to the jail to talk to Cord. No matter what Derrick said, she had to find Shondra. There was no way she'd leave her on the trail, out in the elements. Her heart skipped a beat at what state she would find her friend in, but she steeled herself for the worst with a sinking stomach.

When she arrived at the station, Bryce was nowhere to be found. According to his receptionist he'd gone to question Valerie Patterson's neighbors. At least he was working and not at Haints scarfing down shots of whiskey.

"I need to talk to Ranger McClain," she said. "He might have information about where another victim was left."

The receptionist pinched her face. "I hope you find this creep. My daughter is the same age as the women he's taking, and I'm a nervous wreck."

"I understand," Ellie replied. "I'm doing everything possible. Just tell your daughter to stay home or be with a friend at all times until we catch him."

She pushed through the double doors, making her way to the cells. Her breath stalled in her chest at the sight of Cord staring at the ceiling from that single cot. The cell was dimly lit, and the concrete walls and floors reeked of sweat and urine.

He'd been mistreated as a kid, and now he was locked up for a crime he hadn't committed. She had to do something about that. Make things right.

She'd failed so many times before, her gut twisting at the thought of Shondra, but she wouldn't let down another friend.

Approaching slowly, Ellie met his gaze as he turned his head to face her. Seeing it was her, he sat up, but his rigid posture was defensive.

How could she blame him?

"Hey," she said softly.

"Hey."

She released a breath, aching to comfort him.

"I need your help."

He stood and walked over to the door, then gripped the cell bars. "I told you everything already. Did you find Finton?"

"We went to his house and found evidence. You were right. He's seriously into necrophilia. But at the moment, he's in the wind. Agent Fox may have a lead and has gone to check it out."

A sliver of relief flitted through his grey eyes, but it disappeared as quickly as it had come.

"Cord," she said, her voice breaking as she pulled her phone. "I think he killed Shondra."

Anger flashed across his chiseled face. "You found her?"

"No, but he sent me this." She showed him the photograph and saw him grimace.

"I'm sorry, El. Really."

She nodded. The fact that Cord was in lockup when she'd received the picture should prove his innocence—unless Derrick continued to push Cord and Finton working as accomplices. "I can't leave her outside all alone in the elements."

They both knew that animals would ravage her body if they didn't recover her soon.

"I think I recognize those cypress trees," she said, pointing to the foliage on the hill where Shondra lay. "Do you know where they are?"

His brows creased. "You have your trail map with you?"

"Always," Ellie replied, reaching inside her jacket pocket.

Within seconds, Cord pinpointed an area for her to search. "The area is called Prayer Point. It's at Cypress Hill. That's the area where all the cypresses grow."

Prayer Point was also considered a reverent place, where people went to pray for others.

Friday's child is loving and giving. The location fit, but the perp's twisted sense of irony was way off. Shondra *was* loving and giving. "I have to go find her," Ellie said.

Cord caught her hand. "It's dangerous, Ellie. He may be waiting to ambush you."

Ellie hesitated. If it was up to her, she'd release Cord, but Bryce would have a fit.

She didn't give a damn though. She'd deal with the sheriff later. Besides, she could argue the fact that she'd received the text while Cord was in a cell. Even if Bryce argued that Finton had sent it, that the two were working together, she didn't believe it. Right now, Cord could lead her to the location faster than she could find it on her own. That was what mattered.

Decision made, she rushed to the front and snagged the keys to the cell.

"What are you doing?" the receptionist called after them.

"I need Ranger McClain's help. Tell the sheriff he's in my custody."

CHAPTER 116

Cypress Hill

"Are you sure you know what you're doing?" Cord asked, a half hour later, as she parked at the Approach Trail to hike up to the hill.

"No, but we don't have time to waste and who gives a flying fuck what Bryce thinks?"

Her comment earned a smile from Cord.

Despite her bravado, she was pretty sure Bryce would push for her suspension, and Derrick would believe she was covering for Cord. They'd order her not to set off into the woods with bad weather on the way. But she didn't have time to worry about their opinions. The ranger was her best bet at finding Shondra. That was what counted, she reassured herself as the trees shook violently in the wind, the threat of a tornado becoming more and more real.

"Why would he leave her in the midst of cypress trees?" Ellie asked.

"The dark green leaves of the cypress represent resurrection and immortality. The elongated form gives the appearance of—"

"Fingers pointing towards heaven," Ellie finished. "My father brought me here when one of the kids at high school died suddenly. I was so angry because she'd been hit by a drunk driver, but Dad said we had to pray for everyone."

What little sun had trickled through the cloud disappeared into the distance. Shadows flickered through the narrow paths between the endless rows of pines, oaks, and cypresses in the woods.

With the storm coming, the temperature felt colder here, the air danker, the sounds of the wild more prominent. Eyes peeled for trouble, they made their way into the woods in silence, picking up the pace as the swirling storm clouds gathered above the sharp ridges. The sound of falling rock echoed ahead, and water trickled down the side of the mountain wall.

They stopped briefly to check the map and note identifying markers along the way, Ellie using a compass to guide her.

Four miles in, Cord led her onto a shortcut heading west. They crossed an overflowing part of the creek that had demolished the foliage on the bank. The cloying scent of rotting vegetation filled the air, and the ground was slippery underfoot.

"Don't look down," Cord muttered as they reached a flimsy swinging bridge made of rope and board. Carefully, Ellie eased onto it, testing the fraying rope and carefully stepping over missing boards. She held her breath as she crept across it, and she didn't have to look down to know that if she fell, she'd plunge headfirst into a rocky ravine.

The bridge swayed back and forth, making her dizzy, and she clutched the ropes to steady her footing. When they both made it over, they paused to catch their breaths then take a quick sip of water. Together they hacked away the dense foliage and kept climbing until they reached the summit near the falls. Ellie's pulse raced again as they clambered over stumps, through briar patches, and along a narrow ridge.

As her foot hit a tree root, she nearly stumbled. Cord grabbed her arm and steadied her as they breathlessly crossed the next section. Up another punishing hill, around a steep curve, and… finally she saw the cypresses.

Her calf muscles strained as she raced up the hill, her heart pounding. Suddenly, the daffodils came into view.

Swallowing hard, Ellie bolted into a sprint and headed toward them.

CHAPTER 117

Bear Mountain

Derrick spotted the pick-up truck in the parking lot of a cheap motel on Bear Mountain.

The motel backed up to the forest, and the jagged mountain ridges rose behind it, trees swaying and dipping in the wind. Trash was being tossed across the tumbledown parking lot.

After Angelica's newscast, Finton had to know that the police were looking for him.

Slowing, Derrick pulled into a space in front of the lobby. He inched his way along the front of the row of rooms. Judging from the dark interiors and lack of cars, many were empty. Lights were on in three units, but the vans, SUVs and noises inside indicated families, one with a barking dog.

Finton's truck was parked in front of the last room. Derrick pulled his weapon as he reached the door, pausing to listen. Inside he heard footsteps pacing, then something crash.

The curtain was closed, blocking his view of the interior, and he raised his hand to knock, shouting, "FBI, Finton. Open up!"

The footsteps inside ceased, then something banged against the door. Stepping back, Derrick called out again. "Open up, Finton. FBI."

He twisted the doorknob, but it was locked. There was more noise inside and Derrick raised his foot, kicking at the door. Once, twice, then he slammed his body against it and the door burst open. Inside, he nearly tripped over an overturned chair on the floor.

Angry, he shoved it aside and spotted Finton's back as he dashed through the room.

He looked bigger in person than the photo from the website, his broad body covered in a dark jacket and black pants, and his hair peeked out from beneath a black ski cap.

"Stop, Finton, or I'll shoot." Sprinting toward him, he jumped over the desk, which Finton had thrown into his path. Finton was already climbing out the back window.

Derrick caught the man's leg. Finton kicked out but was dragged back inside and thrown on the floor. Wild-eyed, Finton threw a punch at Derrick, but the FBI agent dodged the blow and pressed his boot into the man's chest, holding him down as he aimed the gun at the suspect's head.

"Move again and this bullet will hit home."

Grabbing his handcuffs, Derrick rolled the man over and snapped them on.

"I didn't do anything," Finton said.

"You defiled the corpses you were supposed to treat reverently. Then you became so obsessed with the dead, you decided to find out what it was like to watch them die, and you killed several women," Derrick snarled. "I wouldn't call that nothing."

Eyes widening in horror, Finton spit out a protest. "I want a lawyer."

Derrick yanked him up and formally arrested him. He'd take him to the station and then he'd make him talk. Maybe by the time they got there, the monster would realize he had no other choice.

As Derrick was pushing a handcuffed Finton in the back seat of his car, his phone rang.

"Special Agent Fox."

"Is Ellie with you?"

The sheriff's voice sounded angry, accusatory.

"No, I tracked down Finton's truck at a motel on Bear Mountain. I'm about to bring him in. Why?"

"Because she fucking let McClain out of jail and took him with her to look for Shondra."

"What?" Derrick's temper flared, and he glanced back at Finton, who sneered at him. "Finton and Cord might be working together."

"You're preaching to the choir, Fox. I'm going to suggest Hale fire her ass when she gets back."

So the sheriff was more enraged that she'd defied him than he was worried about her safety. Why did that not surprise him?

"Do you know where they are, Waters?"

"No, Ellie has a habit of going off on her own."

He wanted to shake Ellie. Couldn't she see that Cord was dangerous? If he was working with Finton, he could be leading Ellie to her death.

CHAPTER 118

Prayer Point

Ellie braced herself to see her friend murdered on the bed of daffodils.

But as she jogged over the crest of the hill, she halted, her heart jumping out of her chest. There was a young woman lying on the flowers, bramble wrapped around her slashed throat, her hands folded in prayer, her shocked death gaze angled toward the cypresses as if she was looking up at heaven. She wore a silk pink blouse, a black pencil skirt, and garish makeup—the MO was the same.

"It's not Shondra," Cord said in a raspy voice.

"No." Relief slammed into her, followed by a wave of grief for the woman—and dread at notifying the victim's mother. "It's Maude Hazelnut's granddaughter, Honey Victoria." *Does Maude even know she's missing?*

Needing a closer look, Ellie walked toward the once perky blonde with pale blue eyes who was the light of Maude's life.

If the killer stuck to his pattern, it meant he didn't perceive Honey as being loving and giving. Vera had once referred to Honey as a "gold-digger" telling Randall that the young woman had let her children run riot at the country club because she was too busy talking to the pool boy.

Ellie had merely rolled her eyes at her mother's gossiping. She knew little about Honey, other than that she was married to an older, wealthy businessman. More than enough to set tongues wagging behind the back of arch-gossiper Meddlin' Maude, Honey's comfortable lifestyle could make her Saturday's child in the killer's eyes—who according to the rhyme "works hard for a living".

"Call it in," Ellie told Cord as she checked out the area. It was quiet, with no hint of anyone nearby. Just the sound of the wind gaining momentum as it roared through the tunnel of trees.

Circling to the other side of the body, she stooped down to examine her more closely, noticing thick bruises around her neck. It definitely looked like the bruises were made from a dog collar, deeper and more pronounced than the previous victims. Derrick's theory about the dog abuser or trainer could be right, and the hair he'd found at the chicken houses had been blonde. Did it belong to Honey?

CHAPTER 119

Bear Mountain

Derrick usually played by the rulebook, as emotions could compromise a case.

But his patience was wearing thin. Ellie's life—Shondra's and God knew how many more women's—depended on him catching the serial killer.

And out here in the middle of nowhere, he had a reprieve from prying eyes. For once, he wanted to take advantage of that.

He pulled Finton back out the car and shoved him up against it. He raised his weapon again, aiming it between the man's beady eyes. "Where's Deputy Eastwood?"

"Who?" Finton feigned an innocent look.

Derrick grabbed him by the collar. "Deputy Shondra Eastwood. She's been missing for days. The Weekday Killer has her, and I believe that's you. I know about your past. About you and your daddy and your sick perversions, how you play with the dead."

Finton went still, radiating a depravity that made Derrick's skin crawl.

"We searched your house and your funeral home and found photos of your activities," Derrick said. "You're going to jail for that. But I want to know what you've done with Shondra."

"I didn't do anything to that cop."

Derrick gripped the man's collar so tightly it cut into his neck and he coughed for air. "The jury might go easy if you stop this nightmare and cooperate."

"I didn't kill nobody," Finton said, baring his teeth in a sneer. "And I don't know where that bitch is."

"I don't believe you. I know about your father and about Cord McClain. The Weekday Killer dresses the victims as if preparing them for their funerals, putting makeup on them and sewing their lips closed." Derrick tightened his finger on the trigger. "That sounds exactly like something a mortician would do. I just want to know if you did it alone or if you and McClain are partners."

"I told you, I didn't kill anyone. I like to play with the bodies afterwards, but that's it." Finton scratched at his face, and Derrick noticed scars pockmarking his skin. The guy was probably a meth addict. "I haven't seen that chickenshit McClain in years," he spat. "But my father disappeared a few months after Cord left, and I think he killed him. So, if you're looking for a murderer, talk to McClain."

Derrick released a heavy breath. Finton was trying to change the tune of the questioning, but he wasn't buying the diversion tactic. "If you thought he killed your father, why didn't you go to the police?"

"Because I had no proof." Finton's jaw clamped so tight the veins in his neck bulged.

"Or maybe you figured your daddy just ran off." Derrick let out a sound of disgust. "And you knew if you did go to the cops, they'd investigate and find out what you and your father were doing with the bodies you were meant to take care of."

"Those people were already dead," Finton hissed.

"Those people had loved ones and they deserved to be treated with dignity." Derrick ran his hands over Finton's clothing. Inside his right pocket, he found keys to his vehicle, but no other keys that might belong to wherever he was holding Shondra.

Maybe the ride to the police station would change his mind. But first he'd let him stew in the car while a crime scene team searched the hotel room.

He locked Finton in the car and made the call, then paced beside the vehicle, waiting while the storm picked up speed. Gray clouds swirled and drifted together forming mountain-like funnels above the trees, threatening to rip them from the ground.

Worry for Ellie mounted in his gut. Had McClain killed Felix Finton? If so, had that whetted his appetite for murder?

He called Ellie, but it went straight to answerphone.

"Ellie," he said when the beep sounded. "Call me as soon as you get this and let me know where you are. I have Finton, but he may be working with McClain. Be careful. Finton claims McClain killed his father."

CHAPTER 120

Somewhere on the AT

Fuck, fuck, fuck, fuck. Everything had gotten messed up. The days of the week were off. It started when that stupid woman escaped and he'd had to kill another one in her place.

Not the seven he planned. Then there was the deputy and detective.

The cops were all over the mountain. Everyone was looking. Although he liked that reporter Angelica Gomez for making him famous.

He'd thought about taking her. She was another ball buster. Another one who needed to be tamed. But he'd decided she'd be more useful making sure the whole world knew his name.

That pretty little Honey was perfect though. She'd gotten what she deserved. And she had been so weak she'd folded like an accordion.

They'd already found her and now it was time to move on. He'd show the detective that she couldn't stop him.

CHAPTER 121

Prayer Point

As she watched the crime scene team search the area, Ellie checked her phone. Another text came through.

I told you that you'd pay for what you did to me.

Her breath caught in her chest. The comment sounded familiar, stirring some sort of memory from the recesses of her mind. She tried to wrack her brain to remember exactly where she'd heard it before.

"What's wrong?" Cord asked.

Ellie hesitated before telling him about the message. "Sounds personal, Ellie. Who did you piss off bad enough to do this?"

"I don't know. There are plenty of meth dealers I arrested. But this type of planning doesn't fit with them."

Looking back at her phone, she listened to the voicemail messages.

The first one was her captain. "*Ellie, what the fuck has gotten into you? Bryce wants you fired for disobeying orders and letting McClain out. I don't know if I can save your ass this time. Get McClain back here right now.*"

Ellie quickly called him back. "I'll be on my way soon, Captain, but we found another victim. She's local, Honey Victoria."

"Jesus," Captain Hale muttered. "Maude is going to fall apart. She doted on that girl."

"I know."

"I'll make the notification."

Ellie thanked him, then clicked to listen to a message from Derrick.

His warning about Cord killing Finton made her uneasy. Not because she was afraid of the ranger, but because she'd seen the pain in his eyes when he'd talked about his past. The evidence was stacking against him, pointing to him and Finton being in cahoots.

And if Finton wasn't the Weekday Killer or acting alone, they were back to square one, with no suspect. What were they missing?

"Agent Fox found Roy Finton and arrested him," she told Cord. "He denies being the Weekday Killer."

"Did you really think he'd confess?" Cord asked gruffly.

"No, but I was hoping. Shondra still needs us to find her." She inhaled sharply. "Cord, the sheriff and Agent Fox think you're working with Finton, covering for each other."

"Is that what *you* think?"

"I don't know what to think," she admitted. "The evidence points to both of you. It also pointed to Hiram and a man Hiram met in the psych hospital. I feel like the killer is some kind of puppeteer, pulling strings and sending all of us running and pointing fingers at each other." And making her doubt everyone.

"Roy Finton could have framed me, although I don't see how he'd know about all the other things."

"The Ghost case has been all over the news," Ellie said, thinking. *And there was the therapist he'd used to get information.*

"Where's Finton now?" Cord's voice was gruff, his look puzzled.

"Being booked at the sheriff's office." Ellie hesitated, before clearing her throat. "Cord, do you have any idea what happened to Felix Finton?"

Cord's eyes darkened and he exhaled through gritted teeth. Then he gave a small shake of his head. "When I was sent away, I never looked back. Why?"

"I'm just looking for the truth." Ellie kept a cool face, studying him for a reaction. "Cord, Roy Finton accused you of killing his father."

Cord went still, then angled his head, staring at the thickening gray clouds above them.

He said nothing, which left Ellie wondering why exactly he was lying to her.

CHAPTER 122

Crooked Creek

"I'm sorry, Cord, but Captain Hale ordered me to bring you here. Finton is being held at the sheriff's office, and we want to keep you separate."

"I understand." The ranger looked resigned, his expression grave. "I didn't mean to get you in trouble."

"You didn't. I made my choice. I needed you. Thank you for leading me to Prayer Point."

Ellie's stomach clenched as Captain Hale pounced on her.

"The sheriff is livid, Ellie, and Maude is a wreck."

"I'm sorry," she replied. While she didn't care for Maude, she would never wish this type of tragedy on anyone. "He still has Shondra, Captain." She explained about the text she'd received. "I'm beginning to think this all centers around me, around someone who perceives I've done them wrong."

The captain rubbed his balding head. "We've exhausted the list of protestors, and I've been looking through your arrests. No one fits the profile of this guy. Can you think of anyone?"

Bryce's face flitted through her mind. They'd been adversarial for years. He liked the attention of being sheriff, enjoyed the notoriety. That part of his personality fit. But he wasn't a killer.

Just then Deputy Landrum appeared, his expression lit. "I found links from the other victims to Kennedy Sledge. They all joined an online group therapy chat too."

Disgust ate at Ellie. The impostor had encouraged her to join that group. "That's how he knew details about them," Ellie said. "They spilled their thoughts and feelings to the fraud therapist and each other, and he was watching and listening."

"Who knew you were seeing a therapist?" Captain Hale asked.

Ellie chewed her bottom lip, thinking. She didn't want to break Shondra's trust, but if it helped save her life, she had to be truthful. "Just Shondra. She suggested Kennedy Sledge." Then something else struck her. As she'd left Haints that night with Shondra, she'd seen Bryce watching them closely. Had he overheard them talking about the therapist?

Meanwhile, the captain was scrutinizing Cord. He'd worked with the ranger enough times that surely he couldn't believe the accusations against him, Ellie hoped.

"I'll take care of McClain. Go home and get some rest," said the captain.

But there was no way she could rest tonight. "I'm going to the sheriff's office. If Finton wants to hurt me, maybe seeing me in person will trigger him to talk."

Cord's eyes darkened. "Be careful, Ellie. He's sadistic."

"I've seen what he can do. He doesn't scare me."

"Go home, Ellie," Captain Hale said more forcefully. "Best if you avoid the sheriff right now."

Anger rippled through her, but the captain's look warned her not to argue.

Still, she couldn't sit on her ass and do nothing while Shondra was still missing.

That latest message from the killer echoed in her head. *I told you that you'd pay for what you did to me.*

A memory tickled her conscious. Back in high school, all those years ago, Bryce had been high from scoring the winning goal at a football game. He'd cornered Ellie as she started to leave, asking for a celebratory kiss. Her refusal, coupled with the beers he'd just consumed with his buddies behind the bleachers, had spiked his temper and he'd gotten aggressive. He'd pushed her into the back seat and reached for her shirt. Said he knew she had a crush on him, that he wanted to be her first.

Furious at him, she'd kneed him in the groin, shoved him from the seat onto the ground, then jumped in the car and taken off.

She'd never told anyone. But he'd bragged that he'd screwed her after the game, the rumor spreading around school. Then his buddies had started coming onto her. She'd had to teach Bryce a lesson after that—she knew she couldn't let him get away with it, do the same to other girls. She'd tricked him into meeting her behind the bleachers and told him he was right, that she'd had a crush on him for years.

Once she got him naked, she'd used the rope-tying skills her father taught her and tied him to the bleachers. At first, he'd laughed, thinking she was playing some kind of kinky game.

Then she'd walked away.

"You can't leave me like this, Ellie!" he'd shouted. "Come back here!"

But she'd kept walking. She'd seen his friends nearby and told them Bryce was looking for them, pointing them to where he was tied up.

The next day, he had been the butt of everyone's jokes. After school, he'd been waiting at her car. "You'll pay for what you did to me," he'd snarled. "You will pay, Ellie."

Ellie shook her head as she contemplated the possibility that he was the Weekday Killer. He'd made no bones about the fact that he'd get revenge on her one day. Had butted heads with her after they both came back to Bluff County to work. He'd been upset at her lack of support over her father's endorsement as sheriff.

He and Shondra had words, and Shondra had threatened to file charges against him. And then there was the smug look he'd given her when he'd made his victory address to the locals.

There was no doubt that Bryce was narcissistic, and thought men were superior to women. With his job and experience, he'd know how to commit a crime without leaving evidence. He knew she was close to Cord, and if he'd hacked into Sledge's files or convinced an impostor to pose as a therapist, he could have listened to her sessions. He also knew the Appalachian Trail and could have easily planted evidence.

Hand trembling, she started to turn back and tell her boss, but Captain Hale's warning taunted her. *Best if you avoid the sheriff right now.*

How could she tell him that she suspected their very own sheriff might be the monster they were looking for?

CHAPTER 123

Ellie cornered Deputy Landrum before she left. Bryce had questioned Carrie Winters' clients and coworkers at the gentlemen's club, but she hadn't seen a list of their names.

"Deputy Landrum, did you ever see the list of Carrie Winters' clients at the Men's Den?"

"I saw the sheriff's, but then Fox's partner sent a list over, too. I haven't looked at it yet." He frowned, then clicked a few keys on his computer. "Here it is."

"Let me see."

Ellie claimed the chair beside him and skimmed it, searching the names. "Some of these look fake," she said.

Heath nodded. "These men value their privacy."

"See if you can connect any of them with the Ole Glory Church." She combed the list again, and she zeroed in on the seventh name—Rocky Henry. Her heart stuttered.

Rocky was the nickname Bryce had in high school, because he was obsessed with the films, and Henry was his middle name.

Her fingers curled around the edge of the desk. Bryce was one of Carrie Winters' clients. No wonder he'd volunteered to question the people at the Men's Den. And he'd intentionally failed to mention that he knew the victim.

Nerves tightened her neck, and she knew that she needed proof first before telling the deputy or her captain. If the sheriff was the perp they were looking for, it would be difficult to take him down. She needed to share her theory with someone, though, so she called Derrick on the drive home. She got his voicemail and left a message.

The scent of death and her own sweat from the hike lingered on Ellie's skin, so she decided to grab a quick shower before she confronted Bryce. It was better to question him at his office rather than at Haints, where he was probably deep in a beer and burger. By the time she made it there, Derrick could meet her and provide back up.

Running on adrenaline, she hurried up to her front door. Thunder crackled and popped overhead, the sky darkening by the second. The wind caught her hair, tearing it from her ponytail, smothering in her face.

Ellie glanced around but nothing seemed amiss, yet she couldn't shake off the sense that someone was out there in the woods watching her.

Hunching inside her jacket against the wind, she shined her flashlight on the porch to see if the killer had left her another present.

She was getting royally pissed at his game. But there was nothing this time.

Flipping on every light in the house, she swept the rooms, breathing a sigh of relief that there was no one inside.

Stripping her clothes, she stepped into the shower, mentally sorting what she would say to Bryce. Before all their trouble at high school, when it had all gone so wrong, she'd known him as a kid, had ridden bikes with him on the trail and built forts in the woods. She tried to recall a time when she'd seen him be violent. One time they'd found a deer that had been shot at Rattlesnake Ridge and he'd run and gotten his father's shotgun, telling her they had to keep the animal from suffering. She'd sworn tears had blurred his eyes when he'd shot the deer to put it out of its misery. That didn't align with the killer on the loose, did it?

Scrubbing her skin raw with soap, she was desperate to erase the images of the Weekday Killer from her mind. But they punished her, screaming that Shondra would be next.

She had to think. Criminals who fit the profile typically had a history of abuse—by a parent, family member or even a coach.

Bryce's father was the mayor, and as kids, she'd never seen anything to suggest Mayor Waters was abusing him. No bruises or cuts. No whispers in their small-town community about it. And his mother had doted on him, thought he hung the moon.

Somewhat calmed by the thought, she stepped from the shower and grabbed a towel.

After drying off, she padded to her closet to snag some clean clothes. The light was off inside, and she flipped the switch, but it didn't come on.

Suddenly all the lights in the house flickered off, goose bumps erupting on her skin.

Ellie froze, pulse pounding as darkness engulfed her. Panic clawed at her. Her heart rushed to her throat.

You're safe, she told herself.

Although her senses warned her she was not.

Outside, the wind snapped branches off. Something scraped the window, and the floor groaned.

Her gun. She'd left it on the nightstand.

Easing backward, she turned to grab it, but in the darkness, someone pounced on her from behind. She clawed for the pistol but knocked the lamp over instead. He dragged her backward, and she flailed and yanked at the bedding, anything to slow him down. But he wrapped his arm around her neck in a chokehold, cutting off her oxygen. Struggling to wrench his hands from her neck, she swung her elbow back to jab him in the torso. He grunted slightly, tightening his hold. His breath brushed her ear. It was warm and sticky, making her shiver in disgust.

"Too late, Ellie. I told you that you'd pay."

A second later, the sharp sting of a needle pierced her skin and the world faded into oblivion.

CHAPTER 124

Stony Gap

Finton banged on the glass window of Derrick's car as Derrick parked at the sheriff's office. Before he headed inside, he checked his messages. His heart thundered as he listened to Ellie's. She suspected the sheriff of the crimes? Seriously?

Confusion rippled through him.

Bryce and Ellie definitely had some kind of tension between them, some kind of past. But that wasn't enough to drive him to murder—surely Ellie knew that?

Anxious and wanting to know more before he saw Waters, he stepped from the vehicle and called her number. The phone rang four times before going to voicemail. Trying three more times, he got the same result. "Call me as soon as you get this," he said through gritted teeth.

Praying Ellie was all right, he phoned Bennett. "Find out everything you can on Sheriff Bryce Waters. For some reason, Detective Reeves has suspicions about him. Any word from the lab on DNA under Dr. Sledge's nails?"

"No hits yet. But we'll keep running it."

Derrick hesitated, before carrying on. "Run it against the sheriff."

"You think Waters is the perp too?"

"I don't know. Just run it, okay."

"On it."

"And see what you can dig up on Felix Finton, Roy Finton's father. Roy claims McCord killed his old man. But there's history between the two of them so who knows if he's telling the truth or not? I'll push him for more after he's been in lockup for a while."

Bennett whistled. "A lot going on in that town."

"Tell me about it." And Ellie Reeves seemed to be at the center of it all.

CHAPTER 125

Somewhere on the AT

Ellie blinked furiously, struggling to see where she was. Panicked, she tried to move and failed. Her body was a dead weight. The sharp sting in her neck… he'd drugged her.

She'd lost time. Had been unconscious for a while. Had no idea if it was still night or morning.

A pungent odor inundated her, but she couldn't define the source. Fighting the fear threatening to consume her, she inhaled several deep breaths, forcing herself to focus.

At least she was still alive. But for how long? She opened her mouth to call out for her friend, but her voice died in her throat. How long would it take for the drug to wear off? She couldn't fight him if she couldn't move.

Closing her eyes, the message echoed in her head.

I told you that you'd pay for what you did to me.

She'd driven home, planned to confront Bryce.

But some bastard had jumped her from behind. His hands had been around her throat, his deep voice in her ear… the sting of the needle… then the world faded to black.

She hadn't seen his face and his voice… it was so low that she couldn't tell who it was. "Shondra," she tried again, but the sound was barely a croak.

CHAPTER 126

Stony Gap

"Where's Sheriff Waters?" Derrick asked the deputy on duty as he escorted an angry Finton into the sheriff's office.

"Probably at Haints grabbing a burger," the deputy said.

Wasn't he always? Derrick thought wryly.

He shoved Finton into an interrogation room, the mortician roaring for a lawyer.

"You're going to need one," Derrick said. "But think about it, Finton. We can work on a deal if you'll tell us where Deputy Eastwood is."

Tearing his gaze away from Derrick, Finton looked down at his clenched hands. "I told you I didn't do anything to her. Did McClain put you up to this?"

"We have enough to charge you and shut down your business for good," Derrick replied, ignoring the question. "If you want the chance to see the outside world again, you'd better start talking."

"I'm not going to confess to something I didn't do," Finton snarled. "Maybe McClain is the one killing women. He always had a weird side."

The animosity between the two men was obvious. Frankly, Derrick liked both of them for the crime, but he needed proof.

"Maybe the two of you did it together," Derrick suggested. "You're trying to cast suspicion on each other to confuse the case." But where did Waters fit into the picture?

"There's no way I'd help that asshole do anything. I'd like to see him hang," Finton replied, leaning back in the chair and barking a sarcastic laugh.

Derrick pinned him with a cool stare. "Then perhaps you framed him."

"I wish I'd thought of that." Finton's eyes flickered with a challenge. "But I didn't. Now, lawyer."

Pushing away his chair, Derrick stood. Moving around the table, he yanked Finton up by the arm. "All right then. Maybe some time in a cell will change your mind."

"My phone call," Finton shouted. "I want my phone call!"

"I'll see what I can do," Derrick said. "Right now, I have to try and save a woman's life."

CHAPTER 127

Bluff County Hospital

Kennedy Sledge's body throbbed, but she had to keep running.

Escape him.

The women's scream pierced her ears. Night after night she'd heard them cry. Heard him beating them. Dragging them from the cages and forcing them to beg.

He'd kept her for days. He said he might need her later, but he'd never said why.

Just like he'd kept Shondra. He'd beat her more than the others, saying he would break her, but the deputy was tough, refusing to beg.

The nameless women's eyes had pleaded with Kennedy to help her. The ones he called Cathy. He called them all Cathy—Monday, Tuesday, Wednesday, Thursday, Friday… She was supposed to be Friday's child. She could hear him chanting, "Friday's child is loving and giving…"

Tears flooded her face. She wanted to help them. That was what she did. But she'd been chained herself, deprived of light and food and water for days on end, so she was too weak to fight back. He'd made her listen to the other women's endless cries. To his sick voice murmuring that childhood rhyme.

Then he'd carried her into the woods and she'd known she would be next.

Tears trickled down her cheeks. She blinked, moaning as guilt seized her for leaving the others behind. She should have run back, tried to save Shondra…

But it was too late now. He'd chased her until she'd come to a ridge overlooking the river, the water crashing below. Then she'd thrown herself over. Death was better than going back to that hellhole.

She snapped her eyes open, her heart pounding. Where was she? Not in her bed. Not in the river.

Her body ached, her limbs felt weak and she could barely breathe for the sharp pain in her chest. Machines beeped. An oxygen tube was threaded through her nose. A cart clanged somewhere. And voices…

A hospital, she realized. She was in the hospital.

The nightmare… it was real. She'd been running from the man who'd abducted her. She'd dived into the river to get away from him—preferring to die than to face him.

Fear suffocated her, but she managed to claw at the bed and find the nurse's button. She had to talk to the police. She had to tell them what she knew.

CHAPTER 128

Haints Bar

Leaving Finton in the cell and the deputy on duty to watch him, Derrick went to Haints to talk to the sheriff. Just as he parked, he got a message that Kennedy Sledge had regained consciousness. The sheriff's car was in the lot.

A killer was on the loose, and he was sitting around drinking whiskey?

Fury made him clench his jaw as he strode into the crowded bar. Country music rocked the room while the scent of beer and fries permeated the air.

Even with the warning they'd issued to women in the area, a few had come to the cop bar, as if a ruthless serial killer wasn't out there.

At the bar, Bryce was chowing down on a burger and flirting with a young brunette. Derrick tapped him on the back.

"Sheriff, we need to talk."

Bryce looked annoyed.

"Where's Ellie?" Derrick demanded.

At the mention of Ellie's name, the woman seated next to him rose, carrying her drink to a table with two other women.

"I asked you a question, Sheriff. Where's Ellie?"

"How should I know? She doesn't exactly keep in touch or follow orders."

"I got a message from her after she found the latest victim. She said she was coming back to Stony Gap to confront you."

Bryce shoved his food away. "Confront me? Hell, I'm going to fire her ass for letting McClain out of jail against my orders."

"Don't fucking lie to me, Waters," said Derrick, gripping his arm. "If you did something to Ellie, then you'd better fess up."

"What does that mean? If I *did* something to Ellie?"

Derrick hated to play all his cards, but every minute counted. "She left me a message saying she liked you for the crimes. If you're the Weekday Killer, saving Ellie and the deputy will go toward leniency."

"Shit. You're serious, aren't you?" Bryce said, dropping his glass down so hard that beer sloshed over the sides.

"Dead serious," Derrick said. "The last thing she told me was that she was going to talk to you and now she's not answering her phone."

Outrage darkened Bryce's eyes. "That's absurd. I'm going to call your superior and tell him—"

"Tell him what? That Ellie suspected you for some reason? That you were drinking on the job while the rest of us were hunting for a serial killer? That you had a vendetta against the deputy and Ellie because you have an aversion to strong women?"

"You're way off base, Agent Fox. Way off."

"Then prove it."

"I don't have to prove anything to you."

"The hell you don't. Either come with me or I'm going to arrest you."

"You'll be sorry you said that," Bryce said.

"Come with me now or I'll handcuff you right here in front of everyone in this bar you like so much."

Bryce spit out another curse word, then tossed some cash on the bar and stood. He peeled Derrick's fingers from around his arm and led the way back outside.

"Give me your weapon," Derrick ordered when they reached the car.

"You'll regret this," Bryce snarled. But he lifted his service revolver, handing it over.

After checking the safety, Derrick gestured for Bryce to get in his car.

"Where are we going?" the sheriff snapped.

"To the hospital. Kennedy Sledge woke up."

CHAPTER 129

Bluff County Hospital

Derrick led the way into the hospital, a steaming Bryce by his side. On the way over, he'd asked the sheriff about the tension between him and Ellie, but Bryce had told him it was none of his business. Derrick had furtively recorded his voice to play to Kennedy Sledge, in case she could identify him.

As his mind churned over everything, Derrick thought about Ellie.

She'd damn well better be alive.

The doctor met them at Kennedy Sledge's room. Another young woman, who looked so much like Kennedy that she had to be her sister, sat beside the bed, stroking Kennedy's hand.

"How is she?" Derrick asked.

"Physically she's going to be fine," replied the doctor. "But she's suffered severe emotional trauma."

"Did she tell you what happened?"

The doctor shook her head. "Just that she was abducted, and she asked me to call the police." Derrick started forward, but the doctor touched his arm. "Be gentle, Agent Fox. Try not to upset her or push her. Let her talk in her own time."

Time was one thing they didn't have.

"The sheriff will stay here with you." He gestured to the guard they'd stationed at her door. There was no way he was taking him in if there was a chance that he was the abductor. "Don't go anywhere."

Bryce gave him a venomous look but leaned against the door-jamb as Derrick entered the room. At the sound of his footsteps, Kennedy opened her eyes, turning her head toward him.

Not wanting to frighten her, he approached slowly, stopping a few inches from her bedside and showing her his credentials.

"My name is Agent Derrick Fox. You're Kennedy Sledge, right?"

Light brown hair framed her oval face, and her pale, bruised features grew pinched. Then she gave a little nod.

The woman beside her looked up at him with imploring eyes then introduced herself as Lara, Kennedy's sister. "She's been through a lot, Agent Fox."

"I know, and I truly am sorry. But the man who hurt her may be holding at least one other woman now."

"It's okay," Kennedy told her sister gently. "I need to do this. Why don't you go get some coffee?"

"Are you sure?" her sister asked, looking skeptical.

"Yes." Kennedy squeezed her sister's hand. "I'll be fine."

Lara fidgeted with her purse and stood, but Derrick read the silent warning in her eyes. "I'll be back in a few minutes," she said before disappearing out the door.

"I'm sorry for what happened to you," Derrick said, again. "Do you feel like talking?"

She squeezed her eyes shut for a second, then opened them and took a breath. "No, but I need to. I know you're looking for the man who abducted me."

Derrick nodded. "What can you tell me about him?"

"He... was sick. He took other women and killed one each day," she said in a raw whisper. "He kept repeating this rhyme about Monday's child..."

"We believe that after he took you, he hacked into your files and your group therapy forum, and then used another woman to pose as you. She took on new clients."

Kennedy gasped. "And since I'm a solo practice, no one realized someone took over my office."

"That's how he chose his victims," Derrick finished, hating the pain on her face. "He even changed the photograph of you and set up a fake profile for the impostor."

Everything looked professional enough to fool even Ellie.

Her eyes widened in horror. "I can't believe a woman helped him. Although…"

"Although what?"

"I knew there were other women there. I never saw them, but I heard them crying."

"Do you recall when he first abducted you? What day it was?"

"What day is it today?"

Derrick glanced at his watch. Twelve thirty a.m. "Technically Sunday."

She rubbed her hand over her eyes, and Derrick took in her jagged nails and bruised skin.

"It was almost two weeks ago. As I was leaving my office, he attacked me at my car."

"Did you see this woman there?" Derrick asked, showing her a photograph of the deputy. "Her name is Deputy Shondra Eastwood."

"I didn't know Shondra. But I heard him with her. She refused to beg and kept telling him she was a cop. He… punished her over and over again." A sob escaped her. "I wanted to help them, but… I couldn't… he kept me chained in a cage."

"Do you know who he is? Did you see his face?"

She pinched the bridge of her nose. "He wore a ski mask all the time. And it was dark, so dark. I think we were held in a basement somewhere. There was no light, but there were steps. I… heard them creaking every time he came down."

"How about his voice? Do you think you'd recognize it if you heard him speak?" Derrick asked, glancing back at Bryce, who was hovering in the doorway.

Biting down on her lower lip, she gave a quick nod.

"Do you have any idea of the location where you were held?"

"Somewhere in the mountains. All I remember was being in the trunk of his car and going around the winding roads. I'm sorry… I'm not being very helpful…"

The woman had been through so much. Yet she'd survived. She was here. "You're doing great."

Sniffing, she rubbed her finger over her throat where the wide band of bruising marred her skin. "He… put a dog collar around my neck…" she said, her voice trailing off.

Derrick bit back a sound of revulsion. That fit with Dr. Whitefeather's findings. "How about sounds? Did you hear a noise outside? A plane or train? Cars? Anything that might help us pinpoint the location?"

She furrowed her brow. "I did hear a plane a couple of times. Like a small one. It sounded close by."

"Okay. I'll have my partner start searching for remote areas near a small airport or where a private plane might be able to land."

"And… I think I heard a dog barking, maybe more than one," she said, rubbing at her neck again.

That also fit with the theory that the killer might have trained dogs to fight. "Did he say why he was holding you hostage or killing women?"

Pain wrenched Kennedy's face, then her cheeks reddened. "Just that he wanted me to beg. He wanted all the women on their hands and knees begging like… animals. And he called us all Cathy. He never said why but he hated her, and said we were all Cathys."

Disgust ate at Derrick, but that might be the lead they needed. "I want you to listen to this voice and tell me if it sounds familiar."

She nodded, clenching the bedsheet in a white-knuckled grip as he played the recording he'd taken of his conversation with the sheriff.

At the sound of his own voice, Bryce burst into the room, his face a picture of fury. "What are you doing? You didn't have my permission to tape me."

Stepping in front of Bryce to protect Kennedy, Derrick's gaze met hers. "Was that the voice of the man who took you?"

CHAPTER 130

Sunday

Somewhere on the AT

After what felt like forever, Ellie felt a tingling in her toes. She struggled to move her fingers, managing to bend her pinky slightly. Hopefully the drugs were starting to wear off.

"Where are you, you coward?" she tried to yell, but her voice emerged as a hoarse whisper.

Silence surrounded her as the darkness swept her into a black abyss, but she fought the fear running through her. She had survived the dark before and she would survive it again.

You survived the coffin, she told herself. *But only because Derrick found you.*

She couldn't count on Derrick this time. He had no idea where she was. He might not even know she was missing.

In desperation, she ordered herself to turn her head. Like the rest of her body, it felt heavy, weighted down.

As she moved, metal clanked, cutting sharply into the silence. Something was around her neck. The collar. Trembling, she realized he'd chained her inside the space, and she squeezed her eyes shut to stem her rising hysteria.

When her breathing steadied, she listened again. A scratching sound echoed from somewhere in the dark.

"Hello, is anyone there?" she choked out.

Nothing.

But seconds passed, and there was another noise.

Suddenly something sounded from above. Footsteps. Shuffling. A thumping noise, as if someone was tapping their fingers on the wall.

A memory flitted through her brain. Someone else used to do that. Another man towering over her. Pushing her against a wall. His fingers tapping on the wood as his breath bathed her neck and face…

A shudder coursed up her spine as the door creaked open.

Then came his voice. "Ellie, Ellie, where are you?"

CHAPTER 131

Bluff County Hospital

Kennedy's sister rushed in on the sheriff's heels, and Derrick raised a hand to her in a silent plea to let Kennedy answer. "Ms. Sledge?" Derrick asked. "Is that the voice you heard?" His heart pounded as he waited for her response.

"No," she whispered. "That's not him."

The sheriff glared at Derrick, but the FBI agent ignored him. "Thank you so much," he said to Kennedy. "You've been a big help. Now get some rest."

Lara rushed to her sister's side, and Derrick started to step into the hall.

"There's one thing he said," Kennedy murmured. "He hated Ellie, said she humiliated him, and that she was the cause of everything."

Derrick contemplated the statement. They needed to look back at other cases Ellie had worked and look for any reference to a woman named Cathy. "If you think of anything else, please call me."

She nodded, and her sister sank into the chair beside her, clasping her hand, as Derrick and the sheriff exited the room.

"Keep guarding her," Derrick told the deputy.

"You had some nerve back there," Bryce growled.

"I'm just doing my job. Besides, it was the fastest way to clear you."

"Ellie's ass is toast."

"Let's find her first, then she can explain," Derrick replied.

Once again Derrick rang Ellie again, but got her voicemail. "I think she's in trouble. I'm going by her house."

"I'll go with you," Bryce said.

"No. I'll drop you at your office. Get a voice recording of Finton and McClain and we'll have Kennedy listen to it. Also, there was DNA beneath her fingernails. Send both men's DNA samples to the lab for comparison."

Meanwhile, he had to find out who Cathy was. She might be the key to finding Shondra and Ellie.

CHAPTER 132

Somewhere on the AT

As his voice boomed down the steps, Ellie was beginning to be able to move her hands and legs again. The cold metal floor where she lay was the bottom of a cage, she realized, and in the darkness she'd managed to reach up and feel the sides. There were bars, she figured, revolted.

Is this where he'd killed some of his victims? In this cage? In this room? Had Shondra sat in this very spot? The questions spun in her head.

Terror bled through her as his feet shuffled across the floor, but she tamped it down with steely determination. She didn't want to give him the pleasure of seeing her fear.

He stalked toward her, a hulking shadow with a black mask. He was tall, with wide shoulders like a linebacker's. Ham-sized hands. Heavy footfalls. She held her breath as he inched towards her.

Keys rattled as he unlocked the cage door. He knelt in front of her, icy black eyes piercing.

"Hello, Ellie, it's good to see you again."

Again? The voice… she knew him.

"Come on out and let's play," he said.

She didn't move.

He yanked the chain connected to the collar around her neck so sharply pain ripped through her.

"I said come out and play." Grabbing her by her hair, he forced her to crawl forward. "It's time you learned you're the weak one. That you have to obey."

She'd never obey him—or anyone else.

The chain clinked as he hauled her toward him. Then he stood, towering over her, and kicked her in the stomach. She bit back a cry, gasping for breath, then braced herself as he delivered another and another, grunting with every blow.

With one big, hard hand, he pulled her head up. "Beg me, Ellie. Beg for your life."

This was what he'd done to the other women before he'd killed them, she realized, lying there at his mercy. This is what he had done to Shondra.

Knowing she somehow had to find a way out, she collapsed into a puddle, staying as still as she could. He knelt in front of her, jerking her face up to look at him again.

"You will beg before it's over. They always beg," he spat.

Fury fueled her, and she pushed away the pain, rolling onto her back and kicking him hard. He groaned, reaching for her, but she kicked him again and sent him flying backward.

"You bitch," he roared. "You'll pay for that."

"Why are you doing this?" she asked, her voice raw.

"Don't you remember, Ellie? It's been a while, but I haven't forgotten. I'll never forget what you did to me."

"What I did?" The murdered women's faces flashed behind her eyes. She was next. Lifting herself to her hands and knees, breathing through the pain, she crawled toward him. But he was fast, wrenching the chain so hard that the collar tightened, choking her. Using it as leverage, he stood and kicked her again, this time in the face. Blood spurted from her nose and mouth, then he delivered a sharp blow to her ribs, sending her to the floor in agony.

"Now you see whose stronger and smarter," he shouted.

Another kick, another punch to her face with his fist, one after the other relentlessly, until she collapsed, the pain swallowing her.

CHAPTER 133

Crooked Creek

"*Folks, this is Cara Soronto, your local meteorologist. The entire North Georgia area is now under a tornado watch, which means conditions are ripe for a funnel cloud to strike the area. Already five people have died in Alabama and trailer homes were literally ripped apart in Tennessee. My best advice; stay home for the next twelve hours as these dangerous winds roll across north Georgia with a vengeance.*"

The car vibrated in the wind as Derrick pulled into Ellie's driveway, where her Jeep sat. He said a silent prayer that she was safe inside, curled up asleep and hadn't yet gotten his messages. Despite his gut instinct telling him otherwise, hope flared in him.

Removing his gun from his holster, he eased toward her vehicle. A quick look inside indicated nothing looked amiss. Checking out the surrounding property, he moved onto her porch. The storm clouds were thickening above him, casting shadows onto the rising mountains behind her house. The wind had intensified, trees bowing and limbs cracking off and thundering to the ground. The flowerpot had blown over, spilling soil, and dirt fluttered through the air.

He twisted the doorknob, and the door opened. Not a good sign.

Holding his breath, he eased inside. The sound of a clock ticking echoed in the tense silence. The floor creaked and wind whistled through the eaves as he entered. "Ellie, are you here?" Just the sound of the windowpanes rattling. "Ellie?"

Gun at the ready, he strode into the kitchen, but no one was there. An empty coffee mug sat on the counter, a half full bottle of vodka on the bar.

Unease burned within him as he crept toward the bedrooms. The guest one was empty. In Ellie's room, Derrick saw with horror that there were three dresses laid out on the bed, as if the killer had been deciding which one she should be laid to rest in. One was a bright fuchsia with ruffled sleeves. The second, an orange low-cut number, and the third, a leopard-skin print. None of the outfits looked anything remotely like Ellie would wear, which meant the killer had brought them here.

A cold knot of fear seized him when he glanced at the closet door. It was ajar, blood spattered all over the floor.

Then he saw the daffodils. Dozens of the petals strewn across the floor like a yellow river.

CHAPTER 134

Pacing the front porch, Derrick made phone calls while he waited on the crime scene team.

"Ellie dropped McClain at Crooked Creek Police Station, then was headed home," Captain Hale said.

"McClain is still there?"

"Yes. What's wrong?"

"The Weekday Killer has Ellie." He relayed his conversation with Kennedy Sledge.

"It can't be Finton, then, or McClain. They're both still in custody."

Dammit. It wasn't Finton or McClain or Waters. It wasn't one of the people who'd sent hate mail to her father. It wasn't Vinny Holcomb; he was dead. And Hiram was still in prison.

"What other enemies has Ellie made?" he asked.

"A few meth dealers and a couple of wife beaters. I'll check into all of them and see what I can find out."

"Dr. Sledge mentioned something about a woman named Cathy. She said he called all the women Cathy and that he blames Ellie for everything. Could be a girlfriend or an ex or even his mother, I guess."

"The name Cathy doesn't ring a bell, but I'll get right on it."

"Has she busted up an illegal dog-fighting operation?" asked Derrick.

"No, why?"

Derrick explained about the dog collars, and the barking Kennedy had heard.

"I'll keep that in mind as I search her old cases," Captain Hale said. "Deputy Landrum is on his way to Kennedy Sledge's office and I sent another officer to her house. Maybe they'll find something there."

"Keep me posted."

As the crime scene team arrived, Derrick explained how he'd found Ellie's bedroom. "We need any and every piece of forensics you can find in there. Be sure to check the tags on the dresses. Maybe he messed up and left a print there."

The team went to work while Derrick paced again, mentally reviewing the evidence they'd found so far. The MO, the victims' past. The mental health counselor, the fact that there was an impostor who'd posed as Kennedy Sledge.

The pieces just didn't fit.

He said Ellie had to pay for humiliating him. That she was the cause of everything.

Other than her current boss, the only person who might know about Ellie's past was her father.

Randall Reeves was the last man on earth Derrick wanted to see. But talking to him might be the only way to save Ellie.

CHAPTER 135

Somewhere on the AT

Ellie had lost all sense of time. She'd drifted in and out of consciousness, only to be beaten again, suffocated by blackness all over again. In between, she'd thought she'd heard a dog barking somewhere.

That was how he treated her, how he'd treated the other victims. But she still refused to beg.

He glared down at her now, pulling at the chain to force her to crawl toward him.

"I told you that you'd pay for humiliating me," he snarled.

He had. Suddenly it all made sense. She knew who he was, what he had said all those years ago. He'd been at the police academy at the same time she had and had tried to bully her into quitting with sexist remarks. He'd tripped her up during their runs, teamed up with two other trainees to mess with her gun so it jammed when she was in a simulation exercise, and groped her by the locker room when he caught her by herself.

All these years later, his words still echoed in her ears. "You're a weakling. But I can put a good word in for you if you cooperate."

"I don't need a good word from you," she'd told him. "I'll make it on my own."

Then he'd shoved his hand up her shirt. "No, you won't. I'll make sure of that."

She'd kneed him in the balls, then punched him and broken his nose. When she'd looked up, two other men had been watching.

They hadn't bothered to help her but she'd heard them laughing at Burton when she'd walked away.

"It was your fault you got dismissed from the academy," she spat, dragging herself away from the memory. "You got what you deserved."

His name was Hugh Burton. She'd filed charges against him for sexual harassment and once her complaint was filed, other female officers had come forward. An investigation revealed his violent tendencies towards women, that he was a racist and a hothead who used unusual and unnecessary brute force on the job. He was also found to beat the K-9 unit dogs during training.

"Women have to be put in their place," he said sharply. "Especially women like you."

"That's the reason you killed those women?" she asked. "Why not just come after me in the beginning?"

"I wanted you to suffer. I saw you on the news. I knew you felt guilty about those little girls dying." A smile curved his mouth. Finally, he'd removed his mask, and she could see his face. He'd aged more than she would have thought. While once he'd been handsome, his thick wavy hair was now thinning. A deep scar on his upper arm looked recent, and his black eyes were menacing.

"It's your fault my wife left me." He gripped her arms and shook her so hard nausea caught her in its clutches. "After you got me dismissed from the academy, I couldn't get another job. When Cathy heard about it, she went crazy." He shoved his face in hers, spitting on her as he spoke. "I tried to explain, but then she said she thought I had a wandering eye and now she knew it for sure."

"Then what did you do?" Ellie probed, fearing what the answer would be.

"I did what I had to do, I taught her a lesson. Then she had the nerve to try and leave me. I couldn't let that happen. But she was insane, she had the nerve to push me, and I grabbed her to keep her from leaving. She said you spoke up against me, and she wanted to be like you. Like *you*," he spat. "That she didn't want to be my wife anymore."

Ellie saw the scene playing out in her mind in sickening clarity. "So you tried to stop her."

"I did," he bellowed. "But she put our little girl in the car and took off, speeding. She was going so fast, I chased after her in my truck, but…" His voice broke. "But she flew around the mountain so quickly she lost control. She crashed and my baby girl… they were trapped." Wild rage contorted his face. "I tried to get my baby out but… she died right there, trapped in that twisted hunk of metal."

"I'm sorry about your little girl," Ellie said, striving to calm him, dreading what was next.

But he wasn't listening. His fingers dug into her arms. "It's all your fault. You killed her. You killed Cathy and my little girl."

Swallowing, Ellie tried to control her emotions. Now he was going to kill her. She had no doubt about that.

"Why wait all these years to get your revenge?" she asked.

"I tried to move on," he said. "Tried to put it all behind me. But then I saw you in the news. Ellie Reeves a hero, for saving two children." His voice rose another octave. "That story aired on the anniversary of the day I buried my girl. You didn't save my daughter, did you? You killed her. You're not a hero."

Despite the monster he had turned into, Ellie couldn't help feeling sympathy for the man in front of her.

"But Deputy Eastwood has nothing to do with any of this, and neither did those other women," Ellie said. "You have me now. Where is she?"

"Oh, she's another one just like you. Thinks she's better than everyone else. She needed to be put in her place. I made her suffer, too."

"Where did you leave her body?"

He scoffed. "You should be worried about yourself."

"Where is she, Hugh?"

"You'll be together soon. I have the perfect place to dispose of your bodies."

"All you've done is prove that you didn't deserve to wear a badge," she spat, thinking of her helpless friend.

Backhanding her, he sent a sharp pain pulsing through her jaw.

"I proved that I'm smarter and stronger than you. All this time you've been chasing different leads. Making arrests. Running all over town like a headless chicken. You didn't have a fucking clue it was me."

It had been years since she'd last seen him. Since she'd spoken to him. How could she have known?

"You found out everyone I was close to and tried to turn me against them," she said. "You framed Cord."

"See how clever I was."

"And you knew about Hiram."

"Oh, yes, Hiram and his friend Vinny. All I had to do was pose as a cleaner and I got to talk to your brother. He told me all about Vinny. And that fell into place. Vinny would do anything for your brother, so I helped him get out of that hospital and pointed the finger at the two of them."

"It was you on the security camera going into Vinny's room," Ellie said.

He chuckled. "All it took was some scrubs and knowing one of the guards liked to slip out for a smoke every two hours."

"You hacked into the therapist's files," she said, piecing together the past few weeks. She'd told the counselor—or the woman she'd thought was the counselor—all her secrets, poured out her feelings of guilt, about Hiram and the adoption, her irritation with Bryce, that one night with Derrick, her history with Cord, and the tension between them. "How did you know I was talking to a counselor?"

He barked a laugh. "You can thank your local sheriff for that one. I met him at Haints. A few drinks in and that man has a loose tongue. He bragged that he heard you talking to the deputy. The rest was easy."

They'd bonded over their animosity toward her. Ellie wanted to scream.

"Did you know that that's my bar?" he asked.

"You own Haints?" Ellie asked, shocked.

"I bought it because it was across from the cemetery where Cici is buried. And to be close to the cops." His fingers dug into her arms. "Where I should have been all along, with my fellow officers." His sinister laugh rang in her ears. "Where I could keep an eye on you."

"You put that blood on my porch," Ellie said. "The blood—"

"I took from your precious friend," he snarled. "Imagine my fun watching it drain from her body. And I didn't have to go anywhere near your house. Vinny did that for me."

"But what about Cord? You put his print on Shondra's truck?"

"Easy peasy." He laughed again.

"How did you know about his upbringing? About Finton?"

Another sardonic laugh, and he shook her so hard her teeth rattled. "Because I'm the best detective," he said sharply. "What a mistake the academy made… Once you spilled your guts to the therapist, all I had to do was a little investigating." He bounced up and down on his heels like a kid with too much energy. "When I learned about his foster family, I knew he'd make the perfect patsy. And finding all those books in his house gave me all the information I needed to plan out the disposal sites."

"And Finton? You let us think he was part of it. Was he?"

"That sick creep. No. But he was the icing on the cake. With his past and McClain's, it was easy to make them look like conspirators," Burton said with a grin. "Really, Detective, I helped you put away a bad guy. I should receive a police commendation."

He was totally deranged.

Keep him talking, Ellie. She needed time. "Tell me this, Hugh. How did you get that woman to agree to be a fake therapist and help you?"

He pulled at the collar around her neck, choking her. "I have my ways."

"You held her hostage and abused her," Ellie said, figuring it out. "Stockholm syndrome."

"You'd be surprised what a woman will do when she thinks she's going to die." He threw his head back and laughed, the ugly sound booming off the concrete walls. "She was easy to manipulate, to train, just like the dogs."

"You're a sociopath," Ellie said, earning another slap across the jaw.

"Once I had her under my thumb, I could make her do anything for me. Not like you or Cathy."

"Where is she?" Ellie asked.

He shrugged, then brushed his calloused fingers across her cheek. A second later, he snatched off the rubber band holding her ponytail and spread her hair over her shoulders. "Your daddy should have taught you how to be a lady."

"And yours should have taught you how to be a man," Ellie said, unable to resist the barb.

He hit her again, this time so hard her head snapped backward and the dog collar cut into her neck. She gagged as he hauled the chain, dragging her after him.

"That's a good girl, Ellie. Good girl."

Tears blurred her eyes at the menacing edge to his deep voice, but she blinked them back. She refused to give him the satisfaction of crying in front of him.

Her body ached as he heaved her into the hallway, into another cold room, where the air was thick with the smell of blood. Three metal cages glinted in the dark.

Two were empty, but she saw the outline of a body in the other.

CHAPTER 136

Bluff County Hospital

Derrick found Randall Reeves perched by his wife's bedside.

He knocked on the door, which stood ajar, the sound of machines beeping and whirring from inside. Randall looked up, surprised, then something akin to suspicion settled on his craggy face.

Derrick motioned for him to step into the hallway, and Randall kissed his sleeping wife, before striding toward him.

Anger darkened Randall's face, his tone defensive. "What are you doing here?"

"It's about Ellie," Derrick said, knowing time was of the essence.

Randall softened somewhat. "What about Ellie?"

"The Weekday Killer has her."

Randall balled his hands by his sides and straightened, looking more like the intimidating man he used to be. "How did you let this happen?" he barked. "You were supposed to be working with her."

Guilt slammed into Derrick. He'd been beating himself up the entire drive over. "I don't have time to get into everything, but the bottom line is that I went to Ellie's house and found signs of a struggle in her bedroom."

The man's face turned ashen. "No sign of Ellie?"

He shook his head. "One of his victims is in the hospital, but she never saw the man's face. But he told her that Ellie had to pay for humiliating him. That means the killer knows Ellie personally, that they crossed paths. Captain Hale is reviewing her old cases, but you know her better than anybody. Is there anyone you can think of who hates her?"

Randall pinched the bridge of his nose. "She and Bryce have some tension, but he wouldn't hurt her or kill all those women."

"He's been cleared," Derrick said, earning a surprised look from Randall. "But think. There has to be someone in her past."

"You know Ellie. She's a ball buster and has pissed off a lot of people, but… to want to kill her. I…"

"If you don't give me something here, it might be too late for your daughter." Derrick barely resisted beating the damn man. "Think about it. This perpetrator forces the victims to wear a dog collar. Perhaps he trains dogs to fight?"

Randall's frown deepened.

"He also said she humiliated him. And he mentioned something about a woman named Cathy. He could have seen Ellie in the news lately, maybe that triggered something in him. We've eliminated the family members of the Ghost victims."

"You mentioned he might have trained dogs to fight?" asked Randall, pacing in the hall.

Derrick nodded.

Closing his eyes, Randall rubbed the back of his neck. "There was an officer at the academy with Ellie. An incident, but it happened a long time ago."

Derrick's pulse jumped. "What kind of incident?"

"He volunteered to train dogs for the K-9 units, but he was caught beating one."

Derrick's heart raced. "Was there anything else?"

Randall glanced back at his wife's room, but she hadn't moved. "Ellie was very competitive and athletic. She ran rings around a few of the men. She was faster, was mentally sharp, and also outshot a lot of them at the shooting range. She filed a complaint against the same man for sexual harassment."

"What happened?"

"She didn't share the details. But after she filed, some other female officers spoke up as well. An investigation ensued, and he was dismissed from the academy." Randall worked his mouth from side to side, his face growing more and more ashen. "After he got kicked out, I heard his wife left him. I… believe they had a child, and they were killed in an accident."

Derrick's blood went cold. "He could blame Ellie for that."

"But why wait until now to try to get revenge against her?" Randall asked. "It doesn't make sense."

"Maybe he spiraled downward after that. Or maybe he got help. Who knows at this point? But seeing Ellie in the news being reported as a hero might have triggered his need for vengeance. What's his name?"

"I think it was something like Herbert— No… Hugh. Burton, that was it. Hugh Burton."

Derrick had started to walk away when Randall called out his name. "Agent Fox? Please find my little girl."

Derrick's gaze met his. He would find Ellie, but not for Randall.

CHAPTER 137

Somewhere on the AT

Ellie swallowed back a sob as she stared at Shondra's lifeless form inside the cage. It was too dark to see if Burton had slashed her throat, but the strong odor of blood and body waste permeated the damp room. Water dripped somewhere close by, pinging on the concrete floor.

Forcing her to crawl over to the cage, Burton unlocked the door and ordered her inside. A clamminess washed over Ellie, and she thought she might pass out. The cage was big enough for a large animal but cramped with her and Shondra inside. It smelled like blood and dog hair, and she bit back a retch.

The door clanged shut, and she felt Burton watching her as she lifted a battered hand to touch her friend. Shondra was only thirty years old—she had her whole life ahead of her. After such a broken past, she'd met a woman who loved her and they'd planned to get married. But she would never get the happiness she deserved.

Now she looked thinner, as if she hadn't eaten in days. Her skin was pale and splotchy, black and blue with bruising. Her hair lay in a tangle, dried blood making the strands coarse. Ellie gently pushed it away from her cheek. Her friend's skin was ice cold.

Derrick met Bryce, Deputy Landrum, Captain Hale, Cord and half a dozen other deputies at the sheriff's office to brief them. Bennett had been fast in investigating Burton. Armed with new information, he asked everyone to meet in the conference room.

Captain Hale hung up his phone as he walked in. "That was Deputy Eastwood's girlfriend, Melissa. She's hysterical and demanded to speak to Detective Reeves."

"What did you tell her?" Derrick asked.

"That I'd have her call her," he said grimly.

Derrick dove straight in. "I believe Detective Reeves has been abducted by the Weekday Killer, and this is him." He tacked Burton's photo on the whiteboard. "Sheriff, can you get an all-points bulletin out for him, send his picture to Angelica Gomez and have her run it?"

The sheriff nodded. "What makes you think he's the killer?"

"He fits the profile and has a vendetta against Detective Reeves. Burton was at the police academy with her. He had trouble there, though. Volunteered to train dogs but was caught abusing them. Later, Ellie filed charges against him for sexual harassment. Her complaint started a wave of others that got him dismissed and ended his career in law enforcement. His life went further downhill from there. His wife, Cathy, left him, taking their six-year-old daughter with her. He chased after them, but the wife crashed and she and the little girl both died."

Bryce made a strangled sound, causing Derrick to pause.

"Do you know him?" he asked.

"I saw him at Haints," Waters murmured, pressing his hand to his forehead.

"You talked to him?" Derrick asked, his jaw tightening.

"Yes… I met him years ago at a weapons training seminar, but I had no idea he knew Ellie." Bryce had paled.

Captain Hale cleared his throat. "What did you talk about?"

"I don't know," Bryce said. "We had a beer, that's all."

He'd probably found common ground by bashing Ellie. "What *did* you tell him?" Derrick barked.

"I may have mentioned she was in therapy. I heard her and Deputy Eastwood talking one day."

"You stupid son of a bitch," cursed Derrick, barely containing his rage. "You fed him information and he used it to find his victims."

"I didn't know," Bryce choked out. "I… thought he was a good guy."

"He used that personal information to make her doubt everyone she knew and to frame me," Cord said gruffly.

Derrick nodded. The ranger had a right to be pissed and walk right out. Instead, he pulled a wall map down for them to study.

Meanwhile, Deputy Landrum looked up from his computer. "I've found an air strip near an old abandoned farm east of here. It's not far from the one where you found that hair. Looks like the farm once belonged to his dead wife's parents. And that air strip was once used for crop dusting planes but hasn't been used in years."

"That's it," Derrick said. "That's where he'd take the victims."

The deputy gave Cord the coordinates. "We should divide up. I'll mark off search quadrants so we can cover more territory."

Derrick's gaze met his. When this was over, he owed McClain an apology. But now they had to act quickly.

"I'll get my people to send a chopper so we have an aerial view," Derrick said. "I'll head to the farmhouse—he might be using it as home base. Sheriff?"

Bryce squared his shoulders. "My deputies will search north of the farm, in case he took them into the woods."

"My guys can search the east," Captain Hale said. "McClain and I will head west."

Derrick clapped his hands. "Let's get to it. The weather is getting wild out there. Shondra may be Saturday's child, but we have to save Ellie before she becomes Sunday's."

CHAPTER 139

As Burton dragged Ellie up the stairs, she felt like she was being led to execution.

Upstairs, he forced her to crawl across the cold linoleum floor. It smelled like a dead animal in here. Like urine and mold and… and the gruesome scent of death from the cages below. Muttering the rhyme in a crazy voice, he threw a duffel back over his shoulder, then forced her through the back door. Wind slapped the screen back against the doorframe as he dragged her outside, down four cement steps.

Tugging her to a standing position, still pulling her with the chain, Burton shoved her towards the woods. With the gray stormy skies, it seemed dark, the wind hurling dirt and leaves around them.

The tornado they'd talked about on the weather. It was coming their way.

As Burton chained her to a metal fence, Ellie realized they were on some kind of farm. An old barn sat to the right with pens that could have been used for pigs or chickens. She heard a dog yelping and realized their theory about him training dogs was on target.

Pure raw hatred churned through her as she watched him gather sticks, piling them at the door of the house and all around the outside.

"Ellie's going to die today, Ellie's going to die. And they will never find me," he muttered. "Die, die, die, Ellie. And no one will ever find you."

Realizing with horror what he planned to do, she struggled with the collar around her neck, yanking and twisting, desperate to free herself. She could see a funnel cloud in the distance, the trees rocking in the wind.

Burton grabbed a gas can and began to spread gasoline all around the edge of the house, dousing the sticks and steps to the porch.

"No!" Ellie cried, knowing that Shondra was still inside.

His laugh punctuated the air as he stepped back, lit a match and tossed it onto the pile. One match after another.

Terror assaulted her as the flames began to spark and spread.

Then he snatched the duffel bag, threw it over his shoulder and returned to unchain her from the fence. She fought, digging in her heels, to try to go back to Shondra. But it was useless. He hauled her into the forest behind the house, and she knew her time was running out.

CHAPTER 140

North Georgia

Derrick swerved onto the shoulder of the road to dodge a tree branch that crashed down, speeding toward the farm. Black clouds raged in the sky, and fierce winds careened through the woods.

The wind beat at the car, knocking him sideways, as if it might lift his vehicle and send it sailing through the air. Clenching the steering wheel, he pulled it back onto the road away from the rocky mountain wall.

Ahead, above the jagged peaks, he saw the clouds spinning and realized he was heading into the eye of the storm. There was no way a chopper could fly overhead now. It was too dangerous.

Praying he wasn't too late, he flew around a curve, but almost lost control and went skidding over the ravine.

A loud roaring rent the air, and suddenly a pine limb was falling through the air, straight at his windshield.

Derrick swerved to avoid it, but the branch struck the passenger side of his car, shattered the window and sent him skidding. A second later, metal crunched and glass sprayed him as the car flipped onto its side.

CHAPTER 141

Somewhere on the AT

"It's almost a shame to end this with you," Burton said to Ellie. "It's been so much fun watching you chase your tail and fail."

Ellie's body ached from the beating he'd given her, but she stifled her emotions. No time for self-pity. She had to get away from him, go back and get Shondra's body out of that house. Her friend deserved a proper burial.

He dragged her through thorn bushes, poison oak and past a barbed wire fence that tore at her clothing, then down a hill behind the old house. Smoke billowed in the air in thick rolling waves of gray, and flames shot toward the dark sky.

Dried brush crackled and twigs snapped, the damp moss adding to the smoke.

The tornado was almost on top of them, the wind making him sway on his feet, almost tumbling down the hill. She clawed at his leg to trip him, but he kicked her hard and she collapsed.

Glaring down at her, he laughed. "Do you know where I've chosen to leave you?"

She shook her head. "Tell me, Hugh. I want to hear everything. Tell me why you chose the rhymes."

"Well," he said, his eyes hollow black holes, "my mama used to say that rhyme to me all the time. She'd point out all the girls and talk about how good they were. But Daddy told me the truth. They weren't what they seemed at all. Just like you aren't, and all the other women I picked to die."

"Was your daddy mean to you?" she asked. "Are you one of those poor little boys who could never live up to Daddy's expectations? Did he beat you or lock you in the closet or starve you like those crooks do to turn dogs into fighters?"

Gripping her chin with one hand, Burton squeezed so hard that she thought her jaw might crack.

"My daddy was a real man. And no, he didn't beat me. But he made sure my mama knew her place."

"So she was helpless," Ellie said. "And you watched."

Burton chuckled. "He had to teach me to be a man. That's what fathers do. Now you're going to be laid on the daffodils, because unlike Sunday's child, who is bonny and gay, you're ugly and cold. You and your stubborn pride. You'd let your own mother die before you'd forgive her."

Hurt swelled inside her, but an image of Vera lying helpless in bed, hooked to machines that were keeping her alive, taunted her.

"Good fathers don't beat their wives or children. They're loving and kind and lead by example," she said, pushing aside the thought.

"Like your daddy?"

Ellie pressed her lips together to keep from spitting at him. "What would your mother say about you now? Would she be proud of the man you've become?"

"My mother was nothing but a bitch. She left me with him," he snapped. "Walked out on us one day—her own husband and son. And when my father went after her, punishing her like she deserved, she killed him. Just like Cathy walked out on me and killed my little girl. Just like *you* killed my baby girl. And you expect me to like women? You all deserve to die."

A tree branch splintered, crashing in their path. Dodging it, he dragged her toward an old well.

"The well is underground, the devil's underbelly," he murmured. "It's the closest thing to Satan and the furthest place from heaven.

That's where you'll spend eternity. Unfortunately for you, no one will ever find your body out here."

Fear coursed through her. He was right.

With his thumb under her chin, he tilted her head up. "Maybe I won't cut your throat after all. Maybe I'll just put you down there and let you rot."

Keeping a firm grip on the chain, he thrust her toward the edge of the well. Then he opened his duffel bag. A bag of daffodils, the petals browning, sat inside, along with a vine of bramble.

"Why the daffodils?" Ellie asked.

Pure evil raged in his eyes. "Because they're the flower of the underworld and that's where you and Cathy belong."

The sharp blade of a knife glinted in the darkness.

It was now or never.

Mustering all her strength, Ellie gripped the collar with one hand, diving for the knife. He swung it toward her and the blade sliced at her arm, pain rippling through her, but she used both hands and every ounce of her courage to grab the knife handle. They fought, the chain tightening, and he punched her in the ribs. With all her force, she lifted her leg and kicked him in the groin.

Their hands were still twined together around the knife as they struggled to take control, and they rolled across the ground. Releasing one hand from the knife, Ellie jabbed him in the eyes. He hollered in pain and momentarily loosened his grip, long enough for her to snatch the blade handle.

He grabbed at her, but she clenched the weapon and brought it down. The blade connected with his cheek and sent blood spurting. The next jab went to his chest. As he staggered to the side, she pushed him down, pressed the knife to his neck and tried to wrangle the keys to the chain from his belt.

Somehow, he managed to flip her over. Suddenly on top of her, he pulled Ellie's own gun from his waistband.

Summoning every ounce of force she possessed, she bucked him off and the gun slid across the wet ground. She crawled toward it. He snagged her foot but she grabbed the gun, rolled over and fired.

CHAPTER 142

North Georgia

Derrick must have lost consciousness. When he came around, confusion muddled his brain and the wind rocked the car back and forth.

But panic quickly set in. He had to get out, get to Ellie.

He blinked through the fog and pushed at the airbag. Reaching inside his pocket, he retrieved his pocketknife and cut it away, then shoved at the door. Dammit, it was stuck. Fumbling for the window lock, he realized it was jammed, so he pulled his gun from the holster and used the butt of it to break the glass. Then he hammered the shards of glass away. Freeing himself from the seatbelt, he crawled through the window.

Pain ricocheted through his chest as he dropped to the ground. He probably had a broken rib and he tasted blood. But he had no time to dwell on it.

The clouds and ground seem to be meeting in the sky as a dizzy spell overcame him. Pushing to his hands and knees, he took deep breaths to stem the nausea and dizziness.

You have to find Ellie.

Clenching his phone, he called Ellie's boss. Had to tell them he needed help. That someone had to go to the farm.

Captain Hale's voicemail picked up. *Dammit.* He couldn't wait.

Fear for Ellie drove him to push aside the pain in his ribs and take off on foot down the road. One foot in front of the other. Another and another.

He struggled for a breath. Every step cost him.

Suddenly the clouds unleashed themselves, rain pummeling him. His boots slipped on the wet asphalt, costing him precious time.

Another painful breath, another footstep, then he froze, heart hammering. He'd reached the turning for the farm, but smoke curled into the night sky, a bright orange blazed against the gray.

Was Ellie in there?

No… fire wasn't the Weekday Killer's MO. Although if the farmhouse was his holding spot for hostages, he might have set it to destroy evidence.

Picking up his pace as much as the pain would allow him, Derrick slogged through the wet grass and mud, taking the most direct route to the blaze. Lightning zigzagged, the storm gaining intensity, although the wind was dulling slightly as it moved toward the east.

Although it seemed like hours, it only took minutes for him to reach the abandoned house, which was now well ablaze.

He was desperate to see if Ellie was inside, but the windows exploded. He staggered back at the intensity of the heat.

Emotions choked him as he screamed Ellie's name.

CHAPTER 143

Ellie crawled over to Burton, checking his pulse. The first bullet had pierced his stomach. The second his thigh. He was covered in blood.

And he wasn't moving.

She had to call an ambulance. But first, Shondra.

Pushing up from the ground, she struggled to steady herself, fighting against the wind. Weak from the beating, her ankle throbbed as she ran, and her chest ached. She tasted blood but swiped at her lip with the back of her hand, heading back towards the house. Flames were starting to ripple along the exterior and smoke curled into the sky.

Breath panting out, she saw sparks shooting from the front door, so she ran to the rear entrance. The weathered wood splintered as she kicked the door in. Smoke clogged the air, and flames were crawling along the door edge.

Hesitating to get her bearings, she searched for the door to the basement. The hallway. It was partially ablaze, but she dodged the burning embers and opened the door. Heat scalded her, and she was pitched into the dark.

Her breath caught. Her head swam. She clutched the wall to steady herself, then raked her hands across it in search of a light switch. She almost cried with joy when she found one and flicked it on.

Her body throbbed as she rushed down the steps, and nausea flooded her as she passed the first room with the cage where he'd held her. Upstairs, she heard wood splintering and the fire hissing as it spread.

Racing to where Shondra was trapped, she dropped to her knees, opened the cage door and dragged her friend out.

An explosion upstairs made her rush into motion. She yanked at Shondra's arms and pulled her through the room toward the steps. But the fire had spread to the doorway and she didn't think she could carry her up the steps.

Mind racing, she ran back through the basement and, to her relief, found a crawl space that would lead to the outside.

Ellie struggled against her fear of the tight space, but it was the only way out. Adrenaline firing her up, she pulled Shondra's limp body into the narrow tunnel.

Panic nearly overpowered her and she had to close her eyes to regain control. She didn't have time to break down.

She managed to slide herself to the doorway. She pushed and shoved at it, but it seemed stuck. A dizzy spell overcame her, and she lifted her head to the ceiling of the tiny space for air.

Ellie gave herself to the count of three before twisting around and kicking at the wooden cover with all her might.

CHAPTER 144

Terror for Ellie forced Derrick into motion. The front of the house was completely ablaze. He had to go around back.

Two of the windows exploded on the side as he ran past. Wood crackled as the roof collapsed. The smoke stung his eyes. "Ellie!" he called.

Another sound broke through the roar of fire and the collapsing house.

Senses alert, he blinked through the smoke. A few feet away from the house he noticed a wooden board covering a crawl space. A fallen tree had partially blocked it.

Pulse hammering, and rain thrashing him, he rushed toward it, and heard the sound again.

Dropping to his knees, he shouted Ellie's name. "Ellie? Ellie?"

"Help!" a muffled cry echoed through the wooden barrier. Fear fueled his strength, and he pushed through the pain, tugging and yanking until he dragged the tree away from the doorway.

Ignoring the pain in his ribs, he wrenched the hatch open. The opening was quickly filling with smoke.

"Ellie!" Leaning over the edge, he made out Ellie's figure a few feet below.

"Shondra's in here." A coughing fit seized her. They had to hurry. "I have to get her body out."

Precious seconds passed as the blaze reached toward the sky, black smoke pouring from the crawl space. He heard Ellie grunting as she pushed Shondra toward the opening.

Grabbing Shondra's shoulders, Derrick pulled her out. He settled her on the ground, then returned to help Ellie. Her hands were already gripping the opening, and he dragged her the rest of the way out.

She rushed to her friend, gasping for air, eyes blurring with tears as she lay down beside her.

Ellie laid her head against Shondra for a moment, her tears dampening her friend. Suddenly she raised her head, a wild look in her eyes. "She's alive, Derrick!"

"What?"

Ellie looked up at him imploringly. "She's breathing. Let's get her away from here."

Scooping Shondra up, Derrick carried her across the yard away from the burning house, then laid her on the ground.

Ellie wiped soot from her battered face then pressed her hands on her friend's chest, starting CPR. "She needs an ambulance."

"So do you."

"I'm fine, just make the call."

Derrick punched 911 and gave the address, before turning to Ellie. "Where's Burton?"

"In the woods near the old well," she said. "I shot him."

But Derrick's relief was short-lived, as suddenly a gunshot echoed from the direction of the barn, loud and jarring. "Stay down and take cover," he ordered Ellie.

She lowered her head, but continued CPR while Derrick gripped his gun and turned in the direction of the barn. The flames that lit the sky flickered off the figure as he darted behind a bush. Trees were down everywhere. The woods looked like a landmine had exploded.

Derrick braced his gun and fired. The bullet pinged off the barn, then Burton fired another round toward him, creeping from one bush to the other as he staggered closer.

"It's over, Burton," Derrick yelled.

"I'm not going to jail," the man shouted desperately as he fired again.

In the distance a siren wailed, and voices reverberated from the woods. Burton pivoted, firing at Captain Hale and Cord McClain as they approached.

Then Burton raised his gun and fired at Ellie. She dropped her head onto Shondra, and Derrick, holding his breath, shot at the man's head.

The bullet hit him square between the eyes, blood erupting everywhere, before he collapsed onto the ground.

CHAPTER 145

Just as she saw Cord emerge from the thicket of trees, Ellie watched Burton drop dead with a mixture of relief and anger. Death was too good for him. But death by cop proved he really was a coward. He'd taken the easy way out.

Limping over to Ellie and Shondra, Derrick's jaw clenched as he looked them over. Then his eyes settled on the damn collar around her neck and Shondra's.

"God, Ellie."

Humiliation flooded her. But at least Shondra was breathing. That changed everything. "Go get the damn keys and get these things off us."

Derrick looked almost as bad as she did. But they'd gotten their man.

He ran back to Burton then returned, keys in hand.

"Shondra first," Ellie said. It was tearing her up seeing her friend so battered and bruised.

Unlocking the collar, Derrick eased it from Shondra's neck, then Ellie held her breath while he removed hers.

"Damn asshole," Derrick muttered as he threw the collars back at Burton's dead body.

Finally, Shondra stirred, trying to open her eyes just as the ambulance arrived.

"You're going to the hospital now," Ellie told her. "I'll be right there with you."

For once, she wanted to leave the crime scene to someone else. Her friend was all that mattered, and she needed to check on her mother, Burton's words still haunting her.

Cord had disappeared into the barn, but he re-emerged, striding toward them. His smoky eyes were troubled, and he was also holding a small pitbull mix. "I found him in the barn. Looks like he's been abused."

"He was training them to fight," Ellie said. "We heard him barking."

"I'll call Animal Rescue," Cord replied.

The paramedics jumped from the ambulance and Derrick waved them over to Shondra.

"Ellie?" Shondra said in a whisper.

"I'm here."

"Go," Derrick said. "We'll take care of things here. You need to be examined."

"Call Melissa and tell her we found her," Ellie said.

Derrick nodded, while Ellie took Shondra's hand and ran along beside the medics as they carried her friend to the ambulance.

CHAPTER 146

Bluff County Hospital

A half hour later, Ellie tolerated her own exam while the doctors continued treating Shondra.

The nurse cleaned and bandaged her forehead, treated her other bruises and cuts, and did a chest X-ray. Her ribs were bruised, but not broken. But it hurt like a mother to breathe, her head ached, and her jaw felt as if she might never chew again.

Still, she had to see Shondra, so she convinced the nurse to let her into her room.

A young, pencil-thin blonde hovered by Shondra's bed, stroking her face. "Shondra, honey, I'm so sorry, so sorry."

Ellie remained at the door, not wanting to disturb the reunion, but watching as Shondra opened her eyes. "Melissa," Shondra whispered. "You're here."

"I am," Melissa whispered. "I've been so worried about you."

Ellie felt dizzy for a moment, grabbing the doorway to steady herself. Something about Melissa's voice sounded familiar. *You talked to her on the phone when she called about Shondra*, she reassured herself.

"I'm here now and it's over," Melissa cried. "He can't hurt you anymore."

As the dizziness passed, Ellie inched inside the room. Melissa turned to look at her, and a twinge of recognition struck Ellie. But no… it couldn't be… She'd never met this woman. Her golden blonde hair hung down her back, and her eyes were a deep violet.

"Kennedy?" Ellie murmured under her breath.

Tears filled Melissa's crystal-blue eyes, and Shondra coughed, spluttering out the words, "No… Ellie, this is Melissa."

Shock stabbed at Ellie and her mind raced. Maybe she had hit her head too hard. Yet unease nagged at her as she stepped forward, her gaze falling to the woman's wrist, at the small cross-like scar.

"No, you're the Kennedy Sledge I talked to," Ellie said, grateful her voice didn't crack. "You wore a short dark wig, and colored contacts, but I saw that scar."

Melissa lifted her arm, rubbing at the tiny mark on the inside of her wrist, and shook her head in denial.

Shondra pushed at the bed to sit up, but she was too weak, collapsing against the pillows. Her face was so bruised, her eyes swollen, and she had stitches in her lip. She swung her gaze back and forth between the two women. "What are you talking about, Ellie?"

Ellie quickly explained about Kennedy Sledge's escape from the killer, and about the impostor. "This woman pretended to be Kennedy Sledge to learn details of his victims for the Weekday Killer. And she sounded so convincing, as if she really was a therapist."

Shondra gasped, confusion clouding her face.

"I didn't want to do it," Melissa cried, finally relenting. "And I do have a background in therapy. He targeted me because of it, then forced me to help him. He was going to kill me…"

"Where have you been all this time?" Ellie asked.

"Locked up," Melissa whimpered. "At first in a cage in an old chicken house, then he moved me because he knew you were looking for him."

Shondra choked on a sob, and Melissa clenched her hand. "Please, Shondra, I love you. I didn't want to help him, you have to believe that I didn't. When I left to go tell my parents about us, he took me. He beat me and tortured me and locked me in one of those cages just like he did to you." Pivoting, she unbuttoned her blouse and lowered the fabric. "See, I have scars. He whipped me and starved me and… I… I didn't want to die."

Melissa broke down into hysterical sobs, and Shondra pushed her hand away, clinging to the sheets in horror.

CHAPTER 147

Derrick rushed into the hospital, where he found Ellie standing beside Shondra's bedside. The deputy looked in shock, bruised and battered, a young blonde sat slumped in the chair beside her, sobbing into her hands.

Ellie looked like hell herself. But at least she was alive, and the Weekday Killer was done.

Tears swam in Ellie's eyes as she turned to him. "I know who the impostor therapist is," she said quietly.

Derrick narrowed his eyes. "Who?"

The blonde looked up with a tormented expression, and Ellie cleared her throat. "Special Agent Fox, meet Melissa. She's the woman who posed as Kennedy Sledge."

Stunned, Derrick tried to assimilate what was going on.

"She claims Burton forced her," Ellie explained.

This case just got more complicated. They'd have to take Melissa into custody, arrange for a psychologist to talk to her. Get to the truth. Either the woman was a great actress or she was telling the truth.

Heading over, he took Melissa's arm. Shondra watched from the bed, shock, anger and confusion streaking her swollen face.

Ellie moved over to comfort her as he escorted Melissa from the room.

CHAPTER 148

Ellie called for a nurse, then soothed Shondra as best she could. It would take time to sort out Melissa's story, to figure out whether she would be charged for the crime or treated as a victim. It would take even longer for Shondra to overcome the trauma of what she'd endured.

"You're going to be okay," Ellie murmured. "I'll be here for you, Shondra."

"I… loved her," Shondra said softly. "I… thought we were a couple. We are—were—in love."

"We'll figure it out," Ellie said. "Right now, you just need to rest."

The nurse slipped in and gave Shondra a sedative to calm her, and Ellie sat beside her until she fell asleep. Wiping away tears, she returned to the waiting room. Her father was standing there, the grooves beside his eyes deep with worry.

"Honey, are you okay?" He rushed to her, starting to hug her, but Ellie stiffened. After everything, she couldn't bear being touched right now.

"I will be," Ellie said. She just needed time. "How's Mom?"

"She's refusing the surgery."

"Why?"

"She seems to have lost the will to live."

With a thud, Ellie realized she had to talk to her.

Derrick appeared, his jaw snapping tight as he took in the scene. He cleared his throat.

"Melissa is being admitted to the psych ward for evaluation. Deputy Landrum is going to stand guard."

Rita Herron

As Ellie thanked him, the sheriff strode in, his green eyes glittering with a myriad of emotions. He raked over Ellie with a grimace as he noted her injuries. Angelica Gomez and her cameraman were close behind.

Anger at Bryce railed through Ellie. Damn him for blabbing to Burton. She didn't know if she could ever forgive him.

"How's Deputy Eastwood?" he asked gruffly.

"She's in a bad way, but she's tough." Ellie crossed her arms. "You told Burton about the therapist. That's how he found out everything about his victims."

A muscle ticked in Bryce's jaw. "I'm sorry, Ellie. I am. I... didn't know."

She shook her head in disgust, walking past him. Burton would have found another way to get to her, but it galled her that the man who'd replaced her father as sheriff had fed a serial killer crucial information.

She'd never trust him again.

Angelica Gomez cornered her father. "Mr. Reeves, is it true that Detective Ellie Reeves is not your biological daughter? That you adopted her?"

Ellie pressed a hand to her mouth—so the truth was out. It could only have been a matter of time, she guessed.

"Ellie is my daughter," he said gruffly. "That's all anyone needs to know."

Angelica didn't miss a beat, sweeping across the room to Ellie.

Bryce stepped up to intervene, but Angelica elbowed him aside. "I want to hear from Detective Reeves."

Ellie had been running from the press for weeks, hiding from her problems.

She was tired of running. Head high, and ignoring the pain in her body, she stepped over to make a statement. "Ms. Gomez," Ellie said. "I can confirm that that information is correct. But my family's personal life is not important. What is important is that we caught the Weekday Killer."

Angelica's eyes glimmered as she aimed the mic toward Ellie. "Please fill us in on the details, Detective."

Running a hand over her disheveled hair, Ellie looked into the camera and described the hunt for Hugh Burton, and how it had ended with his death.

As her father slipped back down the hall to see her mother, Ellie decided to follow.

"I'll let Special Agent Fox fill you in on the details," she said. "Right now, I need to visit my mother."

Her phone buzzed just as she reached the elevator. A quick glance revealed it was an unknown number, making the hair on the back of her neck prickle.

Her finger shook as she answered the call. "Detective Reeves."

"Hey, Ellie."

At the sound of Hiram's voice, she went completely still.

"First you took Mama, and now Vinny," he said in a low sinister voice. "You take everyone from me, don't you?"

"You sent him to kill me."

"Oh, he offered to do that for me," Hiram said. "I have other followers now, Ellie. Friends who'll do anything for me."

CHAPTER 149

Rose Hill

Eula Ann stared at the image of Detective Ellie Reeves on the TV, her knitting needles clacking together furiously as she worked off her nerves.

There was something about that girl that got under her skin. Something about the way she tilted her head when she spoke, or was it the tiny little birthmark on her neck?

She hadn't noticed it before. But when she'd pushed her hair back tonight, there it was. Three tiny little dots below her ear lobe. For a minute she thought they were freckles. And maybe they were.

But the pattern of them was odd. Like something she'd seen before. But no… it couldn't be…

The storm had died down outside now, the wind settling into a calm.

She looked out at the emerging moon, and spotted the three crows on the power line silhouetted against it. Lord have mercy. Their beady eyes bore holes into her, a sign they knew what she'd done.

And that death was not done on the trail.

Ellie Reeves was doing her darned best to fight it, though. The bruises on her face and hands attested to the fact that she was tough.

But evil had a way of growing and feeding on itself. And Eula feared it would get Ellie in the end.

CHAPTER 150

Bluff County Hospital

Ellie was still shaken from Hiram's call as she entered her mother's hospital room. Machines whined, and her mother's breathing was so shallow that Ellie had to lean forward to tell she was alive.

A cold sweat beaded Ellie's skin and she sucked in a breath. It hurt to look at her mother. Her parents' betrayal had carved a deep wedge between them.

But Vera Reeves was still her mom. At least the only one she'd ever known. She'd tended her wounds when she was little, brought her tomato soup and grilled cheese sandwiches, fed her ice cream when she had her tonsils removed.

For a brief second, she put herself in Vera's shoes and her heart gave a pang.

She slowly approached the bed. She wasn't sure she could forgive Vera just yet. But Burton's comment taunted her. She could show her some grace. That, she could do.

The chair her father kept by her mother's hospital bed still felt warm from where he'd been sitting vigil day and night. Her mother lay still and pale, her eyes fluttering open as Ellie sank into the chair. Licking her dry lips, Ellie cradled her hand in hers and stroked it. "Mom?"

Vera's chest rose and fell but she didn't speak.

A memory surfaced in Ellie's mind—she was five years old and had one of her many nightmares. Vera had come in and wrapped her in the quilt her grammy had made for her, rocking her and singing to her until she fell asleep. When she'd woken up the next morning, her mother was still there, holding her.

Tears blinded her, and she stroked Vera's hair from her face.

"Mama, please don't die," she whispered.

Slowly, her mother opened her eyes and looked at Ellie. Tears swam in the deep brown depths, making Ellie's chest clench.

"I want you to have the surgery," Ellie murmured. "When you get better, I'll take you to lunch and to get your hair done."

Then she realized she must look a frightening mess—something her mother couldn't stand. She probably should have gone home and showered.

Maybe she'd even get a trim herself. They could have a girls' day.

Or maybe not.

"Ellie?"

"Yes, I'm here." She squeezed her mother's frail hand.

"I'm s-so sorry," Vera whispered.

"I know," Ellie said, her voice cracking. "We can work on things when you get better."

Her mother squeezed her hand. "I'd like that, sweetheart."

A sound behind her indicated her father was back. "El," he said as he approached.

"I need to go home and clean up, but I'll be back." Ellie turned to leave, but her mother called for her to wait.

"Don't go yet, Ellie."

Ellie clamped her teeth over her bottom lip, returning to her mother's bedside.

Her mother tugged her closer, then spoke in a low whisper. "An envelope, for you, in a safety deposit box."

Ellie narrowed her eyes. "What?"

"There's an envelope. In it, there's the name of the social worker at the adoption agency we used."

Ellie went still.

"Randall has the key."

Stunned, she turned and faced her father. The key lay in the palm of his hand.

"It's up to you if you want to pursue it."

Ellie's throat thickened, and she reached for the key with a shaky hand. Looking for her birth parents would be like opening Pandora's box.

But could she go on without knowing?

A LETTER FROM RITA

Thank you so much for diving back into the world I've created with Detective Ellie Reeves in *Wildflower Graves*! If you enjoyed *Wildflower Graves* and would like to keep up with my latest releases, you can sign up at the following link. Your email address will never be shared, and you can unsubscribe at any time.

www.bookouture.com/rita-herron

As a child, I grew up in the country with no library close by, but the Bookmobile, a mobile unit, brought books to our street, and I devoured as many as I could get my hands on. Fast forward to adulthood and my favorite pastime became browsing bookstores. I'm obsessed with the endless stories, authors, and settings that offer an escape into another world.

One day I stumbled upon a book about customs, stones, statues and symbolism associated with burial rituals. From there, the idea for *Wildflower Graves* was born!

Coupled with the raw wilderness of the Appalachian Trail and the folklore associated with the mountains (some of which is research-based and some totally my imagination!) the setting seemed ripe for a new serial killer.

I hope you enjoyed the second installment of Ellie's journey and submerging yourself in her world as much as I did! If you liked *Wildflower Graves*, I'd appreciate it if you left a short review. As a writer, it means the world to me that you share your feedback with other readers who might be interested in Ellie's adventures.

I love to hear from readers, so you can find me on Facebook, my website and Twitter.

Thanks so much for your support.

Happy Reading!

Rita

 ritaherron

 @ritaherron

💻 www.ritaherron.com

ACKNOWLEDGMENTS

A huge thanks to Christina Demonsthenous and the entire Bookouture team for their support for the series. My mind often races in a dozen different directions and Christina has a way of tapping into the good that's there and cutting the fat!

Again to my agent Jenny Bent and my fabulous critique partner Stephanie Bond for their unfailing support.

Another thanks to my sister, Reba Bales, licensed mental health counselor, for answering numerous questions regarding details of psychiatric therapy and treatment.

And I can't forget my adorable husband Lee, who has always stood beside and behind me in whatever I wanted to do, even when he thinks I'm scary and strange. Love you to the moon and back!

37551911R00220